Puerto Paz

Jefferey J. Reese

ISBN: 978-1-7345725-0-6 (Paperback)
ISBN: 978-1-7345725-1-3 (e-book: EPUB)
ISBN: 978-1-7345725-2-0 (e-book: MOBI)

Library of Congress Control Number: 2020901658

Published in the United States of America by Puerto Paz Entertainment, Medford, MA

First Printing, April 2020.

www.PuertoPaz.com

This is a work of fiction. Names, characters, places, and incidents either are the products of the author's imagination or are used fictitiously. Any resemblance to actual persons, living or dead, businesses, companies, events, or locales is entirely coincidental.

<u>Cover Design & Artwork:</u>
Cover design by James T. Egan of Bookfly Design.
The "Puerto Paz Compass Symbol" is by Jefferey J. Reese and is a copyrighted image © 2016.
The "Shattered Glass USA Map" image is by Jefferey J. Reese.

Thank you to: My wife and parents for being my "Gamma Readers", and to Nate D., Alex F., and Lestra L. for being my Beta Readers, and to my brother for comments on a later draft.

Prologue
Mitosis

Democrats and Republicans. In the early twenty-first century, they never agreed on anything. Constantly bickering, arguing, and disagreeing. One side would take a position on an issue, and the other would immediately take the opposite position, regardless of the issue. Voting was strictly along party lines. Dissent, and you were ostracized from political social circles. Dissent, and you jeopardized your chances in the next election.

On February 3, 2024, in a special Saturday session, Democrats and Republicans finally agreed on something: divorce. Separation. Segregation.[1]

The democratic republic that had survived for more than two hundred years no longer existed, but it was less like a death and more like mitosis. Instead of a cell developing two sets of chromosomes and splitting down the middle, a country had developed two sets of political ideologies and split down the middle—or more precisely, the Mississippi River.

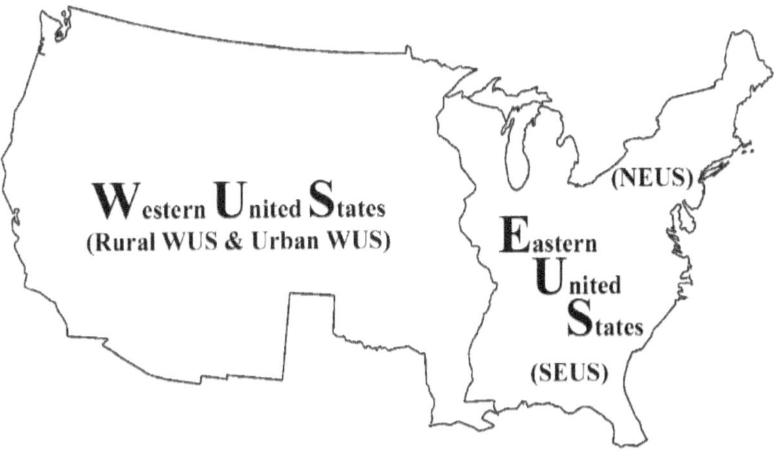

---

[1] A more detailed history timeline is provided at PuertoPaz.com

Part 1: NEUS
Chapter 1: Last Day

Marcus Coleman sat at his desk in English class, his uniform sticking to his body and beads of perspiration dripping down his forehead and temple. He had just come from Phys Ed where he and the rest of his classmates had completed the second day of a two-day decathlon, which the gym teacher considered the final exam.

It was 2:45 p.m. on Friday, June 20, 2053; the last period of the last day of school before summer vacation, and his English teacher was droning on about what books they should be reading over the summer break. Marcus snuck a glance around the room while the teacher was facing the chalkboard. No one seemed to be listening, and since Mr. Clark's jurisdiction ended in fifteen minutes, he knew that no one planned to read any of the books.

The last two days of school were supposed to be for final exams, with half of each class's exam on the second-to-last day and half of it on the last day. Mr. Clark had surprised them by beginning the English exam a day early so that he could reward the students who had studied hard all semester and punish those who thought they could cram during the last couple of days and get a good grade. *Or was his real motivation for starting the exam a day early so that he could spend our final hour of school torturing us?* Marcus wondered.

The books Mr. Clark was describing sounded just like every other book they read. Marcus swore that if he took the character names from one book and plugged them into any other book they read, it would end up being the same story. They were always some variation of the same theme: either a triumphant war-hero saga or a Christian-themed fable. Or both.

Marcus looked two seats to his right, where his best friend, Dylan Callahan, was sitting. Dylan leaned over to the kid sitting between them, flicked the kid's ear, and said, "That's June twenty-sixth." It was the sixth time Dylan had flicked the kid's ear in the last fifteen minutes, each time increasing the date he said by one day.

The kid, Bobby Cisarelli, grabbed his ear and whined, "Quit doing that!"

Mr. Clark spun around from the chalkboard and shouted, "Respect your teacher!" Everyone sat up straight and silent until he turned back to the chalkboard.

Dylan leaned over and quietly taunted Bobby, saying, "But I'm not going to see you all summer, so I've gotta flick your ear once for every day of summer vacation that I won't be here to pick on you, Sissy-really."

Most of the class had chuckled the first few times Dylan flicked Bobby's ear, but it was growing old, and Mr. Clark was getting increasingly cranky.

Poor Bobby, not his fault his last name is what it is, Marcus thought.

Marcus caught Dylan's eye to distract him. He looked down at his watch, looked back up at Dylan, rolled his eyes, and leaned back in his seat. Dylan stopped picking on Bobby "Sissy-really" Cisarelli and started making clicking sounds with his mouth that grew slower and slower, simulating how time seemed to be slowing to a crawl.

Marcus and Dylan, now minutes away from the conclusion of their junior year, had known each other and been best friends since the first grade. Seating arrangements were, as always, in alphabetical order by last name. Thus, from the teacher's point of view, Coleman always sat one seat to the right of Callahan. Until seventh grade that was. In seventh grade their class merged with another middle school's class and moved to one junior high building. Bobby Cisarelli, the kid who Dylan had nick-named "Sissy-really," despite Bobby's pleas to pronounce his last name the proper Italian way, was from the other middle school and had the misfortune of being seated between Marcus and Dylan. Dylan didn't particularly care for having the dorky runt separating him and his best friend, so he had been picking on Bobby ever since.

The school bell rang. Everyone began standing up and running toward the door.

"Sit back down!" barked Mr. Clark. "You know the drill. The last day of school is no different than any other day. End-of-day pledges and prayers first, *then* you leave. Anyone caught moving before final prayer is over gets juvenile detention."

The classroom speaker mounted on the grayish-green concrete block wall in front of them ignited with the screeching sound of feedback, followed by the principal clearing his throat. "Bow your heads for first prayer," boomed the principal's voice. The students obeyed. "Jesus Christ, our Lord and Savior, only son of God, the one true God..."

Marcus bowed his head as instructed. A few seconds later, after hearing him stifle another yelp, he opened his right eye and tried to look over at Bobby without moving his head.

After first prayer concluded, Marcus raised his head, looked at the classroom flag, and placed one hand over his heart while saluting with the other. "I pledge allegiance to the flag, of the Northern Eastern United States..." Marcus turned slightly and cringed as Dylan abbreviated their region's name to the acronym "NEUS" and made a lynching gesture, hanging himself with an imaginary noose. Marcus looked toward Mr. Clark, who had his back turned to them. Dylan had gotten away with his pun this time. Dylan also got away with another ear flick before final prayer completed.

Finally the school bell rang again. Bobby Cisarelli was spared sixty-nine ear flicks. Dylan and the rest of Marcus's classmates started chanting, *"We are seniors and we rule, get out of our way we own this school!"* as they bolted for the door. Marcus refrained from the chanting and slowly gathered his belongings while watching to confirm that Dylan and some of the other boys were unbuttoning their collars. As most of the students cleared out of the room, he too undid the top button of his uniform, releasing the choke hold it had on his neck. He walked calmly out into the hallway where Dylan was high-fiving classmates while waiting for him.

The hallways were a chaotic pinball machine of students bouncing off of one another, running and yelling in a cathartic rebellion against all the hallway rules they had suffered through during the school year. Marcus headed steadily on the most direct path toward his locker. Dylan followed, stopping intermittently to exchange slaps on the shoulder and giddy grunts with the popular kids or to ridicule the unpopular kids, then running to catch back up with Marcus.

"Dude. Can you dial it back with the yelling and running?" Marcus asked. "It's anarchy in here. They're going to turn the guards on us again if this keeps up. I don't want to get maced again."

"Chill, man. It's the last day. School's done. They'll go easier on us today," Dylan responded.

One of their football teammates approached them and gave them each the traditional greeting: a heavy double slap on the shoulder from arm's length. Marcus and the teammate, the only other black boy he knew who hadn't been sent to juvenile detention, gave each other a knowing nod.

The teammate turned to Dylan. "Dude, my sister discovered a treasure trove of 1990s movies in the attic of a house she was babysitting at last weekend. When do you think you'll finish repairing my VHS player?"

"Told ya it's a complex repair," said Dylan. "I'll finish when I finish, man, and if you keep bugging me about it, I'm gonna just keep the damn thing."

Marcus looked around nervously, then at their teammate. "Be careful. You know what they'll do if they catch you with contraband."

"Yeah, I know," said Dylan, connecting eyes with Marcus. "My ass still has scars from Wegener's caning freshman year. I think he enjoys seeing bare boy ass."

Marcus sheepishly looked at the floor, then back up at their teammate. "But a black boy would be caned *and* sent to juvie."

"I'll be careful," their teammate said before giving another nod and going on his way.

They continued down the hall. The principal's voice bellowed through the school's speakers again. "Students! You will behave in a civilized, respectable manner! Ten Hail Marys. All teachers are to report to hallway duty armed with disciplining tools."

A chorus of students dutifully muttered their Hail Mary prayers in unison before moving on in a more orderly fashion. "Told ya," Marcus said.

"It's just the teachers though," Dylan said

"The principal must be in a good mood today," Marcus replied as the teachers began filing out of their rooms and standing next to their doors with arms crossed across their chests and batons, tasers, and cans of pepper spray hanging conspicuously from their belts.

Marcus spotted his least-favorite teacher, Reverend Wegener, the same teacher who had caned Dylan a couple of years earlier, a few rooms away from his locker. "Shit," he muttered under his breath. There was no way to avoid crossing paths with the beady-eyed, rat-nosed man, whose jaw seemed permanently clenched. Marcus tried to avoid eye contact, but the reverend's wrath was inescapable. He heard the reverend shout, "Coleman! Button that collar! You're a disgrace to God Almighty!" Marcus silently fiddled with his shirt button one-handed until he felt the collar choking him again.

Dylan turned to Marcus. "Jesus, does that asshole not even know who you are? For fuck's sake, you'd think he could cut *you* of all people some slack."

"He's always like that," Marcus said.

"Just say the word and I'll pop him one in the face," Dylan offered.

Marcus and Dylan arrived at their lockers and started ripping out all of their books and school supplies. School lockers were also organized by grade and alphabetical order, so Marcus was two lockers away from Dylan. Bobby had apparently taken "the long way" back to his locker so that he could avoid Dylan.

"Books in the garbage or save 'em for the fire pit?" asked Dylan.

Marcus knew there would be hell to pay if he didn't come home with the books his dad had paid for. "Save 'em."

"Nah, I don't feel like lugging a hundred pounds of books around. I'm tossing 'em now," Dylan said. After dumping the contents of his locker into a trash bin, he added, "You want to go to Fonzarelli's to celebrate the start of our reign as kings of the school?"

Marcus nodded. Dylan waited while Marcus finished filling his backpack with books. Marcus hoisted it onto his back like an Army rucksack racer, and he and Dylan followed the hordes to Fonzarelli's, the local teen hangout specializing in old-fashioned ice cream sundaes.

The place was absolutely packed with frenzied high school students when they got there. It took forty-five minutes to get their order taken, and they had to eat their half-melted sundaes while standing on the black-and-white checkerboard floor in a crowd of boys near the bathrooms while the girls sat at the tables and booths.

Marcus closed his eyes and bowed his head in silent prayer before his first bite, but his prayer, along with subsequent spoonfuls of ice cream, were continually interrupted by classmates slapping him on the shoulder and saying things like, "Way to put New Rochelle High School on the map!" or "Way to represent New Rochelle!" The congratulations were for his second-place finish in the 100-meter dash at the previous weekend's state track meet. Other than saying thanks, he stayed fairly quiet and just bounced back and forth between listening to Dylan trying to impress the ladies and listening to the general hum of voices while eating his ice cream.

The boys around him mostly talked about the strength of next season's football team, while the conversations at the girls' table in front of him was centered around summer plans and gossiping about which student relationships people thought would endure the summer break. Marcus found none of the topics of chatter terribly interesting at this particular moment, but the excitement in everyone's voices was contagious. He ate another spoonful of sundae, savoring the moment along with the ice cream.

Marcus surveyed the room. White walls, chrome tables and chairs, and seat cushions the red color of the artificial dye added to Maraschino cherries. The checkerboard pattern of the floor repeated as an accent on the walls. White, black, white, black. His eyes moved from background to foreground, to a swarm of cream-colored faces framed with straight brown or blond hair, then to the dark-brown skin of his own hand dipping his spoon into the sundae bowl for a final scoop.

He rarely came here. Only on special occasions, and only when Dylan invited him. He always tried to convince himself that because of his regimented after-school athletic schedule, combined with a relatively long walk home, he just didn't have time to hang out here, but deep down he knew that this was only part of the reason. It was mostly that he just didn't feel welcome here.

At four thirty, Marcus spotted his girlfriend, Stacie, enter the joint, fashionably late and wearing a rather risqué dress he hadn't seen her in before. It was appropriately full length for public apparel, technically covering every square inch of bare skin, but the forearms were made from a sheer lace fabric, allowing men to see through to her milky white skin. The form-fitting dress was elegantly sequined and stood out compared to the standard plain cotton dress that most girls were wearing. *Must be a pre-partitioning attic find,* Marcus thought.

She was so completely preoccupied by her popular-girl entourage, who had commandeered a table from some freshman girls across the room, that he wasn't able to catch her eye to even wave hello, and the place was so packed that it seemed futile to try to worm his way over to her. He stayed close to Dylan's side, content to be entertained by his best friend's antics.

At five o'clock, Marcus decided he had better get home. His dad commuted home from his work at West Point Military Academy an hour away, and was typically home by 6:15 p.m. on Friday nights. Marcus wanted to be home before his dad arrived to give the appearance that he hadn't had any fun after school. His dad always seemed irritated by Marcus having fun.

"Walk home with me?" Marcus asked Dylan.

"Dude, the party is still going strong here. Curfew isn't for another three hours."

"I need to beat my dad home."

"And you want me to hold hands and walk with you, Nancy-boy?"

"Come on, man, you know bad shit tends to happen to me when I'm anywhere near Duke Estates alone."

Dylan acquiesced, and the two boys began making their way through the bodies toward the exit—Dylan rudely bumping people out of the way like a fullback and Marcus following through the gaps Dylan opened. As he neared the exit, Marcus finally got close enough to Stacie's table for one of her girlfriends to notice him and point him out to her. She looked up, Marcus waved a combination hello and goodbye, and Stacie gave him a half-hearted smile in return.

Marcus breathed a sigh of relief upon reaching the sidewalk outside. He had reached his limit of extroverted frenzy. He heaved his backpack onto his shoulders once more, and the two boys headed toward their usual route home. It wasn't the most direct path home for Marcus, but it was the safest.

Marcus peeked across the street at the tall brick wall and spiked iron gate with the sign for Duke Estates, then fell a step behind

Dylan, crossed behind him, and walked with Dylan between him and the wealthy neighborhood. "Thanks for walking with me," he said.

Marcus and Dylan continued together until Dylan had to split off from Marcus's route. Dylan's home was to the west, in the gritty, blue-collar neighborhoods. Marcus's home was almost another mile to the south. After they said their goodbyes, Marcus glanced down the street in the direction of the dilapidated cottage that Dylan and his father had lived alone in for the last seven years. Despite having been friends with Dylan for such a long time, he hadn't stepped foot in that house in more than four years. *And I suspect I never will again*, Marcus thought.

The image of Mr. Callahan's angry face flashed in Marcus's mind. The abusive, alcoholic auto mechanic was only in his late thirties, but his reckless lifestyle had made his worn-out face look more like that of a gruff man in his late forties. He was tall, fairly well built, and scary as hell when drunk.

Marcus gritted his teeth as he recalled his last time in Dylan's house. Mr. Callahan had come home drunk at 1 a.m. from one of the speakeasy joints he frequented. Marcus and Dylan had fallen asleep in the living room while watching bootleg movies. They awoke to Mr. Callahan throwing things around the room and shouting at Dylan, "Get that fucking nigger out of my house! If I ever catch you bringing another nigger in here, I'll beat you until you're so black and blue that you'll look like a nigger too, and then I'll beat you again for lookin' like a nigger." Marcus had fled out the back door, sprinted away, and then walked home alone in the dark in the middle of the night, well past curfew.

I can't even imagine having to deal with that monster as a father, Marcus thought. *My dad is an unpleasant man, but compared to Mr. Callahan, he's a saint.* Marcus recalled the latest set of bruises he had seen on Dylan's body during gym glass. Dylan had his father's height, but he hadn't filled out his frame with muscles like his father yet. He was just a tall, lanky white kid, and when Mr. Callahan went on his drunken fits of rage, Dylan had difficulty defending himself.

Marcus had learned not to ask about the bruises, though. Dylan didn't like to talk about it. Once, when Marcus had asked him about them, Dylan had lashed out, saying, "What the hell are you looking at my body for? Are you turning into a fag or something, MC?" It was a pleasant response in comparison to what he'd heard Dylan say to other kids. When they asked questions, Dylan threatened to replicate his bruises on their bodies.

He could hardly blame Dylan. He'd lost his mother, a sweet, caring woman, at a young age. *And it was that monster's fault. Couldn't even stay sober long enough to drive his own wife home safely.* Marcus suddenly found himself reminiscing about the peanut-butter-and-honey sandwiches Mrs. Callahan used to make for him and Dylan when he visited. *Did Dylan make them for himself now?* He certainly couldn't imagine Mr. Callahan lifting a finger to make a sandwich for Dylan. *And I don't think the year in jail did Mr. Callahan any good. I think he even got worse. He never would have gone on a racial-slur-laden tirade like that when Mrs. Callahan was alive.* Marcus shook his head. *Mrs. Callahan deserved so much better. How the hell did she even end up with that asshole? They were polar opposites.*

Marcus walked a few more paces. Now that he thought about it, though, he and Dylan were polar opposites too. Dylan was loud, extroverted, and the class clown and part-time bully. *How did we even become best friends?* In the semester that had just ended, the only classes Marcus and Dylan still had together were Phys Ed and English. Dylan barely scraped by in terms of grades at school, with the exception of auto-shop class, which he excelled at—another trait he had inherited from his father. Marcus excelled at math and science, to the point of his school beginning to run out of advanced placement classes to offer him.

Dylan had a rebellious, anti-establishment streak in him. *Probably why he's willing to befriend a black boy*, Marcus thought. *I think he even likes that my skin color aggravates his dad.* By comparison, Marcus was nearly a goody two-shoes. Marcus recalled his parents coming home from parent-teacher conferences and his mom saying that all of his teachers—except for Reverend Wegener— had described him as reserved, thoughtful, introspective, honest, and intelligent. A respectable young man who had his moments of extroversion, especially around people he liked or when he was curious about something and wanted to learn more, but who buttoned up quickly and went into observer mode when made uncomfortable, or when around people he didn't like, or even when he was just tired or hungry. *Dylan is one of those people who can draw out that extroverted side of me*, Marcus thought. Dylan's ability to be outgoing was one of the things Marcus enjoyed most about their odd friendship.

Marcus peered down a street and across a bridge toward the neighborhood to the southwest of Dylan's. It was a drug-infested ghetto, nicknamed "the Zoo," the rug under which society's rejects were swept and where the vast majority of the city's black people lived. *Thank God I don't have to live there*, he thought. He could taste the sugary ice cream residue in his mouth developing into an acidic aftertaste. *Fonzarelli's*, Marcus thought. *That's probably part of why I'm best friends with Dylan too. He's my bridge to the white world.*

Marcus shifted his overloaded backpack full of books around on his shoulders as he entered the commercial district a few blocks from his home. Small strip malls lined both sides of the street. He picked up his pace, partially to lessen the amount of time he had to endure the backpack's straps biting into his shoulders and partially because he hated this section of his walk home, despite the fact that it was the safest place he could possibly be while walking alone.

Superficially he didn't like this block because he thought the buildings were ugly. The faux stone and faux brick storefronts were clean but boxy and plain, and they looked like they hadn't changed since the 1970s. The shopkeepers who tended the stores only exacerbated his dislike of the area. They tended to follow high school sports closely in an effort to demonstrate civic pride and to gain favor with customers, so they always recognized Marcus from his athletic accomplishments and eagerly patted him on the back. They were almost too friendly with him. *Obnoxiously friendly. Fake friendly*, Marcus thought. It had only been a week since the state track meet. *My golden ticket of black respect won't expire for another couple of weeks or so. They'll still be in full ingratiation mode today.*

But the ugly façades and annoying shopkeepers weren't his main reason for hating this part of the walk. The majority of his disdain was reserved for one particular building. He tried not to look at the sign above the Army registration office that had taken residence in one of the strip mall's spaces, but it was instinctive to do so. Every time he walked past that sign, he looked at it and was reminded of the repeated admonishments from his dad throughout the last few months about applying to West Point.

His mind began to echo with the sound of his dad's voice nagging him to finish his application. He had been dragging his heels for months. He couldn't find the words to tell his bully of a father that he didn't want to go to West Point, and his default tactic was to stall. The household dishes had never been washed and dried as promptly as they had been the last few weeks. His bedroom was meticulously clean. His schoolwork had never been as time-consuming or as eagerly performed as these last few weeks. Any excuse to avoid the application was enthusiastically welcomed.

Marcus plodded on, deep in thought that managed to remain uninterrupted by overzealous shopkeepers. A few minutes later, he was startled to find himself standing in front of his house. He'd unconsciously taken his house key out of his pocket a block earlier and had been gripping the jagged metal so tightly that there were indentations in his hand. As he loosened his grip on the key, he looked at the keychain medallion it was attached to that read "Ohio State Football." He paused, and then looked up at his house. His family had lived here for as long as he could remember. A white, two-story house with a picket fence in a sea of mostly Caucasian, white-collar, middle-class families. Well east of the Zoo and well south of Duke Estates and the whites-only neighborhoods near the country club.

Multiple generations of Colemans had called this home, and his mom and dad never dreamed of leaving it, nor New Rochelle, New York. On nights when Marcus's dad came home extra grumpy from particularly long, grinding commutes, Marcus had often wondered why his dad didn't just move the family closer to West Point. He knew the answer without having to ask it, though. NEUS men were stubbornly loyal. Loyal to their homes, their families, their neighborhoods. There was Coleman history in this house that couldn't be abandoned. It had been a huge source of pride several generations earlier, when his great-grandfather had scraped together decades of savings and moved the family out of the Bronx ghetto and to this house in the once-thriving middle-class part of New Rochelle.

Not only would they never permanently move away from this

spot, but outside of his dad's commute to West Point, the family hardly ever left the confines of New Rochelle, even for temporary reasons. They had taken a few family vacations within NEUS, but the family had only ever left the country once, when Marcus's dad had to take the family with him for a temporary teaching project at a newly opened military base in Germany.

Marcus glanced at the house key in his hand again. The only key on the keychain. He looked around at the neighborhood surrounding him, realizing that he didn't really know any of his neighbors, despite having lived there his entire life. *Without a bridge to the white world, there would only be loneliness and isolation,* he thought.

He inserted the key in the lock, turned it, let himself in the front door, pausing to pick up the mail, and walked up the flight of stairs to his family's home, which sat over the part of the house that his parents had converted into a rental unit after his brother and sister had moved out. The smell of some sort of tomato-based pasta dish cooking began to stimulate his salivary glands. He stopped in the kitchen to kiss his mom hello as she was putting the finishing touches on supper before heading to his bedroom. He unloaded his backpack full of books, most of which he assumed he'd never read again.

Chapter 2: Last Supper

The supper Marcus had smelled walking up the stairs turned out to be lasagna. It was one of his favorite foods, and his mom typically only made the labor-intensive dish for special occasions. This time it was presumably to celebrate his becoming a senior. He changed out of his school uniform and started to pick out some comfortable old jeans and a T-shirt before thinking better of it and putting on some nice slacks and a clean, collared shirt. He didn't want his appearance at the dinner table to give his dad an opening to start criticizing him. He walked back to the kitchen.

"How was your day, honey?" asked his mother.

"Fine."

"How did you do in the decathlon in gym class?"

"I got the highest score in the class."

"Congratulations, Marcus! I'm sure Coach Brimbaugh will be impressed with that! He'll probably make you captain of the football team next year!"

"I don't think Coach really cares how I do in the gym class decathlon, Mom. Anyway, I don't care if I'm captain next year as long as I'm the starting running back again."

"Oh, but I'm sure your father would be so proud of you if you were captain. It's such an honor to be chosen captain."

"I'm sure he would," Marcus said unenthusiastically. "When's supper?"

"Your father should be home at around six."

Marcus had been the starting running back on his high school football team the last two years, and had been on the varsity squad since his freshman year. Dylan had finally made varsity team junior year. He played both wide receiver and kicker. Dylan was able to catch the ball over most defenders' heads because of his height, but he was a bit clumsy and slow and was certainly not good enough to play receiver for a college team. He was, however, a very good kicker and had potential to kick for a college team in the future. *If he ever gets his grades up,* Marcus thought.

Marcus was a much better athlete than Dylan. His five foot, eleven inch frame was solid yet lean and quick. He had already had numerous college scouts watching him at games that year and had been told verbally just a few days earlier that his favorite school, Ohio State, was prepared to offer him the ultimate lure for an athlete: a half scholarship.

It would be a great boon for someone in the Coleman family's economic status, but Marcus hadn't yet told them about the impending offer. He felt compelled to continue feigning interest in the only three schools that his father wanted him to consider: Navy, Air Force, and especially Army at West Point, where his older brother, Saul, was currently attending school. His father, Abraham Coleman, was a military man, and he had his mind made up that both of his sons would follow in his footsteps and become military men too.

But Marcus didn't want to go to Army or Navy or Air Force. He didn't want to become a soldier. He didn't want to learn military strategy or yet more combat skills. He wasn't sure what he wanted to study there, maybe some sort of engineering, but he knew he wanted to go to Ohio State and play football, or at least he was pretty sure. One thing he knew for certain was that he wanted to get the hell out of claustrophobic New Rochelle.

On some particularly soul-crushing days, he dreamed of leaving NEUS entirely and escaping to the tranquility of Southern California and going to UCLA instead. Southern California always looked so perfect in old movies: the sun, the beaches, swimming in the ocean. The drawback of UCLA was that it meant abandoning football, since the Western United States had prohibited the sport due to its "excessively violent nature." Beyond the climate and scenery, though, the benefit of California was getting to see his sister, Sharon, for the first time in seven years.

Sharon, his elder by eight years, had moved out to California when she turned eighteen. She had left New Rochelle without saying goodbye to anyone, save for a note she left behind explaining that she didn't want to live in a country that persecuted and oppressed lesbians. Her homosexuality had been a well-kept secret, even from her family. Marcus didn't blame her for that. The day their father read her farewell letter, he disowned her and never spoke of her again. Had Marcus not had household trash duties, he never would have rescued the crumpled note from the garbage can and learned the reason for Sharon's departure.

Marcus heard the front door unlock. His dad was home. Marcus's breathing got shallower as he listened to the heavy-set fifty-four-year-old man lumber up the stairs. The first words out of his dad's mouth were directed at his mom: "Is that lasagna?"

His mother confirmed.

"I thought we only had lasagna for special occasions."

"As of this evening," Wynona replied, "Marcus is a senior in high school."

Abraham snorted. "So now we're giving out participation ribbons for not flunking and being held back a grade?"

"He was getting straight A's before final exams."

"Exam results aren't in yet. Besides, they grade too soft at that school."

"Have a seat, dear. You must be hungry."

"Starving." Abraham sat down at the dining room table in his officer's uniform.

Marcus ran out of reasonable excuses to stay in the kitchen and quietly walked into the dining room, trying not to attract his father's attention and hoping that his mother brought dinner in quickly. His dad was distracted by a newspaper that he put down when his mom brought supper to them. She returned to the kitchen.

Marcus bowed his head as his father began impatiently saying grace before his mother had even returned to join them. As his father began shoving forkfuls of lasagna into his mouth, Marcus tried to time the clink of his fork slicing through his food and striking the plate to synchronize with his father's, and except for a few subtle glances up, he kept his head down, focused on his plate.

Finally, his mother returned with her own meal and sat down across from Marcus. Abraham looked up at her like a dinosaur distracted by the motion of potential prey, then over to Marcus.

"Have you started your Candidate Questionnaire for West Point yet?"

"Final exams have been my top priority, sir. I haven't had time yet."

"You should have started it weeks ago. Early applicants impress Admissions. It says to them that you truly want to go there. I thought we discussed this before."

Marcus felt a rush of heat go to his face, followed by a shiver of cold through the rest of his body. They *had* discussed this before, many times, and Marcus was sick to death of hearing it. He looked down at the remnants of the dimples in his hand from where he had squeezed the key too hard during his walk home. Then, as if disembodied and witnessing someone else say it, he heard himself blurt out, "I'm being offered a football scholarship to Ohio State."

His father dropped his hands to the table and stopped eating, his fork clanking against the plate. "Football?" he asked incredulously. "You think you're going to go to Ohio State to play *football?* And then what? Where is football going to get you? You think you're going to have a career in football after college?"

"I don't know for sure what I want to do after college. I get good grades. I'll find something."

"Coleman men serve their country."

Marcus's whole body was numb. He couldn't believe what he was saying. "I'm not like you and Saul. I don't want to be in the military."

Abraham glared and pointed his knife at him. "Two years of military service is mandatory in this country. You will be in the military whether you want to or not. You think you're going to juggle schoolwork, football, ROTC, *and* a job at Ohio State? You realize that if you go there, you're on your own? No way in hell am I paying what your scholarship doesn't cover."

Marcus could tell that his dad had mentally prepared himself for the possibility that Marcus didn't want to be a military man. It must have been obvious that Marcus's passions lay elsewhere, despite his best attempts to feign interest to mollify his dad. It seemed they had both been trying to avoid this conversation for as long as possible, but the time had finally come, and like a good officer, Abraham had already prepared his strategy for the battle. He launched his final salvo with "You still have several months to make a decision. Go to your room and start your Candidate Questionnaire now. I want it in my hands by Monday 0700. I will hand deliver it myself."

Marcus got up and went to his room. He had completely lost his appetite anyway, but he figured that between the ice cream sundae at Fonzarelli's and the few bites of lasagna he had managed to shovel in, he'd probably be good for the night. After shedding his more formal clothes in favor of shorts and a T-shirt, he got out his Candidate Questionnaire and stared at it.

Marcus's parents were early-to-bed, early-to-rise types. At nine, he heard his dad clear his throat as he walked past Marcus's bedroom door. Marcus looked down at his Candidate Questionnaire in a panic and realized the only progress he had made since walking into his room was to put his name, address, and government ID number on it. He heard a knock at his door. He scrambled to cover up the empty spaces on the form with the pages of instructions. His door opened, and thankfully it was his mom's face poking through. He looked at her, then crossed his arms over his chest, leaned back in his chair, and looked straight forward at the hutch over his desk, his eyes settling on the elaborate cardboard castle he had built in sixth grade, which served as a permanent prison for all the military action figures his father had given him during his younger years.

"Honey, I know you want to play football, but you need to obey your father. Okay?"

Marcus bit his tongue. He wanted to tell her that he was his own man, that he'd been waiting for his dad to show him some sign of respect for years, but it never came. He didn't want to take out his frustrations on her. Nor did he want to start an argument with a woman who would always be fiercely compliant to her husband's demands, regardless of whether he was right or wrong.

It was obvious she could read the frustration on Marcus's face. "I'm worried about you, sweetie. I don't want a repeat of Sharon. She wasn't at peace when she left, and I'm sensing that you aren't at peace now, either. Why don't you pray on it the next few days? The Lord can alleviate your confusion and frustration if you let Him into your heart."

"Goodnight, Mom." Marcus turned away and looked out the window as his mom shut his door.

Chapter 3: Dylan Dilemma

At ten p.m., Marcus heard his phone chirp with a new notification. It was a text from Dylan.

"I'm parked down the street. Gotta get out of here. You in?"

Marcus was perplexed. Dylan didn't have a car. They both had driver's licenses but no cars. Marcus called Dylan. "Got your text. What's up?"

Dylan's voice was panicky. Something was really wrong. "My dad beat the shit out of me. I gotta get out of here."

Marcus sat up, frowning. Dylan's dad had beaten him many times, but he had never reacted this way before. Usually Dylan didn't say a word about it.

"What happened?"

"My dad came home already half-blitzed, and when he found out I had tossed my books in the garbage, he just started wailing on me."

Marcus felt a twinge of guilt for not having tried to talk Dylan out of pitching his books in the garbage at school, not that it would have changed Dylan's stubborn mind.

"I tried to fight back this time," Dylan continued, his voice cracking. "I got a couple of punches in, but it just pissed him off more. This one was bad, Marcus. He even went for my head. He went out to a speakeasy afterwards. I trashed the place and took the Dean. I gotta get out of here, MC. I gotta get far away. I'm never stepping foot in that house again."

The Dean, short for James Dean, was the nickname Dylan had given to Mr. Callahan's vintage 1969 Dodge Charger muscle car. It had been passed down from generation to generation in the family. It was a garage queen, stored on their property in a garage that was almost as big as their house, and it only came out for car shows. It was Mr. Callahan's pride and joy. Dylan had talked about running away from home before, but taking the Charger was taking things past the point of no return.

"You in?" Dylan repeated.

"Give me five minutes. Where are you?"

Marcus scrambled around his room, packing a large military duffle bag. Clothing, cash, passport... He still wasn't sure if he was going to flee with Dylan, and he had intentionally not replied to him with a yes or no, but he was on autopilot now and unable to process the dilemma further. He had spent most of the evening dreaming of running away himself, but he knew there was a big difference between dreaming and doing. *I doubt Dylan could survive more than two weeks on his own,* Marcus thought. *He's impulsive and loud-mouthed, and more like his dad than he cares to admit.* Marcus finished packing and set his bag next to the door, then walked over to the bed, picked up his school books, and put them neatly on his bookshelf. All except for the calculus book, which he stuck in his bag.

He smoothed out the sheets on the bed, then went to his dresser. He pulled the bottom drawer completely out, reached into the void, and retrieved the letter Sharon had left when she ran away. He paused for a moment, remembering that this was the same place where he had found Sharon's unlabeled VHS tape when he had moved into her room after the downstairs had been converted to the rental unit. A wave of guilt hit him. It was the same VHS tape that had gotten Dylan caned freshman year. Their only friend with a working VCR at that time had just been sent to juvie, and Dylan had offered to break into the school's AV room to satisfy Marcus's curiosity about what was on the tape. Wegener busted him. Dylan took the fall without ratting Marcus out, and had likely prevented Marcus from being sent to juvie, which would have irreparably damaged his future. *What did Dylan say the name of the bootleg movie on the tape was? "Better Than Chocolate?"*

He returned the dresser drawer to its proper place and set Sharon's letter on the bed and stared at it for a minute, thinking about how it might have been written in nearly the exact same spot. *Sharon's old room. I followed her into this room, and now I might be following in her footsteps again, running away.* His phone chirped. Dylan was asking if he was coming.

"Just finished packing. There in a minute."

Marcus slipped out of the house. He clumsily fumbled to lock the door, his hands stiff like rigor mortis. He winced at the sound of the deadbolt clicking shut, which seemed as loud as a gunshot. He clutched the keychain in his fist, afraid of it jingling if he attempted to stick it in his pocket. He could feel the key digging into his skin once more. The supracorporeal sensation he had felt a few hours earlier at the dinner table tugged at him again, but the nausea in his belly anchored him back to his body. *Jesus, the last time I felt this way was before the Mamaroneck game.*

He had puked in the locker room before that game and didn't really regain his composure until a hard hit from a linebacker knocked his nerves back into alignment. He considered slapping himself in the face now to try to simulate that experience, but he didn't dare risk making any noises that could alert anyone to his presence. Instead he carefully shifted his keychain around in his hand and silently but vigorously rubbed the medallion. He walked briskly toward the nearest pocket of shadows between the streetlamps, afraid to look back, fearful that every noise he heard might be his father's footsteps.

Mustn't look back, lest I be turned into a pillar of salt, he thought. He looked around the neighborhood. The odds of him being seen increased the longer it took him to get to the car, but too fast and he'd look suspicious if he was spotted. He scanned the street the same way he scanned the line of scrimmage when handed the football, looking for any threats, searching for the best path to take. *I wonder if Sharon felt this paranoid when she snuck away in the middle of the night.*

Nearly a block away from home, he couldn't resist the urge to check behind him. He looked back with a twitchy turn of the neck and saw a light on in one of the windows of his house. *Shit.* He spun forward and darted to the far side of the nearest unlit telephone pole, trying to look as casual as possible as he leaned against it and looked at his house. *Too far from the end to be my parents' bedroom. Is that my bedroom light? Did I forget to shut the light off? Or is it the bathroom?* He counted windows. *Third from the left. My bedroom. Either I left the light on or one of my parents is in there.* He waited and watched. If it was his parents, then other lights would turn on as they looked around the house for him.

The light in his bedroom stayed on, and the rest of the windows remained dark. He decided to wait another minute to be sure. *How could I be so stupid?* He scolded himself while gently head-butting the telephone pole. He'd rehearsed this so many times in his mind, but never in a million years did he think he'd forget to shut the light off. If one of them went to the bathroom in the middle of the night, they'd notice the light and check why he was wasting electricity.

His phone chirped. *Damnit!* He pulled it out of his pocket, shielded the light of the screen with his hand, and muted it. *Probably Dylan wondering what's taking so long. That's my reason for forgetting the light though. I never imagined Dylan involved in this scenario. Surprises are throwing me off my game.* The house lights remained unchanged, so he made a break for it, walking a little more briskly and trying to always keep a telephone pole positioned between him and his parents' bedroom window.

He made it to the passenger door of the Charger, climbed in, and tried to fake some calmness and confidence. "You sure about this? We could go back, put the car in the garage, and clean up the house."

Dylan shook his head. "I'm done. I'm done taking his shit. I'm not letting him lay another finger on me. Besides, he'll know. I've already put a mile on the odometer. He'll murder me. He loves this car more than me. I don't think he even planned to hand it down to me, at least not until he dies. I took all the cash I could find too. I can't go back."

Marcus sensed that Dylan was more confident in the decision to leave than he was. "Where would we go?"

"Don't care," Dylan replied.

Marcus squirmed in his seat for a moment, struggling with the impulsiveness of that response.

Dylan added, "You don't have to come with."

"I told my dad about Ohio State tonight," Marcus said.

"Shit. What did he say?"

"He sent me to my room to fill out the Candidate Questionnaire. He was ready for it. I wasn't." Marcus's tone shifted from despondent to angry. "I'm *not* going to West Point. I am my own man. I deserve *respect*. Fuck him!"

"Fuck yeah, MC! You in? You want to get the fuck out of New

Roach-hell?"

Marcus pursed his lips and nodded several times, as if confirming with himself that he was certain before saying, "I'm in."

Dylan gunned the engine and peeled out of the parking lot.

"Dude!" exclaimed Marcus. "Chill out! We don't want to draw attention! This is a stolen car, for Christ's sake. Keep an eye out for cops."

Dylan eased off the gas. Marcus repeated his question about their destination.

"Away from here. Far away."

"Okay, okay," Marcus said. "Out of New Rochelle. If your dad calls the cops, then we should be out of New York state too."

"The entrance to I-95 is up ahead. Should I take it?"

"Yeah. Do you think they can track our phones?"

"Probably. Give me yours." Dylan took both of their phones, rolled down his window, and tossed them out.

Marcus looked at him, stunned. "We probably could have just removed the SIM cards and shut them off."

"Whatever. It's taken care of. Okay, southbound on 95, what now?"

"Shit. Without the phone I don't have maps. Just stay on 95."

"Okay. Oh, dude, check the map pocket on the door or the glove compartment. I think my great-grandpa's old paper maps are in there. My dad considered them like part of a time capsule."

Marcus rifled through the compartment, found the maps, and turned on a light. "These are from the 1980s. Wonder if they're obsolete. I suppose the Interstate hasn't changed much since then." He fumbled to open the USA highway map. "We have to go through the Bronx and then cross the Hudson. Then we can either go south on 95 or west on 80. 95 goes all the way to southern Florida."

"Southern Florida is party central. I'd go there."

"80 goes to California… San Francisco."

"Isn't that where your sister went?"

"Yeah, and it's WUS. We're in a stolen car, with stolen money, runaways. If we get pulled over, we're toast. We should get out of EUS. Canada's closer, but their borders are tight. WUS has open borders in the westbound direction, and I'm sure Sharon would let us crash in San Fran. Let's go west."

"As long as we're out of New Rochelle."

Chapter 4: The Running of the Boys

After a few minutes of no sound other than the throaty purr of the Dean, Marcus finally broke the nervous silence. "If we get caught, you have to tell them that you told me your dad gave you the car for your birthday and that I didn't know about the money being your dad's, okay?"

"Just like that? You'd throw me under the bus that quickly?" Dylan said with a sly grin.

"No point in us both getting grand theft auto. If I have to go back, I don't want to be suspended from school or kicked off the team. I'd lose Ohio State. Hell, I'd lose West Point too. I'd probably be thrown in jail for the rest of my life. All the money I brought with me is mine from summer jobs, and nothing in my bag is stolen. As long as I'm not an accomplice to something bigger, and as long as we get caught before next school year starts, then the cops won't have anything on me, and school won't have to know. My dad will be the only one I have to deal with."

"We're not going to get caught."

"What if your dad calls the cops and they put out a bulletin looking for this car? The car is distinctive. It'd be easy to spot."

"My dad is getting hammered right now. He won't be home until at least one a.m.—if he makes it home at all. And he won't be in any condition to make sense of what happened. He'll probably black out. He hardly ever goes in the garage, so he might not even realize the car is gone for days. We'll be long gone. We'll sleep in shifts and drive nonstop to the border."

After a couple more minutes of silence, Dylan spoke up as they passed a road sign indicating the exit for Yankee Stadium. "We're in the scrotum of New York City." Marcus didn't respond. "Get it? Manhattan looks like a penis on the map, with the Bronx as the scrotum?"

Marcus still didn't respond.

"Wonder if we'll get to see the stadium from the highway," Dylan said quietly.

After a few more minutes, Marcus finally spoke again. "How much money do you have?"

Dylan wriggled in his seat with one hand on the wheel, pulled a wad of bills out of his pocket, and handed them to Marcus to count. Marcus flattened each bill, sorted it, and added it to how much he had brought. He then asked Dylan how many miles per gallon the car got, leading to an incredulous outburst of "Ten! This thing only gets *ten* miles per gallon? Are you kidding me?" He alternated rustling the map and looking up at the sun visor for a few minutes.

"Whatcha doing?" asked Dylan.

"Calculating how much money we're going to have to spend on gas between here and San Fran." A few seconds later, he said, "Okay, I think we'll have about—COP! COP! COP!" Marcus pointed frantically into the darkness toward a barely visible car ahead of them.

Dylan let off the accelerator and squinted his eyes at the car. "Dude, take some valium or something. It's just a roof rack!"

"Oh shit," Marcus gasped as he sunk back into his seat, closed his eyes, and pinched the bridge of his nose.

"So how much money do we have?" Dylan asked.

Marcus regained his composure and explained his financial math to Dylan, summarizing that with gas and tolls being mandatory costs, food and other items would be on a fairly tight budget.

The next two hours alternated between silence and nervous chatter. Finally, Dylan looked down at the fuel gauge and said, "We're low on gas. I'm going to take the next exit."

"Low already?" Marcus asked, wondering whether his fuel calculations were already off the mark.

"We didn't start with a full tank. My dad must have siphoned some off when his truck was low. He ought to know better than to store a car long-term without a full tank."

After a stop at a gas station in Drums, PA, Dylan continued driving duties. Marcus closed his eyes and reclined his seat, the prickly fabric reminding him that they were modern replacements. He felt a momentary sense of sympathy for Dylan's dad for having had to replace the original seats after they were ripped up by the Gestapo-like police in an unwarranted drug raid. Dylan had said that his dad couldn't afford to restore them properly, so he had to replace them with these cheap cloth ones. The sympathy evaporated. *That shithead probably was involved with drugs at some point in his life,* Marcus thought. *Maybe it was karmic retribution.*

His thoughts transitioned to his own dad and quickly the Ohio State conversation began to replay in his mind on a repeating loop. He kept trying to think of a way he could have approached it differently and gotten a better result, but he was at a loss. His dad was right. Without his financial assistance, there was no way Marcus could handle school, a job, and ROTC on top of football, and he didn't see any alternatives.

He started to get frustrated with NEUS as a whole. The forced military service. The duty, obedience, and strictness. The itchy trigger fingers everywhere, eager to dole out punishment. The constant threat of juvie, mace, or batons. The need for someone like Dylan to be a bridge to the white world, and even then not feeling fully welcome in that world, and having to cash in his athletic golden ticket of black respect in order to be treated with basic human dignity. Having to secretly watch and re-watch fifty-year-old movies because of the complete lack of arts and entertainment other than sports. Mandatory prayer on a schedule dictated by someone else, and the need to feign a state of permanent piety. He was just starting to feel a great sense of relief to be leaving it all behind when the thought of prayer reminded him of his mom's last words to him. He hoped he hadn't broken her heart. She was an anxious woman to begin with, and he was her last child in the house, so he was leaving her with a premature empty nest. She'd be worried about him, there was no doubt about that.

Marcus's mind once again wandered back to the Ohio State conversation with his dad. He needed to stop thinking about it or else he'd drive himself mad. He sighed audibly, alerting Dylan that he was indeed awake and available for a conversation that would distract him from his own thoughts.

Chapter 5: Spoonfuls of Sugar

"You awake?" Dylan asked.

Marcus raised his seat back up. "Yeah. I didn't sleep a wink."

"Did you hear what they were saying on the radio about Randall being in Chicago on top of all sorts of road maintenance projects? It's causing gridlock all over. Sounded like a lot of people were pissed."

"No. I was zoned out. Can't say I'm surprised, though. I've heard that the entire Chicago to Madison corridor is a hotbed of rebellion. President Randall always seems to be visiting the border states trying to rally support." Marcus pulled out the map again and studied it. "We could divert near Youngstown, Ohio to 71 and 70, go through St. Louis and then catch back up with 80 later. It looks like six of one, half dozen of the other in terms of distance, and we wouldn't waste time and gas idling in traffic around Chicago. We'd avoid all the extra security Randall will have in Chicago too. By the time we get there, your dad might have realized the car is gone."

"Six of one, half dozen of the other? So, which is better?"

Marcus crumpled the map back into his lap. "Think about it, dumbass. How much is a half dozen?"

"Six, right?"

"And six is better than, worse than, or the same as six?"

"Oh, I see. Will we get to go through the 'Gay-way' Arch?" Dylan asked in a goofy voice, referring to the Gateway Arch in St. Louis. "We have to go through the Gay-way Arch on our way to gay-as-hell WUS!"

Marcus rolled his eyes. "I don't think the highway goes through it, just near it."

"I'll bet Sharon drove through the Gay-way," Dylan said, guffawing at his own joke.

"Watch it, now," warned Marcus.

"You miss her, don't you?" Dylan said, finally in a serious tone of voice.

"Yeah. Things got a lot different after she left. Sharon was always kind of a buffer between me and my dad. After she left, things declined, and after Saul left for West Point, all of a sudden I was the sole recipient of my dad's..."

"Bullshit?"

"I was coming to the word 'attention,' but yeah, bullshit works too."

"Have you heard from Sharon at all since she left?" Dylan asked.

"Just a birthday card the first year she was gone. The postmark is how I knew she was in San Fran. God, I hope she's still there. I think she's probably called Mom a few times, always during the day when Dad was at work. Once when I stayed home sick, I saw her talking on the phone. She had this glowing smile on her face and was giggling a lot, but when she saw me at the door, she got all weird."

"Yeah, sounds like either she was talking with your sister or she was having an affair. I know what you mean about Sharon being the buffer between you and your dad though. My mom was like that for me and my dad."

"Your mom was an angel. I never understood how she ended up with your dad. I miss her."

"Me too."

Both boys got quiet for a minute. Marcus looked out the passenger window, trying to give Dylan a moment of privacy in case he was feeling emotional and needed to recompose himself.

Dylan finally spoke again. "My dad has always been an asshole, but he got worse after my mom started teaching. I think he was embarrassed that he couldn't provide everything we needed and that she wasn't a stay-at-home mom."

"I thought your mom loved teaching, though. And Cisarelli once said she was the best teacher he'd ever had."

"She did love it." Another moment of silence passed before Dylan asked, "Speaking of missing people, you think you'll miss Stacie?"

"Not really, and I don't think she'll miss me, either."

"Seriously?"

"Yeah. We were like each other's trophy or something. I think

she was only with me because I'm the star running back and it
looked good on her prom queen résumé. She doesn't really need me
as an accessory during the summer while school is out. She probably
won't even notice I'm gone until school starts back up again in
autumn."

"And what, you were only with her because she's smokin' hot?"

Marcus shrugged. "I guess that was part of it. There wasn't any
other girl I was particularly interested in, at least none that weren't
sent to juvie, and I guess I'd rather be with someone than with no
one."

"Aw, man, are you still carrying a torch for Danaë? Dude, you
gotta move on. Just because a chick was the first one to get your dick
wet doesn't mean you have to be in love with her the rest of your life.
Besides, Stacie is way hotter, and I thought you hated going to the
Zoo for dates with Danaë."

"I did hate the Zoo. I feel bad for *anyone* stuck living there…that
place is so depressing. I almost broke up with Danaë because of that,
but it was such bullshit that she was sent to juvie. The only thing she
was guilty of was being black and poor."

"Oh, don't start with that again," Dylan interrupted. "Getting
back to Stacie…"

Marcus sighed. "I don't know. I felt like I was dating Stacie
because I was *supposed* to date her, like everyone expected us to
date, and who was I to defy the tradition of the star athlete dating the
hot, popular girl? I never felt like she really understood me, though,
not like Danaë did, and she's actually kind of a stuck-up bitch."

"Yeah, all the people who live on the north side near the country
club are stuck up like that, but still, she's a *smokin' hot* stuck-up
bitch. I'd tap that ass," said Dylan, sexually gyrating his hips in his
seat. He leaned over slightly. "Did ya fuck her?" except the way he
said it mashed all the syllables together into a single word to sound
more like "dihjafucker?"

Marcus laughed nervously at the unexpected intimacy of the
question. "No, between the difficulties of finding some privacy and
getting my hands on a condom, it just wasn't happening. The one
time we did have some privacy, though, things got weird."

"How so?"

"I probably shouldn't even tell you this. You can't ever share this with anyone. I started taking my clothes off. She unzipped her dress, and then she just started *crying*. I put my shirt back on, tried to hug and console her, and asked her what was wrong, but she just turned away. I kept telling her it was okay, that we didn't have to do anything, and I just asked her to talk to me and tell me what was wrong. A minute later she was done crying, and she just seemed embarrassed. She apologized. I told her there was no need to apologize. And then she just started getting angry. She told me if I ever said anything about what had just happened, she'd have me sent to juvie."

"That's fucked up! What is she, queer or something?" Dylan said.

"I have no idea. All I know is that things were never that great between us, but ever since that night things have been really awkward. I don't know. I tried to make things work, but I guess we weren't really all that compatible."

"I guess if you're not right for each other, then you're not right for each other. Plenty of other chicks to date." After a few seconds of silence, during which Marcus could tell that the gears in Dylan's head were turning by the look of constipation on his dimly lit face, Dylan suddenly laughed out loud. He broke into his best Sean Connery impersonation and said, "'Losers always whine about their best. Winners go home and fuck the prom queen.'" The impersonation ended, and he asked, "Know what movie?"

"*The Rock.*"

"Yeah, you only got that 'cause of my kick-ass Connery impersonation."

This exchange kicked off a ritual they had done many times before: have entire conversations almost purely in quotes from movies. It was the typical young man way to lighten the mood when things were getting too serious—to have a conversation without having a conversation. Movie quotes somewhat related to what was really on their minds either substituted entirely for serious conversation or used as spoonfuls of sugar mixed in with the medicine of a more serious conversation.

The movies referenced were almost always old, from the pre-partitioned era before NEUS's censorship and rejection of imports destroyed the entertainment industry, and when movies came on physical discs or tapes that could be hidden and forgotten. Hardcopy movies would occasionally be found in attics or basements, then bootleg copies would be made and traded in high schools on the black market. With a limited selection available, they had watched most of the movies so many times that the scripts were practically burned into their memories. Marcus had, in recent months, grown tired of the movie-quote game because it was starting to feel like it had been done too many times, and it was a bit childish, but right now he welcomed the exchange.

Marcus responded with another movie quote loosely related to his relationship with Stacie: "'You have a girlfriend?... Ex-girlfriend. We dated in high school.... Do you still see her?... No. She lost some weight over the summer, so she's dating a lot more now. You know how it goes.'"

"*Loser*?" Dylan guessed.

"Yep. I still can't believe Stacie made us watch that at David's house that night. Terrible movie. That was actually the same night things got weird between me and her."

"Oh, yeah! I remember that. She came marching into the room, yanked the movie we were watching out of the player, shoved *Loser* in, and proceeded to be nasty to everyone the rest of the night. God, watching that movie made my teeth ache," Dylan said.

The game continued with a quote from *Dazed and Confused* that combined the topics of football and dating. Then it transitioned to the topic of masturbation and sex in general with quotes from *Chasing Amy*, *My Super Ex-Girlfriend*, and an obscure quote Marcus had remembered from *Annie Hall*. A *Good Will Hunting* quote from Marcus about relationships with women led Dylan to use a quote from the same movie to turn the conversation toward the topic of a smart young man leaving a home that didn't nurture his talents.

"That reminds me, did you bring a math book in case you get stressed out?"

"Yeah. My calculus book was just sitting there on the bed, so I grabbed it. Wish I had said something to you about holding on to your books," Marcus said, finally acknowledging the guilt he felt for why Dylan's dad had beaten him just a few hours earlier.

Dylan briefly resumed the *Good Will Hunting* quotes with an "'It's not your fault'" to alleviate Marcus's guilt. "I'll never understand how the hell you find re-solving old math problems stress relieving. For me it's stress *inducing*. For me, driving the Dean here is ultimate Zen." He shook his head a few times before commencing with another quote from *Dazed and Confused*, which clearly alluded to his relationship with his dad. At this point they both realized they were tired of the guess-the-movie portion of the game, and Dylan tacked on the movie name himself.

Marcus responded with, "'Sons are put on this earth to trouble their fathers.' *Road to Perdition*. Since we're on the topic of sons disappointing fathers, you think we'll ever go back and disappoint ours some more?"

"I can't. Like I said before, he'd murder me. You think your dad would be willing to adopt me?"

"Dude, my dad would chew you up and spit you out. You wouldn't be his son; you'd be his cadet. He's been trying to mold me into a soldier my entire life. You don't want to be in my family. *I* don't want to be in my family."

"At least he gave a crap about your future. And he didn't beat you."

"I got the rod a few times as punishment, but yeah, his brand of torture was more psychological than physical. Growing up, the only games we'd play were *Stratego*, *Battleship*, or something like capture the flag, and not once did he ever intentionally let me win. Now that I'm older, he never misses an opportunity to remind me that Saul followed in his footsteps. The nicest I think he's ever been to me outside of church was on a take-your-son-to-work day at West Point, when he sat me down in the front row of the military history class he taught."

Marcus thought he might have heard Dylan quietly mutter "boo-hoo" under his breath, but he couldn't be sure. A minute later, Dylan changed the topic to running away from home with his next quote: "'What the hell are we doing here, Harry? We've gotta get out of this town! ...Oh yeah, and go where? Where are we gonna go?... I'll tell you where. Someplace warm. A place where the beer flows like wine. Where beautiful women instinctively flock like the salmon of Capistrano. I'm talking about a little place called Aspen.' *Dumb and Dumber*."

Marcus laughed. "I think our route is actually going to take us pretty close to Aspen." He moved on to his next movie quote. "'What would you do if you were stuck in one place and every day was exactly the same, and nothing that you did mattered?' *Groundhog Day*."

"'Oh, oh, I see. Running away, eh? You yellow bastards! Come back here and take what's coming to ya. I'll bite your legs off!'" Dylan didn't even need to mention that the quote was from *Monty Python and the Holy Grail*. It was their favorite and most quoted movie of all time.

Marcus started singing a song from the movie about a cowardly knight who ran away from danger, and one line in Dylan joined in, and they sang in unison.

They both smiled, delighted at the return of a sense of normality from the nerve-wracking past few hours. Marcus could tell that Dylan was still struggling to think of more movie quotes, but the game had run its course. He laid his head back on the headrest, and before Dylan could come up with one, he fell asleep sitting up.

Chapter 6: Everything a Growing Boy Needs

The car engine fell silent, waking Marcus up. "What time is it? How long was I out?" he asked, blurry eyed.

"It's quarter to three. You were out for about an hour."

Marcus looked out the window and saw gas pumps. "Holy shit, I'm starving," he said, realizing how little he had eaten since lunch the previous day.

"Me too. My stomach has been growling for the last half hour, but I didn't want to pull over until we needed gas."

Marcus headed into the gas station store to look for food while Dylan pumped gas. He came back out a few minutes later, munching on some chips, with a couple of small plastic bags full of supplies and tossed them in the car before climbing in the driver's side to take his turn driving.

Dylan started opening the bags Marcus had acquired. "What's for dinner?" he asked.

"Caffeine, sugar, fat, and salt. Everything a growing boy needs."

"The four basic food groups."

"Not many options at a gas station."

Marcus knew that for Dylan this wasn't an abnormal meal, but Marcus was used to a much cleaner diet. Not only was his mother a great cook who looked out for his well-being, but he was also very health conscious in order to maintain peak athletic condition. As they climbed the on-ramp to return to the highway, he glanced at Dylan, who was shoveling chips into his mouth and chewing annoyingly loudly, and said, "You know, if you keep eating this shit after high school, you're going to get fat as fuck!"

"You're not going to have mommy to cook for you anymore," Dylan retorted through a mouthful of food, "so your diet is going to turn to shit too, then we'll both be fat as fuck."

"If you get fat, then you'll finally have a big fat body to match your big fat ego," Marcus said, earning himself a few light punches to the shoulder.

"We don't need to worry about diet yet," said Dylan. "We're young, we play football, we'll be fine. Besides, calories are calories. It doesn't matter what they are, just how many of them there are."

"First of all, we *played* football. Past tense. Who knows whether we'll ever play again. Second of all, wrong about calories being equal. The body metabolizes different things differently, especially fructose. It's only metabolized in your liver. You are what you eat. Maybe that's why I run the hundred-meter dash in 10.41 seconds and you run it in, what, an hour?"

"Yeah, yeah, yeah, MC. You're faster than me, you're smarter than me, but you can't party like me. I have more fun. You're the one with the stick up your ass."

"Speed and intelligence can be measured objectively. Having fun is subjective. Maybe my definition of fun is just different than yours."

"Yeah, like re-solving old math problems is fun, nerd?"

"I really shouldn't get into a battle of wits with an unarmed man."

"Fuck you," said Dylan. "Where did you learn that shit about fructose anyway? I don't remember that in the textbooks."

"Remember when I told you a few years ago how Cisarelli showed me how to bypass the censors to access international websites? I've learned all sorts of stuff from a British health website." Marcus went on to describe the technical details of bypassing the censors and some of the treasure troves of information he'd found beyond the reaches of the censors.

"*Foreign* websites? You think you can trust them? Aren't the Europeans all a bunch of commies?" Dylan mumbled tiredly.

"Well, I used that 'foreign info' throughout high school, and I'm one of the top sprinters and football players in the state. It certainly didn't hurt me. I stuck mostly to stuff that would help me with sprinting faster, so that if I got caught I wouldn't get in too much trouble, but Bobby said he found all sorts of crazy stuff that contradicted what they teach in school.... Evolution, climate change, economics stuff. He was too scared to tell anyone but me, but..."

Marcus looked over at Dylan after a minute of silence to see if he had any stupid or insulting responses brewing. Dylan's hand was still in the bag of chips, not moving, and his eyes were closed and his mouth parted open as he was drifting off to sleep. Pretty soon he was snoring.

"Of course a discussion involving science puts you to sleep," Marcus muttered under his breath. He turned the radio on softly to keep himself amused and to help drown out the sound of the snoring, not that it took much more than the deep rattle of the Charger's engine.

Marcus turned the ventilation fan speed down a notch. Though the day before had been sweltering, the air temperature had dropped precipitously during the night and even more so after they had entered the Poconos. He could tell that the landscape had already transitioned from mountainous to relatively flat. He wished their journey through the hilly regions of New Jersey and eastern Pennsylvania had been in daylight so that he could have seen the Appalachian beauty rather than experiencing the hills merely as an upward or downward tilt of the car in the nighttime darkness. He had always lived in a more urban, small-city environment and had felt mildly trepidatious about the idea of camping or hiking in wilderness. No amount of Young Soldiers Club survivalist training could drive out the fear of being eaten alive by a bear, but viewing natural beauty from the safety of a car appealed to him.

He inhaled deeply, absorbing the odors of the 1960s mixed with modern smells. The sweet perfume of muscle-car gasoline exhaust and hot motor oil with the faintly musty aroma of cracked, old vinyl upholstery mingled in his nostrils, blending with the new-car chemical smell of the fabric replacement car seats and a hint of chip spices from their snack bags. He exhaled deeply, letting his shoulders relax as the air escaped. The dark of the night supplemented only with the dim headlights and an occasional highway lamp left little visual distraction, and the gentle vibration of the powerful engine was soothing. He could see why Dylan found driving the Dean a Zen experience.

He smiled at the old-fashioned and excessively abundant gauges and switches on the instrument panel: tachometer, speedometer, oil pressure, temperature, alternator. He didn't know what some of the gauges were even for, or if they were just for show and machismo.

Being in such an old car, he felt like he had stepped into the past. It was as if he were driving a time machine, but he couldn't decide whether he was moving forward or backward in time. Had sitting in this old relic of a car absorbed him into its past? Or was he leaving behind an old relic of a culture, desperate to revive the 1950s, and heading into the post-1950s future in a new-fangled, rebellious, 1960s street machine? In some ways the car felt more modern than NEUS.

Marcus's thoughts drifted to the future. He wondered what WUS was like, whether it was populated with nothing but dreadfully dreary communists as everyone in NEUS seemed to exclaim with a knee-jerk reaction anytime anyone mentioned WUS. He figured it probably couldn't be too bad if his sister preferred it over the EUS, and the people of NEUS seemed to think *everyone* outside of EUS was a communist.

As he had gotten older, he had also become more suspicious of knee-jerk reactions, especially when it wasn't backed up with any supporting evidence. His suspicions had especially cemented during football camp one summer, where he met and befriended a couple of players from Mamaroneck High School, New Rochelle's big conference rival. He'd thought they were great despite all the hype around his school that everyone from Mamaroneck was a trash-talking punk.

He wondered how his sister was doing, if she had gone to college and started a career. Whether she was happy, had a partner, missed her family at all. He was just beginning to wonder how they would even find her in San Francisco, if she even still lived there, when the markings on a highway sign seeped into his consciousness, and he suddenly realized they were in the wrong lane to take their southern diversion away from Chicago. He tried not to swerve too hard, crossing over the rumble strips just beyond where the highway had started to fork, and drifted into the correct lane. He glanced over at Dylan to see if the rumble strips had woken him, but Dylan was still asleep.

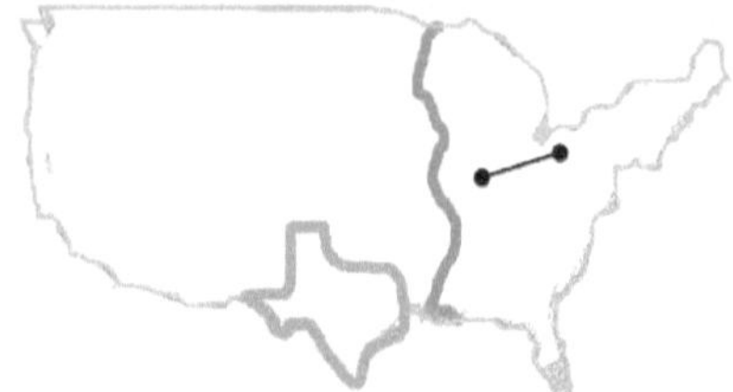

Chapter 7: Does All of Ohio Smell Like This?

"Dude, did you shit your pants?"

These were the first words out of Dylan's mouth after waking up at 5:20 a.m. as they passed through Burbank, Ohio. The light of dawn had just begun to fill the horizon in the rear-view mirror a few moments earlier. The car was flooded with the smell of manure.

"It's a pig farm. We're in Ohio," Marcus assured him.

"Does all of Ohio smell like this? You sure you want to go to Ohio State?" Dylan then muttered something about "not being sure whether this will make things better or worse" before he cracked his window. The unbalanced air pressure hurt Marcus's ears, and he shot up in his seat and began rolling down his own window. As their olfactory senses started to desensitize to the manure, Dylan noticed the daylight, and Marcus informed him that he had been out for close to two hours.

After the next gas stop and change of drivers, they picked up breakfast at the drive-through of the Real McCoy's, a popular EUS mega-chain fast-food restaurant. Dylan held up his food and giddily exclaimed, "Look, orange juice. I'm eating healthy!"

Marcus laughed. "You know that fruit juice is almost pure sugar, right? Most of the fiber that was in the original orange that slows down the sugar absorption has been processed out of the juice, so it's basically liquid candy. That's *if* they haven't diluted it down with artificially flavored sugar-water, which I wouldn't put past a giant corporation like McCoy's. In Germany at least they had to publish nutritional and ingredient information, but who knows what the hell is in the food here."

Dylan's shoulders slumped. "I just can't win with you," he said between one-handed bites of breakfast sandwich while he steered with the other hand.

"Hey, man, I'm just the messenger. It's not me you can't win with, it's nature."

By the end of the brief conversation, both boys had already ravenously wolfed down their breakfasts. The fat and salt of the fast-food breakfast on top of the gas station snacks earlier in the night had Marcus feeling bloated. His head felt numb from lack of sleep and long, monotonous driving shifts. The sugar embedded in their fast-food gave him a temporary boost, but wore off quickly, leaving him even more sluggish. He looked out the windshield at a road mileage sign along the highway that read "Columbus 57" and started to feel a wave of excitement on top of his fatigue, tugging him simultaneously in opposing directions. Dylan noticed the sign at the same time.

"Columbus. Isn't that where Ohio State is?" asked Dylan.

"Yeah. I wonder if we'll be able to see the campus from the highway."

"Want me to drop you off there?" Dylan asked half-jokingly. "You've taken so many AP classes already. And didn't you say something about having to take classes at the community college next year because the high school was running out of advanced classes for you, so couldn't Ohio State just let you in a year early?"

"I doubt it. The registration deadline for this year has probably passed, and even if they would let me in, my scholarship wouldn't kick in until next year. Driving past it today might be the closest I ever get."

"Harsh," Dylan said.

"Real."

"You think you could still get in next year?"

"I don't know. Guess I need to figure out how to graduate high school first. And I'd need to figure out how to pay for it."

"That sucks that they only give partial scholarships. You'd think since the football team brings in a gazillion dollars or so for the school, and players like you are the reason for all that money, they could at least give you a full ride."

"You know the policy. No free lunches. Gotta pull yourself up by your bootstraps," Marcus said.

"Sorry, man. So, if you had stayed in New Rochelle, and Ohio State was a no-go, do you think you would have ended up going to West Point?" Dylan asked.

"I don't know. Maybe. It seems like the only option I was being allowed to choose—if you can call that a choice. How about you? What would you have done if we had stayed? You think you would have become a mechanic or something? Gone to work for your dad?"

"I don't know either. I definitely wouldn't want to work with that asshole, but I hadn't really thought about anything beyond high school much."

After a few minutes of silence, Dylan turned the car radio on at a surprisingly—for him, anyway—low volume and tuned it to some innocuous music station. Forty-five minutes later, they were on the outskirts of Columbus, taking a ring of highways a quarter of the way around the city like a giant rotary. Marcus slipped his keychain out of his pocket and clasped the Ohio State Football medallion in his hand, rubbing it with his thumb. He knew the campus was somewhere in the central-northwest part of the city, and he spent the twenty minutes it took to get from the far northern to far western side of the city looking in the general direction of where it might be, craning his neck to try to see over and around buildings. Alas, it was no use. He wasn't able to identify anything that looked like a college building or stadium. "The buckeye stops here," he muttered disappointedly. He shoved his keychain back in his pocket, slumped back into his seat, and then reclined it back as far as it would go and closed his eyes.

Perhaps it's for the best that I didn't catch a glimpse, he thought. It was kind of like when you were infatuated with a girl who you knew you couldn't ask out on a date. As energizing and stimulating as it was to see her, sometimes it was best not to have the reminder of her burned into your visual cortex, haunting you for days. Now at least he could let go of it and get some sleep rather than obsessing over what the school would be like based on a single, split-second peek at a few buildings. And sleep he did.

Chapter 8: Chicken Bucket

"I've gotta pee like a race horse," Marcus said upon waking several hours later.

At 10:30 a.m., they pulled off the highway for a bathroom and brunch stop at the Terre Haute Chicken Bucket restaurant that was practically nestled into the highway exit itself.

As Dylan parked, Marcus looked around at all the beat-up old pickup trucks surrounding them, wondering whether the people who drove them all actually needed a pickup truck or if it was really just a status symbol, the same way a Porsche was for rich, New Miami investment bankers. And were they all beat up and old because the owners couldn't afford a new one? Or because they valued durability? Or because it was a fashion statement the same way distressed, ripped jeans were sometimes in fashion?

They clumsily climbed their way out of the car, their muscles stiff from sitting so long, and paused to stretch for a few seconds. The temperature was already starting to get quite warm, and the air had a faint industrial, rotten-egg odor. The smell made Marcus briefly second-guess whether he even wanted to eat there, but the pressure in his bladder guided him toward optimism that the interior of the restaurant would be shielded from the stench.

As they walked toward the building, Marcus looked at the mangled rear bumper of one of the trucks. It had a bumper sticker on it that looked as if it were holding the fractured tailgate together like a Band-Aid, reading, "Welcome to *Real* America." He unconsciously clenched his fists and snarled. He unclenched one to point the bumper sticker out to Dylan. "What the fuck is that supposed to mean? Do they not think that New Rochelle is 'real' America too?"

"Maybe they've been to New Rochelle and seen what a shithole it is," Dylan replied.

"Better than this smelly, backwoods dump," Marcus said.

A different truck's bumper sticker that said "Jesus is my co-pilot" caught Dylan's attention, and he pointed it out, saying, "Dude probably gets lost a lot. The owner will be easy to spot, though. He'll be the one with the brown nose from kissing God's ass so much. God's shit is brown like ours, right?"

Marcus chuckled. "I'm all for Christianity, but Conspicuous Christianity is so obnoxious. It shouldn't be something you wear on your sleeve...or your nose."

As they neared the front doors, Marcus looked up at the chain restaurant's distinctive building design. It looked like a box-shaped warehouse with a porch and a phony façade slapped on it in a cheap attempt to make it look like a cross between the veranda of a country home and an Old West saloon. A cheesy, modern sign over the porch declared that this was the Chicken Bucket Restaurant and Olde Country Shoppe.

The front doors led to the old-country-store portion of the building rather than directly to the restaurant—a blatant ploy to sell merchandise to those entering, waiting for a table, or leaving. The wares included things like wicker baskets, quilts, old-fashioned farm implements, metal pails, carved wooden children's puzzles and toys, and candles, all carefully crafted, selected, and displayed to create an aura of being a little mom-and-pop farm supply store. Over the speakers played a twangy country song that made Marcus wince even though the volume was low.

They put their name in for a table and stood near the hostess's station, looking into the restaurant portion of the building. Marcus looked around the dining room, which was half full of patrons. He immediately noticed a trend of body sizes: Everyone was either morbidly obese or rail thin. There did not seem to be any intermediate. Everyone looked grumpy, unfriendly, and probably at least twenty years older than they actually were. Many of the diners were looking back at him and Dylan. Half of the people staring had a blank, defeated look on their faces, but it was the other half who gave Marcus a chill down his spine. They looked at him with a stoic yet disapproving expression that said, "You don't belong here, now do ya, boy?"

He noticed at least a couple of the more rotund men looked

almost identical, and after a few seconds he realized who they reminded him of: an actor from pre-partitioning times named Wilford Brimley, whose 1980s TV shows were often considered safe enough by NEUS censors. These portly old men with their potbellies pressing against the tables all had the same silver walrus mustaches and balding heads like Brimley.

Marcus wondered why they had to wait so long for a table when there were so many empty tables available. Finally, the hostess returned from some back room and explained to them with a sheepish look on her face that customers who weren't regulars had to prepay a deposit before being seated. Dylan began to object, but Marcus interrupted and said he just wanted to pay the deposit and get on with it. They handed the hostess some cash, and she took them to a sticky, poorly cleaned table next to the bathrooms. Marcus wondered whether the deposit and their seating location had something to do with his skin color, but he had to pee so badly that he was relieved to be so close to the bathroom and done with the wait. He excused himself and headed straight there before even picking up a menu.

After returning to the table and studying his menu, Dylan asked him what he could order that wouldn't result in dietary criticism. Marcus rolled his eyes, ignored the question, and resumed looking around the room. Everyone else was eating, mostly silently, as if the other people at their table, presumably their family, were complete strangers. Almost no one was talking. The loudest sounds in the restaurant were the sound of utensils clanking against porcelain plates and bowls, set against that awful, ancient-sounding country music playing over the sound system and the occasional waitress asking if someone wanted a warm-up on their coffee.

The patrons looked like they didn't know what smiling was, like they were a lost tribe separated from the rest of humanity and hadn't discovered smiling yet and were stuck with a permanently grumpy countenance. Marcus was tempted to look one of them in the eyes and flash the biggest, most artificial, toothiest, open-mouthed smile ever, just to see how they would react, but he couldn't muster the courage. For all he knew, it would instigate them to whip out a concealed handgun and shoot him for acting "threatening." Instead he whispered to Dylan, "I think these people might be zombies."

Dylan played along and whispered back, "I didn't bring my machete into the restaurant."

Marcus pointed to some old farm implements strapped to the wall as decorations and asked if any of them would work on a zombie. Just as he was finishing the question, their waitress approached the table and gave him a disapproving look, as if the reason he was pointing at the décor on the wall was because he intended to steal it. *As if all black people are thieves who only go to cheap chain restaurants to steal the top-notch and uber-expensive "artwork" on the walls*, Marcus thought. They placed their orders before Marcus picked up the conversation where he had left off.

"On second thought, they're probably armed zombies. We probably shouldn't attack. Might not be a good idea to bring a pitchfork to a gun battle. If they come after us, we should run."

"Good idea," Dylan said. "I think they're looking at you more than me, though. They probably prefer black brains to white brains, must be healthier or something."

Marcus countered the passive-aggressive snark saying, "Brains are brains. The body metabolizes black brains the same as white brains. Thankfully I don't have to outrun them, I only have to outrun you, and that won't be a problem."

"But you're so much smarter than me. Smarter brains are definitely more delicious than dumb people's brains. I think I should stand up on the table right now and shout that you're a straight-A student and I'm a C student. Then it won't matter that I'm slower. They'll definitely be after you, not me."

"I wonder if they're looking at me because they've never seen a black person before."

"I could go around to each table and take a survey," Dylan jokingly offered.

Marcus didn't doubt that Dylan would carry through and do it if he jokingly accepted the offer, so he ignored it. "Or maybe they're all looking at me because I'm just so damned handsome."

Dylan laughed while sipping his glass of water, almost spraying water out his nostrils. "Yeah, that's it."

Their food arrived surprisingly fast, given how long they had waited to be seated. Marcus surmised that after having failed to discourage the black boy from dining there with a long wait to be seated, they had changed tactics and were trying to rush him out as quickly as possible. Marcus closed his eyes and bowed his head to pray.

Dylan quickly interrupted. "You know, you don't have to do that anymore. No one is going to give you any demerits for not praying at every meal now."

"I know. It's just nice to feel like I'm doing it by my own choice for a change." He opened one eye and looked up at Dylan. "You should join me. I'm praying that I won't be eaten by zombies." He closed his eye again to finish his prayer as Dylan snorted.

Marcus opened his eyes and joined Dylan and the rest of the restaurant in silent ingestion, except for the clanking of their silverware. At one point during the meal, both boys started intentionally striking their plates with their forks increasingly loudly with each bite while looking at each other and trying to hold back the laughter at their secret game of wordlessly mocking the locals. Marcus peeked around the dining room to see if anyone had noticed their game. He saw one of the Wilford Brimley doppelgangers having an animated discussion with the waitress and then pointing at Marcus and Dylan. The waitress shrugged and walked away from the table. Marcus returned his head to facing forward and kept it there, looking only at his food and Dylan, for the rest of the meal.

When the check arrived, Marcus reviewed it carefully to make sure they hadn't tried to rip him off. Satisfied, they paid what the deposit hadn't already covered and left the table, artwork still miraculously intact on the walls. Marcus desperately wanted to leave the building, but Dylan seemed intent on checking out the merchandise in the shop before they exited. Marcus stood at the end of the aisle Dylan was browsing in, as far away from the items for sale as he could, impatiently waiting for Dylan to look up and make eye contact so that he could tell him with body language that he wanted to get the hell out of there. His body language was insufficient, however, as a staff member, an emaciated, pale white man who had the air of a manager, approached them with a concerned look on his face. The manager stopped at Dylan, who was just a few feet from Marcus, and said, "You boys got your food, now it's time to move along so that you aren't scaring off the regulars."

"Scaring off regulars? What the hell?" Dylan responded. "I'm just checking out these candles, minding my own business."

"We both know that you don't need any candles. It's time to move on," the manager said as he gestured toward the door.

The Wilford Brimley doppelganger who had been pointing at Marcus and Dylan earlier waddled over and interjected himself into the discussion. "Is there a problem here?" he asked, looking at Dylan.

"Yeah, I'm just minding my own business, checking out the stuff for sale, and this A-hole is harassing me, telling me to leave," Dylan said.

"It *is* time for you to leave," the man said from behind his furry mustache. "You've disrupted everyone's meals long enough. This isn't your place, and he isn't your kind," he said, pointing at Marcus.

"Are you fucking kidding me with this shit?" Dylan protested. "You don't know him," he said, pointing at Marcus. "He's a star football player. He's going to be huge in the pros in a few years. He's a straight-A student, and a good guy. His dad is a decorated military officer. Who the fuck are you to be disrespecting him like that?"

Marcus took a step forward and touched Dylan on the arm. "'D, let's get out of here. We don't need anything here."

Dylan didn't respond.

The fat man shifted his hand to point at Dylan, nearly jabbing his finger into Dylan's chest as he growled, "I don't give a shit who he is, and I don't give a shit who you are, you loud-mouthed brat. We've tolerated you here long enough. You ain't one of us. You don't belong here, so get the hell out and don't come back."

Dylan turned toward the manager. "So what? You have a problem letting respectable black boys hang around in your building but not flaming fags like this asshole?"

The fat man's face turned red, his fists clenched. He jolted forward, bumping Dylan with his belly, and jabbed his finger into Dylan's chest, making contact this time. "I will whup you, boy. Teach you some manners."

Dylan swatted the man's hand away and shouted, "You wanna go, fat fuck?"

Marcus spotted a knife sheath on the man's belt. The old man's belly bumped Dylan again as he reached toward the case, causing Dylan to lose his balance and take a step backward. Marcus grabbed

Dylan by the arm and used his backward momentum to tug him toward the doors. He shoved the doors open and turned his head—the fat man was giving chase, shouting something about killing them.

Dylan stopped resisting, and they ran through the doors and sprinted back to the car. Marcus reached the passenger door a few seconds before Dylan could reach the driver's side door and fumble with the keys. Marcus turned to see where the fat man was and saw that he had just reached the side of a pickup truck closer to the restaurant and was fumbling with his own set of keys.

Marcus turned his gaze to the rear window of the pickup truck, the same truck with the "Welcome to *Real* America" bumper sticker on it. He spotted two long, dark, horizontal shadows in the window and recognized them as long barreled guns, either rifles or shotguns. Dylan climbed in the car and unlocked the door for Marcus, who quickly jumped in. "He's going for a gun," Marcus said anxiously. He buckled his seatbelt as the Dean roared to life.

Marcus contorted his body to look out the rear window as Dylan threw the car into reverse and backed out of the parking spot. He spotted the fat man's truck rocking back and forth as the man tried to wrestle a gun out of his rack. Dylan shifted gears and gunned the accelerator. The car peeled out of the parking lot and back onto the highway entrance ramp. Marcus turned to look out the side window and saw the fat man pull the rifle out of his truck, lower the barrel, and turn to try to sight the boys. A thicket whizzed by, and Marcus lost sight of the man.

"Holy shit, holy shit, holy shit!" was all he could manage to say. With this much of a head start, and a muscle car versus a rickety pickup truck, there was no way the man could catch them, but he continued to sneak peaks in the passenger side mirror to be sure. The boys continued on their path in silence until the shock wore off and they began chattering excitedly in disbelief about the experience.

"Motherfucking backwoods hillbilly pieces of shit!" Marcus exclaimed.

"We really should have grabbed a pitchfork off the wall. I'd like to shove it right in that fat fuck's belly and watch his guts spill out."

Their profanity-laden tirade continued through the Illinois

border.

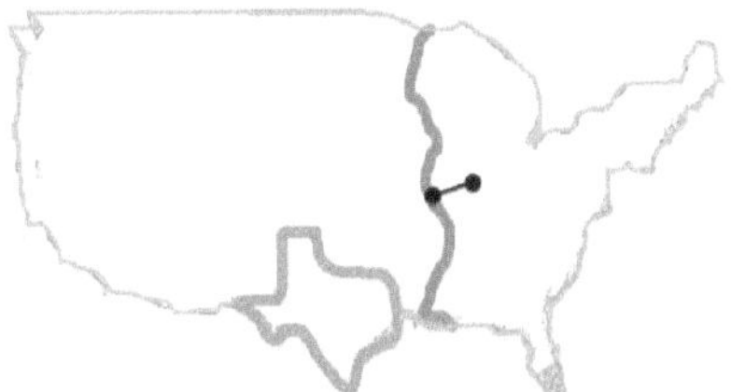

Chapter 9: Borderline

Not far west of the Illinois state line, after their ranting about the Chicken Bucket incident had been exhausted, Marcus took over the driving duties for the two-and-a-half-hour trek to St. Louis. Dylan took a few cat naps, and when he was awake, they mostly listened to the radio, leaving Marcus with little stimulation to keep his mind alert. The driving was tedious, and he frequently had to snap himself out of highway hypnosis.

The scenery was cornfield after endless cornfield as they made their way through rural Illinois, giving Marcus the impression that he was driving on the never-ending loop of a Möbius strip. At least it wasn't pig farms. The sky was nearly cloudless, the sun was strong, and the temperatures roasting hot. Thankfully the Charger had a functioning air-conditioning system, otherwise Marcus worried that they would have been cooked alive in the belly of the light bronze poly steel beast. The summer was already beginning to look like it would have record-breaking highs. Every summer seemed to set a new record.

The frequent zoning out while driving gave this leg of the journey a strange sensation of simultaneously taking both an incredibly long time to complete and flying by in no time. As the highway signs noting the distance to St. Louis started dipping below the sixty-mile mark, Dylan finally broke the silence. "I still can't believe that you just knew to throw me the ball in that busted option play against Mamaroneck. I think that play will end up the highlight of my life."

The game Dylan was referring to was the conference championship against their biggest rivals, the same game Marcus had been thinking of as he ran away from his house. It was an instant classic of a game that Marcus and Dylan knew they'd be talking about for the rest of their lives.

"That was awesome," Marcus said. "I still can't believe I caught your eye and you just knew that I wanted you to break off of your block and run a slant. Mamaroneck had that run stuffed. I can't believe I even threw it to you, but they had been stacking the box all game, and I had to try something different. Probably the worst game of the season for me. I got more yards receiving than I did running."

"Yeah, glad they were focused on stopping you, 'cause it led to me having my best game!" Dylan said.

"Dude, if we hadn't completed that pass, Coach would have kicked us off the damned team!"

"I know! It's like, Coach, dude, shorten the leash a bit and let us improvise a play once in a while, or audible at the line of scrimmage if we see something in the defense. Especially at the end of the season when we've been playing together for months and have gelled as a team. We spent hours, weeks, years practicing as a team, sweating and bleeding together to form a cohesive unit that knows everyone's strengths and weaknesses inside and out. Take a risk and trust us, Coach. What's that he always said about teams at the end of the season?"

"The one that goes 'The strength of a team, like the strength of an army, lies in its loyalty to each other'?" Marcus asked.

"No, the other one. The funny one. 'By the end of this season you boys will know each other so well that you'll recognize each other by the smell of your teammate's panties. You'll be finishing each other's sentences and...' Oh, I forget the rest," Dylan said.

Marcus cackled loudly.

Dylan turned serious. "You know, I think the hardest part of leaving New Rochelle is leaving the team behind. I would kill for each and every one of my football brothers." He paused. "Well, at least I still have you."

Marcus just nodded. He knew what was going on in Dylan's head. He was feeling it too. The approaching border in St. Louis was more than just an imaginary line on a map, or a river carving through land.

Part 2: Rural WUS
Chapter 1: How the West Was One

Not long after reminiscing about what they were already referring to as "the good ol' days," Dylan caught a glimpse of the Gateway Arch in the distance. "Dude, what did those WUSsies do with the other half of that McDonald's sign?" he joked.

Marcus chuckled. "Speaking of...lunchtime? Maybe non-fast food for a change though, like a sit-down restaurant near the Arch or something? Assuming we get past the border without problem, we won't need to be in such a hurry."

Dylan agreed.

As they approached the border, the highway made a long, gentle curve. Just before the curve, Marcus spotted a car on the opposing eastbound side that was pulled over by a EUS highway police cruiser. *Huh, that's odd*, he thought. *There are hardly any cars on the oncoming side.* Their own westbound lanes had both a steady volume and steady speed. Then he spotted a second car pulled over by the police. Then a third. They began to round the curve, and in the wide median he saw a line of about twenty police cruisers hiding from the eastbound traffic behind a long row of shrubbery. As the road straightened out leading to the bridge that crossed the Mississippi River, which was considered a neutral zone between the two countries, Marcus finally spotted the EUS's border patrol station on the opposite side of the road.

"Are you seeing this on the eastbound side?" Marcus asked, looking at what appeared to be miles of cars backed up on the far side of the bridge. "All those poor bastards stuck in line forever, waiting for their brutal car-by-car inspection and security interview at the checkpoint, getting more pissed off every minute they have to wait. Then, finally they get through, they slam on the accelerator in frustration, and to add insult to injury those dicks have a speed trap set up half a mile away."

Dylan shook his head. "That's such a NEUS move!"

"Thank God we don't have to go through that," Marcus said. "I think I'll slow down a bit, though, just in case."

"They probably figure most of the bastards they catch speeding are WUSsies who deserve to be treated like shit."

"Or that the EUS citizens who get caught are disloyal for leaving EUS anyway, so they deserve it. I wonder why WUS doesn't do the same checkpoint going westbound."

"I heard it was because they figure anyone who makes it into EUS has been vetted so thoroughly that the WUSsies figure they can't be a security threat," Dylan said.

"Huh. Kind of like when my family went to Germany. Once we got in, we were free to roam most of Europe. Not that we actually did. My dad had no interest in even leaving the military base." Marcus paused for a moment. "Or maybe the Western Americans don't have a checkpoint just to be perverse...to do the opposite of whatever the Eastern Americans do."

"Whatever the reason, I've heard it's probably the only decision they've made in their entire history that did not increase the level of bureaucracy in their country."

The Dean reached the start of the Poplar Street Bridge, the only remaining bridge crossing the Mississippi into St. Louis that hadn't been closed. Marcus clutched the steering wheel with kung-fu grip, hands at ten and two, squeezing like vises for the duration of the trip across the bridge. Once safely on the WUS side, he exhaled deeply and loosened his grasp. No longer did he have to worry about being pulled over by EUS police, arrested as a fugitive, a runaway, or a car thief, and extradited back to New Rochelle.

Marcus followed the road signs and took the exit for the Arch. The boys navigated to a parking garage and walked in the direction of the Arch in the stifling afternoon heat. Marcus shielded his eyes from the sun and looked up at the giant sixty-three-story, stainless-steel structure. The sensation of time travel renewed. They had just exited the 1969 Dodge Charger, and now they were walking toward a massive 1965 monument, yet despite the Arch being older than the car, he felt like he was walking toward the future. The Arch had somehow managed to maintain a modern feel to it. The dynamic, tapering size and shape remained distinctive and unique, making its form feel futuristic and foreign. It looked like some sort of alien technology that had been dropped from the sky and embedded into the ground like a double-pronged lawn dart. The curving shape and the cross-section that narrowed the higher the Arch rose deviated from all of the rectangular and uniform building shapes he was used to growing up in EUS.

They stopped at the windows of a few restaurants to review the menus on display as they meandered Market Street. "Blech," was all Dylan had to say at each one. After a few rejections, Marcus asked Dylan what it was that he didn't like about the restaurants so far. "No meat," was Dylan's only response. Finally, they stumbled across a quaint little restaurant entrance that advertised "historic St. Louis-style barbecue" and went in. The restaurant was packed, so they gave their names to the hostess. They were stunned when the hostess asked them for their IDs.

"May I ask why you need our IDs?" Marcus asked as he pulled his wallet out of his pants. "We're not ordering alcohol."

"The bean counters in San Fran make us track and limit how many times a Western American citizen can visit a non-conforming restaurant. We have to document everyone's visits," she replied.

"Non-conforming?" Marcus asked.

"Restaurants are required to serve a menu that is ninety percent vegetarian, and they have to meet a certain threshold of other healthy dietary minimums. This restaurant is only allowed to exist because of an exemption to the rule for a limited number of historic restaurants that have served unique, local, cultural specialties since before the partitioning."

Marcus laughed. "Well, I guess bean counting is technically a vegetarian activity."

Dylan just shook his head.

The hostess scanned their IDs in a machine, then handed them a couple of menus and told them to take a seat in the crowded waiting room.

"See anything you like?" Marcus asked after reviewing the menu for a while.

Dylan nodded. "Think I'll get the ribs, assuming that the WUSsies let me. I don't see anything here saying it requires a special permit or anything."

"Ditto," Marcus said. He tilted his head back and craned his neck to get a better view of the Arch down the street.

"After lunch, you want to go up Mussolini's Arch?" Dylan asked.

"Yeah, I think the Arch looks pretty cool. I'd be interested in going up it," said Marcus.

Dylan excused himself to go to the bathroom. A man sitting next to Marcus turned toward him and said, "Oh, you guys better watch what you say with the 'Mussolini's Arch' and the 'WUSsies' comments. The further west ya go, the more sensitive they get, but for insulting the Arch, even these guys here will slap a disparagement fine on ya faster than a UW Madison student can chug a Miller Lite, don't cha know."

"I didn't know. Thanks," Marcus said.

"You betcha. They don't like people sayin' negative stuff about their Arch or nothin'. After the partitioning bill was signed back in 2024, the Gateway Arch became the iconic symbol of WUS. EUS got the Statue of Liberty and all the monuments in DC, and this was WUS's primary man-made monument. Being right at the border, it was considered a welcoming beacon to the poor, misguided souls of the EUS. They just cleaned and restored it a few years ago. Got a nice, shiny patina to it now."

"It is beautiful," Marcus said, turning briefly to admire it again.

"Yah. And secondly, they object to callin' it Mussolini's Arch because they say it conflates communism and fascism. Ya know the history of why Eastern Americans nicknamed it Mussolini's Arch, don'tcha?"

"I don't," Marcus confessed, resting his menu on his lap.

"Oh, yah. It goes way back to the accusations made during the Arch's original design that the idea for it had been stolen from an arch proposed by Mussolini for the 1942 World's Fair in Italy. The one in Italy ended up never being built because World War II canceled the fair. The architect for the Gateway Arch claimed he had never heard of Mussolini's Arch when he came up with the idea of an arch, but the controversy was revived after the partitioning due to the common confusion by Eastern Americans that Mussolini's fascism was the same as communism. They believed that calling the Gateway Arch 'Mussolini's Arch' was akin to calling it a symbol of communism. They're really touchy here about name callin' and stuff, don'tcha know."

"No. I didn't know," Marcus said. "I take it you aren't Western American?"

"Nah. Me an' my family are from Wisconsin. I alternate taking my family west one summer vacation and east the next. This year I did a bad job of timing our trip though. WUS's schools have their two-week summer vacation goin' on right now, so everything is cram-packed tighter than a vacuum-sealed bag of cheese curds."

"I imagine going back across the border is no fun. Looks like the lines for EUS security are brutal," Marcus said.

"Yah, made the mistake of tryin' to cross here in St. Louis once. Never again. We'll be crossin' into what I like to call 'East Minnesconsin' from 'West Minnesconsin,' our separated conjoined twin state. The crossin' usually isn't as busy there."

"You mean Minnesota to Wisconsin?"

"Yah. We're goin' up to Mount Rushmore after this, to see the monument there before they close it down for good. Then we'll head back through Minnesota real quick. Got lotsa family in Minnesota, don'tcha know."

"I didn't know. I didn't know they were closing Mount Rushmore down either," Marcus said.

"Yah. Somethin' 'bout Teddy Roosevelt exterminatin' Native Americans and Washington and Jefferson ownin' slaves."

"You seem to know a lot of the history of the partitioning. Do you know why the conservatives chose the eastern United States and liberals chose the west?" Marcus asked.

"Oh, yah. Some people thought they should split north-south like the Civil War, but the south was so much poorer than the north that the conservatives felt like they would be getting the short end of the stick if they went south.

"Others thought the liberals should get the west and east coasts and the conservatives should get the middle of the country to minimize mass migrations. Mass migrations had been done before though, such as when Pakistan split off from India, and the liberals didn't want their country split in half and separated by another hostile country.

"What really cinched the deal though was that the conservatives wanted to preserve the great American history and heritage of the east, and the liberals wanted to preserve the beautiful environment and wilderness of the western states. By taking the region east of the Mississippi, the conservatives got to essentially rewind the clock back to before the Louisiana Purchase. They got the White House, the historical sites of the American Revolution, Liberty Bell, Plymouth Rock, the historic plantations, Independence Hall. Basically, all the oldest historic sites.

"I'm just thankful that the split and mass migration didn't turn into a bloodbath the way Pakistan's split did. There was more violence here before the split than during the migration. I think partitioning might have saved us from another civil war."

Marcus was about to press his new Wisconsin buddy about the history of NEUS and SEUS informally separating into two distinct regions when the hostess came over and called out the guy's name. They exchanged "nice ta meetcha" salutations, and a new group filled the vacancy on the bench in the waiting room.

Dylan returned from the bathroom, and a short time later the hostess returned for Marcus and Dylan and showed them to their table. Marcus filled Dylan in on what the Wisconsin guy had told him while they waited for their food to arrive, and Dylan filled Marcus in on how weird the bathrooms were, noting that it was a long corridor with probably twenty private unisex rooms that took up at least a third of the restaurant's space.

The meal ended up being bit of a splurge, as there was a surcharge for the historic, meat-based dishes, but they were feeling celebratory for having made it out of the EUS. They enjoyed the decadence of the smoky, heavily sauced ribs and clinked their root beer glasses together to toast to the unknown future that lay ahead.

Chapter 2: Mussolini's Arch

When they arrived at the base of the Arch after lunch, they were dismayed to find out that the guy from Wisconsin had been right about things being packed with families on vacation. The lines for the Arch were fairly long, extending out the doors of the subterranean museum and security check entrance. Perhaps the scorching sun and temperatures had scared away some of the tourists, but not many.

The heavy, carnivorous meal with sugary barbeque sauce sat in Marcus's belly like a load of bricks, making him sleepy, but he was just happy to be out of the sitting position, upright and moving his stiff body a little. The boys entered the line next to a plaque that read "Once the Gateway to the western part of the United States, now the Gateway to the sovereign nation of the Western United States."

Once inside the doors, they saw that the walls along the waiting line were plastered with rules, regulations, and warnings. Whatever the WUS government had lacked in security and bureaucracy at the border crossing, they made up for at the Gateway Arch entrance. After an hour-long process that included signing an eight-page contract to buy tickets and a security gate with metal detectors and x-ray machines, they were finally next in line to board the tram to the top.

At long last, the tram arrived and the doors opened. Dylan laughed at the ridiculously small doorway to the even more ridiculously small five-person tram pod. "Is this the tram or a clothes dryer?" he asked no one in particular.

The boys entered first, and three strangers followed them in. The tram pod lacked air-conditioning and was agonizingly hot. One of the strangers, a woman, immediately scolded Dylan for "man-spreading," as he had his knees spread far apart.

"Didn't you read your contract?" she asked. "It specifically prohibits man-spreading."

"Just tryin' to air out my sweaty crotch," Dylan muttered.

A voice over an intercom speaker spent five minutes reiterating the most important rules and regulations and finally warned, "Caution, the tram pod doors are closing."

"Did he say tram pod or tampon?" Dylan asked no one in particular. "'Cause I feel like I've been shoved like a tampon into a wet, hot, tight pussy."

The woman who had scolded him about man-spreading shot him a look of disgust. Marcus closed his eyes and silently prayed that Dylan would keep his mouth shut the rest of the four-minute ride up the leg of the Arch, and that the top of the Arch would have air-conditioning.

At the top, the temperature in the observation room was slightly cooler than the tram but was still disgustingly warm. It was an improvement, though, and Marcus tried to put aside thoughts about discomfort. As he reached the top of a short flight of stairs that led to the observation room, he found himself fascinated by the unique shape of the room. One of his all-time favorite bootleg TV shows was *Star Trek: The Next Generation,* and the curved floor and ceiling of this room gave him the sensation that he was in the observation lounge of the starship *Enterprise* as it went through a warp in the fabric of space-time.

He made his way to one of the westward-facing observation windows and leaned over to look out. The view was spectacular. He felt like a giant standing over a meticulously crafted model train set's landscape. He crossed over to an eastward-facing window and looked out over the river to EUS territory for a couple of minutes. He walked back and forth between windows several times, alternating between examining known EUS versus unknown WUS. When scanning the distance, beyond the immediate foreground differences of a major city to the west versus a river to the east, from here the two countries looked essentially the same. He spent the better part of twenty minutes trying to absorb every sight there was to see until Dylan complained that he was too bored to deal with the heat anymore.

The three-minute ride to the bottom felt considerably shorter than the ride up. Back at the base they lingered in the air-conditioned museum to cool off, pretending to be interested in the cheesy dioramas showing the history of the Louisiana Purchase, the site the Arch was built on, and the construction of the Arch itself. They wanted to cool off longer, but they noticed the woman who had gotten upset with Dylan in the tram pod talking to a security guard and pointing at them. The guard shrugged a couple of times while talking to the woman before turning, rolling his eyes, talking into the radio pinned to his shoulder, and slowly sauntering toward them. The boys took this as their cue to leave. They hurriedly exited the building and headed toward the parking garage.

Chapter 3: Maybe I'm Just Like My Mother

On their way to the highway entrance they drove past what appeared to be several gas stations, looking for someplace to fill up their tank before they got back on the highway, but everywhere they went the gas pumps were missing. Finally, Dylan pulled into one station and asked where they could get gas. The attendant informed them that in cities gas was hard to find. Most gas stations had converted to a mix of hydrogen fuel and battery swapping and were no longer willing to pay the high fees and taxes for selling gasoline. He advised them to try farther away from the city, where rural farmers might fuel up their farm truck or other equipment with gasoline.

They got back on the highway and headed west. Almost immediately they passed through a toll station. They had gone through a few toll roads in EUS, but the tolls here were drastically higher than in the EUS. Marcus began to wonder how much he had underestimated WUS tolls in his financial calculations earlier in the trip and whether splurging on barbeque in St. Louis had been a bad idea.

He looked around at the rest of the cars waiting to go through the toll station. All of them looked modern, or at least in comparison to what he was used to in EUS. They didn't have particularly sexy styling, and most looked similar to one another, but they all looked relatively new. They were all electric and nearly silent too. The Charger stood out like a sore thumb. Marcus looked at the drivers and passengers of the cars nearest them and saw nearly everyone was looking at them and the Charger. He quickly turned his head forward again, jamming his head into the headrest.

Marcus turned his attention back to the interior of the car. After a minute he said, "Hey, D? Next time we're in a building together or out in public, could you maybe *not* say shit that gets us in trouble with the locals and causes us to have to flee in a hurry? First the

Chicken Bucket, then the Arch. It's getting old."

"Hey, MC?" Dylan responded in a mockingly whiny voice. "Could you maybe not be such a pussy? I mean, come on. I'm not gonna take shit from *nobody*. Someone gives me shit, I give it back to them twofold. I stand up for myself. At the Chicken Bucket I stood up for both of us, and at the Arch I was just being funny, and some oversensitive commie chick got offended. She probably would have gotten offended no matter what I said or did. I could have said 'hello, ma'am,' and she would have gotten offended. That's just how these commies are."

"Yeah, but at the Chicken Bucket we almost got shot," Marcus said, "and at the Arch we probably would have been fined or arrested. Pick your battles, man."

"Life is a battle. You have to fight for everything, otherwise everyone will walk all over you," Dylan replied.

Marcus decided to let the topic go. They were half an hour west of St. Louis when they finally exited the highway again, their car running on fumes, and found a station that sold gas. Marcus's jaw dropped when he saw the gas prices. They were four times what they had been in EUS.

"Are gas prices like this everywhere in WUS? We're going to run out of money before we reach San Fran."

"I dunno," Dylan said.

Marcus went inside to pre-pay for gas and to ask the attendant whether the prices were normal. The attendant confirmed his fears. Marcus came out in shock and confronted Dylan, who was still pumping gas. "We're not going to make it to San Fran. We are hemorrhaging money, and gas and tolls are insane here."

"We'll be fine."

"No, we won't. How can you say that? We have to do something. It's the Charger. We need to trade it in for something electric, or at least fuel efficient. This thing devours money."

"We don't need to trade in the Dean, dude. We'll be fine. It'll work itself out. We'll find the money."

The lack of logic in Dylan's attempts to calm Marcus only flabbergasted him more. "What do you mean it'll work itself out? You think money will just magically appear? Or do you have plans to rob a bank? What?"

"Dude, chill out. We'll figure something out."

"You don't seem to understand how the world works. Shit doesn't just magically fix itself and get handed to you on a silver platter. Things only improve when people put in the effort to *make* them improve. We have to change the situation. The Charger's gotta go."

"We're not selling the Dean," Dylan said, the irritation growing in his voice. "Have we ever failed before? We're not going to fail now." He got in the car, slamming the door a little harder than normal. Marcus climbed in the passenger side and slammed his door shut even harder.

"We've..." Marcus started, but then had to pause as the Charger let out an extra-loud roar as Dylan started it. "We've never been on our own before," Marcus continued. "This is a whole new set of variables. Are you ignorant enough to think that bad things don't happen to good people? Of course they do! Look at the people living in poverty in the Zoo. You think they're poor because they deserved to be? No, something happened...their industry collapsed and they lost their job, or they had a medical emergency and didn't have insurance, so it bankrupted them, or they had mental illness and couldn't get the help they needed. They didn't deserve it; it just happened. We are hemorrhaging money, and this car is causing most of it. We have to stop the bleeding. We have to get rid of it."

"What the fuck is with you, MC? We are not selling the fucking Charger!" Dylan shouted as he slammed his hand on the steering wheel. The tires squealed briefly as the Charger darted forward. Dylan began alternating between using his right hand to shift gears and waving it in the air wildly as he spoke again. "You are absolutely riddled with anxiety. You sound just like your fucking mom. Jesus, and that shit about things not being served to us on a silver platter? I could swear your dad was sitting next to me! What the fuck?" Dylan slammed his palm on the steering wheel again. "You need me to turn the car around and go back home so Mommy and Daddy can fix things? And when you're not paranoid about money or getting caught or hurting commie feelings, then you're ripping me for my diet or calling me dumb. Seriously, dude, what the fuck is your problem? You always have some sort of cold-blooded, mercenary-type way of taking me down a peg anytime I have something to say."

His hand made another thud as it smacked the steering wheel. He paused for a moment. "We're not getting rid of the Charger." *Thud.* "It's mine." *Thud.* "It has been in my family for generations, and I deserve it after the hell my dad put me through, so just shut the fuck up."

Marcus sat in the passenger seat sulking, wounded by the comparison to his mom and dad. He wanted to retaliate by telling Dylan all of the awful ways he was just like his own father too, but he would probably be accused of being mean like his father again if he fired back at this moment. He looked out his window as the car accelerated up the highway ramp. He chewed on his lip and fought back angry thoughts. He didn't want Dylan any more agitated and out of control as they began driving at highway speeds in this 1960s death box.

An image of Dylan's mom flashed in his mind briefly. Marcus looked at the dashboard console, realizing that the car didn't even have airbags. *Didn't the real James Dean die in a fiery car crash?* Marcus thought. He couldn't remember for sure, but it felt correct. *Hope the car's name isn't a bad omen.*

Marcus began to wonder how much truth there was to what Dylan had said about him being like his mom and dad. He had heard his father use the "silver platter" line before, but the context of his own use of it a few minutes earlier was different. The logic of bad things happening to good people was unassailable, and Marcus was just stating facts, not being condescending the way his dad was whenever he used the phrase. He could admit to himself that he had inherited his dad's cold, calculating military logic and strategizing, but not his condescending and controlling nature. *Well, maybe.*

He knew he was highly critical of Dylan whenever he felt Dylan was saying or doing something stupid. It wasn't that he thought Dylan *was* stupid, rather he thought Dylan *acted* stupid. Marcus had numerous theories as to why Dylan might pretend to be dumber than he actually was. Attention seeking, the need to seem cool or tough, or maybe because he thought he was destined to be a blue-collar auto mechanic, so why bother trying to learn anything else. Or maybe it was just something to do with his father's abuse or his mother's death. He had done better in school before her death. Marcus didn't know for sure why Dylan acted the way he did; he just knew it bothered him.

He had no doubt that the reason why he accentuated his own intelligence around Dylan was to serve as an example of how someone Dylan valued could be intelligent without repercussion. He wanted to be living proof for Dylan that it was okay to be smart and to corral Dylan into being the better person that he knew he could be—the carrot of a good role model combined with the stick of criticism for stupid and irritating behavior.

Maybe there was some of Marcus's father in him, but the comparison to his mother couldn't be accurate. He did have a lot of anxiety at the moment, but it seemed like it was warranted. Someone had to worry about their finances. Someone had to have a plan to keep catastrophe at bay. They were headed down a financial dead-end.

Dylan had turned the radio on after their spat, at a volume loud enough to signal that he didn't want to talk anymore. In a moment of synchronicity, Prince's "When Doves Cry" came on the radio. Marcus cringed the first time through the chorus, which mentioned people being like their fathers or mothers. His mind went into high gear, and by the second round through the chorus, he began riffing on the song, singing his own lyrics on top of Prince.

"Maybe I'm just too military.

Maybe I'm just like my father, tactical.

Maybe I'm just like my mother.

She's got anxiety."

Finally, Dylan caved and laughed. "Dork!"

Tension smoothed over for now. Smoothed over but unresolved, Marcus thought.

Chapter 4: Vapor Lock

The monotony of the middle of the continent continued into Kansas. By the time they reached the exhilarating Rockies, all Marcus could remember of Kansas was the Dust Bowl truck stop where they had eaten dinner, slept in the car, eaten breakfast, and where Dylan had wasted precious money on a silly T-shirt during a brief moment that Marcus wasn't with him.

Marcus had said, "You know, if we run out of money, and we're down to our last few dollars for one last meal, I'm going to use all of that money on food for me, and you can eat that fucking shirt."

Dylan had stuffed part of the shirt in his mouth and replied, "Mmm, that's some good shirt!"

As they drove through Denver, Marcus's eyes glued to the mountains from the passenger seat, he pondered why he found oceans and mountains so appealing. Perhaps it was because they were places of change, he decided. The mountains had changes from flat to steep, with a constantly varying landscape of random jagged ups and downs. The shores of the ocean had a change from liquid to solid, along with the perpetually shifting motion of the waves. He wondered whether there were people who actually preferred the static, flat plains of some of the former Midwestern states. Probably people who didn't like change and felt like the flatness was a security blanket, he imagined. Probably people like the Wilford Brimley doppelgangers he had seen at the Chicken Bucket in Terre Haute.

The Dean had gotten relatively poor gas mileage on this leg. Marcus wasn't sure if it was his imagination, but it seemed to be running more sluggishly, and they just barely made it to a gas station in farm country north of Denver. The boys went into the station to grab some lunch and pre-pay for gas. To Dylan's frustration, the options consisted of a dozen varieties of kale chips or some bags of nuts with dried fruit.

The station attendant was a young Hispanic boy about the same age as them. Dylan walked up to him and asked, "You speak English?"

The attendant glared at him. "Do you?"

Marcus tuned out for a minute as he perused the food options. He tuned back in when he noticed both Dylan's and the attendant's voices getting more agitated.

"Don't you have any *real* food here?" Dylan asked.

The attendant replied with a statement of the obvious that they had real food—it was kale chips and nut mixes.

"So you don't have any secret stash of spic food like tacos or burritos or something like that?" Dylan asked.

Marcus shot Dylan a look of horror. Dylan waited for a second before shrugging. "Whatever. We'll take the stupid kale chips and $170 on pump 2."

"I'm not sure we have any gas left," the attendant said. His eyes locked with Dylan's, and his jaw clenched.

Marcus saw that Dylan was about to erupt into more rude comments. He stepped toward the counter and intervened, putting his arm across Dylan's chest. "Dude, I got this. Go back to the car."

Dylan balked at first, but Marcus calmly insisted that he return to the car to wait. Marcus turned to the attendant after Dylan was out the door. "Sorry about that. He gets ornery when he's hungry, and we're from the EUS, so he's not used to healthy foods being sold at gas stations."

The attendant released his jaw. "Why on mother earth would you hang out with a racist asshole like him?" he asked.

"He's always been a bit of an asshole, but that's actually the first time I've ever heard him add a racist component to it. I don't know what's up his ass today."

The attendant looked out the window at the Charger. "You know that car isn't street legal here, don't you?"

"What do you mean?"

"You have to have a special permit to drive a gasoline-powered car, and even then the car has to meet fuel-efficiency standards. I probably shouldn't even sell you gas."

"It's the only transportation we have. We can't go anywhere

until you sell us gas. You want that asshole out of your life, right?" Marcus said, pointing out the window toward Dylan. The attendant's facial expression remained unchanged. "Besides, we're just here to visit my sister, and she doesn't live that far away. We'll be off the roads in no time."

The attendant seemed to be weighing his options. Marcus tried one more tactic to tip the scales in their favor. "There's a twenty-dollar cash tip in it for you if you'll sell us the gas."

"So, $170 on pump 2, the chips, and nuts. Anything else for you today?"

Marcus paid him, tacking on the bribery tip, and went out to the car and pumped the gas. He hopped in the driver's seat. "What the fuck was that in there?" he asked Dylan.

"Dude was pissing me off."

"You almost stranded us. Once again, your mouth gets us into trouble. And what was with the racist shit?"

"I only said it because he was an asshole, and I knew it would get under his skin. I'm not racist."

"You can't say racist shit and claim you're not a racist. How do you think it makes me feel hearing you say shit like that?"

"Sorry. It's just...when people piss me off, I want to get revenge and piss *them* off. Saying shit like that pisses them off."

Marcus shook his head. "Whatever. Eat some nuts. They have protein and will fill you up so you're not so hangry."

Marcus retreated into his own thoughts as he drove, still in disbelief. *Once again, I feel like his chaperone,* he thought. *Man, I'm getting sick of this.* He thought back to numerous incidents of Dylan's bullying, rule breaking, and selfishness in school when he'd felt he had to scold or instruct Dylan on behaving like a decent human being. The teachers intervened when Dylan broke some rules but not when he was bullying classmates. Sometimes they even seemed to encourage Dylan's bullying. *Why did I have to be the one to call him on that sort of behavior?* It was a question that had troubled him several times in the past year but one to which he had found no satisfying resolution. After a few minutes, a theory began to blossom. *When Dylan bullies our classmates, they cower quietly. That's what the teachers want,* Marcus thought. *A room full of kids who are silent and afraid. He's doing the teachers' job for them.* Then it dawned on him how he might fit into the equation. *The teachers used Dylan to control our classmates, sacrificing a few nerds every once in a while, and they used me to control Dylan. I did their job for them too.* He shook his head. *I guess I am my brother's keeper.*

Marcus's introspection was interrupted as he checked his rearview mirror and saw flashing red and blue lights. "Shit. It's the cops."

Dylan turned around and looked behind them. The police car was right behind them, not making any attempt to pass. "Dude, he's driving an electric piece of shit. We could totally outrun him."

"I'm not running from the cops, dipshit. That'll only make things worse."

Marcus pulled over to the shoulder and waited for the officer to run their plates and walk up to the driver's side window. With the engine off, the air-conditioning had shut off with it. It was another scorchingly hot day, and it had just reached the midafternoon peak temperature. He was sweating and nervous, and the thought of the officer running their plates and potentially discovering that this was a stolen car wasn't helping.

Marcus turned to Dylan. "Don't say a word. Let me handle this. But remember, if he asks, you told me your dad gave you the car as a birthday present." He rolled down the window as the officer approached. The officer was a fairly well-built Hispanic man in his thirties, possibly with some Native American heritage. He bowed down toward the window, his wide-brimmed hat nearly hitting the top of the door frame, casting a shadow on Marcus's left arm. He eyed the interior of the car briefly before opening his solidly built jaw and locking eyes with Marcus.

"Do you know why I pulled you over?" he asked, speaking mostly out of one side of his mouth.

"No, sir," Marcus replied. "I was going the speed limit."

"Where are you boys from?"

"New York, sir."

"That explains it. You know this car isn't street legal in the Western United States?"

"No, sir."

"Here we actually give a damn about the environment. The earth is a closed system with finite resources. We have standards for cars to prevent the pillaging of the earth. So, what brings you boys over the border in this toxic atrocity?"

"We're on our way to visit my sister. She moved to WUS seven years ago, and I haven't seen her since, so we figured we'd drive out here and visit her during summer break," Marcus said, hoping his plea for sympathy was subtle enough.

"Hmmm. Well, I guess since you're from the EUS, and you're minors in unfamiliar territory, I can let this slide. I don't want to strand you before you've even reached your sister. But be warned, you're likely to get pulled over again, and the next officer might not be so lenient. You really ought to be in a street-legal vehicle."

"Yes, sir. As soon as we reach my sister's place, we'll stay off the roads. Thank you."

"You have a nice day, and be sure to maintain respect for women and people of different ethnic backgrounds," the officer said.

As the officer began walking back to his car, Dylan muttered, "I'll bet that fucking spic at the gas station narced on us."

"I thought you said you weren't racist," Marcus said as he turned the key in the ignition to start the car. The car remained silent, refusing to start. "What the fuck?"

"Try it again," Dylan encouraged. Still nothing. "Shit. I think it's vapor locked. Probably the altitude and heat." He got out of the car and fiddled with the gas cap.

The police officer got back out of the car and shouted, "Everything all right?"

"Yes, sir. Just vapor lock. We'll be fine." He walked up to the driver's side window and told Marcus to hand him a water bottle and his truck stop T-shirt and then to pop the hood. He took off his shirt, pulled on the new one, doused the old shirt he had been wearing with water, and handed the water bottle back to Marcus. Marcus took a peek back to see whether the police officer was looking when Dylan took his shirt off, hoping that the officer wouldn't see the plethora of bruises on Dylan's torso while he was briefly topless, which would surely have instigated a new round of questioning. Dylan then disappeared behind the hood.

A couple of minutes later, Dylan hopped back in the passenger seat. "Give it some time to cool down a bit." He smiled. "Looks like this shirt came in handy. I think I just earned myself a last meal with you."

"You had other shirts packed in your bag."

Ten minutes later, Dylan got out and grabbed the wet T-shirt from under the hood and prompted Marcus to try starting the car again but to push the gas pedal down completely and hold it there. This time the engine roared to life. He gave a thumbs-up to the police officer and hopped back into the car.

"My hero," Marcus said. He said it like he was being sarcastic, but he was actually impressed by Dylan's skills and quick thinking. But given that the car troubles had only intensified Marcus's desire to get rid of the car, he didn't want Dylan feeling any sense of extra confidence that holding on to the car was a good idea. Plus, his ego didn't need more bloating.

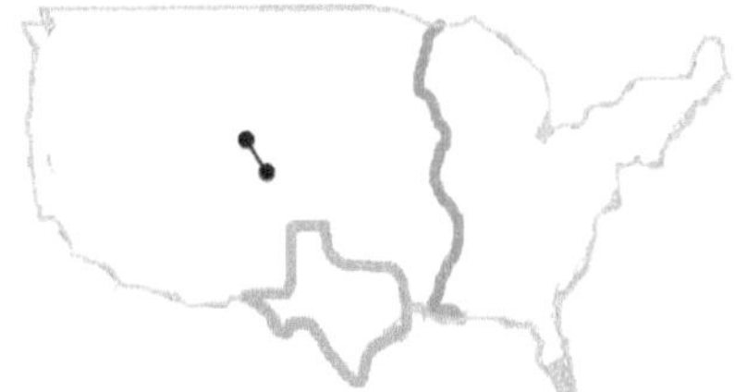

Chapter 5: L.O.V.E. On Elk Mountain

They chugged along for another couple of hours, crossing into Wyoming and onto I-80, the point where the six and the half dozen from their diversion away from Chicago intersected. The car continued to have a sluggish feel to it, but it was operational so long as they kept moving. At close to 5:30 p.m., they pulled off the highway in search of dinner.

Elk Mountain was a small town that felt straight out of the Old West. Their route into town took them over dirt roads, past ranches with horses, and past a tiny town hall that looked like a trailer with a wooden parapet scabbed onto the front façade. Given the scenery, it only seemed appropriate to stop at a restaurant across from the town hall called Wagon Hitch Trading Post.

Marcus pulled into a gravel parking spot in front of the building. He turned the car off. "Think it'll vapor lock again?"

"Probably."

Marcus turned the key just to see. It didn't start. "Yup."

"I need to tune the carburetor. I don't have any tools, though, and mechanic shops are probably closed Sunday nights. Maybe we should stay here tonight, and I can look tomorrow morning."

"Sounds good, partner. Let's get us some grub in this here Wild Wild West saloon."

They lumbered into the restaurant, their bodies stiff again from the long time spent sitting in the car. They walked with a silly, bowlegged, rigid gait partly because of that stiffness from sitting but also to imitate the bowlegged cowboys they had seen on old western TV shows, a staple of NEUS television, walking into saloons after riding their horses all day.

Inside, they discovered that it was both a restaurant and an actual trading company in the same building. Its layout was somewhat similar to the Chicken Bucket in Indiana, except with a sparser décor and a more authentic mom-and-pop feel to it rather than the artificial chain restaurant feel that the Chicken Bucket had. The boys were seated and began skimming their menus. The menu probably met the WUS vegetarian minimums, but Marcus saw that it also had a section of meat-based dishes from the historic ranching west.

"I'm getting a bison burger, how about you?" Dylan asked.

"I was thinking about getting that too, but I've never had bison before, and I don't want to risk wasting our money on something I end up hating."

"How could you go wrong with a burger?" Dylan asked.

Marcus shrugged and took the hedged bet on the burger, assuming that Dylan was right about any burger being good, and figuring that the side of a potato and vegetables could probably suffice even if he ended up hating bison meat.

When their meal arrived, Marcus closed his eyes to silently pray before taking his first bite. He could hear Dylan smacking his lips as he ate and suddenly found himself wishing for some of that twangy country background music from the Chicken Bucket to mask it. He opened his eyes and dug into his burger, then he and Dylan exchanged nods of pleasant surprise— their bets had paid off, and the burgers were delicious.

After their meal, Dylan said he should look around the trading post store to see if they happened to have the tools he needed for the car. Dylan wandered the aisles while Marcus looked at historic newspaper clippings and photos that were posted near the register. He overheard the high-pitched, somewhat squeaky yet soothing voice of a young woman at the register saying, "Oh, wow, these are so much better. Thank you so much."

He looked over and saw the woman, likely in her early twenties, who looked like a hippie from the 1970s. She had dirty red hair in dreadlocks, with beads woven into a few tight braids here and there. She wore a long, flowing, flower-print dress and was barefoot. She was fiddling with the glasses on her nose, which appeared to be what she had been referring to in her comments to the store clerk. Her skin was milky white, and her face was slightly chubby and cherubic despite her body being so thin that she looked like she was a few skipped meals away from being malnourished.

Marcus looked at her a bit longer, trying to determine whether he found her attractive or not. Had he spent the last decade in prison, and she was the first woman he had seen since being locked away, he was sure he would find her plenty attractive. She wasn't at risk of being crowned prom queen anytime soon, but she still had the bloom of youth, and if you looked for it hard enough, you could find attractive features. *Not that physical attraction is everything,* he reminded himself. She looked over and noticed Marcus looking at her.

"Oh, hi!" she said a little too cheerily. "Like my glasses? Bill did a wonderful job fixing them, so I can finally see again. What's your name?"

"Marcus," he said, and before he could say anything else, she stepped forward and gave him a hug.

"Okay," he said, taken aback by her extreme friendliness. She had a weird energy, somehow simultaneously cheery and energetic, yet also mellow. It was like the vibe of a cheerleader who had smoked a joint. She also smelled terrible when she got that close, like she hadn't bathed in weeks.

Dylan walked up and asked, "Do I get one of those too?"

"Oh, hi!" she exclaimed even more excitedly than the first time. "I'm Lily. Lily Opal Vandermeyer-Earhart. My friends call me 'Love' because my initials spell out L-O-V-E. What's your name?" she asked as she gave Dylan a hug.

"Dylan."

"Oh, are you two lovers?" Lily asked innocently.

Marcus and Dylan looked at each other, wide-eyed. "No, but we almost had to spoon in the backseat of our car at a truck stop. Does that count?" Dylan joked.

Lily giggled. "Probably not. So, what's your astrological sign?"

"Aries," Dylan replied.

"Oooh, my forecast said I'd make love to an Aries today!" Lily exclaimed.

Marcus and Dylan once again looked at each other wide-eyed. She turned to Marcus and asked him what his sign was. Marcus had no idea, so she asked him when his birthday was. "I think one of the girls in my tribe might be a good match for you. Would you like to join our drum circle tonight and spend the night at our camp? It's only about half a mile away. We have an extra tent for guests."

Marcus and Dylan looked at each other and shrugged. Marcus was sick of sleeping in the car and found the idea of sleeping completely horizontal with legs fully extended very seductive. He was sick of being in the car in general, regardless of whether he was awake or asleep. He could tell Dylan wasn't about to let a possible opportunity to have sex slip by either, so they agreed.

They all hopped in the Dean, and Lily directed them to Ranger Station Road, or as she referred to it, "the high area," along a cliff above the creek and walking path that she was familiar with. They ended up driving nearly two miles before they finally found the path to the camp. Between not recognizing landmarks from that vantage point, and seeming to be more interested in asking them about their journey and where they were from than she was in staying focused on directions, Lily made for a terrible navigator.

They parked the car in a clearing near the path and walked down. They could smell incense burning before they reached the path but couldn't hear any noises from the camp over the crunching of gravel and twigs under their feet as they descended. Lily had so fascinated the two boys that Marcus only now thought to ask Dylan if he had found any tools at the trading post for working on the car. After Dylan said no, Lily chimed in, saying, "I know a local farmer who has tools for fixing cars. I could take you to him tomorrow."

At the base of the footpath down the escarpment, they turned around nearly 180 degrees to head to the camp. The sun was low, approaching the horizon. Marcus noticed motion to his left and saw the silhouettes of a small group of people hunched over the edge of the creek. It looked like they were washing dishes. Straight ahead in the distance was a random scattering of a couple dozen tents. In front of them were long-haired men and women building a fire in the center of a clearing while some others attended to burning incense sticks in small clay bowls.

A glittering, swirling motion caught his attention, and he turned to see a few people acrobatically twirling sticks, tossing them in the air, and deftly catching them as they spun toward the ground. On the opposite side of the fire pit, a small group skillfully kept a small, leather-clad hacky sack aloft with their feet and knees.

Marcus made a second evaluation of the motley crew, this time admiring the hodgepodge of mismatched clothing. Brightly colored layers of clothing on one person clashed next to someone else in drab earth tones. Primary colors mixed with pastels and chocolate browns. It was an abundance of apparel looking like it had been borrowed from distant foreign cultures and mixed with the occasional familiar item, such as blue jeans. One of the stick twirlers would have likely fit in back home in NEUS better than anyone else, but here his collarless, black martial arts uniform with horizontal gold clasps up the center like railroad tracks made him seem like the misfit of the group.

A plume of smoke rose up behind the trees in the distance beyond the creek. "Is something on fire?" he asked Lily.

"That's the cooking fire being extinguished," she replied. "We keep our cooking area separate from the rest of our camp in case animals are attracted to the food."

Marcus was afraid to ask what kind of animals she was referring to.

"What's with the baton twirling?" Dylan asked. "Are they in a marching band or circus or something?"

"Those are devil sticks. After dinner and before the candle lighting vigil, some people like to do meditative arts to prepare for saying goodbye to the sun and to welcome the moon."

Three young women and a young man who were seated on the ground in front of a devil-stick twirler noticed Lily and the boys approaching, and they stood up and walked toward them. "Love! You've brought us new spirits! Welcome!" said one of the young women as they hugged. The young woman then hugged Marcus and Dylan, repeating, "Welcome."

The other two women and young man followed suit and hugged them too. Marcus squirmed a little as the young man hugged him, uncertain how he felt about that level of intimacy with another male, but he didn't want to be rude. Dylan stepped back from the hug attempt and thrust out his hand for a handshake, creating a bit of an awkward moment between the two young men where neither seemed to know what to do next. Finally, the young man grabbed Dylan's outstretched hand with both of his and limply held them as he closed his eyes, bowed slightly, and said, "Namaste."

Lily introduced everyone, identifying the young woman who

had first spoken as Celeste. Her two female friends were named Willow and Sage, and the young man's name was Cheyenne. Celeste asked the boys if they were hungry, indicating that they still had quinoa and bean stew leftover from dinner.

"Nah, we had bison burgers at the Trading Post in town," Dylan replied.

"But thanks, though," added Marcus.

Celeste put her hand on Dylan's stomach and said in a somewhat forlorn tone, "Aww, poor bison." She closed her eyes with her hand still on his belly. "Dear Bison, we love you and want you to know that we recognize your life and we respect your place in the Universe. We will honor you at our candle lighting vigil tonight."

Marcus smiled as he tried to imagine what was going through Dylan's mind. Probably something like, *These people are total freaks, but this Celeste chick's hand is only a few inches away from my dick. Maybe if I play along, I can get in a threesome with her and Lily.*

Celeste then put a hand on Marcus's shoulder. "Welcome. It is so wonderful to finally host someone of color. We love adding diversity to our tribe, but we so rarely get the opportunity."

The group made their way back to the devil-stick twirlers and sat down. Lily went out of her way to make sure Marcus and Sage were sitting next to each other, which led Marcus to believe that Sage was the young woman Lily had mentioned back at the Trading Post who would be a good match for him. Sage seemed like the sweet but shy type, the yin to Lily's extroverted yang, and she just smiled pleasantly with her lips pressed closed and made no attempt at conversation.

Marcus was feeling a bit overwhelmed by all the new faces and strange customs, so he didn't participate in the conversation either. He listened for a while, but then tuned out of the conversation and just watched the misfit twirler, mesmerized by the athleticism and grace of his movements. The twirler, a young man of Southeast Asian descent, appeared to be the only person in the camp who didn't have hair down to his shoulders or lower. He lunged, spun, and stretched between some sort of martial-arts-type poses as he twirled, juggled, and bounced the three sticks, sometimes seeming to get them to defy gravity.

The heat of the campfire began to pick up in intensity. The odor of the incense was obnoxious and nausea inducing, but soon the burning wood and smoke began to dilute it. The one nice thing about the incense—and now the campfire smoke—was that it masked the body odor of the people around him. Celeste and her friends didn't smell any better than Lily, something he'd noticed when they hugged him.

People who Marcus assumed were the dishwashing crew had joined them around the campfire, and other people were beginning to filter in as the sun set over the mountain peak to the west. He heard a quiet tone, like a mellow air raid or tornado siren, start to ring, growing louder and louder. He looked over to the opposite side of the campfire and saw an older, gray-haired white woman sitting cross-legged on the ground in front of a stack of boulders, rubbing what looked like a thick drumstick along the rim of a crystal bowl, which seemed to be the source of the noise. The people around the fire slowly wrapped up their conversations, and the sound of voices gradually filtered away, leaving only the sound of the singing bowl and the crackling of the campfire. After a couple of minutes, the older woman stopped rubbing the bowl, and the sound ceased. Then she stood and spoke.

"As we bid farewell to the sun, we gather here for our candle lighting vigil to give thanks for our blessings, share our stories, and reconnect with the Universe. Each of us is on a journey. Each of us has a story. Each of us seeks oneness with the Universe. Through our stories, we connect with each other and with the Universe. Please feel welcome to come forward, light a candle, and share your story."

A few more people trickled in to join the circle, and Marcus could see more approaching from the tent area. Sunset seemed to mark the start of this ritual, but no one seemed upset about the latecomers. Schedule, promptness, and timeliness seemed to be values lost on this tribe. Marcus imagined his dad trying to organize anything with this group, like a shepherd herding cats, and he nearly laughed out loud at the image as Lily rose and walked to the stack of boulders to be the first to speak.

She lit her candle and placed it on the boulders. "I am lighting this candle in thanks for two blessings. First, Bill fixed my glasses, and I can now see all of your beautiful shining faces again! Second, I am thankful for meeting the two new spirits who have joined us here tonight, Dylan and Marcus. They have traveled long and far, and the

Universe has brought them here tonight to be with us. Please join me in welcoming them."

The crowd of people turned to Marcus and Dylan and in not-quite-unison said, "Welcome."

Celeste got up next, and as promised, she lit a candle to honor the bison whose life had been sacrificed for the burgers Marcus and Dylan had eaten. Following Celeste, person after person got up, lit a candle, and expressed their feelings about their day. Some counted their blessings, even seemingly trivial blessings like finding a piece of quartz on the ground that was perfect for the piece of jewelry she was making.

Others shared their disappointments, such as one of the cooks for their dinner earlier in the evening, who expressed his frustration with not being able to get the fire steady enough for slow-cooking the beans the way he wanted, and how he worried that it was a sign from the Universe that there was imbalance in his life.

By the fourth or fifth person, Marcus was already starting to lose interest in what seemed to him like inconsequential, normal daily events that didn't rise to the level of interest of sharing with a group. By the time the fourteenth and final person got up to light a candle, he had already gone beyond boredom into irritation, and this last gray-haired, middle-aged woman seemed determined to drive him over the edge into madness. She lit her candle and sighed loudly. She looked down at the ground, not speaking, and closed her eyes. *Come on, lady, let's get a move on it,* Marcus thought. She sighed again. *Oh, for Christ's sake, what a drama queen. Quit sighing and get on with your boring story. You're just trying to get attention.*

"My partner, Sheila, as you all know, has been suffering with fever, cough, and rash," the woman finally began. She sighed loudly again. She began going on ad nauseam about Sheila's symptoms. Marcus stared into the campfire, trying to distract himself with the only other visual source of interest available in order to quiet the voice in his head that wanted to scream at this depression-inducing woman who was wasting everyone's time rattling off symptoms. He tried to amuse himself by coming up with clever ways to describe his agony, finally striking gold with the alliterative phrase "Must every mundane moment be memorialized?"

Finally, after five minutes of symptoms and sighing, the whiny woman sat back down and buried her head in her hands while those around her put their hands on her back and shoulders to comfort her. The older woman who seemed to be leading the ceremony stood up, grabbed several sticks in her hands, and began inserting the sticks into each candle's flame to ignite the ends. She took the flaming sticks over to the campfire. "Each of your stories has been shared with the Universe, and as the light from your candle becomes one with the light from the group's campfire, so do your stories become one with the Universe." She then tossed the burning sticks into the campfire and returned to her seated position at the crystal bowl, where she again rubbed the rim of the bowl with a stick to produce the singing siren sound.

The older woman stood up and took her bowl away, and in her place congregated three young men with bongo drums. They began playing a tribal beat, with the campfire as their stage light. One by one, people around the campfire started dancing to the beat. Lily was second to join in, alternating between spinning around with her arms at her sides and raising them in the air while making a side-to-side wavy motion with her body and tossing her hair back and forth. Dylan jumped up to join her, alternating between mimicking her and mixing in dance moves he did at the occasional illicit basement parties back in NEUS, even though they looked out of place in this hippie love fest. No one cared. Marcus stayed seated and just watched. He didn't object to people dancing, but he didn't find dancing a natural act, and he preferred not to participate in it.

The tribe members who didn't dance were all passing a joint around the outer perimeter of the dance circle. He considered taking a hit. It would be nice to do something that shut off the part of his brain that everyone else seemed to be able to shut off when they claimed to be having fun, but he didn't know whether football at a high school or college level was still in his future, and he didn't dare jeopardize it with a failed drug test, so he passed at his chance.

After a couple of hours of drumming, dancing, and pot smoking, the festivities seemed to be winding down. Some of the older people had trickled away from the circle to the tent area in the distance, and a few more people wandered off after the drums had ceased beating. Dylan and Lily had collapsed into each other's arms, exhausted from dancing, and began making out. Soon they wandered off to the tent area, presumably to fulfill Lily's astronomical forecast. Marcus had no idea which tent he was supposed to sleep in, so he shyly remained at the campfire with the dozen or so people who were still congregated for more pot smoking and conversation.

One of the drummers took a drag off the joint, held in the smoke, and exhaled. "You know, I feel like I still owe my Peruvian drum master teacher millions of dollars. I can never repay him for the gift he has given me of sharing his knowledge with me. I mean, like, it was such an amazing gift."

Marcus finally broke what must have seemed like a vow of silence. "Did your teacher give you lessons for free?"

"No, dude. I paid four hundred dollars, but it still feels like nothing compared to the knowledge he gave me."

"So, teaching drums to students is part of how he makes his living, right?" Marcus said. "I imagine bongo drummers aren't in high demand, so he can't be making a living off of performances, so he teaches to make a living. He probably likes the idea of the music not dying with him, but instead being passed on to a new generation, right? So, he charges a fee that is enough to make a living, but not so much that it prevents students from being able to afford his classes, and the whole thing is mutually beneficial for everyone. I don't understand why you feel like you owe him millions."

"Dude, it's hard to explain. It's like, before, I had no skills and couldn't play the drums. Then I met him, and suddenly I have these skills that I get to carry with me for the rest of my life. I can play the drums thousands of times in my lifetime, and all I gave him for it was a few hundred dollars. I feel like I ripped him off."

"But he only spent a few hours with you, right? So, if you look at the cost per unit of time, it isn't unreasonable. Besides, you had to have the raw skills to begin with, and I assume you had to practice alone for many hours, so he only helped you shape those skills. It's still you playing the drums now, not him."

"Yeah, but it feels so unbalanced. I feel like I got so much more out of it than he did. It's like, you know, karma. Bongo karma, dude."

The conversation wasn't going anywhere, and the drummer was starting to get too stoned to make sense, so Marcus dropped out of it. He saw Sage stand up and start walking toward the tents and jumped up to join her and ask which tent he could crash in. She said she'd walk him there.

Along the way, Marcus's curiosity overcame his introversion, and he asked her just how this group made any money to live off of. They seemed to lack specific marketable skills, and based on the drummer's responses, he wondered if they understood basic economics. Sage told him that they tried to minimize their needs and to live with what Mother Earth provided, but when they needed to supplement that, they bartered, did seasonal farm work, worked at food co-ops, and sold jewelry along the side of the road. She said that about a third of the tribe was currently in a separate camp doing migratory farm work to help support the full tribe, and that which people were on a work crew was voluntary, but that they encouraged a constant shifting of personnel to make sure everything was fair and that members got to mingle with everyone in the tribe at some point in the work season. They also dumpster dove and rummaged through junkyards from time to time, looking for things to fix up and resell or trade, and they often traded for things at thrift shops.

"Do you typically get all your clothing at thrift shops? They don't look handmade."

Sage nodded.

"I suppose if everyone in the world adopted your lifestyle, then there wouldn't be any first-hand clothing to go to thrift stores to become second-hand clothing, and the tribe would have to spend a lot more time making their own. It would be even more like the Pilgrims coming to America with nothing than it is now."

Sage shrugged her shoulders and pointed Marcus in the direction of the guest tent, where he retired for the night, alone, falling asleep the best he could to the muffled sounds of lovemaking coming from several of the surrounding tents.

Chapter 6: Rejuvenation at the Lake

Marcus woke up in the morning to the sound of his tent rustling. He sat up suddenly, jolted awake and fearful that a bear might be trying to get in. The door flap lifted, and Dylan poked his smiling head in. "Dude. I joined the mile-high club. We're probably at an elevation of over a mile above sea level, and I got laid."

"I'm so proud of you, Dyl-weed," Marcus said sarcastically.

"Aww, you're just jealous that I got some ass."

"I'm not jealous of that stinky ass! How could you even stand the smell of her? She reeks!"

"Like either of us smells like a flower right now?"

Marcus saw his point. It was Monday morning, and his last shower had been Friday morning. Since then, he had done half of a decathlon in gym class, walked over a mile home, then spent two days riding and sleeping in the Charger, interrupted only by a dripping-hot ride up the Gateway Arch, followed by sitting around a campfire all evening absorbing smoke in every pore. He didn't even need to duck his nose into an armpit to know that he smelled awful, and suddenly he desperately craved a shower.

Back home, the shower was also his place of morning refuge, where he entered a tranquil trance that smoothed the transition to consciousness. He never truly felt awake and human until after his morning shower, and after several days of feeling like a sleep-deprived homeless zombie, he really wanted to soak in some water and reclaim his humanity. "Yeah, I could really use a shower or something right now. There's gotta be a lake or something around here we could take a dip in. Wanna ask your new girlfriend if there's something nearby?"

"She's not my girlfriend."

"Sure, I believe you," Marcus said wryly. "But pretty soon she'll have you picking out crudely made quartz hippie rings."

Dylan cocked his fist like he was going to punch Marcus, but he had a smile on his face. He jumped on top of Marcus, who was pinned under the blanket he had slept in, and started giving him a noogie. Just then, Lily poked her head through the tent flap.

"Oh my god!" she exclaimed with concern in her voice. "Are you guys fighting? Stop! Stop fighting. We have to love one another!"

Marcus and Dylan stopped tousling and looked up at her and started laughing. "We're just playing around, Love," Dylan said.

"Love?" Marcus asked Dylan. "You're calling her Love now? Told you!"

"Everyone calls her Love because of her initials, you bastard. If she weren't here, I'd whup you!"

Marcus turned his attention to Lily. "Know of any swimming holes around here? I could really use a bath."

"Yeah, I know a good place. We can go there after breakfast. Normally I'd do morning rituals and astrology forecasts with the group after breakfast, but I suppose I can do the rituals at the lake and check my forecast later."

The threesome exited the tent and waded barefoot through the narrow, ankle-deep creek to join a small group on the other side that had gathered near the cooking fire. A pot of leftover bean stew from the previous night's supper was reheating over the fire, and Marcus could see one person in the distance lowering a metal food-storage canister that was suspended from a tree branch with a rope.

Celeste cheerily wished them a good morning and offered them stew, noting with a sideways glance that it was vegan and no animals had died for it, and herbal tea. A few people nearby were smoking clove cigarettes while sipping their herbal tea. Surprisingly, the clove cigarette smoke didn't bother Marcus the way regular cigarette smoke did, and the odor actually paired pretty well with the herbal tea. The warm tea also paired well with the overcast sky, which looked like it could turn to rain any moment.

Marcus's mellow contemplation was diverted by the sound of Dylan's voice asking where the bathroom was. Lily extended an arm and swept it in front of her. "Pretty much everywhere."

"Have any toilet paper?" Dylan asked.

"Mother Earth provides that too. Just watch out for poison ivy," Lily said.

"Seriously?" Dylan asked.

Marcus chuckled. "One is pee, two is poo, but leaves of three, let it be." He stopped chuckling quickly, though, realizing that he could feel something brewing in his intestines too. Thankfully he didn't need to join Dylan just yet.

When Dylan returned, Marcus and Lily got up, and the threesome started walking back to the main camp as an older man started ringing the crystal bowl. They could hear the beginnings of some sort of pagan chanting as they crossed back over the creek. Marcus was relieved that they weren't sticking around for morning rituals, imagining another candle-lighting vigil type of ceremony that they would be missing.

Lily said that the lake was a rather long hike away, so they ended up driving there on Ranger Station Road into the more densely forested higher elevations. The lake was small, perhaps more appropriately it would be called a pond, but it was well worth the drive. It was a pristine, beautiful, and clear body of water plopped in the middle of forest, with a narrow strip of grassy shore near the entrance off the road.

At the shore, Lily immediately threw down the blanket she had brought, pulled something out of her dress pocket, then whipped off her dress and glasses and tossed them on the ground, leaving her completely naked. Marcus and Dylan looked at each other and shrugged as she walked toward the water. Marcus found the sight of her bare body a bit shocking, yet her lack of inhibition regarding nudity was not entirely surprising given everything he had learned about her so far.

"I guess now I've seen everything of her that you've seen," Marcus said to Dylan. "Now I kind of feel like she's my girlfriend too!"

The boys took a "when in Rome" attitude and stripped off their clothes and followed Lily into the lake.

"No peeking, fag," Dylan said to Marcus as they disrobed.

The lake water was refreshingly cool. It was that temperature where if you started swimming hard for a few minutes, it would be perfect, but without the heat built up from activity, it was a tad chilly. Lily passed them a bar of soap—the mystery object she had pulled from her dress pocket. Marcus looked at it. It was crudely shaped by hand, with chunks and swirls of different ingredients and flakes of something embedded into one side. It looked nothing like the perfectly machine-formed, homogeneous bars of soap he knew from home. He scrubbed hurriedly before passing it to Dylan.

"Are these flakes oatmeal?" Dylan asked Lily.

"Yeah, it's all natural, and the oatmeal flakes can be used either for gripping the bar or to exfoliate. We make our own soap."

"Do I wash with it or eat it?"

"You could probably do either!" Lily giggled.

"Wish we'd had these back home when my mom would stick a bar in my mouth when I took the Lord's name in vain," Marcus said.

While Dylan washed with the soap, Marcus began to swim some butterfly stroke to keep warm and to show off a bit. He loved the sensation of gliding and undulating through the water swimming butterfly, but he hadn't gone more than fifteen yards when he realized he was getting fatigued by the difficult stroke that he hadn't swum in years. By twenty-five yards, he had stopped. Alone, he looked across the lake. *I wish I could have been on a swim team at school*, he lamented.

The cool water reminded him of his three summers of swim lessons that had started in fourth grade. His dad had instigated the lessons, saying that a good soldier needed to know how to swim, preferably while carrying a weapon, but he had left it to Marcus's mother to execute the orders. The only pools in New Rochelle were at private, whites-only clubs, so Marcus's mom had to chauffer him to a pool managed by a sympathetic young white woman who was willing to sneak Marcus and a young black girl into the pool at a painfully early hour, long before it officially opened, to teach them how to swim. At that ungodly hour of morning, the pool was always freezing, even colder than the lake he was in now. The summer after sixth grade was his last time in the pool though. His interest in other sports, sports that were deemed acceptable for blacks, pushed covert swimming off his highly regulated schedule.

As Marcus waded back toward Dylan and Lily, he started to ponder why some sports back home seemed to be accepting of blacks and others weren't. Football was very accepting. He pursued the idea that maybe it was aggressive, combative sports that accepted blacks, but then he thought of hockey, which was combative but whites-only. Track & Field was accepting, but it wasn't a violent sport. There seemed to be no rhyme or reason to it. It seemed to be based solely on ancient, arbitrary traditions. There were no written rules expressly stating what sports were for whites only—it just seemed like everyone knew and self-enforced the status quo.

Marcus reached Lily and Dylan. "God, this is refreshing," he said. "I feel like I was a fish in a past life or something, and the water was calling to me."

"We could do a guided meditation to explore your past lives if you want," Lily said while hugging her shoulders and shivering.

Marcus shared a quick smirk with Dylan then shook his head as he took the soap back and gave his armpits a second go. As he finished, the sky finally did open up and release a light, misty shower. Lily started to complain about getting cold, so they all got out and dried off under the tree canopy with the blanket. Marcus turned to Dylan and Lily and in a silly, monotone voice feigning disappointment said, "It started raining while I was swimming in the lake. I got soaking wet." Neither of them reacted or seemed to get the joke. Marcus continued. "But my sense of humor managed to stay dry." Still nothing. Marcus laughed at his own joke. Dylan and Lily looked at him cockeyed, curious as to why he was laughing, which only made Marcus laugh more.

The light sprinkle stopped shortly after it had started. Lily walked out from under the tree canopy and onto the grassy shore. "Want to join me for some yoga?" she asked the boys. "It is very spiritual and brings a sense of oneness with the Universe."

At first the boys resisted, thinking that it was too weird and hippie-ish for them. Lily changed her tactics of persuasion and appealed to Marcus's intellect, saying that studies showed yoga and meditation chemically changed the brain and de-stressed people and suggested that there was no harm in trying it. They had nothing better to do, so they relented and joined her.

Neither had ever done any yoga before in their lives, so Lily patiently walked them through some of the basic poses, adjusting their body positions with her hands. Marcus was surprised by how suddenly sexy Lily seemed at that moment. It wasn't just that they were all still naked during the yoga practice, either. As their yoga teacher, she was calm, patient, nurturing, and confident. Her hands on his hips adjusting the angle of twist in his torso was oddly sensual as she rattled off commands to breathe in or out and how to move each limb, all while telling them the foreign, ancient-sounding names of the poses they were doing. Goose bumps formed as she touched his body. He had no desire to jump in a tent with her or anything, but he found himself amused by the sudden shift in perspective.

Lily's attractiveness wasn't the only surprise. Yoga was surprisingly strenuous. Marcus was still in superb shape from spring track and field, but somehow the yoga poses Lily was guiding them through managed to use hidden little muscles that he didn't know existed before. Suddenly the minor muscles used for balance and support were being asked to do work that his powerful quads and hamstrings couldn't help with. Exacerbating the issue was that the altitude was also affecting him more than he had expected it to. Not fifteen minutes into the practice, his lungs began to feel dry and inflamed and screamed for oxygen. He was embarrassed by his weakness, especially after a couple of falls he took while trying to maintain balance in a particularly challenging pose, but Lily was supportive and reassuring. At least Dylan was struggling just as much as he was, if not more.

After the yoga session, Marcus did a mental inventory of his muscles and remarked at how rejuvenated and refreshed he felt. "It's like my muscles have been wrung out, squeezing out all of the tension," he commented.

Lily encouraged him to continue learning yoga beyond that morning, advising that his difficulties with balance were a sign that he "wasn't in balance with the Universe," that he needed to "clear and realign his chakras," and that he needed to continue to practice. She continued her morning rituals with a meditation involving pagan chanting, but the boys had explored their hippie spiritual boundaries enough for one day with the yoga, so they begged off from joining her and instead walked back to the tree canopy and sat on the blanket admiring the natural beauty of the lake and mountains, and inhaling the pleasant pine aroma that had been stirred up and strengthened by the light rain.

After a few minutes of only the sounds of nature and Lily's

chanting in the distance, Dylan spoke up.

"Yoga was tougher than I expected."

"Yeah, my body felt like it vapor locked!" Marcus said.

Dylan chuckled for a few seconds before getting a serious look on his face. "Speaking of…you're right about the Dean. We should sell it. It was fun while it lasted, but it's only gonna cause problems."

Marcus leaned back onto his elbows, then succumbed to gravity and lay on this back, looking up at the gray skies. Had Dylan come to this conclusion the previous night, Marcus probably would have chastised him for being so slow to come to his senses. This morning, he didn't feel the need. "Yeah, Sage said that the tribe does a lot of bartering and trading. I wonder if they know someone we could trade the car with for something more fuel efficient, or even electric. We could probably make a lot of money in the trade too. You know how much the car is worth?"

"My dad has told me on many occasions that the Charger is worth more than my life. So yeah, I know exactly how much it's worth. Well, at least in NEUS. I'm not sure what we can get for it here, especially with a questionable title involved in the sale. We might have to sell it for a lot less."

Marcus closed his eyes and lay there for a few more seconds before he noticed the sound of sniffling. He turned to look at Dylan. His face was red, and his chest was shuddering with erratic breaths. A tear dribbled from the corner of his eye. Marcus remained frozen, not knowing what to do or say. He instinctively turned his head away and looked for Lily. She was still engrossed in her own world quite a distance away. Marcus sat up and looked back over at Dylan, who was now sobbing uncontrollably. He wanted to reach out, to touch Dylan's arm, to tell him it was okay, but his arms remained bound by an imaginary straitjacket. His mouth opened, but no words came out.

"Sorry…" Dylan blurted out. He turned his back to Marcus and scrambled to his feet, grabbed his clothing, and ran toward the car.

A few seconds later, Marcus heard the car door click shut. He sat there feeling ashamed and embarrassed—angry at himself for his emotional impotence.

Soon Lily wrapped up her morning rituals and returned to where Marcus sat.

"Where's Dylan?" she asked.

"Uh, we decided we should sell the car, and, uh, he's really attached to that car, so, um, I think he wanted to spend a few minutes with it to say goodbye in private or something. Like a ritual or something."

Marcus and Lily gathered the blanket and soap and started re-cloaking their bodies before heading back to the car. Marcus, hoping to delay their arrival at the car until Dylan had cried himself out, dressed and walked slowly as he filled Lily in on their car situation and asked her whether she knew anyone they could trade the car with. Someone who wouldn't ask a lot of questions.

"Oh, I know just the person!" she exclaimed. "Tom! We're lovers, but I haven't seen him in such a long time. Oh, I can't wait to check my astrological forecast now. I'll bet it says something about how new lovers lead me to reconnect with old lovers!"

Marcus turned his head to roll his eyes.

"His place is right in town, not too far from where we met last night."

Marcus and Lily reached the car and got in. Dylan appeared to have recomposed himself, including having put his clothes back on, but he seemed to be avoiding eye contact. Lily repeated what she had just told Marcus. Dylan just nodded.

"If he trades cars, does he also fix them? Would he have the tools Dylan needs?" Marcus asked.

Dylan broke in before Lily could answer. "I don't want him to have any doubts about the condition of the car that could affect his offering price. When he turns the key, I want the car to start, and for him to not know we've had easily fixable vapor lock issues. Let's stick with getting the tools from the farmer Lily mentioned yesterday and get it fixed before Tom sees it."

The threesome drove back down the mountain road toward town, with the plan being that Dylan would drop Marcus and Lily off near town on his way out to the farm. Marcus and Lily would walk to Tom's place to talk trade and see what he had available for electric or fuel-efficient cars. Dylan would tune the carburetor, and because Lily didn't know how to describe to Dylan how to get to Tom's place, they would all meet back at the camp.

Chapter 7: Live Free and Die

After Dylan dropped them off near town, Marcus and Lily were truly alone together for the first time since they met at the Trading Post the previous night. Lily broke the silence by asking Marcus if he had beat up Dylan, referring to the bruises all over Dylan's body.

After making Lily promise that she would keep it confidential, Marcus filled her in on Dylan's history of abuse at the hands of his dad and why they had run away from home. Marcus took the opportunity to satisfy his curiosity about Lily too, asking her why she had slept with Dylan just a few hours after meeting him. She explained that sex was a spiritual experience for her, and a way to both make a deeper connection with another being and to "spread love across the world." She reminded him that her astrological forecast had foretold it too, and she asked him if he wanted his forecast read later when they returned to camp. Marcus declined and confessed to her that he didn't think the alignment of planets and stars had any influence on people's lives.

They meandered past the Wagon Hitch Trading Post and the town hall and began cutting through people's yards rather than following the roads.

"Should we be on these people's property without their permission?"

"No one should own the earth," she responded. "It belongs to everyone."

"Do you think the people who live here believe that?"

"I don't know. They've never said anything to us about it."

They meandered on a bit more, and now Marcus understood why Lily couldn't give directions to Dylan. She had simply never even been on the roads needed to drive there. Finally, they walked onto a dirt road, and a few houses down they encountered a coarsely carved wooden sign in the front yard that read "Trader Tom's."

"This is it," Lily said.

Marcus looked around. There was a beat-up, rusting Volkswagen van parked in front of a small log cabin down the dirt driveway. Across from it was a large, rusting, metal-clad shed—presumably Tom's workshop where he fixed up the things he traded for—which looked like it could collapse in a gentle breeze. Parked in the grass in front of the shed were four cars. One was an ancient, rusting Volkswagen Beetle on cinderblocks with no wheels. Three looked like the asexual, modern electric cars they had seen on the highways of WUS, in various states of repair. Surrounding the shed were random pieces of unidentifiable metal and wood scattered all over the place. They walked up to the front door, and Lily knocked. No answer. They could hear loud voices, though. They knocked again. Still no answer. Lily tried the handle, and it was unlocked, so they walked in.

"Tom?" Lily shouted. "It's me, Love!"

A gray-haired man darted out into the hallway, and with a wave of one hand beckoned them to come toward him, while with the other hand he held a finger up to his lips to request silence. He darted back out of the corridor to where the loud voices were coming from. It sounded like a radio.

They walked to where the man had been, then turned and walked into his kitchen, where he was already seated at a table listening to a radio at a loud volume. He repeated his motion requesting silence and pointed to the radio. It was some sort of political talk show, with a call-in guest talking about how the government was tracking him and watching him, and the show's host kept saying, "Uh-huh, uh-huh. That's big brother government for you. Trying to hold down the nonconformists." After a minute the caller hung up, and the host declared the end of the show until tomorrow—if the government didn't shut him down by then.

Tom flipped off the radio and chuckled a phlegmy smoker's laugh, stood up, and gave Lily a hug. Suddenly he stopped laughing and looked at Marcus. "You with the Feds?"

"I'm not with anyone," Marcus responded confusedly.

"He's with me, Tom," said Lily. "He's on his way to San Francisco from New York to see his sister."

Tom stepped toward Marcus and wrapped his arms around him,

giving him a big bear hug, his hairy arms chafing the skin on Marcus's triceps. Marcus nearly gagged from the stench of old sweat, stale cigarette smoke, and some other pungent earthy smell that he couldn't identify.

Marcus looked Tom over as he and Lily exchanged pleasantries and Lily began explaining Marcus and Dylan's situation. He found Tom almost as visually repulsive as he did olfactorily. He looked dirty. He had on a tattered old olive-green vest with pockets everywhere and ripped blue jeans with stains all over them. The scrawny, middle-aged man had gray hair growing everywhere except the top of his head, where he was balding. He had his remaining long gray hair in a loose ponytail, and his shaggy, foreign appearance was accessorized with a bushy gray beard, bushy gray eyebrows with rogue long hairs crawling up his forehead like spider's legs, and more gray hair sprouting from his ears.

Tom turned to Marcus after Lily had finished explaining why they were there. "I only got two working cars. Both are electric, and right now I got the Coulomb Magnétisme running better than the Tesla X300."

"As long as it works and gets good mileage, I think the Coulomb would be fine," Marcus replied.

Lily invited Tom to join the tribe for dinner and catching up, and he accepted. They made a plan to have Marcus drive them all to the campsite in the Coulomb as his test drive, then Tom would take a look at the Charger and decide how much to offer on top of the trade while Dylan looked at the Coulomb. They'd dine with the tribe, Tom would spend the night with Lily, and then on the boys' way out of town the next morning, they'd stop at Tom's place to make the trade and get their cash.

On the drive back to the campsite, Tom sat in the back and Lily in the front, and they chatted back and forth, catching up on each other's lives since they had last seen each other. Marcus kept his window cracked open to keep from being overwhelmed by Tom's stench in such close quarters. He listened briefly to them talking as Tom confirmed that his niece, Celeste, still hung out with the tribe and expressed excitement about getting to say hi to her, but when they started discussing their past lovemaking, Marcus tried to distract himself from consciously hearing what they were saying. He was trying desperately not to picture Tom naked, but there it was, the image of Tom naked in his mind. He fought back his gag reflex. He had no idea what Lily saw in him. Even beyond the physical aspects, the odor aspects, and the age difference, he couldn't even see what Tom had to offer in terms of personality.

After further pondering, his opinion on Lily and Tom's relationship settled into a stalemate. On one hand was the sensible conclusion that so long as *he* didn't have to have sex with Tom, what difference did it make whether Lily did? It didn't impact his life one way or the other. On the other hand, he couldn't fully vanquish the resurfacing thought of, *Come on, though. Tom? Really?*

At last they pulled over to the side of the road behind the Charger, near the path down to the campsite. Dylan wasn't in the car, so they wandered down and found him at the eating area across the creek for a late lunch of dandelion-green salad with pine nuts and wild-berry dressing, along with some hummus and flatbread. Dylan discreetly noted to Marcus that the carburetor tuning was easy and had gone smoothly. Dylan and Tom talked cars for a bit while eating. Marcus was relieved to hear Dylan telling Tom that his dad had given him the car for his sixteenth birthday, but that since it was in the family he had never formally transferred over the title. He was even more relieved to hear Tom reply, "Stuff enters our lives, stuff leaves our lives. It's like a yin and yang. No one really owns anything, man, and we don't get to take any of it into the next life, so it doesn't matter. I'm just a conduit for the Universe."

He also revealed that he didn't need to go to a bank to withdraw the cash to give them to make up for the difference in car values because he didn't believe in banks, and kept his life savings hidden all over his property. As repulsive as he was to Marcus, he was the perfect person to be dealing with in their situation. He smiled to himself as he briefly toyed with the idea of lighting a candle to thank the Universe for bringing Tom into his life at this evening's candle-lighting ceremony, but he didn't think he could pull it off with a straight face, and he didn't want to insult these people who, despite being complete freaks in his opinion, were overwhelmingly welcoming, kind, and generous. He especially appreciated the vegetarian meals they were eating that helped make up for the malnutrition of fast food and gas station meals. And they were free, too, as was the lodging. They were likely to come into some money during the car trade, but he didn't want to count his chickens before they hatched.

Thinking about how generous the tribe had been to them, Marcus started to flounder as he tried to come up with a way he could even attempt to partially repay them. He had no money to give them at the moment, and besides, the tribe didn't seem to care much about money or the objects it could buy. He was intelligent, but lacked experience or skills that might be useful to them. He looked down at his earthenware plate. Eureka! All the times his parents had made him wash dishes after dinner was finally providing him with useful life experience. He joined the dishwashing crew after lunch while Dylan and Tom checked out each other's car.

Between lunch dishwashing and dinner, he had a chance to hang out with Dylan a bit while Lily was off reviewing her astrology forecast. Without Lily there to referee, they devolved into their usual teasing insults. Marcus uncharacteristically started it, saying, "Hey, man, sorry about your girlfriend hooking up with her ex-boyfriend right in front of you, man. You want me to light a candle for you tonight?"

Dylan snorted. "You want me to light one for you in hopes that you have a speedy recovery from the beating I'm going to give you if you don't stop calling her my girlfriend?"

"Dude, I thought Tom was ugly, but if Lily is choosing him over you, then you must be even uglier than I thought."

"Who got some last night? You, or me?" Dylan countered.

"Got some what? Sexually transmitted diseases from a promiscuous woman with indiscriminate taste in partners?"

"You're lucky that putting up with your shit is the lesser of two evils when compared to dealing with a kumbaya, 'let's all love one another and not be violent' lecture from the tribe, otherwise you'd be in serious pain right now," Dylan said.

After the insults ran their course they got down to the more serious business of the car. Dylan noted that they would be making less money on top of the trade for the Coulomb than had they sold it in the EUS, but given the circumstances, it was a decent deal. They would end up with a much less expensive car to maintain, plus they'd get a nice chunk of change for other expenses. Getting to San

Fran would be no problem.

Later, after Marcus finished up with the dinner dishwashing crew, they walked toward the campfire and he heard the sound of the singing crystal bowl. He felt the temptation to run in the opposite direction. Perhaps death at the fangs of a bear or a pack of coyotes, or whatever other beasts awaited out in the dwindling light beyond, would be more enjoyable than another candle-lighting ceremony. His feet kept marching toward the campfire, though, and soon he found himself seated next to Dylan, who had thankfully elected to sit relatively far from the stacked rocks where the ceremony took place.

Marcus saw the drama queen from the previous night's ceremony stand up and walk to the rocks before the ceremony leader even invited anyone to speak. She had her head down, with her long, frizzy, wild hair obscuring her face. *Well, rip the Band-Aid off quickly, I guess*, he thought. The ceremony leader invited her to light a candle, but the woman didn't move. The leader brought a candle to her and lit it for her where she stood, holding it in her right hand while reaching out and taking the woman's hand with her left. The woman whimpered. Suddenly Marcus realized that it was no drama queen act for attention. Something serious was going on. The woman sputtered before finally gasping the words, "Sheila died."

Marcus's jaw dropped while the leader turned to embrace the now weeping woman. Several people rushed up to join in the embrace. Marcus noticed that Sage was still nearby, so he turned to her and whispered, "What happened?"

"Her partner, Sheila, died this afternoon. She had measles," Sage responded.

"Holy shit! That's awful! How did she get measles? I thought vaccines had eradicated measles decades ago. Is it some sort of mutant strain or something?"

"Vaccines are just a way for the government to inject people with tracking chips, and they have chemicals that make you sick. We refuse to put those toxins in our bodies. Besides, if you keep your chakras open and maintain balance with the Universe, then the Universe will guide you down a path that is free of disease."

Marcus almost shouted "you're fucking kidding me" at Sage, but he managed to bite his tongue. Instead he said, "We had a car here. We could have taken her to the hospital. Why didn't she go to the hospital?"

Sage just shrugged. "She was getting regular acupuncture and had taken herbs prescribed by a Native American healer. Western medicine usually does more harm than good. Plus, her long-range forecast said to just go with whatever the week brought her, and not to resist nature."

Marcus was dumfounded. He looked over at Dylan, who was looking down at the ground and fiddling with a blade of grass like he was bored. He nudged him and asked him if he had heard what Sage just said. Dylan acknowledged but seemed indifferent. Marcus, feeling like he had no one to whom he could vent his outrage and disbelief about his feeling that the tribe had essentially just been an accessory to suicide, started to bottle his feelings. He got up and walked away from the campfire. He didn't know where to go, but he knew he just wanted to be away from such stupidity. He reflexively walked in the opposite direction of the tent area and found himself at the foot of the trail up the escarpment. He walked up and saw the two cars parked along the road. Both were unlocked.

He went into the Charger first, grabbing his calculus book out of his duffel bag. Then he crawled into the Coulomb, shut the door, and pressed the start button to turn on the electrical system so that he could turn on the radio and the interior lights. For the next twenty minutes, he sat there with the radio tuned to a news station while re-solving old calculus problems until he felt calm and centered enough to be able to speak to any of the tribe members without accosting them.

He walked to the edge of the escarpment and sat down. He could see the fire burning below, smell the incense and hear the music, which tonight was a melancholy medley of acoustic guitar folk songs instead of tribal dance beats on the bongo drums. *Maybe if that stupid bongo drummer had spent his four hundred dollars on immunology classes instead of bongo drum lessons then they'd be playing happy music tonight instead of sad music,* he thought.

He sighed. He wasn't as calm and centered from the calculus as he had hoped, and the more he thought about it, the angrier he got. He walked back down the trail and made a wide, arced path to steer clear of the campfire and climbed in his tent. It took him a couple of restless hours to fall asleep, and he was soon woken up when Dylan climbed into the tent, reeking of pot, and crawled under the other blanket. They didn't say a word to each other, and Marcus spent a couple more restless hours trying to fall back asleep again.

The boys awoke Tuesday morning to the sound of birds squawking in the trees. "You want to go get breakfast?" asked Dylan.

"I'm not hungry," said Marcus. It was a lie, but he didn't feel like being around the tribe today.

Dylan got up and went to join whoever from the tribe happened to be awake and at breakfast. Marcus remained in the tent daydreaming about finding a way to explain to the tribe that vaccines and western medicine were good things. He knew it was a lost cause, though.

Dylan came back from breakfast with more bad news. Sheila's partner, the woman formerly known to Marcus as the drama queen, had developed a fever and rash overnight. So had the acupuncturist who had treated Sheila. The woman who led the candle-lighting ceremonies wasn't feeling that well either. News of a few other people with symptoms had been trickling in too.

"Great. Now it's an epidemic of stupidity," muttered Marcus. "Can we finalize the car deal and get out of here? I don't want to be here to watch as everyone dies."

"Yeah. Tom was at breakfast, and we're going to all drive back to his place first thing to close it out. We'll drive the Coulomb back, and he'll take the Charger as sort of a last test drive."

They got up and walked to Lily's tent to meet Tom, and Lily came out with Tom to say her goodbyes. She wrapped her arms around Marcus and gave him a big hug, but he could only muster a half-hearted, one-armed light squeeze in return. He thanked her through gritted teeth for all of her generosity and asked her to say goodbye to the rest of the tribe for him.

The boys and Tom drove the two cars back to Tom's place to finalize the car deal and get their cash. Tom made them wait in the kitchen as he ran around the house alternating between making rustling and banging noises and bringing them small wads of cash. At one point they saw him through the kitchen window digging in the yard with a shovel before he came back in with his final installment.

As they walked to the Coulomb Dylan said, "You drive. Driving this electric piece of shit would bum me out too much right now."

Marcus obliged, stopping in town at the Trading Post to grab a bag of granola mix for his breakfast while Dylan waited in the car.

"Grab some for me too?" Dylan asked upon learning of the reason for the stop. "At breakfast all they had was tea. They ran out of food last night."

After Marcus reemerged from the building, he tossed the bags on the driver's seat and told Dylan he'd be back in a minute. He walked across the road to the Town Hall building and disappeared inside for a few minutes. After he returned to the car, Dylan asked what he had done.

"I took a dump in a real toilet and used real toilet paper to wipe my ass. Oh, yeah, and I reported the measles outbreak at the camp and told them the tribe is in need of doctors, and that someone had already died."

"You know the tribe isn't going to be happy if doctors with their 'Western medicine' and tracking chips show up," Dylan said.

"I don't care. Someone needed to intervene, or they're all going to die. I had to do *something.*"

"But shouldn't they be free to choose whether they get treated?"

"Well, I don't know if the town will actually do anything, and if they do send doctors, then the tribe can always refuse treatment, but it's ridiculous to not even try. God, they are so fucking *stupid!*" Marcus ranted. "Vaccines have been around for what, a hundred fifty years or something? And they still haven't figured out that they protect you from disease and cause no harm? How could anyone be so fucking stupid as to reject vaccines? I swear to God, they've rejected every advancement the human race has made in the last two hundred years. Hell, even the ancient Romans had indoor bathrooms with plumbing so that you didn't have to go shit in the woods and wipe with a leaf. They've rejected two-thousand-year-old technology! And instead, what do they do? Follow the advice of the stars? How fucking stupid! I swear to God if the alignment of Jupiter in Scorpio told them to jump off a bridge, they'd do it."

"Yeah, they're weird, but they live life on their own terms. They don't do anything they don't want to."

"So, just fuck 'em? Let 'em die by their own stupidity? Live free and die?" Marcus asked.

"Isn't it live free *or* die?"

"It's supposed to be, but '*and* die' seems more appropriate given the suicidal path they've chosen."

"So some chick you never met died. People die every day. Why you getting so worked up about this?"

"Because it's a problem with such a simple solution. A solution that has been around for ages, and people are dying because they refuse to acknowledge the solution. The problem shouldn't exist. You realize Lily could be next, don't you? She was hugging Sheila's partner last night; she could be getting a fever and rash right now. Do you care whether Lily lives or dies?"

"Well, we're probably never going to see them again, so we'll never know. What I don't know can't hurt me," Dylan said.

"Genius," Marcus muttered sarcastically.

Chapter 8: Alien Territory

The boys spent the next ten minutes in silence. The Coulomb, unlike the Charger, was nearly noiseless, and it was difficult to tell whether it was even on while driving, making the journey even more lonesome.

"It has better acceleration than I expected," said Marcus. "And it's nice to feel like I'm not pissing away money every time I press the accelerator too. With the Dean I felt the same sensation as when I'm running low on shampoo and I don't have a new bottle waiting in reserve. Like I'm trying to work a miracle getting the remaining drops to last until Mom brings home a new bottle. The Coulomb here is like the extra-large squirt of shampoo I always splurge on when I finally get that new bottle."

"Maybe," Dylan grunted. "But if it's like a new bottle of shampoo, then it must be some of that stinky prescription shampoo for scalp conditions or something. The Dean was the good-smelling stuff that left your hair looking perfect."

"Yeah. The Coulomb is more utilitarian and just good for getting from point A to point B," Marcus admitted.

"They didn't have to make it so fucking ugly. They could have slapped a sexy body on it even if it doesn't have much muscle."

Marcus ran out of small talk, and Dylan quickly got bored and turned on the radio.

As they drifted farther past the Utah state line, Marcus began to notice the landscape looking more and more foreign. East of Salt Lake City, they crossed through Red Rock Canyon in Summit County, which felt like Martian terrain with its large, rust-red rocky formations. Farther west they traversed the Bonneville Salt Flats. The vast expanse of snow-white crust felt lunar, and despite wearing sunglasses, Marcus found himself squinting in the bright sun reflecting off the sea of salt. If the Gateway Arch in St. Louis had been some alien technology dropped from the sky, then surely this was that alien's home planet. Marcus had never seen anything like it, and he couldn't believe this was the same North American continent he had lived on his entire life.

The bizarre scenery continued into Nevada, where infinite desertscapes that felt like sets for the original *Star Wars* movie spanned as far as the eye could see. Occasionally, mixed into the unusual natural beauty, they passed acres upon acres of solar farms and wind turbines clustered like shrubs and trees forming man-made forests.

At a quarter to nine at night they pulled off the highway in Reno and found a motel. Dylan's spirits sank when the motel manager told them that the dozens of casino billboards along the highway like a row of giant dominos were obsolete and that gambling had been outlawed decades earlier. Marcus's spirits sank when the manager told them that the tap water wasn't potable, and that due to the severe drought it was metered and cost four dollars per liter. He had been looking forward to a refreshing shower in the morning, but at those prices, he would have to do without. Both boys were disappointed by a late meal that tasted like a microwaved TV dinner from the 1980s minus the salt. Still, it was nice to finally sleep in a real bed again. A real mattress, in a real room, in a real building. The boys had their best night of sleep yet and rolled out of bed feeling fairly refreshed for their departure Wednesday morning.

Part 3: Urban WUS
Chapter 1: The Red Tape Army

As they got into the Coulomb in the parking lot of the Reno motel, Dylan grabbed the driver's seat headrest, yanked it up and out of its socket, flipped it around, and reinserted it. Marcus looked at him wide-eyed. "You can do that? I had no idea. My neck is so stiff from that thing jamming my head forward." He grabbed the passenger seat headrest and did the same.

"I know. I wish I had thought of it yesterday. My neck is stiff too. It was like there was a dude standing in front of me shoving my head into his crotch forcing me to give him a BJ the entire ride."

"Why the hell do they make them so uncomfortable like that?" Marcus asked.

"To get higher ratings on safety tests. If they jam your head forward, then it can't snap back and give you whiplash in an accident."

"That's dumb. Having my neck jammed forward like that is more likely to *cause* an accident in the first place. It restricts movement and gives my neck spasms, making it harder than hell to check my blind spots."

"That's liberal designers for ya."

With some traffic jams here and there and a quick lunch outside of Sacramento, it took four and a half hours to get to San Francisco from Reno. As the highway skirted the San Francisco Bay on the Berkley-Oakland side, the view opened up over a large expanse of water. Even though his parents' home in New Rochelle was a mile and a half from the Long Island Sound, the coastal property there was almost exclusively private property, so he rarely caught glimpses of the sea, and it set his pulse racing. As they crossed the Bay Bridge, his heart was pounding like he had just sprinted a hundred-meter dash.

He knew that the water he was looking at in San Francisco Bay wasn't technically the ocean, but it was close enough. It was the ocean to him. For a brief moment, he could even faintly make out the Golden Gate Bridge to the north. He knew from his love of football history that Candlestick Park once stood to the south but that it had been demolished long ago, and WUS had since erected their national capital on its site. He strained, but he couldn't identify the national capital building from the highway from so far away, and besides, he had heard that it was an ugly, modern monstrosity that looked like heaps of metallicized Spanish moss draped over a collapsed building, so he didn't feel like he was missing out.

Between the 1980s San Francisco overview map they had and street signs they saw along the way, they were able to fumble their way through the streets of San Francisco to City Hall, where they found visitor parking a few blocks away. They had decided City Hall was the best place to find out whether Sharon still lived in San Francisco, and if so, where.

Approaching the building, Marcus was impressed with the beauty of the massive, historic domed structure. The only thing detracting from it was row upon row of eight-foot-tall vertical slabs arranged in a winding maze from the sidewalk to the main entrance, all plastered with rules and regulations for the building copied into dozens of languages. It took several minutes to navigate the labyrinth to the entrance and walk up a large switchback ramp to the front doors.

In the main entrance lobby they had to wait in line for several minutes to go through security, which included documents to sign attesting that they were there for peaceful purposes and waivers to hold the city harmless for a ten-page list of problems that could potentially transpire inside the building. Beyond the security checkpoint was the information desk. There they discovered that everyone entering the building was required to take a mandatory guided tour to familiarize themselves with the layout of the building and to assure their safety.

They were then sent to the guided tour waiting area with about twenty other people to wait for the next scheduled tour. Marcus asked the information desk if he could use the bathroom during the wait but was told that, for safety reasons, he was not permitted to go beyond the waiting area until he had taken the tour. Dylan passed the time waiting by standing along the waiting area border and continually shifting his foot until it was over the boundary. Every time, he earned himself a scolding from someone for violating regulation 530M.

"This is fucking hilarious," Dylan said. "Did you see that? When I put my foot even a fraction of an inch over the line, one of them was always there to yell at me."

"Dude. Can't you just follow the rules for like five minutes? I just want to get Sharon's address and get out of here," Marcus said.

"Yes, sir, boss, sir," Dylan said.

Their tour guide was a young, slender, Caucasian man wearing a collared shirt with a small flower print that was buttoned up to the top. He announced that, unless anyone had a separation anxiety trigger, the tour would be split into three groups depending on how recently one had been to the building, and everyone would be given badges to wear to identify their group. As he began to gather their group for the tour, a chubby, sloppily dressed, middle-aged white woman raised her hand like she was a student waiting for the teacher to call on her in class.

"Yes, please, you have a question?" the tour guide asked.

"Yes, I wanted to check to be sure that the badges aren't organized by color? I was on a tour at a different facility not long ago where they did that, and I feel like separating us by colors is prejudiced against the color-blind, and possibly racist too."

"May I ask what facility it was that did this?" asked the guide. He quickly jotted down the name she gave him. "Typically, we use badges organized by endangered species animals to remind people of the work needed to protect our planet. Is that satisfactory?"

The woman wrinkled her nose. "I feel like separating by animals could be racist too."

Dylan turned to Marcus. "Hey, MC, you're black. Do you feel like the badges are racist?"

Marcus shook his head.

"Hey, lady. My black friend here doesn't think they're racist. He oughta know. Can we just use the animal badges and get on with it?"

The tour guide nearly interrupted Dylan before he had even finished speaking. "Sir, sir, everyone has a right to their opinions and feelings, and we have to work to make people feel more comfortable and accepted, and we need to increase awareness of how our biases affect others." He paused for a second before putting his hand to his face. "I'm so sorry. I didn't mean to call you 'sir.' It is a non-gender-neutral and biased word. Please accept my apology." He then turned back to the woman and asked her if she objected to letters or numbers being used to differentiate the groups, which she did because it implied that some people were ranked higher than others. Finally, she agreed to badges that were based on San Francisco monument icons, so long as the icons were not in color and had Braille descriptions of the icons. After waiting for the new badges to be printed, Marcus and Dylan were finally able to hang their "Golden Gate Bridge" badges around their necks and get moving.

The guide started with emergency exits and safety procedures, including noting that use of the elevators required a mobility impairment permit, after which the recent-visitor "Transamerica Pyramid" group was released to go about their business. Next, they entered the grand interior rotunda, a stunning and cavernous space that reminded Marcus of an elaborate cathedral he had visited in Germany, minus the religious iconography. The tour guide described the history of the building and pointed out the portrait of the mayor, Victoria Timball, hanging on the wall before moving on to one of the corridors.

Next, they entered the South Light Court, where a large blue curtain divided the room nearly in half, and the guide described the current museum-style exhibits on display. On one side of the curtain the exhibit was about former San Francisco resident and Puerto Paz founding father Michael Debroux and the *Renaissancity* online game he had developed while living there. The guide indicated that on the other side of the curtain there was a modern-art exhibit featuring local artists.

After the Light Court tours, the less-recent visitors in the "Victorian House" group was released from the tour.

The newbie Golden Gate Bridge group had to continue on, walking every corridor of the five-story building and being told what every office they walked past was for and where the nearest exits were. Finally, the tour ended back at the lobby waiting area, and they were instructed to form a line. One by one, they were asked what department they were there to see and then told where to go. After they made it through the line, the boys speed-walked to the bathrooms near the South Light Court.

After they finished, they made a beeline for the stairs and marched up to the third floor Registrar of Voters department, where they had been instructed to go to find out whether Sharon still lived in San Francisco. There they had to wait in a line for ten minutes before speaking with a gray-haired, make-up-free, Caucasian female clerk in a rumpled, beige gingham coat, who was buried behind unorganized stacks of paper documents.

"ID cert 426P," the clerk said with a dry, emotionless voice.

"I'm sorry?" Marcus asked.

"I need to see your ID permission certification before I can check your IDs."

"I don't know what that is. Can I just show you my ID? You have my permission to look at it."

"I'm forbidden from looking at your ID until you've shown me your Form 426P," the woman said with a slight whine in her voice. "Department of Permissions. Ground floor. Next."

They descended the stairs to the Department of Permissions, waited in another line, signed waivers and permissions documents, and got their certificate before heading back to the third floor to stand in the same line for another ten minutes to see the clerk again.

Marcus handed the clerk his certification and two forms of ID.

At long last, the woman started searching the voter rolls for Sharon. After scrolling through, she looked up and said, "I can't find a 'Sharon Coleman' on the list. What is her birthplace?"

"New Rochelle, New York," Marcus said.

"That might explain it. She may have antiquated views of marriage and may have taken her spouse's last name," the clerk said.

Dylan piped in and said, "She can't be married, she's a lesbian."

The clerk stared at Dylan with disgust. "Lesbians have every right to marry, just the same as anyone else. Your lack of sensitivity and awareness is very distressing." She turned to a computer monitor and keyboard that were hidden behind her stacks of paper and began typing. "Are you Dylan Callahan? Known associate of Marcus Coleman?" she asked.

"Why do you want to know?" Dylan asked.

"Seems you have quite the record of anti-equality behavior in just the last few days," the clerk said. She typed some more, then turned her attention back to Marcus. "Go to the Marriage Licensing Department on the fifth floor to see if your sister got married and took her spouse's name. If you get a different last name there, then you can come back here to see if her address is on file."

"I guess this is how they enforce mandatory physical fitness," Dylan grunted as they trudged up a couple more flights of stairs. "A wild goose chase up and down a million stairs."

Marcus challenged Dylan to a race up the stairs to keep his mind off the tediousness of their hunt for forms and documents, but at the fourth floor they were yelled at by a City Hall employee for violating rule 703M against running. Marcus had beaten Dylan to that floor, but Dylan caught up to share in receiving the verbal admonishment, and from there the race changed to speed-walking up the next flight of stairs. Dylan's long legs gave him the advantage at that point, and he beat Marcus to the fifth floor.

The marriage license clerk found Sharon's name. She had gotten married and changed her last name to combine hers with her partner's to "Cruzeman." Armed with this new information, they returned to the Registrar of Voters department to wait in that line a third time.

Dylan began singing to pass the time. "I'm dreaming of a white Christmas..." he crooned.

"Christmas carols?" Marcus asked with arched eyebrows.

"Yeah. I figured we've been waiting in lines so long here that it must be getting close to Christmas by now," Dylan said. He started singing again before being shushed by the clerk.

Finally, it was their turn to speak with the clerk again, and they found out that the clerk did have an address for Sharon Cruzeman, but that she couldn't just hand it to them. They would have to go down to the ground floor again to the Documents Release Department to sign paperwork and a waiver before Sharon's address would be handed to them on a slip of paper. Another fifteen minutes later, they finally had Sharon's address in their hands. They headed straight for the ground floor exit, and onward toward the car, eager to head out to the suburbs to find Sharon's home.

"Shit," Marcus said as they walked past the City Hall entrance.

"We don't know where this street is, and our map isn't detailed enough to find it."

They headed back to City Hall, went through security, and to the information desk to ask whether they had any city maps. They were informed that they'd have to go to the Cartography department, but that because they had left the building and returned, they were considered "recent visitors" and would have to take the first part of the next guided tour before they were allowed to proceed to Cartography. Marcus and Dylan looked at each other and without a word, turned around and attempted to walk back out the entrance. They were stopped by security and told it was a one-way entrance only. As they sat in the waiting area for the next tour, Marcus turned to Dylan, grinned, and started singing. "Just like the ones I used to know."

Dylan laughed before squinting at Marcus. "Am I going to have to report you?"

After a mini guided tour and a stop at Cartography, at last they had everything they needed.

"Wow, getting Sharon's address only took four hours!" Dylan exclaimed sarcastically.

"That was exhausting, but I guess I should be relieved that I can finally go see Sharon now. What's four hours after seven years of waiting, right?

Chapter 2: Renaissancity Exhibit

The City Hall expedition had lasted so long that by the time they were ready to exit the building a second time, they were already in need of a bathroom again. They stopped at the bathroom across from the South Light Court a second time as they headed toward the exit. Marcus was in and out in no time, but he left Dylan behind grunting in a stall. Curiosity got the best of him, and assuming he had some time to kill before Dylan was done doing his business, he wandered across the hall into the *Renaissancity* exhibit.

The room was arranged with a rectangular-shaped perimeter of exhibits surrounding a bronze statue in the middle of the exhibit space. The statue had caught his eye during the tour, so he headed to it first. It was of Michael Debroux, father of Puerto Paz. A sign in front of the statue indicated it was a replica of a larger statue located at the main seaport in Puerto Paz's capital, New Athens. Debroux was looking down and to the left with a look of melancholy, at what looked like an award trophy he was holding in his hand. His right arm hung at his side, the hand clutching a sheet of paper. Marcus looked back at the sign's title, which read "Debroux Receiving Academy Award."[2] A plaque in front of the statue read:

> *Exhibit 2: The Hollywood movie industry was another group vehemently opposed to Skrelin's divisiveness. They cherished the* Renaissancity *game and collaborated with Debroux to make a movie based on it. Debroux won an Oscar for his role in co-writing the movie, although most people recognized that the*

---

[2] More information about the founding of Puerto Paz can be found at PuertoPaz.com

*award was more political statement than
meritorious. This statue commemorates his
acceptance of his award in 2023, less than a year
before Skrelin's political wedge-tactics succeeded
in splitting the country.*

A chiming noise behind him diverted his attention away from
the statue. He turned around and saw several large video screens
playing a simulation of a video game. A plaque under the monitors
stated:

*Exhibit 1: Prior to the partitioning of the
United States, during Rupert Skrelin's rise to
power, not everyone was apathetic, and not
everyone was caught up in the anti-communist
and anti-Cuban hysteria of the Neo-
McCarthyists. One such group of people was a
start-up software engineering company here in
San Francisco led by a young man named
Michael Debroux. Tired of the partisan bickering
in Washington and across the country, and in
particular with Skrelin's repulsive rage, Debroux
founded the company to create a virtual-reality
utopian society called Renaissancity.com. The
software, released in late 2020, was part
massively multiplayer online game and part
idealistic sociology experiment.*

*These monitors are playing a recorded
session of the* Renaissancity *game. The game
involved collaboratively building a virtual
online city and society with all of the other
players. Set in a virtual Cuba as a slap-in-the-
face rejoinder to Skrelin, it provided escapism
from the depressing reality that had enveloped
the United States in a cloud of doom and gave
people an opportunity to feel like they were
doing something productive in a futile,
corrupted political system. Little did Debroux*

*know how apropos the Cuban setting would be
just a few years later.*

Marcus continued on to the next bank of monitors hanging on the wall. They had been blank, but as he approached a motion sensor turned them on, and suddenly he could feel the low rumble of a subwoofer vibrating his chest cavity. The screens lit up with a bright flash of light. The flash was followed by a white cloud, and as the image zoomed out it became clear that it was the mushroom cloud of a nuclear explosion. The gravelly voice of a male narrator began over the dissipating sound of the explosion as the images on the screen showed entire neighborhoods of buildings vaporizing and blowing away under the heat and force of the blast. Marcus saw a control panel in front of the monitors and pressed the pause button on it, stopping the movie. He read another plaque under these monitors.

Exhibit 3: In the post-partitioned era, with the liberals essentially evicted from EUS, Skrelin and the Neo-McCarthyists rose to un-checked power and focused their tirades on Cuba. Using phony statistics to claim that the "evil communist Cubans" were the source of the EUS drug infestation, they rationalized their invasion of Cuba. Most of the world recognized the invasion as a pathetic attempt to demonstrate that EUS hadn't been weakened by their split with WUS by bullying a small, poor country, and as a way to create a scapegoat in order to engender citizen loyalty and alleviate the burden of introspection.

By July of 2029, the invasion hadn't gone as smoothly as desired. Cuba had too much land area for the destruction of drug crops to be effective using conventional weapons. EUS's culture of tightly hierarchical organization with rigid conformity and sense of duty, combined with their psychologically unstable leader, resulted in a lack of a mechanism for resistance. Just as Hitler's commands were executed by faithful minions in Nazi Germany, so were the maniacal EUS president's commands to drop nuclear bombs on Cuba. Cuba was completely destroyed.

After the nuclear annihilation of Cuba in 2029, EUS claimed control of the land as occupiers. The soil was radioactive, making the entire country uninhabitable, so EUS had no interest in redevelopment. After the EUS's establishment leadership impeached President Skrelin and regained control, they were eager to appease United Nations demands to relinquish control of Cuba in order to lift sanctions. Both the EUS and the United Nations were at a loss as to what to do with Cuba.

The Cuban survivors, who numbered less than one thousand, had all been resettled in other countries. The land was unusable. In stepped Michael Debroux and a conglomeration of wealthy Hollywood elites. The Renaissancity Coalition, as they called themselves, offered to purchase Cuba from the EUS. The EUS had just finished paying retribution damages to the Cuban survivors and had spent a tremendous amount of money restocking its military after the Cuban invasion, leaving them desperate for new sources of income that didn't involve breaking their pledges to keep taxes low. They were eager to offload Cuba, and in July of 2030 they relinquished it for a bargain price.

Most observers of the deal assumed that the Renaissancity Coalition, especially since it involved so many Hollywood filmmakers, was purchasing the country to film it and create a documentary memorial to shame the EUS and pay tribute to those who had perished. These observers were partially correct, as the coalition did indeed create such a documentary. That documentary is the movie you see playing on these monitors. However, their goals extended far beyond merely filming the land.

Marcus moved on from the wall with the monitors to a series of six-foot-tall partial partitions standing in front of the blue curtain that divided the South Light Court into two rooms. His eyes wandered over the photos, historical artifacts, and plaques on the partitions, sequenced to create a timeline of events, starting from life in Cuba before the United States partitioned, then to the "Bay of Pigs Avenged" invasion by EUS and the nuclear annihilation of Cuba. Marcus continued past a gap between partitions that allowed visitors to cross through the blue curtain into the adjacent art exhibit. The timeline continued with information about the birth of Puerto Paz. Another plaque read:

> *Exhibit 4: Shortly after the filming of the Cuba documentary concluded, the coalition announced plans to try spraying Cuba with experimental bacteria that had been engineered to digest and neutralize radioactivity.*
>
> *By December of 2032, the experiment was declared a success. The Renaissancity Coalition now had a 42,426-square-mile blank slate and twelve years of virtual utopian sociology experiment data from which to build a new country from scratch. Construction of the capital city began nearly immediately based on the Renaissancity game. City planners, architects, engineers, and other professionals had spent countless hours playing the game in past years, making the game's virtual city as realistic as possible, which accelerated the final design phase that preceded groundbreaking.*
>
> *Funding of construction was opened up to a diverse group of idealistic investors and*

*entrepreneurs from around the world, who were
all screened and required to take a pledge of
anonymity for the first decade to avoid pay-for-
play favoritism. The world was eager to see
Cuba rebuilt.*

"Dude!" Marcus heard Dylan shout. Dylan entered the room from the corridor and trotted over to him.

"Dude! I couldn't find you! I came close to initiating City Hall Emergency Procedure 113J to get a search-and-rescue party out looking for you!"

"Sorry. I was reading this history narrative. It's completely different from what we learned in school. I'm not sure what to think of it."

Dylan showed no sign of interest in reading the history, so they decided to peek on the other side of the curtain at the modern-art exhibit out of curiosity. The art piece closest to them consisted of what looked like either a white dog turd on the floor, or a pile of toothpaste wound into a spiral with a trail leading from a toothpaste tube.

"This is art?" Marcus exclaimed.

"Please tell me this was done by kindergartners," Dylan said. "This is shit! I literally could have shit on the floor here instead of in the toilet a few minutes ago and called it art!"

They stood next to the curtain, refusing to step any further into the room, surveying the exhibit from where they stood. Hanging on the walls were large canvases painted all one color. Marcus continued their shared rant. "I could have painted those. Where is the talent?"

After the shock of disbelief at what passed for art in WUS wore off, they headed back through the blue curtain into the Renaissancity Exhibit. A male and female in the beige gingham coats that Marcus now associated with city employees were standing at the hallway entrance looking at the two boys. The two employees broke eye contact and started examining the exhibit. Marcus had a fleeting moment of déjà vu, thinking back to the reaction of the Chicken Bucket waitress in Terre Haute looking at him like she thought he was going to steal decorations off the restaurant wall.

"Let's get out of here," Marcus said.

Chapter 3: Out of the Frying Pan

As Marcus and Dylan rounded the corner after exiting City Hall, Marcus saw that the city employees had followed them out. They were standing near the rear door looking at the boys but appeared to have broken off pursuit. The boys continued on.

Back at the car, Dylan pulled three parking tickets out of the windshield and threw them on the floor at Marcus's feet before starting the car. Marcus picked them up and skimmed them.

"Jesus, they don't even let you park in a City Hall visitor's space long enough to get in and out of City Hall in a reasonable amount of time. I think the first ticket was placed while we were on our first mandatory tour."

Dylan just shook his head and kept driving.

The ordeal at City Hall had lasted long enough that their quest to find Sharon's home began in rush hour traffic. Yet another test of Marcus's patience, and he was in no mood for more delays. He was so close to seeing his sister for the first time in years. He practically prayed for Moses's powers to part the traffic and create a lane that they could quickly drive down for the nearly six miles that separated him from Sharon.

Forty-five minutes later, they were finally in the southwestern Parkside neighborhood, pulling into a street parking space alongside the address they had been given at City Hall. Marcus looked up and down the street. Everything looked the same. It was house after house of semi-attached row houses. The property size was the same for every lot, as was the general shape, size, and architecture of each house. It looked like every house had been built by the same builder, in the same era, using the same construction drawings. The only variations were relatively subtle differences in the front façades and paint colors, plus a different street number affixed to each house.

Marcus thought of the whiny woman at City Hall who had

complained about prejudiced tour badges and wondered if, even among all this uniformity and equality of property, she would object to the street numbers implying some sort of intolerable ranking and superiority of houses, or to the different house colors being prejudiced. There was probably a petition filed somewhere at City Hall to have this injustice remedied.

They walked up a tall flight of stairs—one last mountain between him and his sister—to the front door and knocked. A few seconds later, a curtain covering the small window in the door was pulled back, and Sharon's eye could be seen sizing them up to see whether they were friend or foe. The door opened, and out walked a short black woman wearing a beige pantsuit.

"Oh my god, what are you doing here?" Sharon asked with a muted enthusiasm that seemed to communicate as much annoyance as pleasant surprise.

Dylan spoke up first. "Oh, we were just in the neighborhood. Figured we'd stop by and say hi."

Sharon looked at Dylan like he had two heads. "Who are you?" she asked. They had met before a couple of times, but Sharon hadn't seen him since he was nine or ten years old, and he had changed drastically since then.

"We ran away from home," Marcus blurted out. "It is so good to finally see you again. This is Dylan, my best friend since first grade." He stood there not sure what to do next. In his experience, women were usually the ones to initiate hugs, and the elder of the two people would control the interaction, so he felt like it was Sharon's role to make the first move—plus he had spent five days building up in anticipation to this moment, but he knew Sharon had just been completely blindsided by his arrival.

Instead of hugging him, she put her hands on his shoulders and looked him up and down like she was visually ingesting him from head to toe to confirm his identity and process all of the ways he had physically changed in the last seven years. Marcus wanted her to pull him near and embrace him, but her body language was like that of a running back stiff-arming a defensive back to thwart a tackle.

"Wow. I can't believe it's you. I can't believe you're standing here at my front door," Sharon said before quickly shaking her head back and forth and blinking forcefully, as if clearing the cobwebs from her mind. Finally, she invited them in. "I was just starting to prepare supper. My wife will be home in about twenty minutes."

Seven years. They hadn't seen each other in seven years, and her top priority was preparing supper? And no hug? He tried to find a rational justification for why she would be so standoffish. Was it something minor like the surprise of him unexpectedly showing up? Annoyance at the interruption of supper preparation and a wrench thrown in her plans? Or was it something major like her having felt like she had already burned all bridges to her past and her family, including the ones to him, and she didn't like the reminder of the past here in her home? Marcus was at a loss. The only excuse he could think of for her behavior that he felt he could do anything about was the interruption of supper preparation, so he asked her if there was anything he could do to help. Maybe it would give them time together to talk while they worked.

"Sure. You could chop vegetables for the salad."

Dylan plunked down on the couch and flipped on the television uninvited. "Please keep the volume low," Sharon instructed Dylan. "If the neighbors on the other side of that wall hear it and file a noise complaint, and the police come here and find that it isn't a state-registered TV, then we're in big trouble."

"State-registered TV?" Marcus asked.

"All electronic devices have to go through rigorous safety testing and get State approval. We couldn't afford a State registered TV, so I had to get one...by other means. Let's just keep that among the three of us. My wife doesn't know."

Marcus and Sharon went in the kitchen. Sharon got out the vegetables, a cutting board, and a knife for Marcus to start cutting before attending to some pots and pans that were already heating on the stove.

"So, what have you been up to the last seven years?" Marcus asked.

Sharon described matter-of-factly how when she moved here, she went through a year of paperwork, applications, and background checks to become a citizen and enroll in college at San Francisco State. For a while she lived in a State-run homeless shelter because she was legally an adult but had little money and no income because she wasn't allowed to work or go to school until her paperwork cleared. She was mid-sentence in describing her years at college when she looked over at Marcus and said, "You're cutting the cucumbers wrong. Cut them in half the long way and then slice them thinly. Don't dice them so small."

"Same old bossy Sharon. You haven't changed a bit!" Marcus smiled wryly at her, trying to inject some humor into the conversation.

Sharon looked at him with horror on her face. "Do *not* call me bossy! That is a sexist word that demeans women!"

Marcus took a step back from the cutting board, still looking at Sharon. She didn't seem to be joking. "Why is that sexist? You *were* being bossy. What's wrong with me saying it?"

"Men only call women that, not other men. It means that they don't want women to be assertive, confident, or strong the way men are. It's sexist."

Marcus furrowed his brow. "Bullshit," he said. "Bullshit on both accounts. I would just as soon call Dad bossy as I would you, and I love strong and confident women. I prefer them to weak or submissive women, in fact. I've eaten dozens of salads with the cucumbers cut exactly the way I was cutting them. You didn't need to tell me how to cut them. The way I was doing it was just fine, so that means you were being bossy. If you want my help, let me do it my way."

"Agree to disagree. Please don't use the word 'bossy' in this house, though, and don't compare me to Dad." Sharon continued where she had left off, describing college. She had attended San Francisco State University, which like all colleges in WUS had free tuition, and she had earned her bachelor's degree and a paralegal certificate before doing an internship at a law firm. She and her partner, Elena, had met at San Francisco State during her sophomore year, and they had been together since. They had bought this house together a year earlier. It would have been way too expensive for them, but because she was an African American first-time homebuyer and the State wanted to diversify the mostly Asian American neighborhood, they were given a tremendous amount of government assistance to buy the house.

Now she was a paralegal, and this evening was her date night with Elena, a weekly appointment they made with each other due to how much time they had to spend at work and how little time they felt like they spent with each other during the work week. She'd had to threaten to sue her own company for overtime violations in order to make it home on time for her turn to cook date night dinner tonight. She punctuated the end of her story with an exasperated grunt and a shake of her head. "So, what have you been up to? You just finished, what, your junior year of high school?"

"Yeah. My life the last few years has revolved around football and track and field on top of schoolwork. In football I was all-state, conference MVP, and Ohio State was about to offer me a partial scholarship before we left home. In track I finished second in the hundred meter at State. In school, I've been getting straight A's. I've been thinking about going into some sort of engineering in college, but I don't know what type. I'm not sure how I'm even going to get into college now."

Just then they heard keys in the front door, and Sharon darted out of the kitchen toward the front door, undoubtedly to avoid her wife freaking out upon seeing an unexpected stranger, Dylan, alone in the living room with no one else in sight. Marcus continued chopping vegetables while he listened to the muted voices coming from the other room. The feminine murmurs of his sister and Elena greeting each other, a pause presumably for a kiss hello, more feminine murmurs followed by a grunt from Dylan that was likely him greeting Elena with a "hey," and then more feminine murmurs growing increasingly louder and intelligible as they approached the kitchen.

"Marcus, this is my wife, Elena. Elena, my brother, Marcus."

Marcus exchanged hellos with the olive-skinned woman in a gray pantsuit standing in front of him, and Elena thrust her hand forward for a handshake. Marcus found himself missing Lily and her exuberantly friendly hugs. Elena excused herself to go change out of her work clothes.

Marcus finished assembling the salad and delivered it to the dining room table, and then set the table as Sharon finished the main course. The room was relatively sparse. No décor on the walls. A simple, unadorned table and chairs. A simple, off-the-shelf, flush-mount ceiling light. He realized that the living room and kitchen had also lacked decoration. He hadn't cared for the décor in his parents' home in New Rochelle: a Revolutionary War musket, Christian crosses, various family portraits in which his father was never smiling, and portraits of scowling, long-dead relatives. But at least there was something of visual interest there. This felt sterile.

Sharon mentioned needing government assistance to buy the house only a year ago and has only been in the workforce for a couple of years, so maybe she couldn't afford to decorate it yet, Marcus thought. *Or, since she mentioned her and Elena both working long hours, maybe the issue is lack of time. Or maybe they paid thousands of dollars to have an artist paint the walls a single color of light gray and it's meant to be "modern art."* He stifled a snicker and made a mental note to check the bathroom for a matching "toothpaste turd" art installation later as he joined Dylan in the living room.

A summons from Sharon that dinner was ready brought everyone to the dining room table. Laid out in front of them was a small dish of eggplant parmesan, surely originally meant for two. It was supplemented with large bowls on each side. One bowl had saffron-infused rice and beans and the other bowl had the salad that Marcus had helped prepare, and both had clearly also been augmented to account for unexpected guests. Elena grabbed the eggplant dish, served herself, and passed it to Sharon.

"So, you two ran away from home?" Elena asked just as Marcus had begun to bow his head and close his eyes for prayer.

Marcus reopened his eyes and looked at Elena. She was glaring at him, reminding him again of family portraits back home in New Rochelle. "Yes, ma'am," answered Marcus.

"You don't need to call her ma'am," Sharon interjected. "She's family."

"I can speak for myself," Elena snapped at Sharon before returning her attention to Marcus. "What caused you to flee?"

Marcus looked at Dylan, feeling like he had the better reason for running away. "You want to tell her your reason?"

Dylan kept chewing, and without lifting his eyes up from the table to look at anyone, said, "My dad's an asshole who beats me."

Marcus waited a beat to see if that was all Dylan had to say before adding, "Dad and I were fighting about me going to West Point instead of Ohio State. I want to play football and maybe become an engineer. I don't want to go into the military. He's trying to make me be what he wants me to be instead of letting me choose my own path. He has no respect for me."

"I see. And how long do you plan to stay here?"

"I don't know. We hadn't thought that far ahead. I need to figure out a way to get back into school somewhere next year, but Sharon was telling me earlier that when she moved here it took a year to get the paperwork cleared for her to go to school or even get a job, so I'm not sure what I'm going to do."

As soon as Marcus said "I don't know" to Elena's question about the duration of his stay, he caught her glance sideways and raise an eyebrow at Sharon, who responded with a subtle shrug. Dylan had been unusually quiet and withdrawn since their arrival, perhaps because his mind was being blown by the concept of married lesbians in his presence, but now Marcus was starting to feel less talkative too. He looked at Elena to see whether her body language was expressing any more about how she felt about him being there. Her straight, chocolate-colored hair fell across her cheek as she leaned forward to take another bite of food. She was taller than Sharon, and more slender too—a very attractive woman with deep, dark-brown eyes. She spoke with an accent that Marcus couldn't identify. Sharon had done well in her partner selection in terms of physical attractiveness, but Marcus still didn't have a good sense of her personality or her level of kindness. He was definitely getting a weird vibe from the two women.

Sharon looked at Elena and said softly, "We're blood relatives. The State will mandate…"

"I know," Elena interrupted her curtly. "Have you checked their equality classification?"

"No. I'll look it up now," Sharon said, pulling her phone out of a pocket.

After a significant pause in the conversation, Elena looked up from eating and made eye contact with Marcus. "It would seem you might be here a while, then. I'm an architect. I work with a lot of engineers. Maybe I can get you some contacts for internship opportunities. They sometimes have more relaxed regulations for interns than they do for permanent positions. A lot of immigrants start as interns. Do you have a significant other?"

"No, ma'am. I mean, no. I mean, ma'am. Sorry. Not really."

"If you are heterosexual, I could set you up with my coworker's daughter. It would be good for you to make as many contacts, both professionally and socially, as you can. You will need references who are citizens and who have high equality classifications. Do you have any money?"

"Well, some. We traded in Dylan's car for a cheaper one and made some money in the deal."

"Good. Then you won't be completely dependent on us for everything. We have a spare bedroom that we use as an office. You'll have to share it. At the moment, we only have one air mattress, so one of you will have to sleep on the living room couch for a couple of nights until we have time to buy a second air mattress this weekend."

Elena turned to Sharon, who had set her phone down on the table. "Anything?" Elena asked.

"Marcus is level two, but Dylan is level seven," Sharon said.

"Seven?" Elena said, her eyes opened wide. "*Desigualdad!* How on earth did he get to a seven after only a few days in our country?"

"Big Mother will—" Sharon began to say.

Elena cut her off again. "You know I don't like it when you call them that."

"Yes, dear." Sharon turned to Dylan. "You're going to need to lay low and keep your nose clean for a while. Any more complaints and Equality Defense is likely to send you away to reeducation camp. At level seven they might already be considering scheduling a hearing."

"Reeducation?" Marcus asked. "Is that like juvie back home?"

"Yes and no. It is like juvie in that it is intended as a place of reformation. Unlike juvie, though, the State here focuses on rehabilitation, not punishment. They don't just throw you into a cell with a toilet, shove food at you once in a while, and hope you learn a lesson from imprisonment like back in EUS. Here there is nurturing and education. The reeducation camps focus on increasing awareness of how behaviors affect others and how to coexist and be a good citizen."

"So, what does 'lay low and keep my nose clean' mean?" Dylan asked. "Am I supposed to just stay locked up here so that I don't offend anyone out there?"

"We'll discuss your situation another day," Elena said. "For now, I am exhausted, and do not have the energy to continue thinking about this." She turned to Marcus. "I will talk to my coworker tomorrow morning about setting you up on a blind date with her daughter."

Marcus had thought earlier that Sharon was bossy, but it was clear Elena was in charge here, both of the household and apparently his and Dylan's life decisions too.

Chapter 4: Apples and Oranges

"Yeah, you go fetch me some coffee and a newspaper, sugar tits," Marcus said to the back of his blind date's head, intentionally trying to piss her off as she strode toward the restaurant door. "Maybe that newspaper will have an article in it about what sexism and feminism *really* are, and you could learn a thing or two."

Simone spun around and shot him a dirty look. Marcus opened his eyes wide, raised his palms to the ceiling while shrugging, and sarcastically said, "What? Was that sexist?"

The people at nearby tables within earshot were all staring at him as Simone stormed out. Marcus wished he could have insulted her without them hearing it. Public insults were more Dylan's modus operandi than his own, but after the way Simone had treated him, he felt she deserved it. He was somewhat proud of himself for having not uttered the word "bitch," though. He suspected the police would have been called had he let that word slip.

The blind date Elena had set him up on had been a disaster. He sat there for a few minutes just digesting what had happened. Eventually he noticed his keychain in his hands, his thumb rubbing it steadily, and wondered when he had taken it out of his pocket. He stuffed it back in his pants.

He paid the bill in full and headed back toward Sharon's house, a mixture of regret and fury intensifying the farther he walked. *Shit. What's that incident going to do to my Equality Rating*, he thought. *Am I going to be put on house arrest like Dylan now too?* As he reached Sharon's house, he decided to continue walking to clear his head. He wasn't ready to face any questions about the date yet.

Dusk had ended, and a heavy blanket of fog had rolled in, drastically cooling the temperature. He hugged his chest and tucked his hands under his armpits for warmth for a minute before spontaneously accelerating from a walk to a trot to a steady jog, right there in his new good shirt, good pants, and good shoes, which he'd spent half the day shopping for just for this one miserable date with Simone. *Simone,* he repeated in his head. *Some-moan.*

In the dark and fog, no one could see him. It was both a benefit, as he worried about how people would perceive a young black man running in street clothes, and a detriment, as he couldn't see cars coming as he approached intersections, nor could they see him. He didn't feel like risking his life crossing streets, so he began circling Sharon's block, doing counterclockwise half-mile loops. He had hardly done anything in the last week that qualified as exercise, save for the stair workout at City Hall a couple of days earlier, and breaking a sweat felt refreshing, both physically and mentally.

Running his first lap triggered a memory of the last time he had run on the sidewalks of New Rochelle. A young black man wouldn't dare run in street clothes there unless forced to. He shuddered as he relived the experience. His father had already yelled at him for getting home late from school multiple times in the preceding weeks, and he was on the verge of getting home late again, so he had decided to speed-walk the shortcut through Duke Estates. Halfway through, he heard a loud *pop*, like a fire cracker, then the ping of something hard striking the street sign just ahead of him at high velocity. Another loud pop and then a puff of dust and the cracking sound of concrete being struck in the sidewalk next to him. He took off sprinting toward a wooded park area and kept running until he was through the south walls of the neighborhood. He was pretty sure he had run faster that day than he had at the State track meet, keeping that pace for a full quarter mile.

He had no idea who had shot at him, and there had been no warning. It could have been a suspicious homeowner, their vigilante-cowboy security force, or a trigger-happy racist police officer. He had no time to turn around to find out. That incident had happened the previous autumn, and he hadn't dared step foot in that neighborhood since.

Marcus definitely felt safer here in San Francisco. After all, the State had basically paid Sharon to move to this neighborhood. But it was difficult to shake the feeling that if someone saw him now, they'd assume he was doing something wrong or that he was running away from the scene of a crime.

The fog was rolling in waves, with alternating bands of dense and diffuse mist. He approached Sharon's home again as a lighter wave rolled through. Visibility was still relatively poor, and he could barely make out the street number on Sharon's house. He took note of a white van parked on the street as his marker for where his stopping point would be on future laps when he felt he was ready to terminate his run.

As he kept making left turn after left turn, he was reminded of a dorky joke he had crafted a few years earlier, that "two wrongs don't make a right, but three lefts do." After every three left turns, he would think to himself, *If I continued straight right now, it would be as if I had originally made a right turn instead of my first left.* Finally, he had something silly to distract himself and to smile about. He was already starting to feel considerably better than he had just thirty minutes earlier.

By the end of lap number two, a wave of heavier fog had rolled in. He couldn't see Sharon's house, but the white van marked the transition to lap number three. As he passed the van, Marcus noticed a faint light in the driver's-side window. *Shit,* he thought. *They might drive away during this next lap. If they leave and the fog doesn't let up, I'll have to navigate by feel and estimate how far up the block I've run.* He began counting the steps it took to get to the next turn. Another turn later, he began counting the steps it took to run the entire backstretch block that was parallel to Sharon's street. He subtracted one count from the other to estimate how many steps it would take to get to Sharon's house from the final turn onto her street.

At the end of lap number three the fog was starting to lift a bit. The white van was still there and its interior light remained on. He confirmed that his estimate of steps to get to Sharon's house was relatively accurate.

At the end of lap four, visibility had improved considerably. He was about to break stride and slow to a trot to cross the imaginary finish line when he caught movement inside the van in his peripheral vision. He turned his head as he passed it and saw a woman looking at him. Her shirt had a light-colored collar, and he recognized it as the beige gingham jacket of a City Hall employee. His neck flinched as he turned forward and kept running, trying to maintain a uniform speed to look like he had intended to do another lap the whole time.

A moment later, his brain caught up with his eyes. It was the same woman who had followed him out of City Hall. *What the fuck? Are they here spying on me and Dylan?*

He continued running halfway around another lap, counting his steps on the backstretch to stop at Sharon's rear neighbor's house. He cautiously worked his way through the neighbor's yard to Sharon's house, hopping a couple of fences en route, and let himself in through her back door. He shut the door, locked it, and leaned back on it to catch his breath. He closed his eyes and tilted his head back against the door, pressing a finger into his wrist until he felt his pulse drop from a chaotic drum solo to a steady metronome.

Am I being a drama queen? he wondered. *Anxious like my mother?* He didn't know whether the government employees were outside for him or Dylan, or if it was just coincidence. *It's nothing. If they wanted to, they could have stopped me during my run.* He waited a moment, listening for a knock at the front door, then when no knock came, quietly climbed the back stairs. He found Dylan lying on the couch, right where he had left him before his date, still watching the boring public television shows that seemed carefully crafted to assure they wouldn't offend anyone. He verified that the curtains were shut. Dylan muttered something, and Marcus just said, "I'll be back in a minute."

He headed to the kitchen and, leaving the light off, looked out the window toward the street. A tree was blocking the view. He fumbled in the dark for a glass in the cupboard, turned on the faucet, stuck it under, and listened for the change in pitch signaling the glass was nearly full. He returned to the living room and sat down on the edge of the couch next to Dylan's feet. He looked at the front door, then back at the TV. He decided not to tell Dylan about the van. He didn't want to rile him up and get him foaming at the mouth about commie minders, and since they hadn't knocked on the door, he figured it would probably be okay to assume they were benign.

Dylan informed him that Sharon and Elena had gone to bed early, exhausted from rough days at work, and then asked him how the date went.

Marcus rolled his eyes. "You remember that time I went on a

date freshman year with the girl you ended up calling the Jesus freak? The one who took me on our date to her Bible-study group where we watched a terrible movie about the Rapture, and then the group leader spent the rest of the night telling us what horrible sinners we were and demanded that we sign chastity pledges before we could leave?"

Dylan laughed. "Yeah."

"This was twice as bad."

Dylan suddenly sprang up to sitting position and started paying full attention to Marcus. "Do dish!" he exclaimed.

"Oh, good Lord," Marcus began. "Where do I start? Just about everything about the date was awful. She was completely prejudiced against guys from NEUS, and everything I said or did she took offense to. She just danced from one perceived atrocity to the next and kept giving me this wrinkled-nose look of condescending disgust every time I said anything. At one point I even thought that maybe you had intercepted her before the date and put her up to acting that way, and I looked out the window to see if you were outside laughing your ass off at me."

Dylan let out a loud chortle. "Well, was she at least hot?"

"Stunningly beautiful. Smokin' Asian girl with a killer bod in a skin-tight, short dress. Unfortunately, I made the mistake of telling her she looked cute, though. She got all pissed at me, saying women weren't pieces of meat to be objectified, and that she had a personality and intelligence too. I tried to explain that I didn't know her well enough to comment on her personality or intelligence, and all I had to go on at the moment was physical looks, but she wanted nothing to do with that."

"What the hell?" Dylan interjected. "Chicks love being told they look cute."

"Not this one. She even got mad at me for being a gentleman and pulling out her chair for her."

"You're kidding me! The girls back home would dump you on the spot if you *didn't* pull out their chair."

"I know!"

"Well, was the food at least good?"

Marcus nodded. "At one point during the night I bowed my head and prayed for something, just one thing, to go well during the date, and I think the food was the one thing that God gave me in answer to my prayer. The service was incredible too. The host and waiter absolutely showered me with attention and constantly checked to make sure I was pleased with everything. Simone said it was 'cause I was black and she was a woman of Asian descent, so if we complained then their Equality Scores could go down and they might get shut down for a while."

"I forget, what kind of restaurant did you finally choose? You hemmed and hawed about that forever."

"Well, I kept having to check restaurants versus the government's lists. Half the restaurants were shut down for some violation or another. I finally picked Japanese because I'd never had it before and wanted to try something new, but all that got me was an accusation of racism from Simone. Can you believe that? I didn't even know her ethnicity when I chose the restaurant. And like the black guy from NEUS is going to be racist."

Dylan chuckled. "Was it all vegetarian bullshit?"

"Mostly. The dish I ordered was vegetarian. After Simone asked the waiter whether something on the menu was vegetarian, then asked whether it was also gluten-free, and then dairy-free, I figured I'd better order something vegetarian and dairy-free to avoid more criticism from her."

"Hah!" Dylan exclaimed while jabbing his pointer finger at him. "Now you know how it feels to choose your meal based on avoiding being criticized, asshole!"

"Oh, please," Marcus begged. "Simone is some sort of whack-job who thinks you can't ever let a molecule of junk food enter your mouth. The shit I criticize you for eating is garbage with no nutritional value that you eat on a daily basis. I eat healthy for like ninety-five percent of my meals, and I just splurge on junk once in a while. Apples and oranges, buddy."

Dylan gave him the finger.

"It was pretty funny at the end of the meal though. She was dumping out vitamins onto the table from a pill bottle like she was playing a game of Yahtzee or something, and I asked her why she took so many pills and whether she didn't get enough vitamins and minerals from her diet. She said something about how her body is a temple, and you have to put nutrients and superfoods in and keep poisons and garbage out, and then she accused me of not caring about my health, and said that my occasional unhealthy splurges were poisoning my body and mind. Then the waiter came over and asked if we wanted dessert, and I said no, we'd just take a check, and Simone got all bent out of shape about me not asking her if she wanted to get dessert. I was so baffled. I mean, you just said you thought junk food was poison, make up your mind, chick!"

"What a hypocrite," Dylan said after another laugh.

"Oh, just you wait. I'll give you hypocrite. The check came. I looked at it and did the math for splitting it evenly, and she said that I should pay the whole bill. I was all, 'What the hell. You spent the entire meal telling me what a giant feminist you are and accusing me of being sexist. You rejected me pulling out your chair for you, but now suddenly you want me to "be a gentleman" and pay the bill? Are you an à la carte feminist or something? You pick and choose which feminist principles you subscribe to based on whether they benefit you or not?'"

Dylan cackled again.

"Then she claimed my paying her share would be part of reparations for centuries of sexism," Marcus continued. "I told her if anyone should pay the full bill it should be her, to compensate me for putting me through such an awful date where she did nothing but alternate between ignoring me, criticizing me, and falsely accusing me of racism and sexism."

Dylan's laughing began to crescendo, and as the words "go fetch me some coffee and a newspaper, sugar tits" rolled off of Marcus's tongue, Dylan erupted into a loud and rambunctious guffaw. He laughed so hard he threw his torso back down onto the couch and rolled off, hitting the floor with a loud thud.

"I'm glad my misery was at least amusing to *somebody*," Marcus said. "I'd hate for it to have been a complete waste."

Elena appeared at the living room doorway wearing a revealing tight black tank top and skimpy black underwear. With her hands on her hips she said, "Could you please keep it down? We're trying to sleep."

The boys quieted down, and after Elena had disappeared back into her bedroom Dylan broke the silence whispering, "Damn! Elena be smokin' hot! I wouldn't want to be dating her or anything, 'cause, you know…" Dylan made a whipping gesture and sound effect. "But damn!"

Marcus wrinkled his nose and did his best impersonation of Simone, saying, "That is so sexist. You shouldn't objectify women like that, and the reason you wouldn't want to date her is because you can't handle strong, assertive women."

"Oh, shut up and pass me the remote, sugar tits. Maybe I can find a re-run of the feminist sensitivity training show I saw earlier on PBS-2. Sounds like you could use it."

Marcus gave Dylan the finger with one hand while passing him the remote with the other. "At least see if there's anything more interesting than this flower gardening crap."

There wasn't, and soon the two boys were lying on the couch in opposing head-to-toe position, with their eyelids drooping as the gentle whispers of PBS gardeners lulled them to sleep.

Chapter 5: Sexism on the Beach

Saturday morning, Sharon told the boys that both she and Elena had to go to work for a few hours to tie up some loose ends, but she asked them if there was anything they'd like to do together as a foursome in the afternoon. Marcus immediately spoke up, saying he wanted to go to the beach and see the ocean. Sharon confessed that she had meant something together at home so that Dylan didn't get in any more trouble, but she conceded to going to the beach if Dylan and Marcus promised to be on their best behavior, emphasizing that the beach might have a heavy government presence.

After the ladies left for work, Marcus and Dylan spent most of the morning watching more boring PBS television, or as they now called it "PCBS" for "Politically Correct Bull-Shit," with Dylan busting Marcus's chops about his bad blind date every once in a while. The entire morning, they only got up from the couch to go to the bathroom, get food, and make a brief trip to a local thrift store to buy a couple of cheap pairs of swim trunks for their beach trip. Marcus peeked out the front window a few times to see whether the white van was there, but it had apparently moved on.

After a few hours, Sharon came home and started preparing lunch with Marcus's help. Elena was going to be a little late and had texted to say they should go ahead and eat without her.

"So how did your date go last night?" Sharon asked after they had finished making sandwiches and had sat down to eat.

"Awful. She was a horrible person. I started out being as polite of a gentleman as I possibly could be, but not once did she smile or say anything even remotely friendly or nice. Any compliments I tried to make, she took as an insult. She spent the entire night criticizing me and my upbringing and looking for excuses to take offense at anything I said. She was absolutely awful."

"I'm sorry to hear that," Sharon said, not seeming terribly upset by the news, as if her mind had been elsewhere the whole time.

The rest of the meal was eaten in a mysterious awkward silence. As they were finishing eating, Marcus heard Elena walk in the door. She walked into the kitchen, dropped her keys into a bowl on the counter, and glared at him. She walked past Sharon, ignoring her puckered lips waiting for a kiss hello, and went straight to the fridge. The boys had finished lunch but were politely waiting with Sharon so that Elena would have company while she ate. Elena sat down at the table with her sandwich and glared at Marcus again.

"If you two are done with your lunch, then why don't you go get ready for the beach," Sharon said. The two boys left the kitchen and could hear the murmurs of Sharon talking to Elena.

"Shit," Marcus said as they put on their new swim trunks. "I think Elena is pissed at me."

"Isn't she always pissed at somebody? It's just your turn, dude. Don't worry, I'm sure she'll switch to being pissed at me soon. She's just permanently vagitated."

"No. I think she was at work with Simone's mom this morning. Simone probably told her some BS sob story about me being a sexist and racist date who had the audacity to try to be a gentleman when she wanted a feminist, and a feminist when she wanted a gentleman."

They wandered into the living room where Sharon had started to gather up beach supplies. Sharon glared at Marcus as the two boys entered the room before returning to her tasks. Soon Elena entered the room and began delegating things for each of the boys to carry, telling Dylan to carry the two large beach umbrellas.

"Doesn't an umbrella defeat the purpose of going to the beach?" Dylan asked.

"The State mandates beach umbrellas. You aren't allowed on the beach without one," Elena replied. "We are also not allowed to stay for more than an hour due to sun-exposure risks, and sunblock is mandatory. The UV index is very high, especially given the way the EUS continues to pollute the air and destroy the ozone layer."

"Unbelievable," Dylan muttered.

Marcus offered to carry the beach chairs. Elena turned her attention to Marcus. "You can carry our purses to the beach, sugar tits," she said grimly. "Sharon and I will carry the rest, given that we are strong women, and you are just a boy."

"I only called her 'sugar tits' to intentionally piss her off after she was so awful to me the entire night," Marcus protested. "I was a perfect gentleman up until that point, despite how horrible she was being to me. Had you been there you'd be on my side right now."

"You jeopardized my relationship with my coworker, a woman who has more authority at work than I do, I would add. I was late getting home because I had to spend thirty minutes smoothing things over with Simone's mom because of what you did last night. She was talking about filing a legal complaint. I had to tell her that I would talk things over with you, and I assured her if you did not show any remorse, then I would enroll you in feminist sensitivity training. If she files that complaint, then your equality classification is likely to shoot up at least a couple of points."

Dylan piped in to stick up for Marcus. "Marcus told me the details of the date last night. The whole reason you had to come out and shush us was because I was laughing so hard at his misery of having to deal with such a bitch all night. You should hear his side. He shouldn't have to carry purses to the beach. Besides, you're not our moms."

"You do not call a woman a bitch. You do not call a woman sugar tits. Carrying our purses is partial penitence. You do it, or we do not let you use the beach umbrellas and the beach warden will not let you onto the beach. And because you are minors, if the State finds out you are here for more than just a brief vacation, we would automatically be assigned to be your legal guardians until you turn eighteen, so in a way we *are* your moms."

Dylan relented and turned to Marcus. "Well, half the dudes in San Fran carry purses anyway—I guess you'll just blend right in."

Elena crinkled her brow. "You know, now I'm not even sure I can trust the two of you to behave in public. Maybe we shouldn't even leave the house."

Sharon gently put her hand on Elena's elbow. "Oh, I think relaxing in nature and listening to the calming waves for a while would be a good way for everyone to reduce tensions. After we re-center ourselves in nature, we can have a productive discussion about respectful behavior toward women."

Elena looked pensive.

Sharon turned to Marcus. "Are you willing to give us the sign we need that you are willing to behave by carrying our purses?"

Marcus accepted his punishment, Elena agreed to give the boys a chance, and they started off toward the beach on foot.

About three quarters of the way through the walk to the beach, Dylan pointed to a sign directing people to the beach that had the words "la playa" on it. He turned to Marcus, grinning. "Finally! We're going someplace where a playah like me can be a playah, without all the playah hatin' I've been gettin' in the rest of this city!"

Sharon broke her silence and cracked what Marcus thought might be an actual joke, saying, "Maybe you should petition for protected class status for playahs due to the terrible discrimination they face."

Elena sighed loudly. "It is Spanish. It means 'the beach,' not player, and that isn't even how you pronounce it. You would know this if the EUS allowed recognition of anything beyond its own borders."

"Are you from a Spanish-speaking country originally?" Marcus asked.

"I am from Málaga, Spain. I moved here for college, and when I graduated, the unemployment rate in Spain was a problem, and I had already been in a relationship with your sister here for a couple of years, so I stayed."

"Did you like it there? Do you like it here?"

"I love Spain. Málaga not so much because it is a tourist trap for nightclubbing misogynists. But the rest of Spain I love. Here it is okay. The weather is okay, and the government helps open many doors and provide many opportunities, and protects from discrimination, including discrimination from sexist pigs." She peered over her sunglasses disapprovingly at Marcus as she finished her last sentence.

Dylan chimed in, "But the government here is up your butt with a periscope about everything!"

"Up my butt?" Elena asked.

"He means oppressive," Sharon said.

"It is the price of order and civility," Elena responded. "If you don't provide rules and enforcement, then there is lawlessness and chaos."

"Sounds like something Reverend Wegener would say," Dylan commented.

They arrived at the beach check-in facility and got in line under the massive open-air structure. There were rules and regulations signs everywhere, hanging from the roof framing above. Marcus began reading. There were the rules Elena had told them about—the mandatory beach umbrella and the one-hour limit. Then there was the mandatory sunblock that had to be applied in front of a designated "beach warden witness," and had to contain zinc oxide, which explained why all the people Marcus could see on the beach in the distance had a shiny, silvery-white, ghost-like appearance. Then he got to a rule that made his jaw drop. *No swimming in the ocean.*

"What the hell?" he nearly shouted. Everyone around him turned and looked at him. He stood there motionless, looking at the sign until only Sharon, Elena, and Dylan were still looking at him.

"'Sup?" Dylan asked.

Marcus pointed to the sign. "We're not allowed to swim in the ocean? What the hell? I don't want to just sit there on the beach like a lump. I want to swim! In the ocean! That was the main reason I wanted to come here! What the hell?"

Sharon frowned. "Of course we're not allowed in the ocean. It's dangerous. You could get a cramp and drown, you could be attacked by a shark, stung by jellyfish, pulled out to sea by a rip current. People used to die all the time in the ocean before they banned it."

Marcus just stood there stunned, unable to speak. Finally, disgusted, he said, "Yeah, I could potentially die all of those ways, or I could die of boredom on the beach."

Marcus trudged forward through the line with Dylan, Sharon, and Elena until they reached the sign-in table. The beach warden took their IDs and, while scowling at Marcus, jotted something on a piece of paper on a clipboard and told Marcus that he needed to refrain from outbursts of profanity and insults while on the beach. They signed the waivers and acknowledgement forms, slathered themselves with zinc-oxide sunblock in front of a beach warden's witness, and moved through the turnstile to the beach, grabbing a timer clock that would let them know when their hour was up, before seeking out a spot in the sand.

They set up their umbrellas and plopped down in their chairs in the shade. Marcus started out his time on the beach stewing about the no-swimming rule, then tried to relax and forget about everything and just enjoy the beach. He got up and went for a short walk along the shore to at least get as close to the ocean as legally permitted and to listen to the relentlessly roaring waves for a while. His expectation had been of gentle rolling waves, but today the ocean was considerably more aggressive and tumultuous. Perhaps this really wasn't the time or place for an open-water swim after all.

Upon returning to the group, Dylan laughed and pointed to a wooden pier that had a chicken-wire fence blocking access to it. "Look at that useless bridge to nowhere," he said. "Typical liberal waste of taxpayer money."

"That's a pier, dumbass," Marcus chastised.

"Do not call him a dumbass," Sharon and Elena said in unison.

"That is actually one of my projects," Elena continued. It is the future Lurline South ferry stop. I inherited the project from a coworker who retired after fifteen years on the project."

"The project has been going on for more than fifteen years and it still isn't finished?" asked Marcus. "Can't they even let people walk on part of it for fishing or for leisure?"

"It has gone through many rounds of redesign," Elena said. "Some redesigns had to be done when the State changed their mind on things, others because people started petition campaigns to make changes. Several times we had to redesign because the building code changed during the project and things that were designed previously became illegal per the new code. It has gone through two rounds of construction, but right now it is again halted for another redesign, so no one is allowed on it because it does not fully conform to code yet."

"See," said Dylan, "it *is* a bridge to nowhere. Told ya."

"The Western United States actually does a very good job with public transportation," said Sharon, sounding a little defensive. "I take the Muni all the time. When the ferry stop is done, it will have been well worth the wait."

"Will they actually let people walk on the pier and board and ride a ferry boat?" asked Marcus. "I mean, a big wave could crest over the top of the pier and knock people into the ocean, where they would drown or be attacked by a shark. Or the ferry boat could spring a leak and sink."

Elena peered over her sunglasses at Marcus once again with a disapproving look for his sarcasm. "The boats and the pier will be designed with many factors of safety, and they will be closed during bad weather or rough seas. Speaking of sinking ships, let us speak of your sexism problem. I want to be able to report back to Simone's mother that we do not have a problem needing a legal complaint."

Marcus sighed. "Okay, school me on this sexism thing. First of all, define sexism for me, 'cause I completely disagree that I was sexist last night with Simone."

"This is basically what I do for a living," Sharon said. "Sexism is prejudice plus power. It is discrimination based on gender, and it includes the stereotypes and cultural elements that promote that discrimination. There are different types of sexism: hostile, benevolent, unintentional…and there are many ways in which sexism can be manifested, such as sexual objectification, restriction of gender roles, denigration to second-class citizenship, the use of sexist language, denial of sexism, et cetera.

"Now, I know you have a good heart, Marcus, and that you would recognize and reject hostile sexism. Things like, if you were a boss at a company, you wouldn't hire a less-qualified man versus a more-qualified woman, or you wouldn't pay a man more for doing the same job as a woman, or you wouldn't catcall at a woman walking down the street, and you wouldn't say or even think something awful like 'a woman's place is in the home, barefoot and pregnant,' am I right?"

"Of course not," Marcus responded.

"So, we're left with the less-obvious forms of sexism," Sharon said, continuing her Sexism 101 lecture. "Benevolent sexism is where you treat a woman like a fragile creature who is to be protected and adored, and who is dependent on a man to do things for her. This type treats women like they are weaker than men. Things like insisting on holding the door open for a woman or insisting on paying the bill for both of you."

"I would agree that those things are sexist," Marcus said, "but in the EUS women demand to be treated that way. Every girl I've dated would have dumped me on the spot had I not been chivalrous and done those things. I also hold doors for anyone walking behind me, regardless of their gender, so if it happens to be a woman behind me that I hold the door for, is that considered sexism? Plus, last night Simone objected when I tried to pull out her chair for her, but then insisted that I pay for the date and refused to split the bill. How am I possibly going to make a feminist happy if there aren't any consistent rules? Simone was completely hypocritical making me pay for dinner. I feel like I'm in a no-win situation."

Sharon and Elena quietly conferred with each other for a minute, and then conceded that Simone should have split the bill with Marcus. Sharon continued her lesson. "So, moving on, next is unintentional sexism, where the oppressor is often completely unaware of their own sexism. It is where they convey stereotypes, rudeness, and insensitivity that demean a person's identity, or they exclude, negate, or dismiss the thoughts, feelings, or experiences of women. Unintentional sexism starts branching out into dozens of sub-categories. Examples include things like asking a female coworker how she got her job, which implies she's less qualified than a man. Or always looking to the male coworker of a female client for confirmation of what the female just said, implying that he is superior. Or calling a woman 'aggressive' when you would never say that about a man when he is being assertive, or saying a woman is too emotional whenever you argue with her. It can be sexist language like using the word 'mankind' instead of 'humankind,' or using terms for female genitalia as derogatory remarks. It is criticizing women for the way they talk, mansplaining things to women like they are less intelligent, or objectifying women and treating them like pieces of meat."

"Okay," said Marcus, "I know EUS is sexist as hell, and I can see how things like looking to a woman's male coworker to validate what she just said is wrong, but some of those things don't seem legit to me, and others seem completely dependent on the specific situation. Like they could be sexist in some situations, but not sexist in others. Like the mansplaining thing…. Isn't that exactly what you did to me when I was cutting cucumbers for the salad the first night we were here? I knew exactly what I was doing, there was nothing wrong with my way, yet you felt the need to correct the way I was doing it. Why is it that when you do that to me, it's fine, but if I did it to you, it would be considered sexist?"

"The point you are getting at, of reverse sexism," said Elena, "is invalid because women do not have the history of privilege that men have in order to have enough power as a class to be sexist. There has been a historical imbalance of power that denies women the privilege men have of sexist traditions, assumptions, and legal rulings and means that the impact of a man being prejudiced against a woman is an order of magnitude more extreme than a woman being prejudiced toward a man. Women, in effect, cannot be sexist."

Dylan snorted. "That's convenient. Women automatically get a free pass? You do know that we males don't get together to discuss how to oppress women, don't you? I only control my own actions and behaviors, not the actions and behaviors of my entire gender, so don't lump in their actions and behaviors with mine. Doing so is, in effect, sexist of feminists."

"A free pass, no," Elena responded. "We can be gender-based prejudiced, just not sexist, and believe me, historically we have definitely not had anything resembling a free pass. You would not last a day as a woman. You have no idea what true sexism feels like."

Marcus tried to corral the conversation away from Elena and Dylan, who seemed to be taking it down a path that would end in a yelling match. "So, is this example sexist? I had a group project at school with three girls in my group. Two of the girls were great. Very intelligent and hardworking and made great contributions to the team. One of the girls was awful. She was a stupid, lazy twit who whined anytime anyone asked her to do anything. Is it sexist for me, a guy, to complain about her, or even to explain things to her that she doesn't seem to get?"

Sharon said no, so long as he isn't criticizing a lot of women like that, but Elena said yes, because guys have institutionalized power that women lack.

"You see!" said Marcus. "If the two of you can't agree on whether something is sexist, then how do guys like us stand a chance in figuring out what is sexist?"

Sharon and Elena didn't have a good answer for him, so he moved on. "You are asking me to treat women differently than men. You want me to only criticize men and never criticize women, which is treating women differently and therefore sexist, isn't it? When it comes to criticizing the way women talk or dress, why is that sexist? I criticize men for that all the time, and I've heard women do it all the time too. There is a male football announcer whose voice irritates me so much that I mute the TV and listen to the radio broadcast instead. My ex-girlfriend made me watch a movie where I spent half the movie agonizing over how irritating the sound of the lead male actor's voice was. I criticize this guy who does ads on TV all the time for looking like a homeless alcoholic bum. Why is a guy criticizing a woman for the way she talks automatically considered sexism? Isn't it possible that the way she talks is just truly wrong or irritating? Are you saying it is wrong for me to even feel irritated by irritating things? Am I not entitled to that opinion?"

"Yes, it is sexism," said Elena. "Women face death by a thousand paper cuts of criticisms and comments that devalue them, and the accumulation means that you should not say those things. You have male privilege, so you cannot even see how those things affect women."

"Well, I have experience as a black male. Have you ever walked into a restaurant and been given bad service while everyone else around you got good service, or had an employee look at you like they were suspicious that you were going to steal the artwork off the walls?"

"You are trying to trivialize and negate my experience of sexism by equating your experiences to it. That is in and of itself sexist of you."

Dylan snorted again. "There you go again, acting like you're above criticism and that you're the automatic winner of the victim contest."

Marcus turned to look out at the ocean. He selected a wave and watched it move steadily to shore as Elena went on. "Privileged groups always think they get to decide what is and is not abusive. They have no idea what it feels like to be disenfranchised."

Marcus's wave fizzled out, and the wave that followed leap-frogged it before they both retreated back to the sea.

"Common sense decides what is and isn't abusive," said Dylan, "and I'm not buying a lot of what you're selling. When it comes to objectification, women are just as bad as men. They go for good-looking rich guys with six-pack abs just as much as men go for attractive women with big tits. Back home at school, I'd constantly overhear girls talking about which guys are hot and which ones aren't. Everyone thinks their looks matter, and everyone judges everyone else on their appearance. It's human nature, so don't be so damned offended by it." Dylan's hand made a loud noise as he smacked it against the arm of his beach chair. "We're all biologically programmed to want sex, and part of sex is physical attraction. I mean, shit, look at the two of you. You expect me to believe that Sharon married you because you're Miss Congeniality and that it had nothing to do with the fact that you're smokin' hot and she was physically attracted to you?" Dylan began gesticulating wildly with his arms while he spoke. "You've been nothing but nasty since the moment we arrived! What the feminists want is for all men to be neutered and deny their own biology. They want everyone to be treated exactly equally so bad that they refuse to recognize that there are legitimate differences between men and women, and then they conveniently ignore the way they act on those same biological impulses themselves." Dylan's hand smacked the chair again.

Elena began looking forward intently, only turning her head slightly toward Dylan while keeping her eyes locked straight ahead. "Looks matter to both sexes, but women are taught that their entire worth is determined by their looks, and that their power comes from their ability to give or deny sex. Men don't get that."

Dylan continued, practically ignoring Elena's comments. "You know, there are real differences between the genders. You can try to deny them all you want and say everyone is the same and equal, but it doesn't stop them from existing." He punctuated the end of his sentence with another thud on the arm of the chair. Then he raised his arms like an orchestra conductor and began again. "If someone down the beach wanted to report Marcus for having shouted 'what the hell' at the beach warden check-in station, how do you think they'd identify him from a distance? We are a group with one white boy, one black boy, one white woman, and one black woman. Of course they'd say 'the black boy.' It only takes two words to accurately describe which one of us four they are referring to because the four of us are different from one another."

Marcus furled his eyebrows at Dylan's hand, as if the hand were its own entity capable of comprehending Marcus's contempt, after another dull thud emanated from the chair. Elena jerked her head further away from the group.

Marcus had to admit that he was impressed that Dylan was actually making an effort not to sound like an idiot for a change, despite being annoyed with some of his emotional responses that bordered on personal insults. *Perhaps all the time Dylan spent watching PBS the last few days has benefited him*, Marcus thought. He wasn't sure if he agreed with everything, or even anything, that Dylan was saying, but at least he was making sense. "I'd argue that our differences can be a good thing," Marcus said. "I mean, I imagine that's why WUS works to diversify neighborhoods, right?"

Dylan continued where he had left off, as if Marcus hadn't interjected at all. "We're not all perfectly the same. If women were the same as men, then we'd all have the same genitalia and play in the same sports leagues. And the thing Sharon said about using women's genitalia as a slang insult is absolute bullshit. Men's genitalia get used as a slang insult too. I get called a 'dick' all the time."

Marcus chuckled. "Speak for yourself!"

"But 'pussy' refers to someone weak, 'dick' refers to someone strong, so it is still sexist," Elena said while Sharon fidgeted with the umbrella to cover a spot on Elena's legs that were now exposed to the sun.

"'Cunt' isn't a reference to weakness. It's pretty much the female equivalent of dick. Is it okay for me to use 'cunt'? For Christ's sake, if you liberals keep taking words away from us, we're going to run out of words to use, and we'll all end up mute," Dylan said with another drum beat on the chair.

Elena stood up, wrestled the umbrella stand out of Sharon's grasp, picked it up, and violently spiked it back into the sand to embed it in a new position. "Your continual questioning of things we are telling you are sexist is a form of sexism itself called 'gaslighting,' where men dismiss and deny—"

Dylan almost smacked Marcus in the face while splaying his arms out sideways like Jesus on the cross as he interrupted Elena mid-sentence. "What, men aren't allowed to have or express opinions? Only women are? Accusing a man of gaslighting sounds like yet another awfully convenient way of trying to shut men up."

Marcus looked down and began picking up clumps of sand and letting them sift through his fingers like an hourglass, keeping his eyes focused on the sand as he tried again to adjust the course of the discussion to avoid an emotional shouting match. "I feel like feminists here put me in a no-win situation where no matter what I say or do, it is wrong. I love strong, intelligent women, I want gender equality, and I feel like I'm pro-feminist, but I feel like I couldn't even ask a woman out on a date here without being accused of sexual harassment. How do lonely single guys even get dates here? I mean, I get that when a woman says 'no' you have to drop it and leave her be, but I feel like here it isn't even okay to make an effort to ask a girl out. It's not okay for me to compliment her. It's not okay for me to do nice things for her. It's not okay for me to approach her and start a conversation unless I have ESP and can read her mind and tell that she wants me to start a conversation. I feel completely alienated by this brand of feminism, like I don't even want to try fighting for women's equality when an extremist feminist is just going to smack me down and accuse me of sexism for it."

Dylan took this line of reasoning and ran with it. "Yeah, it's like the little boy who cried wolf. You extremist feminists say everything men do, even breathing, is sexist, and we stop paying attention to the things that actually are sexist because we're so sick of hearing about the bullshit things that aren't really sexism. WUS sucks the life out of people. No one here has a sense of humor. Everyone has to walk on eggshells because everyone is so damn hyper-sensitive. Everyone is stuck in permanent victim status. The State tries to protect everyone from everything, which, by the way doesn't that mean the State is benevolently sexist? You all just want to go through life without anyone ever criticizing you for anything you do, even if what you're doing is clearly wrong. You want to be able to commit murder and get away with it just because you're a woman. This country is full of whiny, crybaby wimps who want participation ribbons even when they do a shit job, and you try to legislate away the risk of any harm whatsoever."

Marcus saw that Dylan's Irish complexion was especially ruddy, and he knew it wasn't from sun exposure. He looked at Elena and saw that she had her lips clamped together hard, like she was winding up to unleash a verbal assault on Dylan in response, but they were saved by the bell as the beach timer rang and Sharon announced that they had seven and a half minutes to gather up their things, return the timer, and depart the beach before they received a fine.

"Seven and a half minutes?" Marcus asked. "Why such an exact number? Why not something round, like ten minutes or five minutes?"

"The city council members disagreed about how much time to allow. Some wanted a longer limit to allow handicap people a little extra time; others were more concerned about UV exposure and skin cancer and wanted less time. Seven and a half was the compromise."

"Is there a bathroom nearby?" Marcus asked as they packed up the umbrellas and chairs.

"Not anymore," Elena replied, seemingly distracted enough to have put aside the disquisition she had in store for Dylan. "There used to be one where the beach warden check-in is now. You see that beautiful pink-granite, waist-high kneewall around three sides of the check-in pavilion? Those are from the original building. My boss won a preservation award for adaptive reuse of historic materials for that."

"She won a preservation award for destroying an old building?" Dylan asked.

"The building was slated to be demolished due to non-code-conformance. She saved parts of it and used it to express the history of the original building."

"Why didn't they just build bathrooms in the beach warden pavilion?" Marcus asked.

"Enclosed buildings require a minimum number of bathrooms per property size. Given the large size of the beach, that would have meant a lot of bathrooms. My boss designed the pavilion as an open-air structure to avoid the bathroom requirement and therefore keep the footprint of the building reasonable."

Dylan rolled his eyes. "So rather than have a few small bathrooms and risk someone having to stand in line for a few minutes, they decided to have no bathrooms at all? Un-fucking-believable. This place is insane. It's like we need permission from the government just to go to the bathroom. I can't wait to get out of here and away from all of these fucking ridiculous rules."

Marcus's ears perked up. *Does he just consider San Francisco a temporary stop on the way to somewhere else?*

The two women had stopped and were staring at Dylan in silence.

"You are certainly welcome to leave," Elena retorted. "These are the rules of our society. If you are going to live here, you better get used to them."

Marcus noticed a shakiness in Elena's voice as she spoke her last sentence. He couldn't see her eyes behind her sunglasses, but her forehead was creased. She dropped her bag and turned away from the group. Her head tilted down, and she buried it in a hand for a moment as her shoulders shuddered. "You can both go to re-ed for all I care!" she burst out in an unsteady voice and began walking away empty-handed.

"Elena, honey..." Sharon began. Elena kept walking.

Chapter 6: Walk Back Home

Sharon, Marcus, and Dylan finished packing up. As they turned in their clock at the beach warden pavilion, Marcus saw the beige gingham jackets again—the same man and woman as at City Hall. The man had something electronic in his ear and was scribbling furiously on a clipboard. Marcus quickly looked away. The threesome commenced their walk back to the house as Elena began to vanish in the distance.

"I carried the purses here, and after that conversation, I think it's definitely your turn to carry them back," Marcus said to Dylan as they left the beach.

"So now you're on their side? And you think you're my mommy too? Whatever. They're lighter and easier to carry. You suffer with the stupid umbrellas and chairs." Dylan took off with the purses tucked under his armpits like footballs and was soon out of earshot.

After a few minutes of silence, Marcus was desperate for some small talk. "So, tomorrow's Sunday. Are you going to church?"

"Churches are illegal here," Sharon said.

"You're shitting me!" Marcus cried. "Sorry. Seriously, though?"

"Organized religions have historically done a tremendous amount of harm. They are extremely divisive, and they are responsible for a lot of wars and violence." She turned to look behind them for a second before saying, "But I know some informal prayer groups that get together, if you're interested. I have a Bible hidden away at home too."

"Let me guess: We need to keep that between us. Elena doesn't know?" Marcus asked.

Sharon nodded. "That reminds me, you need to watch it with the pre-meal praying, especially in public. Elena has commented to me about that."

Marcus just nodded. During a moment of silence, he shifted the beach umbrella to his other arm. "Why is…" he began. "Sorry."

"Go ahead," Sharon encouraged.

"No. I don't want to pry or be rude."

"You shouldn't bottle up your feelings and thoughts. If you have a feeling you want to explore, explore it. We need to increase awareness of each other's feelings," Sharon said.

"Why…why is Elena always so angry? Is everything okay with you two?" Marcus asked.

Sharon sighed. "There isn't a simple yes or no answer to that. We both have a lot of work stress. Long hours. Strained relationships with bosses. Financial stress."

"Me-and-Dylan stress?"

"I'll be honest. A little bit. Your arrival caught us by surprise, and Elena's not good at sharing her space for long periods of time anyway. Plus, Dylan does seem to have a knack for pressing her buttons."

"I think I can relate to that. Both Dylan pressing buttons and the trouble sharing space. Is Elena's space issue why when we first showed up you seemed, I don't know, almost disappointed to see me? You seemed so distant. You didn't even hug me. I thought maybe you felt you'd burned all your bridges to home and didn't want me reminding you of New Rochelle."

"Actually, I think that had more to do with being startled by how much you look like Dad now, at least a younger version of Dad. You've changed so much since I last saw you. When I saw you at my door, I was just stunned. Maybe I was transferring some of my anger toward him onto you because of that. And the hugging thing was because physical contact between men and women in public is frowned upon here. We feel it sets precedent for some of the other bad behaviors of men that we discussed on the beach."

"Great. I look like that asshole? No wonder." He shook his head. "So, do you think you and Elena would get along better if Dylan and I left?"

"You don't have to leave. Just try a little harder to understand our culture. There are a lot of advances that WUS has made." Sharon's voice turned dead serious. "When it comes to sexism back in NEUS, though, you don't even know the half of it. Marcus, you see the benevolent sexism in public there, and because you have a good heart, you think others have good hearts too, but you don't know what goes on behind closed doors. The repressed elders who preach chivalry and putting women on pedestals turn into entitled monsters. Sexual harassment and assault are rampant. I've experienced despicable things multiple times myself. Every female friend of mine in NEUS has."

"Stacie," Marcus mumbled.

"Sorry?" Sharon asked. Marcus just shook his head. Sharon continued. "You know, I was thinking about how you were trying to equate racism to sexism before, and despite Elena's comments, I think that is actually a good way for you to empathize with women. You've experienced being profiled. It's something everyone does automatically, but the problem is that black men are constantly being profiled as dangerous threats, and they constantly have to prove to one person after the next that they aren't a threat. A similar thing happens with women, where they get profiled as being weak, submissive, a piece of meat to have sex with, and easily taken advantage of. Women have to constantly prove over and over that they are strong equals. It is exhausting. And it's something that Dylan, as a white male, has a very hard time understanding because he is typically profiled as 'normal.' People automatically see him neither as a dangerous threat, nor as a pushover. He doesn't have to prove himself during every interaction he has."

"So here you don't have to constantly prove you are a strong equal?" Marcus asked.

Sharon nodded.

"But don't all of the rules and red tape here drive you mad? It seems like it's a burden that's stressing your relationship with Elena."

Sharon looked him in the eyes. "Marcus, trust me, my life is better here. Yours could be too. But as for me and Elena, I think we'll make it through this rough patch, but it's impossible to know for sure. I've been considering asking her to go to couples therapy with me, but I have no idea when we'd find the time. Finding the time might actually make things more stressful. Que será, será, I guess."

Chapter 7: Crisis of Confidence

Days turned into weeks, but time seemed to be the only thing changing for Marcus and Dylan. Elena hadn't been able to drum up any internships because they had all been filled weeks earlier, before the school year had ended. She didn't bother setting him up on any more blind dates either.

Marcus went to City Hall again, budgeting a full day to obtain the documents he and Dylan would need to fill out in order to transfer to a local high school, get low-skilled jobs, and apply for citizenship, but once he had the thick stacks of paperwork in hand he found himself procrastinating and unmotivated to fill them out. Every time he got them out to start, a sense of déjà vu would come over him, and he'd start thinking about his West Point candidate questionnaire. It was especially demoralizing when he found out that kids his age from other countries were considered "disadvantaged" and didn't have to fill out this paperwork in order to get into high school here—they qualified for an amnesty waiver. Marcus didn't qualify for the waiver because EUS was considered a privileged country.

Shortly after Marcus's City Hall outing, Sharon was alerted that the Equality Defense Commission had assigned case numbers to both of the boys and that the commission would be discussing their statuses at their next monthly meeting. Much of the boys' time from there on was spent trying to lay low and keep their noses clean. They spent most days lying on the couch or floor in the living room watching PBS. Marcus felt himself slipping deeper and deeper into depressive doldrums. The PBS shows that had once bored him to tears grew increasingly entertaining, as they filled the metastasizing void of not having anything meaningful to do with his time.

Thoughts of the future began to flood his mind. Since leaving New Rochelle on his first night of summer break from school, after the initial shock of abandoning his home had worn off, his journey had felt a bit like a mix of vacation and exciting adventure. Driving across NEUS in a stolen muscle car had been daring and exhilarating. Crossing the border and stopping in St. Louis had been uplifting and inspiring. Until the measles catastrophe at the end, the stay with the Wyoming tribe had been pleasant and refreshing, albeit unusual. Seeing his sister for the first time in ages had been comforting and healing. Since their arrival in San Francisco, however, his satisfaction had diminished. He worried about how he was going to continue his education, and whether he would be able to get back into either football or track and field. His competition had surely been working hard through the summer, and he had barely moved from the couch in several weeks. The bureaucracy he had to navigate, and the time it took to do so, felt like an unscalable obstacle.

He also worried that he and Dylan were becoming freeloading dead weight to Sharon and Elena. So far, they hadn't asked him for a dime to help pay for groceries or as rent to apply to the mortgage. He tried to jolt himself out of his funk from time to time in order to help out his sister with work in the vegetable garden, or cleaning dishes or laundry, or food preparation, but he found himself absolutely exhausted by every effort.

Elena moved around them as if the living room had a quarantine barrier erected around the couch, adjusting her routine to avoid them as much as possible. Most weeknights she got home so late that she didn't even join the boys for dinner. At first Sharon mostly left them alone too—not that she had much time away from work to interact with them—but as each week passed, she seemed to try to shoehorn in more conversations with Marcus between the time she got home from work and the time Elena got home. At least a couple of times per week, she'd ask how the paperwork was going. Not with the condescending scolding of their father, but more with a tone of concern about Marcus's emotional state.

A few weeks after their beach trip, Marcus was helping Sharon prepare dinner when she announced, "So, I called Mom today."

"Oh yeah? How's she doing?"

"She's doing okay. She's worried about you, of course, but then again, I'm a bit worried about you too. That's kind of why I called her. You seem very discontented lately."

"Yeah," Marcus sighed. "I'm feeling frustrated. I'm worried about how I'm going to get my future back on track. Everything seems to be stalling out here and getting stuck in the bureaucracy."

"Mom wants you to come home."

"I can't. Dylan *really* can't. We stole his dad's car. We're probably in deep legal trouble."

"Mom and I talked about that. She said that the police were never notified. She talked Dad into not reporting you missing because it would jeopardize your chances of getting into West Point when you came to your senses and returned. Dad said he'd give you until the end of summer to make the right decision and take your punishment 'like a *man*,' but after that, he'll disown you." Sharon rolled her eyes. "Mom talked to Reverend Fallar about Dylan, and the reverend called Dylan's dad and learned that he hadn't reported the car stolen because of his history with the police and not wanting any further scrutiny from them." Sharon lowered her voice. "Mr. Callahan did threaten to kill Dylan if he ever saw him again, though. But the NEUS government has no idea there's anything wrong. As far as they're concerned, you are both EUS citizens, not missing persons, and in no legal trouble."

Marcus paused for a moment, digesting the surprising information that his paranoia at the start of their trip had been for naught, and that a return home would be easier than he had expected, at least for him, but less so for Dylan. "I don't want to go home," he found himself blurting out unconsciously. "I don't want to go into the military, and I don't want Dad controlling my life."

"But clearly you're not happy here," Sharon said while reaching into the fridge.

"Well, yeah. Here I can't get into school for over a year, and my athletic career is pretty much destroyed. I might be able to get back on a path for college and an engineering career in a year, but it won't be easy, and the football dream is definitely over. If I go back, I can buy myself one more year of high school and athletics, but after that my life is over, plus I'd have to deal with Dad for another year or more. I don't really feel like I belong in either place. I hated the conformity of NEUS, but here the culture is just so...I don't know, weird. Like Dylan said, the government is so up your butt with a periscope, and everyone is so hyper-sensitive."

Sharon nodded. "Both New Rochelle and San Francisco have restrictive, order-based governments, but the rules in each place are very different. In New Rochelle I could see that if you were a wealthy, white, hetero, Christian man you might find their brand of restrictive order appealing because it aligns with and promotes everything you are or that you believe in. They're at the top of the caste system. If you're not one of those things, though, and you're at the bottom of the caste system, then they oppress you and make your life miserable. I have no desire to live in the Republic of Gilead. That's why I really appreciate San Francisco. Here, as a black, middle-class, homosexual female, they help me out and protect me. Everyone is equal. I don't know about you, but I'm not okay with being at the bottom of a caste system through no fault of my own. My quality of life drastically improved when I left home and moved here. Even during my first year in the homeless shelter, I was treated better than at home. People here actually care about society and random strangers. Plus, here, at least the rules are written and enforced by a neutral State, and they apply equally to everyone. Back in NEUS the rules were often unwritten and enforced by small, selfish segments of society who had more power, and the rules were applied unequally."

"Yeah. I see what you mean," said Marcus. "NEUS really sucks, but I'm not sure I find Urban WUS any better. There are so many rules here it's ridiculous. They're so quick to tell people what they can't do or how what they're doing is wrong, but when it comes to deciding what can or should be done, they suffer from paralysis by analysis. Like with that ferry stop at the beach. They have to study everything to death and it retards progress. Plus, I think Dylan might have been on to something when he was talking about how everyone is in permanent victim status. Everyone is looking to blame someone else. I can see how it is beneficial that here, for example, the sexism of NEUS is essentially wiped out by the rules and the culture, but they seem to take things too far and treat men as permanent oppressors no matter what their actions, even actions that aren't oppressive or anti-women. It's like *men* are at the bottom of the caste system here. I thought it's supposed to be about equality."

Sharon wiggled her head side to side like she was trying to say yes and no at the same time. "We don't use the R-word here, by the way, but getting to your point, NEUS has progress hindered by their obsessive desire to return society to some idealized notion of what the 1950s was. They claim to be protecting their culture and values, but really they are just protecting their place in the caste system and are deathly afraid of change, even if it is change in a positive direction. Here things are so bureaucratic because whenever something goes wrong and someone gets physically or emotionally hurt, then they have to legislate to address that problem, and legislation keeps piling on top of past legislation, creating a larger and larger list of rules and laws. It's why my paralegal job demands such long hours. But what else would they do? Not make the problems illegal? Accept bad or damaging behaviors? I mean, if you want an orderly, civilized society that doesn't discriminate against part of its own population, then you need rules, and those rules have to be enforced."

"I agree and somehow disagree," Marcus said. "Rules are necessary, but somehow here the rules seem to have gone haywire. They are out of control."

"You said you stayed in rural Wyoming with a nomadic tribe, right?" Sharon asked. "They lack the order that NEUS or San Francisco have. What did you think of them?"

"They were freaks. Absolutely sweet, kind-hearted, and loving, but freaks. There, progress didn't just seem to be retarded, er, sorry, hindered, but they seemed to have rejected all progress made since about the 1800s. They are absolutely nuts. They had people dying from diseases that were eradicated a hundred years ago, and they put their faith in where stars and planets happened to align. I liked them, but I could never live with them."

"Have you ever considered Puerto Paz?" Sharon asked.

Marcus shook his head. "I don't know much about that place. Didn't Dad always say that place was full of commies?"

"You going to trust Dad's judgment on that? You know he was a young officer when EUS invaded Cuba before it became Puerto Paz. He had superiors to impress. He accepted the propaganda he was fed, and he has never let go of it."

Marcus stopped chopping vegetables and stared off to the side of the cutting board. It was the first time he had heard anyone speak of his dad in less than noble terms, especially regarding his military career. No one in NEUS would ever dare criticize a military officer like that. "I've never heard about Dad's early years in the military," he said, "and I've never heard anyone talk about him like he was a follower instead of a leader. He's such a bully. I can't imagine a time when he might not have been a bully. So, he didn't just terrorize his superiors until he got to the position he wanted?"

"From what I've been able to piece together, no," said Sharon. "I think he was scared and obedient when he was young. His superiors bullied him, and he learned from them how to bully his subordinates in order to keep them in line and maintain discipline. Once he was swallowed up by the war machine, there was no turning back. I don't think his mind could process the concept of the war on Cuba having been started in deceit or that his superiors could lead him astray. I don't think he was capable of confronting the idea that there was anything wrong with the organization that had helped him move up a rung or two in the caste system."

Suddenly Marcus could see his dad in a new light. It reinforced vague feelings he'd had for years, but he had never before been able to transform those feelings into coherent thoughts, nor did he feel like he would have had anyone safe to express them to in order to develop them. *My dad uses fear to mask his own fear*, Marcus thought. Abraham's forceful and dominating temperament was the use of fear and intimidation to mask his own insecurity and weakness. He wasn't a bully by nature, and he was just as weak as anyone he bullied, but he had somehow created the illusion that he was stronger. Marcus also found himself relating a little bit more with his dad in terms of seeking respect as a black man in NEUS. It was now clear that his dad considered being a military officer as a golden ticket to black respect, the same way Marcus had considered football stardom as his golden ticket. It was an inconsistent respect with limits that neither of them could exceed, but it got them both through some doors and seated at some tables that they otherwise wouldn't have had access to.

Marcus resumed his vegetable chopping. A few minutes later, he re-focused his thoughts and spoke again. "I saw the Puerto Paz history exhibit at City Hall. There was information there that contradicted my history books from school."

"Your 'history' books from NEUS are mostly propaganda," Sharon replied.

Marcus shrugged. "I wasn't quite sure what was real and what was propaganda. A classmate of mine showed me how to bypass the NEUS internet censors. I'd search for athletic and nutrition info beyond the censors, and what I found there often contradicted what they teach in NEUS, but I didn't look much further than those topics. I guess I was too afraid of getting caught. I'm not sure what to believe now."

"Well, Cuba used to be communist, but Puerto Paz isn't. Supposedly Puerto Paz attempts to find a balance point between order governments like San Francisco and NEUS and freedom governments like rural Wyoming. Their founding father was from here. We revere him as a great leader here, although we view Puerto Paz as being too lenient and tolerant of improper behavior. If you're not happy with the order of San Francisco or NEUS, and you're not happy with the freedom of rural Wyoming, then you might want to consider Puerto Paz."

"I don't know. I'll have to mull it over some more," Marcus said. He continued chopping vegetables. "Hey, Sharon?"

"Mm-hmm?"

"Do you ever feel guilty about running away from home? Like you've been disloyal, or like you're weak for having run away from your problems?"

Her expression hardened. "Never. You can't be loyal to immoral people or oppressors. In WUS, we believe that blind loyalty leads to corruption. Our strongest loyalty is to our beliefs that everyone deserves to be treated equally and with respect."

Marcus had noted Sharon's use of the words "we" and "our" when describing anything to do with San Francisco. It reinforced something he had been feeling more and more about Sharon lately: that she was fairly well integrated into the local culture, save for the occasional black-market TV or Bible. She had changed a lot in the seven years since he last saw her in New Rochelle.

A few more minutes passed before Marcus asked, "Do you know if they allow football in Puerto Paz?"

Chapter 8: The Devil You Know

A few more days went by, and Marcus had found no resolution to his dilemma of discontentment. Angry at himself for his lethargy, he knew he and Dylan needed to shake things up and do something to reinvigorate themselves. He turned to Dylan one morning while watching PBS on the couch and said, "Let's go get a football and toss it around in the park."

Dylan, just as desperate for something fun to do, agreed.

Failing to find any sporting goods stores nearby, they walked to a local toy store and entered through a crowd of sweaty people wearing poorly fitting, off-the-rack business attire. The tiny store hardly had anything in it, and most of what they did have was educational. All they could find that was even remotely sports related were round, spongy foam balls the size of a small child's head. Eventually they asked a store employee where they could find footballs and were told that footballs were illegal because the State didn't want children trying to imitate the violent game if they saw it while traveling abroad.

After filling out a twenty-page document outlining limitations of liability and rules of use at the checkout desk, they left with one of the round foam balls, hoping that it would be good enough for tossing back and forth in the park. Upon exiting, the sweaty hordes of suits approached them, each shoving a business card at them and encouraging the boys to call them if they got injured while playing with whatever they had just purchased in the store. Marcus and Dylan tried to ignore the lawyers, swatting away the business cards like they were mosquitoes buzzing around their bodies.

A short jaunt later, they were at Pine Lake Park. Near the entrance, they walked past an empty, fenced-off area with a sign saying it was a children's park and that adult men needed a permit to enter. The entire fenced-off area was nothing but a soft, foamy rubber surface. Even the fence was covered in soft, spongy material. Dylan and Marcus looked at each other and shook their heads.

"A playground without a single piece of equipment for kids to risk getting hurt on," Marcus noted.

"I bet if I did a baseball slide on that rubber surface, I could get a nasty rug burn on my legs and I could sue the State. Dare me?" Dylan joked.

Marcus smiled. "Notice how there isn't a single kid in there. Fun place."

They walked past the children's pen to a grassy clearing and started throwing the foam ball back and forth, getting farther apart with each pass and throwing it progressively harder and harder as they tested how far they could throw it before the wind caught it and stopped its progress.

A few minutes after they started, a middle-aged, silver-haired man walking through the park looked over at them and diverted his path to intercept them. He was holding up his phone like he was filming them with it, and he had a look of great concern on his face as he approached them and announced, "You're not allowed to throw hard overhand passes like that. You are only allowed to gently lob the ball underhand. Didn't you read the park rules at the entrance? Do you even have a permit to be playing here?"

"Do you have a permit to be filming underage boys, pervert?" Dylan responded.

"This is all on record. The video will clearly show that I was only approaching to enforce the rules. My lawyer will easily…" The boys looked at each other and just shook their heads in disbelief and started walking back toward the park entrance. The man seemed sufficiently pleased with himself for having broken up the illegal fun and continued back on his original trajectory. The boys stopped at a bench and sat down in the sun.

"Are we allowed to sit here?" Dylan asked. "I mean, we're in the sun. Are we going to get in trouble for not wearing zinc-oxide sunblock here?"

"I know. This is ridiculous."

"Insane. This place just sucks the life out of everyone."

"I hope that track and field is still an option for me even if I can't throw a football here," Marcus said.

"I can just imagine the track meets. They probably have an equality council pick the winners based on how oppressed they are, and never actually have a running competition. Either that or they force everyone to finish simultaneously so there is no winner and they just hand everyone a participation ribbon."

A few minutes of silently enjoying the sun and nature passed before they spoke again. Dylan broke the silence, speaking in a high-pitched, lispy, feminine voice. "We need to, um, like, increase awareness of people who were born in human bodies but identify as kangaroos, and provide them with a safe and welcoming environment. Will you sign my petition to make it illegal to deny them free, State-sponsored kangaroo-pouch-attachment surgery?"

Marcus chuckled and replied in his own lispy, feminine voice, "I'll sign your petition if you sign mine to, um, like, increase awareness of, and provide protected class status to white Irish Eastern-American assholes."

Dylan cocked his fist like he was going to punch Marcus in the shoulder for having insulted him, then looked around and retracted his hand. "I'd probably be thrown in jail, or whatever they've substituted for jail, if I got caught punching you. These people here are so fucking uptight, man. No one has a sense of humor. They wouldn't know funny if the guys from *Monty Python* put it on a fish and slapped them in the face with it."

Marcus laughed loudly and doubled over, then suddenly stopped laughing and sprang back up into sitting position and looked around to see if anyone had heard him laughing. "True," he said, getting more serious, "but it's just like home in that respect. How many adults back home do you know who have a sense of humor?"

"Yeah, basically none, but this place is just crushing my soul. It is so boring here. You know where they do know how to have fun? New Miami. I've heard it's a nonstop party there. You said the other day that the EUS government had no problems with us, so we could get back in and go to SEUS, no problem."

"Sharon suggested Puerto Paz."

"The place full of commies? No thanks."

"She said they aren't commies. That's just EUS propaganda."

"Maybe she's just feeding you WUS propaganda," Dylan said.

"Commies stick with commies. Either way, I'd still rather go to New Miami. I've never heard of Puerto Paz being a party place. We did your thing of visiting your sister, now let's go party on Daytona Beach. Besides, if you want to get back into school and football, then Miami U is the place. I've heard they'll accept anyone, especially anyone with football talent. You could probably skip your senior year of high school and get in this fall. Hell, even I could get into Miami a year early. Football is a fucking religion there. We could be gods. Even if we can't get into college early, we're EUS citizens—we could find a way to get into a local high school. Plus, they'll have beaches and ocean there too, and I'm sure they won't have the stupid fucking 'no swimming' rules there."

Marcus was torn. Part of him felt like he was a quitter if he gave up trying to make things work in San Francisco, especially on the heels of having given up on New Rochelle, but he knew he wasn't happy here. Another part of him was curious about Puerto Paz and whether his sister was right about it being a good match for him. There were so many unknowns about Puerto Paz, though. Dylan did make a compelling argument about getting into Miami University. He didn't know a lot about SEUS, but he certainly knew more about SEUS than about Puerto Paz. He had heard rumors that the elders of the religious community of NEUS didn't think highly of the people of SEUS, and that they supposedly violated the seven deadly sins on a regular basis. Still, it was worth a shot if it meant getting back on track with school and football, and Dylan clearly wanted to go there and felt he had suffered enough in WUS.

Better the devil you know, I guess, he thought. Marcus relented and agreed they'd go to New Miami, but only if they sold the Coulomb and used some of the money for airfare. He couldn't stand the thought of another transcontinental drive in an automobile, and it would have been a less-than-direct route to avoid going through the Republic of Texas. No way in hell would Marcus be caught in that country, which brought out the obligatory "you don't look like no steer" comment from Dylan.

That night at dinner, Dylan was fidgety until finally he turned to Marcus and asked, "Can I tell them? Please, please, can I tell them? I want to look at Elena's face while I tell them and see if she smiles for the first time since we got here."

Marcus rolled his eyes and gestured at him to proceed.

"I've thought long and hard about this, and I've decided I'm going to take my talents to Daytona Beach and join the New Miami party scene." Dylan stared intently at Elena as he spoke, and Marcus couldn't help but look at her out of curiosity too. He thought he saw her lower lip quiver a little as she tried desperately to keep a straight face and not smile or laugh and give Dylan the pleasure he was looking for.

"Really?" said Sharon in disbelief. "New Miami? You're going to absolutely hate it there."

"The Málaga of EUS," Elena chimed in.

Chapter 9: Caveat Emptor

For the next few days the boys continued to plunk themselves down in front of the TV for much of the day, but Marcus spent less time watching PBS than he did sketching out their plans for going to New Miami.

Sharon bought the boys mobile phones to make communication, planning, and navigation easier, noting that WUS mobile carriers were required by law to allow roaming in foreign countries at no extra charge. Elena surprisingly offered to buy the Coulomb from them, presumably to hasten their departure with plans to resell it later, or to keep it and resell her own junker of a car so that she and Sharon would have one decent car between the two of them.

Marcus purchased their airfare and schemed what they would tell EUS Border Control about their trip to San Francisco having been purely to visit family and what they would say at Miami University to have the best chances of both being accepted for school and getting on the football team. Dylan occasionally interrupted his television viewing to relate his daydreams of being a college football kicker, making a winning touchdown catch on a fake field-goal attempt, taking over the city of New Miami, becoming kings of campus, partying nonstop, and hooking up with hot chick after hot chick.

Time seemed to accelerate, and the day of their flight arrived faster than Marcus felt like it should have. Despite all of his planning, he still felt completely unprepared. Bright and early on a Monday morning, Sharon drove the boys to the airport. She walked them to the entrance to say their goodbyes. This time Marcus didn't wait to see whether Sharon would initiate a hug. He dropped his bag, stepped forward, and pulled her into a hug. He felt her arms wrap around his waist, and he spoke quietly into her ear. "It was so good to see you again. I missed you a lot the last seven years. Thank you for putting up with us the last few weeks. I love you."

"I love you too. Best of luck. I hope you find what you're looking for," Sharon said.

They went their separate ways. Marcus excused himself from Dylan and ducked into a bathroom to get a moment alone to recompose himself without Dylan squawking excitedly at him about flight information. He exited the bathroom to find Dylan focused on his new phone and a pair of security guards standing next to him. One of the guards looked like he was trying to inconspicuously peer at Dylan's phone screen from a few feet away. The other guard spotted Marcus, tapped her comrade on the shoulder, and then spoke into a walkie-talkie. Then they were both looking at Marcus. Marcus got Dylan's attention, and they carried on through the international terminal. After walking for a few minutes, he stopped to look at a bookstore display as an excuse to cautiously glimpse behind them to see whether the guards were following them. They were.

Just before they reached the line for airport security, Marcus felt his phone vibrate. It was a text from Sharon. "Told you men touching women in public was frowned upon. Am late for work because security had to interview me to make sure I was okay after seeing our hug."

Marcus texted back an apology, then turned around and was relieved to see the backs of the two guards as they walked away.

WUS airport security was followed by a EUS immigration pre-check station, where everyone potentially entering EUS had to be screened to confirm they met the criteria for entrance. Dylan was pulled aside for extra scrutiny and interviewed by the EUS security personnel because he only had a driver's license, not a passport. In the end, since he was a EUS citizen—which the security personnel was able to confirm in their database—plus a legal minor feigning ignorance about passport requirements, he got admitted through to their terminal.

Once in the terminal, they bought some breakfast and sat down to absorb the commotion of the airport. Marcus was still feeling a bit melancholy from saying goodbye to Sharon, but looking around, he was reminded of how much he loved airports. Much like the coasts or the mountains, airports were places of change. Everyone around him was scurrying to get to someplace else. A businessman in a hurry to get to a meeting. A family going on vacation. People traveling to weddings or funerals or baby showers. Everyone had a story, and he found it amusing imagining where they were going.

He also loved looking out the windows at planes taking off and landing. Despite knowing the physics of airplane flight, he always found it amazing that hunks of metal that weighed several hundred thousand pounds could fly with relative grace and safety. His meditative state of awe was suddenly broken by the sound of Dylan drumming his fingers on the table. Dylan looked a bit nervous. Then it dawned on him. This would be Dylan's first airplane flight ever. "You doing okay, buddy?" he asked.

"I'm fine. I didn't get much sleep last night. I'm just excited to go party," Dylan responded unconvincingly.

"Maybe one of the travel stores has sleep aids. It'll be a long flight; you could knock yourself out and get caught up on sleep," Marcus suggested.

While Dylan hunted down some sleep-aid pills, Marcus felt his phone vibrate again. It was Sharon once more. "You're getting out of WUS just in time. Equality Defense just contacted me and asked if you and Dylan were staying with us. They scheduled a hearing for you two to see whether they feel they need to send you to re-ed camp. If airport security posts their report about our hug, then EDC will know you're at the airport and might look for you."

Marcus closed his eyes and put his head in his hand.

"Okay, my turn to ask. You okay, buddy?" Dylan said as he returned from the travel shop.

"Yeah. I'm fine," Marcus said. He toyed with the idea of telling Dylan the news but decided he didn't want to add to Dylan's anxiety right as they were being called for boarding. "It is *definitely* time to go, though."

Dylan popped his pills as they began boarding. On the plane, they found their seats in a side row of three. Dylan called dibs on the aisle seat because he had longer legs and might be able to use the aisle to stretch out a bit, so after stowing his bag overhead, Marcus plopped down in the middle seat. He stuck a bottle of water and his headphones in the pocket of the worn and faded fabric seat in front of him and pulled out the safety instruction manual.

After finishing the manual, he leaned over the empty window seat and looked out at the flurry of activity of planes taxiing, workers scurrying about, and people walking past the jet bridge window to board their plane. He looked down at a worker wearing a brightly colored safety vest, and there they were—the man and woman in the beige gingham jackets.

Marcus froze. They were talking with the worker. They held up a piece of paper. The worker shrugged. The beige-clad woman pointed up at the jet bridge, and the worker lifted a walkie-talkie off his belt and spoke into it, then led the pair to a ground-level door, got out a set of keys, and let them into the building. The pair disappeared. Marcus pulled out a magazine, buried his head in it, and sank into his seat.

Marcus's feeble attempts to hide behind the seat in front of him were interrupted when he heard a voice ask him to stand up and step into the aisle. He looked up, bracing for a beige gingham coat, but instead he saw a light-blue polo shirt with a company logo on the breast. Filling out the polo shirt was a somewhat petite but fit-looking black man who appeared to be in his late forties or early fifties. After an instant of panic, Marcus realized it was just his seatmate wanting to get to the window seat. The man nodded and smiled politely at him as he slid past Dylan to take his seat, and then again as Marcus sat down again and he helped Marcus untangle their seat belts.

"Thanks," Marcus said.

"No problem. My name is Isaac," the man said as he extended his hand for a handshake. "Is New Miami your final destination, or are you just passing through on your way to somewhere else?"

"I think it's my destination." Marcus peeked over the seat in front of him to see whether boarding was nearly finished. "Were there many people boarding after you? Do you know if we'll be pushing away from the gate soon?" Marcus asked.

"My connecting flight was late. I just barely made it to this gate in time. I think I was one of the last to board. We should be leaving soon," Isaac said.

Marcus nodded and tried to peek out the window again. He saw a flicker of motion at the jet bridge window but couldn't identify what it was.

"Have you ever been to SEUS before?" Isaac asked.

Marcus shook his head. He looked over at Dylan, who had already put his headphones on and had his eyes closed, looking like he might fall asleep any second. He did a quick check of the three people he had identified on the walk to his seat as most likely to be air marshals. None appeared to be stirring.

"Ahh, caveat emptor, my friend. Caveat emptor," Isaac said.

Marcus wasn't sure if he was in the mood for chatting with a stranger, but the man's demeanor conveyed a calm, controlled energy and a somewhat nerdy but friendly personality, and he figured he could use a distraction from his anxiety. There was nothing he could do now to change whether the Equality Defense pair found him or not. Besides, at least the guy wasn't obnoxiously invading his space, hogging the armrest or the legroom or wearing any insufferable, toxic cologne. "What does that mean?" he asked.

"It's Latin for 'buyer beware.' SEUS can be a shocking place if you've never been there before. Especially if you're from someplace like NEUS or Urban WUS." Isaac chuckled. "Saying the acronym 'SEUS' always makes me think of Dr. Seuss. The people there are kind of like Dr. Seuss characters too. Cutthroat though. It's like the Wild Wild West."

"Are you from there?" Marcus asked.

"No. I'm from Puerto Paz. I'm a product engineer for a company that makes a lot of specialized equipment. My company has a philosophy of having engineers follow the products we design throughout their lifespans. It gives us a sense of customer needs and product weaknesses to design for in the next product we engineer. Anyway, every few years I end up doing a lot of travel. SEUS is my absolute least-favorite place to go. The people there are horrible...selfish, thoughtless, careless...ugh. Sorry, I don't mean to talk your ear off or get you depressed about where you're going."

"No, you've got me curious now," Marcus said. "I was considering trying to skip my senior year of high school and get into Miami U, maybe to major in engineering and play football, but I don't really know that much about Southern EUS. My sister said I'd hate it there, but I didn't press her for an explanation."

"Well, if you are any good at football, then you'll have no

problem getting in a year early at Miami U. Just be careful about the contracts you sign, though. SEUS businesses, and Miami University is definitely run as a business just like everything in SEUS is, will not care about you one bit, and will only care about getting as much money out of you as they can. Everything is like that in SEUS. You need to read the fine print of every contract very carefully. If you don't have a contract, get one. Sometimes even a good contract won't help you, though. The government there is kept intentionally weak, and there isn't much legal enforcement to fall back on if someone powerful tries to screw you over. The only threat that anyone truly responds to there is the loss of profit. Money is valued above all else. They idolize the wealthy there, and they believe the myth that the wealthy are smarter and harder working, but the truth is that you don't have to be smart or hardworking to make a lot of money there. You just have to be an unscrupulous asshole who will do the unethical things that your competitors won't. And conversely, you can work really hard and not make enough to live off of because those in power won't give you your fair share."

"Jesus," Marcus exclaimed. "That sounds awful!" He could feel the plane begin to move backward. He peeked over the seats and couldn't see any beige-clad people in the aisle. The three potential air marshals appeared calm from what he could see. Surely they were in the clear now, yet his anxiety levels continued to feel elevated. "Why does your company even do business there?"

"Puerto Paz encourages interaction of its citizens and businesses with *all* cultures to keep the lines of communication open and the exchange of ideas flowing. We do business all over the world, but in SEUS they are such voracious consumers that we have a lot of sales opportunities. Right now, I handle a lot of product support in North America, so I've been traveling all over Canada, EUS, and WUS."

"My friend and I have done a bit of traveling across EUS and WUS this summer. It's been eye opening. Sounds like I might be in for some more surprises in SEUS," Marcus said.

Isaac nodded. "Every region of the former United States is drastically different. From a business perspective, I can say that one thing they all have in common is that they all experienced a stagnation of innovation after the partitioning. In NEUS, they value the past so much and are so fearful of change, that there is little to no innovation. Plus, they are so insular that there isn't much exchanging of ideas between them and other cultures, and they are so homogenous that there isn't enough internal diversity to foster new ideas from different sub-cultures. In Urban WUS, they have difficulty with innovation because of the stifling rules. So much of innovation is happy accidents, and with all those rules, there aren't many opportunities for happy accidents. In Rural WUS, they have a life philosophy that shuns innovation and technology. In SEUS, innovation is impeded because no one will invest in research because they don't want to put money into anything unless they see an immediate profit in it, and there is no government grant system to fill the research gaps that businesses won't invest in. They rely heavily on foreign research and development, and then they try to steal the design and make knock-offs."

"I know what you mean about Rural WUS's life philosophy. They don't even believe in plumbing! I can't imagine you make many sales there," Marcus said.

"True, but except for SEUS, the former United States market in general is rather difficult."

"How so?"

Isaac held up a finger. "Hold on. I'll tell you more after the flight attendants are done with their preflight safety routine."

Marcus nodded and turned his attention to the attendants. *I wonder if flight attendants are part of WUS security...do they get security alerts? Coordinate with the air marshal? Better keep an eye on them too,* he thought.

After the flight attendants finished, Isaac picked their conversation back up. "So, as I was saying, WUS and EUS are tough markets. In NEUS, they are so xenophobic that they typically reject any foreign products, unless maybe when those products have a military application. Given their history with our nation, we aren't very keen on selling them military technology though. A lot of people there still wrongly associate Puerto Paz with communist Cuba too. Urban WUS we do a moderate amount of business with, but it is almost impossible to avoid losing money there. They are okay to deal if you have a lot of patience and once you navigate all their legal hurdles, which are often moving targets. In SEUS, they have such a disposable culture and strong appetite for anything new that will make them seem superior to their competition that we actually have to suppress our sales to them out of concern for the environment. If we didn't, they'd just keep buying and buying and tossing their old products into landfills, or worse, they'd just dump it anywhere they please if they don't feel like paying for disposal.

"My company, and Puerto Pazians in general, can't stand that. We'd rather send an engineer to figure out how to adjust and tweak the technology that is already in place until there's nothing left to tweak and it becomes necessary to buy something new. We try to influence them to be more environmentally friendly as much as possible, but their whole culture is just so destructive. I'm not sure our policies are entirely effective, though. They are constantly pirating our technology."

"They don't have any regulations in SEUS?" Marcus asked, the volume of his voice rising to be audible over the ear-piercing scream of a baby a few rows behind them.

Isaac shook his head. "Practically no regulation in SEUS at all. Like I said, the government is kept intentionally weak. Businesses run things there, not the government. There are a few monopolies that have a tremendous amount of power and that have destroyed most small businesses. The environment is a disaster. Definitely do not drink the tap water anywhere. I don't know what your plans are for local transportation, but getting around can be a nightmare. There is no public transportation, and the roads are all rabbit's warrens of private toll roads. And the toll operators can charge arbitrary prices. Once a toll operator saw that I was black and told me 'the toll for niggers is one thousand dollars,' even though it was only a quarter-mile-long road. In my experience, racism there is unusual...usually people only care whether you have money, but it just goes to show you how inconsistent it can be. You have to expect the unexpected."

"Christ. Glad we sold our car and didn't drive there!" Marcus shrieked. "How do you get around?"

"The best bet is walking, but even then you'll encounter dead ends, where private property blocks your path. There are private drivers who make a living navigating the shapeshifting routes and working out deals with landowners to get through obstacles, but just like the toll operators, you never know what you're going to get from one driver to the next. The drivers are probably your best bet for getting from the airport to wherever you're going. Make sure you have a pen with you. A common trick the drivers pull is to claim they don't have a pen to sign a contract, and they'll tell you to just trust them. Do you have lodging set up for when you get there?"

"No. My friend talked me into just figuring it out when we got there. He thought we could chat up college students and see if anyone needed roommates."

Isaac nodded. "I'd recommend you go straight from the airport to Miami University. During the summer session they have a lot of extra dorm room space, and you could negotiate a good deal on a room while you apply as a student. You could probably get into summer session classes late if you wanted, so long as you have the money. If you can't get a room, here's my business card and a company pen with my contact info on it. Call me, and I'll put you up in my hotel room for a few days until you find something."

Isaac scribbled on the back of the card and handed it and the pen to Marcus and continued. "Another tip for SEUS first-timers: People there tend to either be really rich or really poor, and they segregate by economic status. The wealthy hire security to keep the poor out of their territories. Try to stay in the wealthy zones as much as possible. The wealthy are assholes, but they'll mostly leave you alone if you don't get in their way. The homeless in SEUS are the most aggressive and dangerous of any place I've ever been. You and your friend look like you could physically defend yourselves pretty well, so they might not try to assault you, but be alert for guns. Guns are completely unregulated, and they are everywhere."

Marcus felt a wave of regret washing over him. He now understood why Sharon had said he'd hate it in New Miami. It sounded worse than "taking it like a man" back in New Rochelle. A sickening feeling was pooling in his stomach, and he a felt pressure in his head that he thought was the start of a headache until his ears began to pop. Then he realized that parts of his physical symptoms were being caused by the airplane having already taken off. He had been so engrossed in Isaac's tales of caution about SEUS that he hadn't even noticed the plane accelerating or lifting off. He looked over at Dylan, who had thankfully fallen asleep. He checked the front of the plane again for beige gingham jackets and saw none. He reconfirmed the nearest exits and began scanning the plane forward and backward to verify that there wasn't anyone who looked like a threat. He faced forward again and saw the two flight attendants beginning beverage service. *If the flight attendants are part of security, and they recognized me, would they turn the plane around? Which is worse? Being delivered back into the hands of Big Mother? Or into the hell-hole my seatmate is describing?* Marcus thought.

Marcus saw Isaac looking at him apologetically. "Sorry to be so depressing. I'm usually not such a negative downer, but people from Puerto Paz place a high value on knowledge and truth, and I didn't want you to walk out of the New Miami airport unprepared for the experiences that lay ahead. New Miami will eat the unwary alive. By the way, on the back of the business card, I wrote the names and phone numbers of a couple of reputable private drivers you could use."

"Thanks. I'm okay," Marcus said and nervously chuckled. "Just surprised. I get now why the church elders back home would describe the people of SEUS as sinners, though."

Marcus spent some time processing Isaac's counsel. Ten minutes later he leaned over to Isaac. "Do you know why it's called *New* Miami instead of just Miami?"

Isaac nodded. "Florida used to have a lot more land area. I think about a third of it, the entire southern tip, was wiped out by floods caused by global climate change. The original Miami was in the part that is now completely underwater. The wealthy of Miami started gobbling up real estate in inner Daytona after it became clear that flooding would wipe out Miami, but the flood prediction data was never released publicly. Only those in the wealthy good ol' boy network who could afford to pay for information knew that flooding was imminent.

"Once they owned the land and had a monopoly in Daytona, where the flooding was limited to small parts of the coastline, they colluded to drive up real estate prices as people attempted to move to there from the parts of the state that were flooding. Poorer people who owned land in southern Florida couldn't bear the expense of home insurance or flood insurance, so they were financially devastated and couldn't afford the new housing in Daytona. The gap between rich and poor widened even further, and the ranks of the poor and homeless swelled. The new landowners from Miami had no interest in assimilating into Daytona. They just bulldozed everything that was in their way and built anew, and they informally called it New Miami until the name stuck, and eventually it was officially changed."

The airplane shuddered momentarily as they crossed through a patch of turbulent air. Marcus clutched his armrest and looked over at Dylan, who had his head cranked into an awkward position and had a spot of drool at the corner of his open mouth. He started to feel a little queasy. *So much for Dylan being the one needing reassurance,* he thought. He briefly wondered where Dylan had stashed his sleeping pills and whether he could take some to knock himself out for the rest of the flight.

Isaac continued. "Miami University was actually one of the first businesses to buy property in Daytona, since it was their climate professors who had the flood prediction data. The first building they built was the football stadium, since football was so profitable for them. They kept the Miami University name instead of changing it to Daytona University in order to maintain brand recognition, so they kind of kick-started the change in the name of the city."

The pit in Marcus's stomach didn't improve any as he listened to Isaac explain the history of New Miami. During their drive from New Rochelle to San Francisco, he had noticed on the old 1980s map they were using to navigate that Florida looked weird on the map, but navigation had been his main focus, so he hadn't had time to think about it. "They didn't mention any of the flooding in my classes at school back home in NEUS."

"Not surprising. They like to whitewash over the parts of history that don't make them look good. The northeast didn't get flooded nearly as badly as the southeast either. There were places like Boston, where the underground highway tunnels flooded before they started treating the flooding as a security threat and they built a lot of sea walls, dams, and levies in a hurry, but in general the topography wasn't as bad. In WUS, the topography was even better, and the flooding was pretty minor. That's part of why they chose the west when the USA split up. In SEUS, though, they have such a disposable culture that they just scrapped the parts that flooded and started over in the unflooded areas."

Marcus was starting to feel like he was on the verge of vomiting due to the toxic levels of pessimism he was now feeling. He rifled through the seat pocket to make sure he knew where the barf bag was. Isaac asked if he was okay and noted that if he needed to go to the bathroom, he should do it before they crossed into SEUS airspace, at which time there would be long lines for the bathrooms before they all converted to pay toilets at the border. Marcus got up, delicately straddled over Dylan's comatose body like a thief crawling over a laser security beam, and headed to a bathroom near the front of the plane, where he promptly sacrificed half of his breakfast to the toilet.

Upon return to his seat, he started to feel a little better but decided to avoid the topic of New Miami. He began to notice that the cabin air already had a stale odor and feel to it. His skin felt oily and dirty. He remembered thinking on his flight to Germany a few years earlier that body perspiration and odor must work on an accelerated clock inside of airplanes. Isaac had begun watching a movie on the seatback entertainment console, and Marcus picked up his airplane headphones and plugged them in and started watching one too.

About thirty minutes into his movie Marcus pressed the pause button and pulled the earphone off of his left ear and raised his hand a little to get Isaac's attention. Isaac paused his movie and removed his headphones.

"Does Puerto Paz have football?" Marcus asked.

"Yes," Isaac responded. "We have both the version that we, and the rest of the world, call football but you call soccer, and we have American football, which we call 'gridiron.' Our version of American football is a bit different from yours, though. We've changed some of the most dangerous and violent parts of the game to try to find a balance point between entertainment and safety. There are still some violent collisions between running backs and linebackers that we haven't been able to get rid of, but the passing game is a lot different. I know that the first reaction of people from NEUS is that we've turned it into a game for sissies, but we look at it as a matter of being a fan of sport versus being a fan of violence. In basketball, for example, violence was never built into the game, and it has always been successful because people enjoy it for the athletic ability. We've tried to replicate that in gridiron."

"Huh," Marcus responded. "I guess I'd have to watch a few games to see if I still liked it with the rules changes." He put his headphones back on and zoned out for the rest of his movie. At the end, he pulled the headphones off his left ear and requested Isaac's attention again. "Did you go to engineering school in Puerto Paz? What branch of engineering are you in?"

Isaac asked him to hold on for a minute while he started and then paused his second movie, noting that once they reached SEUS airspace they would start charging for movies. "I'm an electrical engineer, and yes, I went to UNA, the University of New Athens, in the capital city of Puerto Paz."

"Is that a good school for engineering?"

"It consistently gets ranked up there with Cal Berkley and Stanford by the people who care about rankings. Personally, I think as long as the school is a part of a culture that values truth and education, then you'll get about the same level of knowledge out of just about any school. The highly ranked schools have a mix of good and bad professors, just like the lower-ranked schools. A lot of it has to do with how much effort you put into it."

Marcus nodded and slipped his left earphone back onto his ear. He pulled his keychain out of his pocket and religiously rubbed the medallion with one hand while scrolling through the movie selection with the other hand to pick out a second movie before they entered SEUS airspace.

<u>Part 4: SEUS</u>
Chapter 1: Blonde at Three O'clock

An hour after Marcus's second movie ended, and after he had retrieved his math book from the overhead compartment and spent some time re-solving problems to settle his mind, they landed at New Miami International Airport.

As they disembarked, Marcus said his farewells to Isaac, and he and Dylan hustled the best they could through the crowded, narrow paths between sales kiosks that littered the corridors. Marcus wrinkled his nose and sneezed a few times as they wandered through clouds of cigarette smoke and perfumes being sprayed from the kiosks.

At one point, the path between sales displays lined with fragile beer glasses was so narrow that he had to remove his NEUS army duffle bag from his shoulder and awkwardly walk while holding it in front of him to avoid hitting the shelving. It was is if they wanted people to bump into the merchandise and break it so that they could charge for damages.

Marcus looked at the duffle bag and realized it stood out like a sore thumb. Was it a dead giveaway that he wasn't from the area? Would that lead to local con men identifying him as an easy target? He talked Dylan into stopping at one of the airport stores to buy new luggage for both of them, filling Dylan in on his conversations with Isaac about SEUS culture as they shopped. Dylan still seemed a bit groggy from his long, medicated nap and hardly acknowledged anything Marcus said to him. They hurriedly settled on a pair of overpriced designer knock-off bags.

Marcus fished his new cell phone out of his pocket and checked that it was working on the SEUS mobile networks. After his conversations with Isaac on the plane, he couldn't imagine trying to navigate the contracts and headaches involved in getting a local

SEUS phone carrier. He found Isaac's business card and called one of the numbers for a private driver, asking if they could be picked up at the airport and driven to the Miami University registrar's office.

Isaac's recommendation had been a good one in terms of the driver not trying to rip them off, but the drive to the university was hectic and noisy. Nearby car horns startled them every few seconds, as one driver after another in gas-guzzling SUVs and souped-up sports cars tried to cut off everyone around them in a free-for-all battle to get even one car farther ahead. In addition to the noise of the honking, it seemed like every other vehicle had an overcharged stereo system blasting, only partially drowning out the noise of extra-loud sport mufflers and the thousands of brightly lit video billboards playing commercials over speakers. Marcus was amazed they made it safely to their destination without an accident.

By 4:30 p.m., they were walking in the doors of the Miami University Administration building. They proceeded directly to a row of windows with bulletproof glass and small intercom speakers. They walked up to the nearest staffed window and greeted a disgruntled-looking woman who looked like she had undergone several rounds of botched elective plastic surgery and was wearing way too much makeup. She had bangs that stood straight up at least six inches and had so much hairspray in them that they looked like they could withstand a hurricane.

They began asking her about getting housing in a dormitory and signing up for classes even though they hadn't graduated from high school yet. The woman hardly spoke to them, asking only a few questions and using the bare minimum of words mixed with grunts. She began gathering contracts and paperwork, seemingly unconcerned about their lack of a high school diploma.

As she gathered the paperwork, Dylan nudged Marcus. "Check out the blonde at three o'clock."

Marcus turned to his right to look at the only other people in the corridor on their side of the bulletproof glass. Two college-aged white girls were standing a few windows away. The one in back, seemingly uninvolved in the administrative transaction, was a blonde in an extremely skimpy, tight red dress. Her hair was teased out, and she was wearing a ton of makeup, including bright, ruby-red lipstick that matched her dress. She was staring at Marcus and

Dylan with her lips slightly parted and her tongue touching the corner of her mouth with a "come hither" look of flirtation.

The young woman in front of the blonde was a slender but athletic brunette with her hair up in a loose bun, wearing khaki shorts and a sea-foam-green tank top. *She has the body of an 800-meter runner*, Marcus thought, noticing her perfectly sculpted calves and the gently curved nape of her neck. She had her back turned mostly toward him, so he couldn't see her face, but he could hear her voice.

"This is the fifth time Professor Barnum hasn't shown for class," she said. "This is unacceptable. I want to transfer to another class."

She was clearly not happy, but there was calmness in her voice that seemed to go against the grain of everything he had experienced in SEUS so far. She turned to say something quietly to the blonde, and Marcus got a good look at her face. She was stunningly beautiful. Marcus stood there frozen, unable to turn away in time as she looked to see what her blonde friend was staring at, and her deep-brown eyes locked with Marcus's.

He was certain he must have some horrid, wide-eyed look of panic on his face, as she flashed a quick little smile and turned back to the administrative window to continue her debate about transferring classes. Marcus suddenly found himself gasping for air, not realizing he had been holding his breath the entire time. He shook his head as he heard the administrative clerk in front of him ask him something, and he had to ask her to repeat it.

The clerk shoved a stack of papers through a drawer to his side of the window, and he pulled them out and started trying to read them. He couldn't maintain focus, and he peeked over at the brunette in the tank top a couple of times. As he was about to peek a third time, suddenly she was standing just a couple of feet away, looking right at him, with her blonde friend standing next to her looking at Dylan.

"Are you registering?" she asked.

"Y-y-yeah," Marcus stammered.

"Are you new here?"

"Yes."

"You have the blue forms," she said. "Those are no good. Here, let me help you."

She put the stack of forms back into the drawer and pushed it in, sending the forms back to the clerk's side, before saying to the clerk, "We'd like the pink forms. The ones with the standard rates, without the five-year-minimum contract, and without the university-selected arbiter."

She turned to Marcus and Dylan and asked, "You two want to room together?" Marcus nodded. The brunette turned back to the clerk and said, "And these two would like to room together, so we want the roommate-finder-fee waived. Oh, and they don't want the TV that plays commercials 24/7 that you can't shut off or mute."

At first Marcus worried that the brunette had just blown his chances at getting admitted. The clerk scowled at the young woman for a while before slowly retrieving the blue forms and filing them away, and then getting up to go find the pink forms in some other part of the office.

The young brunette closed her eyes and started taking some deep breaths in through her petite, narrow nose and releasing the air slowly through pursed lips. Marcus looked at her as she breathed. He couldn't tell if she was wearing any makeup. If she was, it was very subtle. He definitely found her physically attractive, but after the horror stories he had heard Isaac tell about SEUS people, he wondered whether he could trust her. For all he knew, she could be running a scam on him with the pink paperwork thing. Maybe the pink paperwork was the paperwork that got her a cut of his registration fee. The young woman gave him a good vibe, but he decided he'd need to read the new contract extra carefully when the clerk returned with it.

"Is that yoga breathing?" he asked.

She opened her eyes and turned to him. "It's meditative breathing, so yes, the same sort of breathing you might do in yoga. I'm impressed that a young man from SEUS would even know what yoga breathing is."

"I'm not from SEUS. I'm from NEUS."

"Oh, I just assumed based on your luggage that you were from SEUS. Well, in that case, I'm even more impressed! Sometimes SEUS women know about yoga, but I wouldn't have expected anyone from NEUS, especially a male, to know about yoga."

"I only discovered it a few weeks ago." Marcus began filling her in on their transcontinental trek, and especially their yoga experience with Lily in Wyoming, as they waited for the clerk to return. Dylan meanwhile flirted with the blonde. "I'm Marcus, by the way."

"Havana. Nice to meet you," the brunette replied as she extended her hand to shake.

"So, I take it you're not from SEUS, either, given the way you described the lack of knowledge about yoga around here?"

"Nope. I'm from Puerto Paz."

Marcus smiled. "The guy next to me on the airplane was from Puerto Paz. He scared the bejeezus out of me telling me about how cutthroat it is here."

"Yeah. It is pretty brutal here. The university is pretty much just a loan shark wearing a professor's tweed jacket. Wait until you see how many students are in your classes. They stuff lecture halls beyond capacity."

"What brought you here?"

"Puerto Paz encourages study abroad for college students to broaden their horizons and give them alternative perspectives." Havana turned to look at her friend before leaning into his shoulder and going up on her tippy toes to whisper into his ear. "I had heard so many bad things about SEUS that I just had to experience it for myself to see if the rumors were true."

The skin on Marcus's arms stood up on end as goosebumps began to form in reaction to the warm, gentle exhalations into his ear as she whispered.

The goosebumps retracted in a hurry as the loud clank of the drawer being slammed to his side jolted Marcus out of his trance. The clerk had returned with the new paperwork and shoved it through the drawer and was now conspicuously looking at her watch. Marcus and Havana stood side by side reading the new contract together, while Dylan continued flirting with the giggling, hair-twirling blonde who Marcus had overheard introducing herself as Kelsey.

"Okay, this isn't perfect, but it's as good as you're going to get," Havana announced.

Marcus and Dylan signed the contract, and Marcus carefully withdrew the cash needed to cover the registration fee out of his bag, being careful to shield the money with the side of the bag so that the young women couldn't see it. Who knew whether she was being honest about being from Puerto Paz. That could be a scam too. He slid the paperwork and cash to the clerk through the drawer, and the clerk shoved a couple of plastic key cards back to them along with more paperwork.

"Here are your keys. You're in Rourke Oil building, room 426. Fill out the class-selection paperwork and bring it back tomorrow. We're closing now," the clerk said as she pulled down a shade over the window and shut off the intercom.

"Kelsey said she and Havana are going to the beach after this," Dylan said. "She'd like us to join them. You in?"

Marcus finally noticed that the bag Kelsey was holding had beach towels in it. "Sure, but we need to drop our gear at the dorm first and change into our swim trunks."

"You need help finding your way to the dorm?" Havana asked.

"I guess we do. No campus map, no directions, no nothing from Miss Happy there." Marcus chuckled. "Thanks for your help, by the way. Those contracts are a rough read."

"Well, at least we got it resolved right here in under four hours without having to go to twenty different departments," Dylan piped in, slapping Marcus on the back. "In San Fran, it would have taken like a year to register and get keys to a dorm room."

Chapter 2: Penalty Card

The foursome headed out to the Rourke Oil Dormitory. Marcus and Havana were walking a bit faster than Dylan and Kelsey, giving Marcus a chance to discreetly ask, "So is SEUS as awful as you heard?"

"Definitely. I'm in pre-med, but I get through it by pretending I'm an anthropology student on an expedition. It is a hedonistic free-for-all here. Complete social Darwinism."

"My sister told me I'd hate it here. She actually suggested Puerto Paz."

"I miss home," Havana lamented. "Can't wait to be back with my Puerto Paisans."

"So, do you live in the dorms too?"

"No. Kelsey and I are in a sorority. The Greek system is yet another crucible of egos and narcissism."

"Why did you join, then?"

"Well, partly because I figured it was a good way to meet new people. There are forty-six fraternities and thirty-two sororities, so a lot of people and a lot of opportunities for interaction. It was partly also for the cultural experience. I was told Greek life was highly representative of the SEUS culture, and if you're going to come here to experience the culture, you might as well go all in. I look at my whole experience here in New Miami as a learning opportunity."

"When we were back at the admin window, it seemed like you didn't want Kelsey to know how you felt about SEUS. Is she a native?"

"She is, but she's one of the nicer ones. Nice, but a tad naïve, and completely obsessed with popularity. It is a combination of personality traits that often gets her taken advantage of. I try to look out for her as much as I can."

It wasn't long before they reached the dormitory, a plain, boxy, unadorned, dilapidated bunker that Marcus could swear was leaning. The boys entered their eight-foot-by-eight-foot room and began remarking at how appalling the size and conditions were. It was nothing but a cheap bunk bed and two flimsy armoires, and it was stiflingly hot. The building was depressing inside and out. All function and no form, and even the function was questionable given the appearance of shoddy materials and workmanship that Marcus saw evidence of.

Marcus went to the window to try to open it but discovered it wasn't an operable window. "Jesus. Is this to prevent people from jumping out of this depressing shithole?" he muttered to himself. They didn't want to keep the girls waiting long, so he put aside his disbelief, and the boys quickly rifled through their bags to find and change into their swim trunks before rejoining the girls in the cramped entrance lobby.

Havana noted that they were unlikely to encounter a bathroom for several hours that didn't require a fee to enter, so the girls used the lobby bathroom before they left the dormitory. Havana exited the bathroom first, remarking, "I still can't get over how they use the same potable water for toilets that they use for faucets. What a waste." Several minutes later, Kelsey rejoined them, and they headed for the beach.

Marcus and Havana picked up where they had left off as they wandered off campus. Between being engrossed in conversation with her, and having to constantly look down to dodge debris and dog poo, Marcus quickly lost track of their route.

As they reached a pause in their exchange, he started to look around a bit. The street they were on was essentially abandoned, and it appeared to be the dividing line between a wealthy neighborhood and a poverty-stricken neighborhood. All of the doors and windows facing this street had been sealed off, with the openings on the wealthy side bricked in and nicely stuccoed over, and the openings on the poor side haphazardly covered with plywood.

Havana explained that the street that paralleled this one on the wealthy side had posh businesses and boutiques, with the entrances only on that street, and that the buildings on the poor side of this street had all been purchased by the owners of the buildings on the wealthy side but were left unoccupied and deteriorating, creating a sort of neutral zone between the rich and the poor.

Marcus peeked down a side street that led to the poor neighborhood and spotted a few dilapidated storefronts that had crudely made signs with words like "Dollar" or "Value" in them. As they continued, a large building came into view straight ahead, blocking the street. It had billboards on top of it plastered with multiple advertisements. More advertisements and blinking neon signs and video ads were in the windows and plastered all over the façade. As they got closer, he realized it was a pharmacy.

"Why did they build that right in the middle of the street?" he asked. "It's blocking the path."

Havana snorted softly. "That's the point. They want you to be forced to look at the advertising and to feel like walking through the building is the path of least resistance. They've built them like that all over the city. They're often right on the border between rich and poor neighborhoods because rich and poor alike need pharmacies. They have rich-people entrances on one side and poor-people entrances on the other side, then this entrance in the middle with advertising covering everything."

Marcus and Havana slowed down to let Dylan and Kelsey catch up, and then started to walk close enough to the pharmacy building to be able to read the smaller print advertisements, many of which were for pharmaceutical drugs being sold inside.

Havana pointed to one. "Lyrica. I think that's the drug that musicians take when they have writer's block."

Marcus cackled loudly, but Dylan and Kelsey remained silent. Marcus pointed to another drug advertisement. "Invokana. That's for witches having difficulty summoning spirits."

Havana smiled and chuckled as they started walking alongside the building toward the rich neighborhood. She pointed to another drug ad. "Latuda. That's to help Latin women who've lost their spunky attitude get their groove back."

Marcus smiled and pointed to another. "Stelara is for interstellar travelers so they don't get space sickness."

"Eucrisa is what you take when you can't make it to church on Sunday but still want to partake in the Eucharist," Havana said.

"Januvia is for people who become bitter recluses during the month of January due to snow," Marcus said.

Marcus looked at Dylan, who hadn't chuckled once during his banter with Havana. Dylan was looking behind them, fixated by something down the side street at the poor end of the building. Marcus followed his line of sight.

"Check out the crazy chick," Dylan said.

Marcus's eyes landed on a woman standing across the street. As he looked, the woman turned her head and locked eyes with them. She began to quickly waddle toward them with presumably arthritic hips altering her gait. Her long, frizzy gray hair nearly stood straight out from her head, and it bobbed from side to side as she hustled over to them. As she got closer, Marcus could see that her excessively tanned and leathery skin had numerous pockmarks and moles, and she looked like she hadn't bathed in months. His mind flashed back to Tom in Wyoming. He hoped the woman stopped before she got within smelling distance.

As she reached them, she extended a pointer finger and jabbed it in their direction. "I seen you lookin' at me. I seen it. You're lookin' at me 'cause I'm famous. I'm famous, you know. You want my autograph 'cause I'm famous, but I ain't gonna give it to you. No. It's mine, and you can't have it. I'm famous, and my autograph is mine. I found it." She retracted her finger and stood up straighter. "Well, five bucks. I'll sell it to ya for five bucks. Deal?"

Dylan snorted and began taunting the woman. "I'm famous. I'm more famous than you. I'll sell you my autograph for only ten dollars. That's a bargain."

Marcus looked at Dylan, wide-eyed, and shook his head. "Dude."

Dylan continued, perhaps misinterpreting what Marcus was saying "no" to, and told the woman, "I take it back. I don't want you to have my autograph. It's no longer for sale."

The woman's eyes grew twice as big as she looked at Dylan in shock from the insult that she wasn't worthy of his autograph. As she stared at Dylan, a young man in a three-piece designer suit and designer sunglasses walked out the pharmacy doors, passed the group, and turned and spat on the woman. The woman threw her hand into the air in a delayed effort to swat away the spit, but it had already landed in her hair.

"Stay on your side," the young man barked as he continued on his way without ever breaking stride or looking back.

The woman turned and mocked spitting in his direction, but he would have already been too far away to reach even if she had saliva available with which to spit.

Havana shouted "asshole" at the man, but he just gave her the finger over his shoulder without even turning around. Marcus turned to Dylan and the girls and nodded his head in the direction of the rich neighborhood to indicate his desire to continue on while the lady was distracted.

As they made their hasty getaway, Marcus asked, "Did a psych ward just let out for recess or something? Wow."

"She probably does belong in a psych ward," Havana said, "but SEUS doesn't have public institutions to care for the mentally ill, only private for-profit companies, and the poor can't afford the care. All of health care is like that here. The poor typically have relatively short life spans."

Dylan pulled himself away from his conversation with Kelsey long enough to chastise the poor. "Why don't those lazy bums get jobs? Then they could pay for health care."

"A lot of them *do* have jobs," Havana said. "Multiple jobs. But they don't pay enough to make a living. The ones who have mental health issues can't get hired or keep a job, and the ones without mental health issues sometimes give up because there isn't much difference in lifestyle between working your ass off and not having a job at all. The wealthy in power collude to set wages. They stack the deck in their favor, and those at the bottom of the totem pole don't have any power or say at all."

"They could start their own businesses," Dylan replied.

"You can't have a functioning society made entirely out of CEOs," Havana retorted. "Society needs janitors, waiters, and auto mechanics just as much as it needs CEOs and hedge fund managers."

Marcus saw Dylan flinch when Havana lumped auto mechanics into the poor-people category. She didn't know his history with cars, nor his likely future with them, so he knew it wasn't meant as a personal attack, but he could see a look of pain on Dylan's face, like he'd taken offense. Dylan suddenly got quiet and withdrew from the conversation.

As they made their way around the corner of the pharmacy building, Marcus found himself being smacked in the face with sensory overload. Every store on this street had music blaring through outdoor speakers simultaneously with noisy video advertisements on the walls combined with moving and blinking lights and perfumes belching out of the front doors. He stopped abruptly, like he had just walked into a brick wall, and turned from side to side to absorb the chaotic scene around him. Every door had a pair of muscle-bound bouncers in sunglasses watching over scantily clad women, who appeared to be some sort of live mannequins sexualizing whatever product the store was selling, rubbing the product all over their bodies while they bit and licked their lips. He turned to look at Havana. He could see her lips moving but couldn't make out what she was saying over the noise.

"What?" he shouted as he leaned in to try to hear her repeat whatever she had said.

"Now you see why I chose the border street?" she shouted. "The poor streets are too dangerous, and the rich streets are too chaotic. The border streets are the only place to get any peace and quiet."

"Yeah," Marcus shouted back. "I can barely hear you. This is nuts!"

The sound of screeching tires and a car horn caused him to whip his head back around just in time to witness the tail end of a red BMW running a yield sign at high speed as a tan mini station wagon skidded just short of broad-siding it. The driver of the station wagon reached into his console before sticking his arm out the driver's-side window toward the red BMW, which was now immediately in front of Marcus.

Marcus instinctively swung his body around to turn his back to the station wagon, centering Havana's body in front of him with his hands and shielding her from what he assumed was going to be a gun being fired. A couple of seconds later, after not hearing any gunshots, he looked over his shoulder and saw that the driver of the station wagon was sticking a red index card, not a gun, out his window at the BMW.

Havana was laughing. "Brilliant!" she shouted. "A football referee's penalty card for bad drivers. I love it!" She leaned forward, gave Marcus a half hug, and with her cheek pressed against his spoke directly into his ear. "Thank you for saving my life." Then she withdrew from the hug and gave him a teasing smile before continuing on down the street.

Marcus was about to start following her when he saw the tan station wagon complete its intended turn and pull over to their side of the road a short distance ahead. Two bumper stickers on the rear bumper read, "You're not a VIP, you can follow the rules just like everyone else" and "Turn signal lessons $5, prerequisite: 1st grade."

He chuckled a little and said to himself, "I feel ya, bro."

Chapter 3: Anthropology Expedition: Peacocks on the Beach

The group rounded the corner at the end of the block that the pharmacy building had interrupted and headed back to the quieter neutral street to continue on to the beach.

"That was crazy," Marcus said.

"Welcome to Anthropology 101," Havana said.

"So, what's up with the traffic lights around here?" Marcus asked. "None of them are functioning, and half of them have small yield signs hanging from them."

"They were abandoned a long time ago," Havana said. "In the parts of the city that remain from old Daytona, a lot of things formerly operated by the government have been abandoned. The yield signs were hung by a citizens group trying to reduce the massive number of accidents at uncontrolled intersections, but a lot of jerks ignore them, or they hire people to go around and change which streets the signs face so that they have the right of way their whole route. The direction that the signs face is constantly changing because of that. Be careful crossing the streets, by the way. Drivers do not stop for anyone. My first week here I forgot that they don't have autonomous cars like back home, and I almost got hit."

"The cars where you live are all self-driving?" Dylan asked. "You just give up all your control to a computer?"

"The vast majority of cars are, and in the city centers, only autonomous electric City Cars, City Vans, and small City Trucks for businesses are permitted. My grandpa used to complain about giving up control of the car to a computer, but then my grandma would always remind him of how back when they lived in the United States, he would complain about what assholes and idiots other drivers were before autonomous cars, and then she would remind him of how the traffic fatality statistics plummeted after the switch to autonomous cars. He would stop complaining after that."

Marcus began to smell a sort of rotten-egg smell in the air, far more intense than the similar smell at the Chicken Bucket in Terre Haute several weeks earlier. "Is there a gas leak nearby?" he asked, somewhat alarmed.

Havana made a face. "That's the beach you smell. Don't worry, your olfactory nerves will desensitize to it in a while."

In short time, Marcus could see the ocean ahead of them. He was once again looking forward to swimming in the ocean, but now he was nervous about the rotten-egg smell. He probed Havana's knowledge of it further. "So, what's causing that smell? Am I going to be okay swimming in the ocean?"

"Oh, god, no," Havana replied. "You don't want to do that here. The water here is crazy polluted. It's disgusting. They pump raw sewage into the ocean, and people throw their trash and hypodermic drug needles in there. The sewage attracts algae blooms, then the algae destroys the local ecosystem, and all that is left is jellyfish and trash. The smell is from algae that has washed up on the beach and is decaying."

Marcus's shoulders slumped and his head sunk down in disappointment. "Unbelievable. What do you do at the beach if you can't go in the ocean?"

"Kelsey likes to sunbathe and scope out hot guys. You're welcome to scope out guys with her, but I like to play beach volleyball." Havana gave Marcus another teasing smile. "We have a deal with the frat boys that they bring rakes and trash bags, we bring the ball, and we clean up a sand court together before playing co-ed games. At this time of day, though, the cleanup will be long over with, and the games will be winding down."

Kelsey finally spoke up to the group as a whole. "Are we, like, going to play with Alpha Sigs this time? They, like, literally have the hottest, most popular guys. I, like, heard that they, like, are having a raging kegger in a few weeks too. I, like, literally, am dying for an invite."

Marcus immediately noticed that Kelsey had a habit of making the end of every declarative sentence sound like a question. There was something else odd about the way she spoke, but Marcus wasn't able to identify it quite yet. Havana told Kelsey she much preferred playing with the nerdy Beta Pi boys because they were much nicer guys.

The foursome approached the edge of the beach, which was surrounded by a chain-link fence and had a security gate along the street. The boys hadn't realized that this was a private beach requiring an entrance fee, so they had to spend all of the money they had brought for snacks and drinks on gaining entrance to the beach.

Once through, Kelsey picked out a spot to lie down a good fifty yards away from the court that Havana, Marcus, and Dylan would be playing on. She seemed to intentionally make her selection based on the location of the Alpha Sigs, who could be seen farther down the beach, presumably in protest of Havana choosing to play with the nerdier Beta Pi guys.

Havana asked the group of Beta Pi guys and a mix of girls from different sororities if she, Marcus, and Dylan could work into a game, and the three newcomers were welcomed into what they were told would likely be the last game of the day. Marcus and Dylan had only played volleyball in gym class once per year, so they lacked experience compared to everyone else, but between Marcus's raw athletic abilities and Dylan's height, they were quickly able to get themselves up to the abilities of most of the people around them.

Havana was one of the better players on the court, even laying out for a dive to save a ball from hitting the sand. At one point she interrupted the game to patiently give everyone a lesson on bumping the volleyball, which did actually improve the quality of play.

After the game, while the group was socializing a bit more, and the young men of Beta Pi were clearly trying to angle their way into dates with the sorority girls, Marcus started feeling like he was on an anthropology expedition of his own. He started noticing the same weird accent or speech mannerisms in the rest of the sorority girls that he had noticed in Kelsey. He began consciously paying attention to it to figure out what it was. There was the up-talking he had already identified in Kelsey, where every sentence sounded like a question. Then he noticed how quickly they spoke, with a very staccato rhythm interrupted by pauses, but during the pauses, they often dragged out the last syllable of the previous sentence, not allowing anyone to break into the conversation. They also seemed to have a permanently snotty or snobby, sarcastic, and overconfident attitude, and they spoke exceedingly loudly.

It vaguely reminded Marcus of his dad's bullying, and he wondered whether the girls were trying to overcompensate for insecurity with faux confidence. It wasn't until he stared intently at the mouth of one of the young women as she was talking that he figured out the last piece of the puzzle. Instead of lowering their jaws and opening their mouths to form words from a default position of closed, they seemed to have a default slack-jawed, open-mouthed position all the time, and they would close their mouths as needed to form words. He turned his attention to some of the guys from Beta Pi and realized they were using a similar staccato, up-talking speech pattern.

Marcus's attention was broken by the sound of Kelsey giggling. He turned around to see her approaching with five moderately muscular guys. All five had fully shaved bodies and were covered in baby oil from their necks down. They had nearly identical spiky faux-hawk haircuts and all wore identical gold-rimmed aviator sunglasses. They strutted with their shoulders pinned back and their chests protruding forward, with their shoulders twisting in a slightly exaggerated motion with every step. The guy who appeared to be the leader had his head tilted back like his head was too heavy to carry around fully upright. Havana turned to Marcus and rolled her eyes. "Here come the peacocks."

"Peacocks?"

"That's what I call them. Peacocks, or you can just shorten it to 'cocks.' They're from Alpha Sigma, the frat that thinks their shit smells like roses. They strut around like they own the place, trying to seduce all the girls."

Marcus smiled, partially because of Havana's cleverness and sense of humor in the face of a situation she clearly did not enjoy, but also because she swore in front of him. He swore all the time when it was just him and Dylan talking, but he always cleaned up his language whenever anyone else was involved in the conversation. To Marcus, swearing was a sign of feeling at ease with someone else, and he liked that Havana felt at ease with him enough to swear in front of him.

His smile didn't last long, though, as four of the Alpha Sigs broke apart into two groups of two, each heading off to chat with different sorority girls. The lead frat boy, the alpha Alpha, so to speak, broke off on his own and started chatting up Havana. He stepped slightly between Marcus and Havana, turning his back mostly to Marcus in an obvious power-play move to try to assert dominance, announcing himself as "Brock" before he broke into what sounded like a well-practiced small-talk routine for ladies he was hitting on.

Marcus briefly recoiled at the overpowering odor of cheap cologne before the wind shifted and carried it away. Havana politely but tersely responded to every question, occasionally trying to include Marcus in the conversation, subtly sliding a little closer to Marcus every time she shifted her weight from one leg to the other.

Marcus mostly stood and observed with a mixture of annoyance and fascination. Brock, undoubtedly recognizing that he would need to work on Havana a lot longer than he had time for today, abandoned his pursuit of her and switched to talking about the kegger the Alphas were having near the "end of sesh," which apparently meant at the end of the summer session, suggesting she should come with a bunch of her sorority sisters. Havana asked whether Marcus, Dylan, and the Betas were invited too.

"Well, maybe a few," said Brock, "but we don't want it turning into a total sausage fest."

Havana told him she'd think about it, and she grasped Marcus's arm. "Want to go for a walk?" she asked as she led him away with her eyes wide, like someone being kidnapped begging for help with just their eyes.

After they had walked out of earshot of the group, Marcus told Havana that he saw what she meant about pretending to be on an anthropology expedition.

Havana nodded. "I know. I mean, Brock, dude, you think I'm impressed by your dick move of stepping between me and the person I'm talking to?"

"And he looked like he was trying to cheat at a slip-and-slide contest with all that oil all over his hairless body," Marcus added, eliciting a laugh from Havana.

Havana, impersonating a British television nature program narrator's voice, excitedly but quietly said, "We've just now entered the coastal sand area of New Miami, the home territory of *Fraternicus douche-bagus*. Our anthropologists need to be on high alert. They don't want to trigger *Fraternicus*'s sexual hormones. It is when *Fraternicus* is looking for a mate that he is most dangerous."

Marcus, impersonating a British journalist, jumped right into Havana's fantasy conversation without hesitation, shoving an imaginary microphone in front of Havana's mouth. "I'm here with world-famous anthropologist Havana. Miss Havana, tell the audience, please, if you would, about the speaking patterns of *Sororitus uptalkitus*. Why, for example, does *Sororitus* stand with her mouth agape, and only close it to form words as she speaks?"

"Well, Sir Marcus, we have narrowed it down to one, or possibly two reasons. First, they might be signaling with nonverbal communication to potential mates with delicate egos that they are slack-jawed simpletons who pose no intellectual threat. The other option is that they are signaling that they are in a constant state of readiness to perform fellatio."

Marcus howled with laughter. Havana smiled at him. She clasped Marcus's hand, intertwining her fingers with his. With her free hand, she started twirling a strand of hair that had come loose from her bun, then turned to him and let her jaw hang slack. In her best imitation of one of her sorority sisters, she said, "I, like, um, like romantic walks? On the beach? And like, candlelight dinners? And like, um, BMWs and stuff?" She ended the impersonation, but their hands lingered together a little longer.

Marcus laughed and called Havana a dork.

"Hell yeah, I'm a dork!" Havana retorted. "I fully embrace my inner dork. Embracing your inner dork is the key to happiness."

Marcus and Havana got quiet for a while and just listened to the ocean waves crashing on shore as they walked. Secretly he was incredibly turned on by her having held his hand briefly, but after an unfulfilling relationship with Stacie, followed by his awful blind date with Simone, he was feeling uncertain about the prospect of dating someone. His life being so tumultuous, with cross-country treks and with no idea where his future was going wasn't helping, either. Marcus broke the silence with a more serious question. "So, you said you're pre-med earlier. What year are you?"

"I'm between my freshman and sophomore years." She looked at him and then quickly added, "But I'm advanced placement, so I'm only eighteen. Only one year older than you, I imagine."

"In NEUS, an older woman would never go for a younger guy,

but in the last few weeks, I've seen all sorts of topsy-turvy things that make me question whether any of the rules of NEUS apply anywhere outside of NEUS. So, I've gotta ask..." Marcus's voice drifted from serious to a goofy sorority-girl impersonation as he continued. "Now that we've, like, gone for a romantic walk? On the, like, beach? Would you be interested in, like, joining me? For, um, like, a candlelight dinner?"

Havana laughed. "Dork."

"Hell yeah, I'm a dork too!"

"Yes. I'll go out to dinner with you. Not tonight, though. I have to study for an exam, but I'll go out with you another night. Speaking of another night, the sun is about to set on today. We should get back to campus before it gets dark out. After dark, the security guards go home, and the homeless invade the beach. As much as I feel for them, they are desperate and ruthless, and unfortunately it just isn't safe to be here at night."

They rejoined Dylan and Kelsey and headed back toward campus, with Kelsey dominating the conversation for a change, talking nonstop about the upcoming Alpha Sigma kegger and how she couldn't wait to go, and how everyone just had to go with her. "It's going to be the most important party of the summer," she insisted. Everyone who was anyone would be there. Dylan eagerly confirmed he was a "yes."

"An evening in Tartarus?" Havana whimpered before unenthusiastically saying, "I guess."

Marcus suspected she viewed it more as going as a chaperone for Kelsey than to enjoy the party, but if Havana was going, then so was Marcus. *Like Havana said, if you're going to immerse in the culture, might as well go all in,* he thought. It was agreed.

They reached the girls' sorority first, allowing the boys to pretend they had been chivalrous and walked the girls home before Havana pointed them in the right direction to get back to their dorm. Havana asked Marcus to hold on a minute while she wrote down her phone number on a piece of paper and slipped it to him.

Walking through the doors of the Rourke Oil Dormitory, the cloud nine that Marcus was walking on was yanked out from under him, landing him in a sinkhole of chaos. Of the eight stories in the building, every room on the bottom three floors, plus more than half of their fourth floor, were occupied, and almost every room that was occupied had a stereo blasting different music and cigarette smoke billowing out into the hallways. The giddy, hormone-driven energy he had from asking Havana out on a date gave way to the reality of having traveled on an early-departing transcontinental flight, and a headache brought on by noise, smoke, and fatigue ensued.

As they walked to their room, they passed the open door of a neighboring room with at least eight people crammed in it. One of the occupants jumped to his feet and stuck his head out the door, revealing his bloodshot eyes as he invited them in for "Rasta pasta." Dylan pounced at the opportunity, but Marcus declined and headed back to the room.

He sat on his lumpy bed, crammed wads of toilet paper into his ears, and put his airplane headphones over his ears like earmuffs before starting to pick classes and to fill out more registration contracts and paperwork. He was hungry, but he didn't feel like finding out what Rasta pasta was, nor did he want to shout over loud music or inhale smoke.

He dug through his bag to find a couple of granola bars that Sharon had given him in case he got hungry on the flight from San Francisco and ate them while he picked out classes for the four-week summer mini-session that had already started that day. He texted back and forth with Havana a few times, asking if a class he was considering was good, relying on the class data her sorority had compiled over the years and the experience she had gained in the eight weeks she had under her belt for her full-summer session. He picked out a couple of classes that he thought might be appropriate for Dylan too, since time was of the essence for getting into classes that had already started, and Dylan clearly wasn't going to be selecting any that evening. Sleep that night was delayed and intermittent at best.

Chapter 4: Competitive Food Ordering

Tuesday morning, Marcus woke Dylan up early and forced him to go back to the registrar's office as soon as they opened to select classes and pay tuition. That afternoon, while Havana took her exam, Marcus attended his first class in a sleep-deprived fog without any of the required books. Dylan skipped his first opportunity to attend a class and went back to bed hung over. Marcus suspected he had learned as much in his first day of class as Dylan had, and he took a late-afternoon nap just before the evening noise kicked in, leading to another night of poor sleep.

Wednesday night, Havana made good on her promise to go on a dinner date with Marcus. He asked Havana to pick a restaurant she liked, saying that he didn't know the area well enough to pick one. It was true, but at the back of his mind was his date with Simone and her immediate criticism of his choice of restaurants. If Havana picked the restaurant, then at least that particular catastrophe wouldn't repeat itself. Havana alleviated another fear of a Simone catastrophe by immediately rejecting Marcus's offer to be a gentleman and treat and insisting that they go Dutch and split the bill.

Marcus walked over to the Sigma Lambda Tau sorority, and then they strolled together to the restaurant. Immediately upon entering, they both coughed as they were greeted with billows of cigarette smoke. Marcus, trying his best not to sound like Simone with immediate criticism of her restaurant choice, asked, "Do you know if they have a non-smoking section?"

"Sort of. Not really," Havana replied. "All restaurants in New Miami are like this, though. Smoking is allowed everywhere. It's awful. I think I'm going to end up with lung cancer just from this one summer of study abroad."

Marcus looked around the restaurant. It was fairly large in

footprint but not very full. Rows of booths flanked the side window-walls, with a line of square tables down the middle of each row. It seemed excessively well lit for evening dining. "So, what inspired you to pick this place?" he asked.

"It is one of the few remaining mom-and-pop operated mini-chains left in the region," Havana said, "and they offer a relatively eclectic menu. Everything else has been gobbled up by large corporations and only has a limited selection of comfort foods, such as hamburgers, fried chicken, or some slight variation of those two dishes, all loaded with plenty of sugar, fat, and salt. All volume and profit and no quality, diversity, or healthiness. For a region that prides itself in freedom of choice, it is amazing how few options there are to choose from."

The hostess seated them in a window booth after Havana prompted Marcus to give her the customary small bribe for service. Marcus had requested the non-smoking section, but apparently that just meant a row with a couple of ceiling fans in operation, which didn't help the situation at all. In fact, it seemed to make things worse, as it sucked in smoke from the next row over and blew it back down to their row.

As they reviewed the menu, Havana made a suggestion. "Let's do what I like to jokingly refer to as 'competitive food ordering.'" Marcus raised an eyebrow. "We each pick a meal and a side dish, and then trade bites of each and judge whose main dish and side dish tasted best, and therefore who the 'winner' of ordering is for the evening."

Marcus smiled. "Sounds dorky and wonderful, just like you! I'm in."

Havana went with what Marcus thought was a daring main dish: some sort of alligator-meat dish in a sauce that he was unfamiliar with. For a side, she got sautéed spinach. Marcus ordered a carbonara pasta dish with a side of coleslaw.

Throughout the evening's two-hour dining experience, they immersed themselves in conversation. The topics meandered from Marcus and Dylan's coast-to-coast journey and back to Havana's travels in Europe. From Havana's love of theater to their discovery of their mutual love of the *Star Trek: The Next Generation* TV show. From favorite and least-favorite childhood memories to Marcus's athletic endeavors and his friendship with Dylan. From analysis of their educational experiences to Havana's desire to become a doctor and Marcus's thoughts about going into engineering of some sort.

During the discussion of Havana's trips to Europe, she revealed that she was fluent in Spanish, about seventy-five percent fluent in French, and that everyone in Puerto Paz who was born and raised there was at least bilingual, often trilingual. "You speak French, Spanish, English, *and* Sorority Girl?" asked Marcus. "Very impressive. And here I barely speak English, my one and only language."

When they were nearly finished, Marcus watched as Havana took a piece of bread and mopped up the leftover sauce on her plate with it, leaving behind a nearly clean plate. She looked up at Marcus's plate, which still had plenty of oily sauce on it. "Mind if I saucer?"

"So-say?" Marcus asked, repeating the sound of the word she had said but not understanding its meaning.

"It's a French word. It means to clean the sauce off a plate with a piece of absorbent food. Why waste perfectly good food? It's inefficient."

"Yeah, right. Like you aren't asking to saucer my plate because I won the competitive food ordering and you just want more of my awesome meal!" Marcus said teasingly.

"Oh, you think so, do you? Well, I think you are half right. You won the main dish, but I won the side dish, so we are tied."

"But come on, the main dish has to be worth more points than the side dish...it's the *main* dish."

"Nope. Equal points for main and side. We tied. Plus, I ought to dock you for ordering a dish with bacon in it. That's practically cheating," Havana replied, clearly trying to keep a straight face but failing.

"I think I need to find myself a copy of the rule book for competitive food ordering," Marcus said, squinting his eyes in faux distrust.

Marcus didn't want the date to end, so he suggested that they splurge and order dessert, even though he was already pretty stuffed. Havana agreed on the grounds that they needed a tie-breaker to decide the ultimate "winner of dinner." Marcus ate his fudge and ice cream dessert as slowly as he could, and Havana seemed to be in no hurry to wrap things up either. As their desserts diminished and the dinner portion of the date was winding down, Marcus felt a little safer, knowing that if he said something too intimate at this point in the evening, then at least the two of them wouldn't be trapped there for all of dinner, feeling awkward because of it.

He watched her dip her spoon into her bowl as he tried to muster up the courage to tell her how he felt. She turned the spoon upside down and slowly licked it clean as her gaze lifted and met with his.

"It is so nice to spend time with someone who understands me so well. I...I feel I can truly be myself with you," he stammered. "I'm not sure I've ever felt that way before. You are stunningly attractive, and I feel like you are my equal in all ways. Except maybe you are my superior in terms of emotional intelligence and language skills. It is just...such a pleasure talking with you."

The pleasant, unassuming smile on her face kept Marcus from breaking eye contact. "Aww," she said. "That's really sweet. Or really sad that you haven't experienced that feeling before. Or both really sweet and really sad at the same time." She smiled again. "I feel the same way about you. You are like a breath of fresh air in a land full of narcissistic and obnoxious frat boys." She leaned forward, inviting him to meet her at the middle of the table. "You are intelligent"—she interrupted her sentence to give him a quick peck on the lips— "inquisitive"—another kiss—"sensitive"—another kiss—"and caring." She ended with a final kiss.

"Don't forget athletic and stunningly handsome," Marcus joked before flashing a cheesy smile.

"Oh, did I forget to say modest? Good. I meant to forget to say modest," Havana sassed back.

They paid their bill, and Havana asked, "Waddlamos?"

"Huh?"

"Waddlamos. It's a Spanglish word I invented that combines the English word 'waddle,' as in, I've eaten so much food that I can no longer walk and instead have to waddle, with the Spanish 'we' form of the verb conjugation 'amos.' Technically it should probably be 'waddlemos,' but I just like the sound of 'waddlamos' better. I figure if the founders of Puerto Paz can drop the 'de' from the country's name, then the precedent has been set for me changing which letter a Spanglish verb I invented uses."

They waddled out of the restaurant together, having completely forgotten to decide the ultimate food ordering winner.

On the way back to campus, Marcus lamented going back to the dormitory for another night of noise, smoke, and insomnia. Havana told him that the rules of the sorority house were that guys weren't supposed to stay overnight or even enter the bedrooms, but that the rule was broken on a nightly basis by the majority of the girls. With the caveat that there wouldn't be any hanky-panky, she offered to let him stay over with her. He jumped at the chance to both get a decent night of sleep and spend more time with Havana.

As they walked past the sorority's lounge, Marcus spied a TV playing and asked Havana whether she wanted to stay up a bit later and watch something. "Unfortunately, everything here is pay-to-play garbage," she said. "Only some vapid, over-the-top melodramatic reality-show entertainment, heavy on the product placement, mixed in with an extraordinary amount of advertisements and infomercials. The remote control doesn't even have a mute button to block out the ads. Even the news is garbage. They only report what the corporations tell them to, and they even control which political candidates get airtime. It is nothing but crap."

After sneaking up to her room and slipping into their underwear for bedtime, Marcus kept his promise of no hanky-panky and didn't even try to snuggle with her. Havana read from a textbook by the light of her bedside table lamp, and Marcus nearly immediately passed out from exhaustion.

Thursday morning, they stumbled groggily down to the kitchen, where Havana greeted the Mr. Coffee-brand coffee maker by saying, "Well, hello, Mr. Coffee. I thought for sure we knew each other well enough by now to drop the formalities and just call each other by our first names."

Marcus giggled, which caught the attention of one of the girls in the adjacent dining room. She entered the kitchen in her silk pajamas and with excessive amounts of makeup around her eyes that made her look like a raccoon, and immediately smiled and said, "Havana! You slut! It's about damn time you got into the Boyfriend Bingo game! He's black, and is he younger than you? Are you younger than Havana? That is like, literally, a double bingo score if he's both black and younger than you, you slut!"

"Morning, bitch," Havana replied.

"I'm Reagan, chief bitch in this house," she said to Marcus. "Come on in the dining room, and I'll introduce you to a few more sluts." She beckoned them with a hand gesture to follow.

"Gimme a sec. I need my coffee first," Havana replied.

"Boyfriend Bingo?" Marcus asked after Reagan had returned to the dining room. "Slut? Bitch?"

Havana took her first sip of coffee and sighed with relief. "They use the words 'slut' and 'bitch' like terms of endearment for some reason. Don't ask me why. I have no idea. I once asked if calling each other 'sluts' had to do with the sorority's acronym, but I just got blank stares in response. I just play along to not disrupt the culture and make the natives suspicious. Boyfriend Bingo is a game they play, where they all have the same bingo card with different types of guys in each square, and they compete to see which sister can bang guys fitting the descriptions to fill up a row on the bingo card."

"You gonna break her heart and tell her we didn't sleep together?"

"I'm sure it won't be long before I can dearchive my bingo card and mark you down. It'll be true soon enough," Havana said. She smiled wryly at him.

"I can live with that," Marcus said, trying to play it cool and stifle his arousal.

Marcus got his cup of coffee, and they walked into the living room to a rowdy chorus of "woo-hoos" from all the girls at the table. Marcus buried his face in his coffee mug. Reagan settled them down, saying, "Okay, like, listen up, bitches. Havana's gonna introduce her new boy toy to y'all."

Havana smiled tightly. "Hey, everyone. This is Marcus. Marcus, this is everyone."

Reagan spoke up again, saying, "Well, part of everyone. A bunch of bitches are still in bed, and other sluts aren't attending summer sesh. Kelsey said you two already met. Going around the table, there's Cassidy, Chloe, Chelsea, Britney, Whitney, and Abbey."

Marcus noticed the now-familiar sorority-girl speech pattern as Reagan spoke, plus a new wrinkle. The girls' names typically ended with an "ee" sound, except the way Reagan pronounced them it was with a drawn out "ay" sound. "Brit-nayyy." "Whit-nayyy." He looked around the table and wondered whether the dead-behind-the-eyes look he saw in them was just because it was morning and they weren't fully awake yet or if that was normal. The raccoon-eye makeup that most of them had on wasn't helping.

One of the girls, Something-ayyy, said she didn't have the black-guy space on her bingo card filled in yet and asked whether she could have Marcus after Havana was done with him. Havana just rolled her eyes. Marcus gave Havana that same wide-eyed kidnapping victim "help me" look that she had given him at the beach volleyball court a few days earlier and said, "Breakfast?"

Havana walked him back to the kitchen to get some food, and later Marcus headed back to the dorm to grab a shower and some fresh clothes before going to his first class of the day.

Chapter 5: It's a Standard Contract

Before his date with Havana, Marcus had called the athletic department and scheduled a meeting with the head coach of the football team for him and Dylan. Thursday afternoon, after his class was over, he headed back to the dorm to rouse Dylan from a nap and head to the meeting with Coach Somers.

At New Rochelle High School, his coach's office had been a dingy, poorly lit little box with a cheap, beat-up metal desk left over from the 1940s, so he was quite surprised when he walked into Coach Somers's office to see an expansive parlor with gleaming, ornately carved matching cherry furniture and a leather couch off to the side facing a large screen, wall-mounted flat-panel TV.

Coach Somers motioned for them to come in and sit down without saying a word or looking up from the paperwork he was working on and made them sit there quietly for a couple of minutes as he finished what he was doing. Finally, he looked up and with a slow, Southern drawl, said, "So you think you got what it takes to play football at Miami University?"

"Yes, sir," Marcus responded. "At New Rochelle High, I was an all-state and conference MVP running back, and Ohio State had verbally committed to offering me a scholarship next year. In track I finished second in the 100-meter at State. In school, I've been getting straight A's. Dylan here is an excellent kicker, and he plays wide receiver too, so he'd be good for trick plays on special teams."

"Coleman, you said your name is?"

"Yes, sir."

Coach Somers rustled some papers in front of him, then placed his index finger on one of them. "Our recruiters seemed to think you'd end up in the northern conferences. Said it wasn't worth the money it would take to go after you. You're a year early too."

"Yes, sir."

Coach Somers proceeded to explain to the boys, with what Marcus perceived as a condescending attitude, that the team's roster was full for the year. They had already started practices two weeks ago, they had no scholarships to offer this year, and that the best they could do was try to walk-on and then redshirt. He added that he was more likely to cut players to make roster limits than he was to add them.

The boys both nodded that they understood and said they still wanted to try to walk-on. Coach then opened a desk drawer and pulled out a couple of thick booklets. He tossed one in front of each boy, placed a silver pen on top of each, and told them they'd have to sign the contracts. Dylan took the pen, flipped the book open to the last page, signed it, and tossed the book back while Marcus opened the book and started reading it.

"What the hell did you just do?" Marcus asked Dylan.

"I signed the contract that will let me play football."

"You didn't even read it. We're in SEUS. We have to read every contract very carefully."

"It's all boilerplate mumbo jumbo. I'm sure it's fine. I just wanna play." He turned to Coach Somers. "You need anything else from me, or are we all set?"

"We're all set. Practices start at seven a.m. every weekday at Vaughn Field. We'll deal with equipment and playbooks later."

Dylan got up and left, but Marcus continued reading. Coach Somers returned to the paperwork he had been doing when they first arrived. As he read, Marcus made a mental note of a clause stating that the athlete must accept all treatment offered by trainers. In NEUS, there were rumors that SEUS schools all had steroid programs for their athletes. It was likely why NEUS schools refused to play SEUS schools. If the rumors were true, then this clause seemed to be making it mandatory that he take steroids. He continued reading.

"Hey, Coach?" Marcus asked. "What does this five-year non-compete clause mean?"

"It means what it says it means," Coach responded without looking up.

"Well, it seems to be saying that I'm not allowed to play for any other school for five years from the date I sign this contract."

"Yup."

"If you don't give me a scholarship now, and I sign this, then what happens next year? Why would you give me a scholarship next year when you have me locked into this non-compete clause as a walk-on? My choice would be either continue playing here without a scholarship or quit football entirely."

"It's a standard contract."

Marcus tossed the contract back on the desk. "I'm not signing this."

Coach Somers finally looked up. He slammed his hand down on the contract and stood up, hunching over and pointing his index finger at Marcus. "This is the fucking contract!" he shouted. "Everyone signs the fucking contract! You think you're special? You want to play, you sign the fucking contract!"

Marcus initially recoiled into the back of his chair, clutching the seat, shocked by the sudden aggressive shouting. Midway through the coach's rant, he remembered the conversation he'd had with Sharon in San Francisco about their father and how he had realized that his father's bullying came from a place of weakness, not strength. He folded his arms, let the muscles in his face relax, and watched the coach finish his rant with detached amusement.

Marcus thought of the assertive way that Havana had spoken to the registrar's office clerk the first day they had arrived and did his best imitation of her now. "I am pretty special," he said calmly. "I'm one of the top prospects in the country, and this is a shit contract. I'm not signing anything that requires me to take steroids, and I'm not signing anything with a non-compete clause that lasts more than one season. You want me? Give me a fair contract."

Coach sat back down in his chair and muttered, "Fuck. Admin's gonna have my head." He sat there muttering quietly to himself some more. "Okay, good for you. You're a smart kid. Come to practice tomorrow morning. We'll draw up a different contract by Monday morning that removes the mandatory trainer treatment and reduces the non-compete to one year."

"One *season*. One year would still put me into next year's season."

"Yes, one season. We'll draw up the new contract, and you can sign it Monday."

Chapter 6: Frat Party Punch

By the third week of Marcus's four-week summer session, he found himself adjusting to his college classes. The "pull yourself up by the bootstraps" mentality of NEUS that had been instilled in him throughout his childhood had trained him for this type of setting, where the professors really didn't care whether their students passed or failed and often didn't put much effort into lectures. It was basically a self-taught curriculum, with a deadline and an exam at the end to prove you had learned the material on your own. Marcus quickly realized that the tuition he was paying wasn't for an education but rather for a piece of paper saying he had an education.

Football practices had, to this point, been mostly conditioning, weight training, learning plays, and watching the starters. The non-starters hardly did any practices with pads yet. Coach Somers still hadn't gotten a revised contract together for Marcus. Marcus didn't mind, though. It felt great to be physically active again, and if he wasn't going to play this season, then a contract didn't really matter since it left him free to do whatever he wanted.

He had been spending most nights at Havana's sorority, and a few days after his first sleepover they had consummated their relationship and confirmed that they were seeing each other exclusively. He hadn't seen that much of Dylan the last couple of weeks. In the mornings, when Marcus went back to the dorm to shower and change, Dylan was usually hung over and sleeping in. They were in different classes, so he never saw him on campus. At football practice, the special teams squad almost never interacted with the offensive squad.

Dylan and Kelsey seemed to still have a casual relationship going, and once in a while he would see Dylan at the sorority, but usually just in passing. They spent a little time together on the

Thursday night preceding the big Alpha Sigs party that Kelsey was still all aflutter about. She had invited Dylan over for a mini fashion show with some of her sisters to help her pick out what outfit to wear to the party, and she dragged Marcus and Havana in as judges too.

Friday night arrived, and Marcus and Dylan finally got some time together at the dorm while preparing for the party. They mocked Kelsey a little behind her back by putting on a two-person boys' fashion show where they kept taking off and putting on every shirt they owned and commenting on how "hot" or "not hot" it was before finally putting on exactly the same shirt they had started with. They walked over to the sorority together for a pre-party dinner with the girls, making small talk and catching up on each other's last few weeks a bit as they walked.

After dinner, the entire sorority together with their various dates and plus ones headed out as a group to the Alpha Sigma fraternity house. Havana told Marcus that it was tradition for each sorority to show up as a group at their appointed time and be officially greeted by the upperclassmen of the fraternity outside of the house before being received into the house.

Upon arrival, they were met by the welcoming crew. A large group of Caucasian peacocks stood on the front porch, all dressed in similar-looking plaid shorts, deck shoes with no socks, and the same navy-blue polo shirt with the fraternity shield monogrammed on the chest and their collars turned up. Marcus saw the asshole from the beach, Brock, front and center on the porch with a clipboard in his hands, but tonight it appeared he wasn't top dog. Below him, at the bottom of the porch stairs, stood an excessively muscle-bound young man with his head tilted to the side and a cocky, lopsided smirk on his face. Marcus's first thought when he saw him was *steroids*. He was fairly tall, had the sunken eyes and thick eyebrows of a caveman, a chiseled jaw, and his dirty blond hair was spiked into the obligatory faux-hawk.

Reagan spoke up in a loud voice over the muffled sound of a rock band playing inside the house, declaring, "Men of Alpha Sigma fraternity, I present to you the women of Sigma Lambda Tau and their guests."

The frat leader at the bottom of the stairs responded, loudly announcing, "Women of Sigma Lambda Tau and guests, the men of

Alpha Sigma welcome you. I am Apollo, president of Alpha Sigma. Assembled in front of you are the upperclassmen of our fraternity. I present to you our council members: Brock, Cody, Zayne, Blake, Brody, Connor, Vince, Conrad, Spencer, Cameron, Trey, Tanner, and Tyler. Please enter."

As the group from the sorority began filing up the porch stairs to the front door, the upperclassmen on the porch stood aside to make a path. Apollo made another announcement. "Inside you will find that the Alpha Sigma plebes are at your service. They are unworthy of introduction. Anything you need, just grab a plebe and order them to do it. If the plebe does not comply or displeases you, feel free to spit on the plebe. They are also here to clean up puke, so don't let puking stop you from drinking more."

As Marcus and Dylan stepped onto the first tread of the porch stairs, Apollo leaned toward them, flexed his pecs, and glared at them, maintaining the lopsided smirk on his face the entire time. Havana was just behind them, and after Marcus passed Apollo, he heard him cheerily say, "Hi, Havana!"

At the top of the stairs, Brock was furiously scribbling tick marks as people walked past him. As he checked off Marcus and Dylan on his clipboard, he nodded at each of them and gave them a "Hey, brah" greeting with a tone of voice that conveyed that he was surprised to see them at the party. Marcus caught a glimpse of the clipboard and saw that it was a tally of males and females.

As they reached the middle of the crowd of frat boys, Marcus was overwhelmed by the stench of cheap cologne. He held his breath mid-inhalation until he crossed the threshold of the front door. Upon entering, he took a deep breath, which drew in a large volume of thick cigarette smoke from the partiers who had arrived before them, and he began coughing.

The volume of the music coming from the basement more than doubled once inside, and he could feel the drums and bass through his feet as he walked, but the floor was still muffling the sounds, making the vocals undecipherable. The makeshift bar was on this level, so they queued up on their way to the stairs to the basement and each got a plastic cup of beer on the way down.

"Disgusting!" Marcus said as he pointed at the second option for a drink: a tub of spiked red punch that had a sign hanging above it that said "menstrual punch." A ring of people surrounded the tub, grabbing unused tampons that had been dangled in the punch and then dipping the soaked tampons into their mouths and sucking the punch out.

"I give them kudos for originality, at least," Havana said, seemingly unfazed.

The music clarity crystallized as they walked down the stairs. It was some sort of rock-dance music hybrid. Rock guitars and vocals but set to a more techno-dance drumbeat and a bass line that bridged the two sounds together. A banner hanging from the ceiling over the band identified them as Mute Button. The music was surprisingly good, but as they reached the basement floor, Marcus felt a tightness in his lungs as he breathed in air that was smoky, stale, and damp with perspiration and respiration. Most of the other attendees had preceded their arrival, and the basement was growing hot and crowded with all of the dancing bodies. The odors of cheap men's cologne, women's perfume, and cigarette smoke became even more overpowering than they had been upstairs.

Dylan and Kelsey wormed their way toward the center of the dance floor and disappeared into the orgy of rhythmically writhing and rubbing bodies. Marcus and Havana clung to the wall, sipping their beers and observing the horny chaos around them. The smokers were mashed up along the walls with them, not that being at the center of the dance floor would have helped escape their plumes in this confined habitat.

Marcus could hear bits and pieces of shouted conversations of the people nearest them. It seemed to all be hormone-driven small talk. Young men saying things like "you're hot" or "that's a smokin' hot dress"—anything shallow and trivial that might arouse the young woman and get them laid. The young women were mostly talking to each other, asking vapid questions about each other's lipstick or perfume. When the young men would hit on them, they would either dismiss them with a "K, bye" or smile flirtatiously and say "yeah" or "you're hot too" before heading off to the dance floor together.

Halfway through his beer, Marcus started feeling ill. He touched Havana's shoulder and shouted, "I think I need some fresh air."

"Me too," she shouted back, pinching her nostrils.

They shimmied their way through the crowd to the rear exit of the partially submerged walk-out basement and stood in the fresh air under the frat house's rear porch.

"Good lord," Marcus exclaimed after a few breaths of unscented air. "Everything around here is so loud. The music is loud. The speaking voices are loud. The advertisements are loud. Everyone even *smells* loud. They all smell like they dumped an entire bottle of cologne or perfume on themselves. It's like everyone is making a desperate plea for attention with an assault on all senses. It's obnoxious!"

"Welcome to Flori-duhhh," Havana responded. "I've tried over and over again to give the locals chance after chance to prove that they are more than just vacuous, shallow idiots, but they keep failing to prove me wrong."

"Ugh!" Marcus grunted in frustration. "This place sucks! I can't stand all these arrogant, immature narcissists!" He paused for a minute to calm himself down and sighed. "I shouldn't be so negative, I suppose. What good is complaining about it going to do, anyway?"

Havana shook her head. "Complaining isn't all bad. Sometimes it can be a good thing. It identifies what's wrong, which is the first step in making positive changes. Complaining leads to wishing, and wishing leads to action and change. The trick is to not get stuck in the complaining phase of the cycle."

Marcus nodded and leaned forward to give her a hug. "You are a very wise woman," he said.

Havana pulled her head back from the hug. "And don't forget smokin' hot and a great athlete too."

Marcus laughed. "Did I forget to say you were modest?"

Havana smiled, got up on her tippy toes, leaned her head forward, and closed her eyes to kiss him. They stood there embracing and kissing for several minutes. Finally, they pulled themselves away from each other. As Marcus opened his eyes, he caught the flash of a Caucasian ankle through the riserless porch stairs as it stepped from the top stair onto the porch above them. "I think we have company," he said, pointing up to the porch.

"You want to go back in?" Havana asked.

"Sure. The band is actually pretty good. It's funny that their name is Mute Button. They're the first thing in New Miami I've heard that I *haven't* wanted to hit mute on."

They went back inside through the basement door, standing against the wall near the door after inserting a plastic cup between the door frame and the door to keep it propped slightly open in an attempt to mix some cleaner air into the room. Dylan had danced his way near them, and they watched as a frat plebe delivered another beer to him. He grabbed the plebe's shirt at chest level with one hand while chugging the beer in a matter of seconds with the other. Dylan then thrust the empty plastic cup into the plebe's hand and signaled for another before returning to dancing, presently with no partner.

Marcus shook his head with disgusted amusement. The basement suddenly flooded with light, and he looked toward the stairs, where a group of a dozen Alpha Sigs, led by Apollo, descended the stairs with pissed-off looks on their faces. They began shoving their way through the crowd toward Dylan. The band leader halted the music and heads began to turn toward Apollo. Marcus took a couple of steps forward to see whether he needed to get Dylan's attention before they reached him, but as the frat boys got closer to Dylan, one of Apollo's minions leaned over Apollo's shoulder and pointed at Marcus. Marcus could lip-read the N-word well enough.

Apollo shifted his gaze from Dylan to Marcus, and the frat boys diverted their path toward Marcus. Marcus stood there frozen for a moment, not knowing what to do. He peeked to the side to check the path to the door, then as Apollo's full body came into view, he scanned him for signs of weapons.

Apollo scowled at him and started barking. "What the fuck? You think you can come into our house, at our school, and talk shit about us, you fucking nigger?" He reached Marcus and thrust his arms out, shoving Marcus in the chest.

Marcus took a couple of steps back to keep from falling over, regained his balance, and took one step forward.

Apollo barked again. "What the fuck's your deal, brah? You think you can come onto our turf and start making out with our sisters?" He shoved Marcus in the chest again, this time sending Marcus crashing into the basement wall. "You're gonna feel some pain, nigger!" Apollo shouted.

Marcus leaned away from the wall, planted his feet in a wider, bent-knee stance, tucked his chin slightly, and clenched his fists. He observed Apollo's stance, and his mind raced with possible next moves Apollo might make and how to counter each one.

If he rushes forward, then left knee up the center. Another shove against the wall, then clear the right arm, go left under his armpit for an arm drag, and reverse position to shove him head first into the wall. He glanced up into Apollo's furious eyes, noticing that his now-familiar peacock head tilt left his chin up and unprotected.

"You're gonna pay—"

A flash of white came streaking in from Apollo's right side. Dylan dove forward with a superman punch that landed squarely on the button, connecting with the side of Apollo's chin. Apollo's head spun to the side, and he went limp and collapsed forward onto the basement floor. He lay there unconscious, his chest robotically expanding and deflating with each autonomic breath.

Dylan squatted over Apollo's flaccid body, clutching his right hand. "If I wanted to hear an asshole, I would have farted!" he shouted.

Marcus looked up and then around toward the basement door. There were three, maybe four frat boys who could easily catch him and Havana before they could reach the door. There were an additional two or three who could grab Dylan before he would be able to reach the door. He teetered on the edge between fight or flight, unsure whether either option would get him out safely.

Several frat boys grasped Dylan's shirt. He squinted his eyes and prepared for them to start whaling on Dylan, but instead they grabbed Dylan and hoisted him up into the air, his head almost hitting the ceiling as they positioned him on their shoulders and began cheering. They all turned away from Apollo, still lying on the floor unconscious like he was yesterday's trash, and began chanting, "Ares! Ares! Ares!"

Marcus stood there, stunned. No one was attacking him. No one was punching Dylan. They were treating Dylan like he was a hero, even giving him the nickname of the Greek god of war!

Marcus turned to Havana. "I don't want to be here when Apollo wakes up." Havana nodded. Marcus jumped up and down, waving to get Dylan's attention. After a few seconds, Dylan spotted them. Marcus jabbed his thumb toward the basement door. Dylan shook his head and waved goodbye at them.

Marcus and Havana ducked out the door as the lights were turned down and the band started playing again. They quickly started walking in the direction of Havana's sorority.

"They need to add another 'Sigma' to the end of their name, 'cause those guys are a bunch of ASS-es!" she roared as they walked past the fraternity's yard sign and onto the street. They walked quickly, silently holding hands, heading away from the chaos. When they arrived back at Havana's sorority, the house was empty. They headed straight for Havana's room, disrobed, and crawled under the covers to cuddle.

"I still can't believe they didn't start beating up Dylan after he knocked out Apollo," Marcus said. "He's their leader, and Dylan attacked him."

"I don't think any of them like Apollo any more than you or I do. I think they just live in a culture that has a system of alpha-male bullies versus submissive subordinates. They followed Apollo because they felt obliged to follow him, and when Dylan knocked out Apollo, Dylan became the de facto alpha male," Havana replied.

As Marcus spooned her under the bedsheet, he could hear and feel Havana begin some meditative breathing to calm herself down. Marcus followed her lead and did a few rounds of controlled breathing himself. After Marcus felt a bit calmer, he spoke again. "You know what I don't get about people here? SEUS people believe in freedom from government, right?"

"Yeah," Havana replied.

"Well, why do they then turn around and hand that freedom over to a different group, like fraternities or corporations? It's just weird how rigidly conformist their culture seems, given their supposed love of freedom."

"I don't know. Maybe it's a sense of strength in numbers," said Havana. "I would guess that their culture of social Darwinism has led them to the idea that they need to be a part of a group in order to thrive, but they are only loyal to whoever has power at the moment. If the power shifts, so do their allegiances. What they don't seem to realize is that if everyone treats everyone else as a member of the same tribe rather than warring rival tribes, then together everyone achieves more. This whole 'us versus them' tribal mentality is unnecessary bullshit."

Havana rolled over to hug Marcus. They lay there silently for a while just holding each other and processing what had happened. Havana, with her face buried into Marcus's chest, finally broke the silence. "There's only one week of summer classes left."

"I know," Marcus responded.

"I go home next weekend. For good."

"I know. I haven't wanted to think about it, but I know."

"I don't want us to separate." Havana lifted her head up to look at Marcus's face. "Do you like it here?"

"At Miami U?"

"Miami U. New Miami in general. Florida. SEUS in general. Do you like this region?"

Marcus thought for a minute. "Except for meeting and spending time with you, no, I hate it here. If you weren't here, I think New Miami would be my least favorite of all the places I've been." Marcus paused for a second. "Now that I say it out loud, though, I'm realizing that I haven't really been happy anywhere I've been. New Rochelle, Wyoming, San Francisco, and now New Miami. Four different places, and the only thing in common is that I've been unhappy in every place. Is there something wrong with me? Dylan didn't seem unhappy everywhere. Am I just an unhappy person, and he's just a happy person? It's like he's a social chameleon who can fit in wherever he is, and I'm this rigid, stick-up-my-ass square who fits in nowhere."

"You've seemed pretty happy to me since I've met you."

"Yeah, but as soon as you go, I'll be miserable," Marcus said.

"Maybe you have higher standards than Dylan. He just accepts whatever garbage he's handed, but you expect better. Although I thought I remember you saying that he was pretty miserable in San Francisco."

"Yeah, he really hated San Fran. He hated New Rochelle too."

"Both order governments. And he has thrived where there are freedom governments. And he's immature as hell. Immature people often thrive in hedonistic settings where no one is trying to stop them or make them think about consequences and how their behavior affects the people around them."

"Hmm. Yeah. But I haven't thrived in either type," Marcus said.

"Maybe that's because they are too extremist. What do you think about going to Puerto Paz with me? I think you'd really like it there."

"My sister thought I would too. But I've just started getting established here with school and football. Football is my life, and this seems to be the only place where I can pursue it."

"You can do those things in Puerto Paz too. Listen. After summer session ends, there is a two-week break before fall session starts. Why don't you come with me to Puerto Paz for those two weeks and at least see it with your own eyes. You can treat it like a combo vacation and test run."

"What about Dylan?" Marcus asked.

"He's an immature asshole. Leave him here to be with all the other immature assholes."

"I can't do that. He has been my best friend since, well, forever. Since I can remember. We've been through thick and thin together. I can't turn my back on him like that. Especially given what he's been through in his life. Plus, he would absolutely flounder if I just abandoned him. He'd end up a homeless addict on the beach."

"What do you mean 'what he has been through in his life'?" Havana asked.

Marcus began filling her in on Dylan's rough childhood, between losing his mom at a relatively young age, and his dad's abuse.

"Shit," Havana said. "I think I've been in New Miami too long. This place has desensitized me into thinking that everyone who acts like an asshole *is* an unredeemable asshole who has bought fully into the bullshit culture. I had no idea Dylan had such a history of abuse and trauma. I can't believe I didn't recognize it. SEUS really brings out the worst in me. If Dylan is going to grow past this stunted level of personality development, then he needs psychotherapy and a healthy environment to grow in. He's not going to find that here. He should really be in Puerto Paz, getting the help he needs."

Marcus nodded and thought for a minute. "Coach hasn't been doing much with me, and he hasn't even gotten me a contract yet. I guess it couldn't hurt to go to Puerto Paz for a couple of weeks. I need to talk to Dylan about it, though. He's going to be a tough sell."

Havana hugged him tighter and said, "Yay!" before they drifted off to sleep.

Chapter 7: Caribbean Vacation

Saturday afternoon after brunch with Havana, Marcus headed back to the dorm to shower and to get his books to study for that week's upcoming final exams. After showering, while Marcus was still wearing nothing but a towel, Dylan walked in reeking of cigarette smoke and stale beer and looking like he hadn't slept the entire night. Dylan smiled sleepily at Marcus and gave him a nod and a "Hey, brah."

Marcus nodded back and said, "Hey."

Dylan collapsed into his bed, his face mushed into the pillow. He rolled onto his right side briefly, then shouted in pain, quickly rolling back over to his left side and clutching his right hand and groaning. "Oh my god. That was so much fun, but I'm gonna pay so hard for it today."

"You okay, buddy?" Marcus asked. "Looks like that punch hurt you almost as much as it hurt Apollo. You want me to go down to the vending machines and buy some ice for it?"

"Yeah, sure."

Marcus threw on some clothes, grabbed some cash, and retrieved some ice down the hall for Dylan's hand. Handing the ice to Dylan, he said, "Thanks for jumping in there last night. I was shitting my pants until you did that."

"Dude was an asshole. I just did what everyone else wanted to do."

"Hell of a shot. One-punch knockout. Good thing too. 'Brah' probably would have gone on a roid-rage had you not knocked him out with that first punch. What happened after I left?"

"Ugh. More partying. Heavy drinking. Other fun chemicals. I don't remember."

Marcus moved around the room, collecting books, pens, paper, and his calculator in preparation for going in search of a quiet place to study. He knew Dylan was on the verge of passing out and wasn't in any state for a conversation about the future, but he also knew that he was unlikely to cross paths with Dylan much in the final week of classes. If they were going to go to Puerto Paz the following week, they had to get planning underway ASAP.

"Hey, D?" Marcus asked. Dylan grunted. "Summer session ends this week, and after that there's a two-week break before fall session. Havana told me campus turns into a ghost town for those two weeks. What do you think about going on vacation to a Caribbean island with me and Havana? Maybe Kelsey too?"

"Yeah, sure. Sounds awesome. Talk to me about it in the morning. I mean the afternoon. What time is it? Talk to me about it later."

Marcus left to go study and didn't return to the dorm room for the rest of the day. At night he found himself back in Havana's room looking for a good night of peaceful sleep and Havana's companionship. Marcus lay in bed reading his physics book while Havana scurried around, doing the last of her bedtime preparations. When he noticed her bedtime routine winding down, he folded his book onto his chest and told her about his brief conversation with Dylan in the dorm room.

"A Caribbean vacation?" Havana asked.

"It's technically true. Puerto Paz is a Caribbean island, isn't it? And it might just be a two-week vacation."

"Yeah, but you're inviting him under false pretenses. You need to come clean with him about where he would be going and why you guys are going there."

Marcus sighed. "I know. But I don't want to. I know what his reaction is going to be already."

Havana just tilted her head to the side and gave him a look that said, *You should know better.*

Marcus thrust his head back and looked up at the ceiling. "Okay, okay...I'll tell him it's Puerto Paz, but I'm not ready to tell him it's to see if I want to live there permanently. I'll cross that bridge when I come to it, if I ever actually come to it. But I need you to help me sell Puerto Paz to him. He's going to start going off on a rant about commies and shit like that, and I want selling points that he'll go for. What can he do there that he'd consider fun? Parties? Hot girls?

Beaches? Alcohol? Illegal drugs, apparently?"

"One of the beach areas is known for being a bit of a party zone," Havana said while crawling into bed. "We don't have a drinking age for wine or beer, and for hard liquor it is eighteen. Marijuana is legal. Other drugs are available, but for harder drugs you have to register to use a drug room."

Marcus's eyes widened. "Really? They allow marijuana and hard drugs there? That's crazy! So, are all rumors from back home that Puerto Paz is one of the sources of the drug problems true? Are half the people just walking around high?"

Havana repeated her disapproving head tilt. "Puerto Paz isn't some sort of drug haven. Abuse of alcohol and drugs is usually a symptom of distress, and we have a healthier, more supportive society than here."

"I just can't believe they allow it at all. NEUS has a zero-tolerance policy about drugs."

"And how is that working for them? I've heard there are entire boroughs of cities that are too dangerous to walk in, even during daytime, because of the drug-related gang wars. Banning it only creates black markets and makes things worse."

"But as a medical student, you must know how drugs destroy lives and communities."

"We aren't heartless bastards like SEUS where they let people in trouble rot and die. If you make soft drugs legal and provide training and counseling along with a better functioning, fairer society, then people don't have the desire to abuse them. And if you make hard drugs legal to use at drug rooms staffed with medical personnel who control quality and dosage, and can advise on counseling, then in the rare case that someone somehow gets addicted, they have a safer path to recovery. Pragmatically, it is the best solution."

"Maybe.... So, what else can I sell Dylan on?" Marcus asked.

"Well, there are specific districts that allow nightclubs and loud music. Puerto Paz is consistently ranked one of the physically healthiest places in the world in terms of diet and exercise, so the women tend to have great bodies. They are also psychologically healthy, though, so they won't be into him unless he goes through some serious therapy and recovery. We also have plenty of free public beaches, but most are more family friendly."

"Is the water polluted? Are people allowed to swim in the ocean?" Marcus asked excitedly.

"The water is very clean, and yes, you can swim in the ocean."

"Yes!" Marcus nearly shouted, pumping his fist in the air. He picked his physics book back up and began reading again. A few minutes later he said, "I thought about having him invite Kelsey."

"Yeah, sure, I think she could use a break from the stress of trying to impress frat boys," Havana said. She paused for a moment, then added, "I still think you should tell Dylan your motives for going, though."

"In time, if it's needed." He closed his book, set it aside, and went to the bathroom to brush his teeth before going to bed.

The next time Marcus saw Dylan was Monday afternoon of exam week while back at the dorm room to restock his study materials. Dylan was lying in bed, sporting a new cast on his right hand and appeared to be on some sort of pain medication that numbed his personality and slowed his speech a bit. After Marcus inquired, Dylan informed him that he had been seen by the football team's trainers, and that they had x-rayed his hand and found that it was broken. The coach had kicked him off of practice squad until his hand healed because he couldn't recover botched snaps or do fake kicks with a broken hand, so Dylan was useless to the coach as a kicker, and they didn't want to waste supplies and staff time on him while he recovered. Marcus said he felt sorry for Dylan but simultaneously recognized this as an opportunity to sell Dylan on a trip to Puerto Paz.

"So, if you can't practice for the next few weeks, then Coach won't miss you if we go on that Caribbean vacation I mentioned Saturday, right?" Marcus asked.

"Yeah, man," Dylan responded in a haze with his eyes only half open. "Groovy, dude."

"I have to confess something about the vacation, though. The Caribbean island I want to go to is Havana's home country."

"Of course you do, man. You gotta follow that pussy wherever it goes, man."

"You remember where Havana's from, don't you?" Marcus asked. Dylan paused for a minute and seemed so deep in thought that Marcus wondered if he had gotten lost. "Puerto Paz," Marcus reminded him.

Dylan got a look on his face like a three-year-old about to throw a tantrum, but it quickly passed and he was back to loosey-goosey all of a sudden. "Commie Central? We're going on vacation to Commie Central?"

"It's not communist. It actually sounds really great. I think you'd like it too. Havana said the chicks are all hot, they have nightclubs, free public beaches with clean water and swimming allowed, no drinking age for beer and wine, legal pot. What harm can it do to go there for two weeks to kick back and relax?"

Dylan rolled over onto his stomach, buried his face in his pillow, and just muttered, "Meh."

"You in?" asked Marcus.

"Yeah," muttered Dylan.

"You want me and Havana to invite Kelsey too?"

"Yeah."

"I have an exam tomorrow morning, but after it's over, are you free to go to the passport agency?"

"Yeah."

"Okay, I'll text you after my exam to remind you."

"Kay," muttered Dylan.

Marcus left the room to go study, feeling simultaneously elated by the ends but guilty about the means. Had his father witnessed how Marcus had just convinced Dylan to go to Puerto Paz, he would have been proud of Marcus for the way he had prepared himself for battle with Dylan, preyed on his weaknesses, and attacked when his opponent's mind was enfeebled by pain medication. He wouldn't have *admitted* pride, but he would have been proud. *If only I had been so lucky with the Ohio State conversation with Dad. If Dad had been on strong pain medication, maybe that conversation would have been like shooting fish in a barrel too,* Marcus thought. *At least I get to spend another two weeks with Havana, and besides, if the situation were reversed and Dylan were trying to talk me into going somewhere I didn't want to go, I don't think Dylan would feel the slightest bit of guilt about manipulating me while I was at a disadvantage.*

Tuesday, after his exam, Marcus texted Dylan, and they met up and walked over to the passport agency. Like most things in SEUS, the agency had been privatized. Getting a passport for Dylan was

simpler than Marcus feared. Dylan's driver's license, his NEUS high
school ID, the expedited passport fee, plus a bribe to convince the
agent to look the other way while they forged Dylan's dad's signature
on his statement of parental consent after claiming his birth
certificate had been lost got them Dylan's passport in less than an
hour. It took longer to take the photos and make the passport
booklet than it did to get the minimal paperwork approved.
Corruption certainly is efficient, but at what cost? Marcus thought as
they walked out the doors of the agency.

The following Friday evening, Marcus, Dylan, Havana, and
Kelsey were all standing at the docks, luggage in hand, ready to
board the overnight ferry to Puerto Paz.

Part 5: Puerto Paz
Chapter 1: New Athens

The overnight ferry took nearly thirteen hours and arrived at Port Camille in Puerto Paz's capital of New Athens at eight a.m. on Saturday morning. Marcus, Havana, Dylan, and Kelsey disembarked and followed the herd of people toward the Customs and Immigration building's massive doors, each of which was flanked by tall, fluted Greek columns and capped with intricately carved pediments.

Marcus looked up at a series of domed cupolas, each enveloped in rings of smaller Greek columns that spiked the top of the gable roof, then back down at the oversized doors that seemed somewhat out of scale on the beautiful pink limestone façade. As they reached the doors, he focused on an intricately carved ornament centered in the pediment. The circular emblem was formed by curving olive branches, with an eight-pointed star, like the points of a compass, inscribed within the branches.

"What is that?" Marcus asked, pointing at the emblem.

"It is my reminder that it is good to be home!" she responded. "It is the symbol of Puerto Paz. We try not to get too crazy about symbols and flags and patriotic things like that, but the meaning embedded into that symbol always stirs my soul when I look at it. You see the small circle at the center with the six wedges that alternate light and dark colors? That is the radiation warning symbol that represents the birth of Puerto Paz having come from the nuclear annihilation of Cuba and the scientific and engineering work that had to be accomplished to make the country habitable again. The compass points indicate balanced and uniform progress in all directions. The olive branches surrounding everything represent peace being found in every direction."

They continued on through one of the garage doors. He looked up at the cavernous interior. Sunlight filtered through the cupolas and dormers spotlighting streams of tiny particles floating steadily up toward the cathedral ceiling. Hiding in the shadows, cranes hung from massive steel trusses that spanned the width of the building. He turned to look at Havana, who was looking back at him with an admiring smile.

"This building has won a lot of Pippas," Havana said. Marcus tilted his head in puzzlement. "P-P-As. The 'P.P.' is for Puerto Paz, the 'A' is for Award," Havana clarified.

"Pee Pee Awards?" Dylan said, laughing at the acronym. "Sounds like a potty-training award or something!"

Havana rolled her eyes. "Every December there is an award show on TV where the best works of all fields are presented. Entertainment, arts, engineering, science, you name it. I remember this building getting awards for multi-use and green tech. The floor you are standing on retracts to reveal docks that boats can be stored in during hurricanes. It also has passive ventilation and evaporative cooling systems, along with translucent solar collectors and tidal generators in the sea floor to make it hyper energy efficient."

Marcus raised his eyebrows and nodded while continuing to survey the interior. They moved farther into the building to where there was a sign indicating which roped-off lines were intended for what people. The sign had several major languages on it in smaller print under a bizarre language at the top that was in larger print. The second language down from the top was English. "The queue for North American citizens forms to the right in lanes 6 through 12."

Marcus pointed to the top of the sign, where the bizarre language read: "ðə kju fɔr nɔrθ əˈmɛrəkən ˈsɪtəzənz fɔrmz tu ðə raɪt ɪn leɪnz 6 θru 12" and asked, "What language is that?"

"Russian," Dylan said. "Told ya they were a bunch of commies here."

"It isn't Russian," said Havana. "It is IPA American English. It uses the International Phonetic Alphabet, but the words are almost all pronounced the same as American English. It is the official language of Puerto Paz, although we also use Spanish on everything to pay homage to our Cuban roots."

"It's so weird looking. Why not just use regular English?" Marcus asked.

"The country's founders believed in questioning all traditions and tossing the ones that don't make sense and fixing anything that was poorly functioning or inefficient. They saw the English language as being ridiculously and unnecessarily complex with completely inconsistent rules about spelling, pronunciation, and grammar. IPA was an opportunity to simplify the language. Every letter of our alphabet has a specific pronunciation that never changes no matter what the word. Every word is spelled phonetically and sounds exactly the way it looks."

"Let me guess," Marcus interjected. "Puerto Paz uses the metric system too?"

"Naturally. EUS is the only country in the world that doesn't."

Havana paused to look at the signage. "I have to go through a different line down here for citizens, but meet me at the Michael Debroux statue on the other side of the building, okay? After you get through immigration and customs, you will find a currency exchange kiosk where you can exchange some of your American dollars for Puerto Paz ergons."

As Havana disappeared, Dylan said to Marcus, "Dude, I think this might be the first time you and I have been together without Havana in like, forever. Let the Caribbean brah-cation begin! Two weeks of beaches, babes, and beer! Welcome to Fun 101, I'll be your party professor!"

"Um, like, hello?" Kelsey said. "Brah-cation? What about me?"

"Bros and babes," Dylan said. "But MC needs some special mentoring in the party arts without the Dictator of Dullsville getting in the way."

The threesome proceeded through the line, at one point going through a mini tunnel that a sign said was the security checkpoint. Marcus looked around for security guards but didn't see any. A monitor above was showing scanned images of people walking and carrying their baggage. Apparently the tunnel had scanned both him and his luggage as he casually walked through it without even needing to stop.

After the tunnel, two attendants directed people to available computer kiosks for brief immigration and customs interviews. Marcus, Dylan, and Kelsey each went to a different kiosk scattered throughout their designated area and filled out the survey. The kiosk screen asked them to scan their passports and confirmed their names and methods of contact before asking standard immigration questions such as how long they planned to stay in Puerto Paz and the purpose of their visit. Marcus struggled to answer the duration-of-stay question: "Do you plan to stay in Puerto Paz for two months or less, more than two months, or uncertain?" He looked around to make sure Dylan couldn't see his selection before finally choosing "uncertain."

Immediately upon exiting the kiosk area and reuniting with Dylan and Kelsey, the threesome each received an automated text message welcoming them to Puerto Paz and recommending that they download the official Puerto Paz app for emergency alerts, such as hurricane warnings, to get help, take surveys, and make or receive other important communication.

"What the fuck?" Dylan muttered. "I gave them a fake phone number. How the hell did they get my real number? Do I even need to download the app, or do those commies just force it onto my phone to track me without my permission?"

Marcus shrugged. "Guess you better behave or else they'll know."

They walked past a video monitor playing a welcome message from Puerto Paz president, Maria Pérez.

"Another chick leader," Dylan said, "just like San Fran. Sure sign of a liberal nanny state."

"I'm sure she's smarter than you," Marcus retorted.

They exchanged some dollars for ergons. Dylan laughed upon receiving his cash. "Dude! Is this real money? It looks like play money from a board game!"

Marcus looked at the cash with amusement. Every bill was a different size and color, and each had an electronic sticker embedded into it with a caption that read: "Scan here to convert to e-credit. Symbol will alter appearance and texture after conversion." He shrugged at Dylan. "I'm sure it will still buy you all the beer you want."

They continued out the exit to a grand courtyard with stone benches and well-groomed shrubbery. At the center was the statue of Michael Debroux, which Marcus recognized from the replica at the San Francisco City Hall exhibit. Havana was sitting at a bench not far away and stood up to greet them.

"Welcome to my home!" she said cheerily. "Welcome to Puerto Paz. I need to run to the bathroom, anyone else? The bathrooms are over thuhr," she said, pointing to one side of the courtyard.

"Thuhr?" Dylan said in a mocking tone.

"There," Havana clarified. "It is one of the words we had to change the pronunciation of for IPA English because it is a homophone."

"A gay word?" Dylan asked. "I thought you touchy-feely commies were pro-homo. You ban gay words here?"

Havana tilted her head and wrinkled her forehead. "No. Homophones are words that sound the same but are spelled differently. In our version of IPA American English, we've adjusted the pronunciation of some of those words so that they don't sound alike anymore, to make the language less ambiguous. For example, we kept the pronunciation of the 'their' indicating possession, adjusted the pronunciation of the 'there' indicating location to sound like th-uhr, and we have eliminated the 'they're' contraction and just say 'they are.' So, we would say something like 'They are putting their baggage over thuhr' instead of 'They're putting their baggage over there' with three different words all sounding the same."

"Huh. Makes sense, but I don't know how well I'd do learning a whole new alphabet at this point in my life," Marcus said.

"I think you'd be surprised at how easy the transition is. Just learn how to pronounce a few letters, and from there on, it is all phonetic. First-generation immigrants might struggle with it a little, but for later generations, it is so much more intuitive."

Dylan and Kelsey followed Havana to the bathrooms while Marcus volunteered to watch the baggage. He stood guard and began looking around at the building and grounds, and then the Debroux statue. This version was considerably larger than the one in San Francisco, and it had an inscription at the bottom quoting Michael Debroux's Oscar speech from February 2024 that read:

> *Life is rarely black and white. Typically,*
> *when viewed through a truthful lens, things are*

> *simultaneously both black and white, and appear as shades of gray. It is through that lens that I view this award. On one hand, I'm flattered, thankful, proud, and happy. On the other hand, every time I look at it, I'll be reminded that a police officer and firefighter whose jobs are to protect us, a farmer whose job is to feed us, a doctor whose job is to cure us, a teacher whose job is to educate our children, and a structural engineer whose job is to make sure buildings like this one we're in now don't collapse on us, could all work extremely hard for fifty years and be good at their jobs, and after that fifty years, they could pool all their money together and still not have as much money as actor Leonardo DiCaprio, whose job description is to pretend to be someone he's not for peoples' entertainment, makes for one single movie. Any society that allows that scenario to happen is backward. If you want a meritocracy, America, then first let's have a discussion about the definition of "merit."*

Marcus raised an eyebrow. It did sound a bit communist, he had to admit, yet he found himself agreeing with the sentiment. While living in NEUS, he had sometimes dreamed of becoming a professional football player. They made extraordinary amounts of money, despite only having careers that lasted less than ten years on average before retirement. His other career option likely involved some sort of engineering, a field that only made mediocre income, started at base salaries that weren't even enough to live on, and he'd have to work well into his seventies before he could even think about affording to retire. *What value does a football player provide to society compared to the value an engineer provides?* he wondered.

Havana, Kelsey, and Dylan all returned to the statue, and Havana led the group to the Port Camille subway stop across the courtyard. Havana stopped at a sign outside of the subway head

house with a large tourist map[3] on it and began playing the role of
tour guide, explaining the layout of the city to the foreigners.

"We are here, to the east along the New Athens Channel at Port
Camille." Havana pointed to the right side of the map. "There is the
East Train Station immediately to our southwest, and the
international airport across the harbor to the south. The heart of the
city is here at Central Park."

Havana pointed to a spot near the center of the map that had a
large green circle. "The Central Subway Station is in the middle of
Central Park, and the city is laid out in rings that radiate out from the
park. There are eight main avenues that emanate from Central Park
in the eight main compass directions, similar to the country's
symbol, that divide the city into eight different sectors. Unlike the
rest of the roads, these eight avenues were built straight as an arrow,
regardless of topography. Under each of the eight main avenues are
the four major subway lines that crisscross and go through Central
Station, plus a rail line in the east-west direction."

A small crowd of foreigners began to form around the map to
listen to Havana explain the layout of the city further. She went on to
describe the various coastal boardwalks that connected to linear
parks throughout the city and the two concentric circles of ring roads
that split the city into the Inner Ring and Outer Ring areas, as well as
the eight pie-shaped sectors that the major avenues and subway
lines sliced the city into.

"Where are the beaches and the bars?" Dylan asked. "That's the
part of the city I'm interested in."

"Right, mate!" chimed someone from the crowd with an
Australian accent.

"The good beaches are all across New Athens Channel, about
twenty kilometers to the east of where we are now. There is a direct
train to the beaches from the East Train Station. Playa Nueva is the
party area with a lot of clubs, but the rest of the beaches are more
family oriented. We can worry about beaches later, though. For now,
let's grab a subway into the center and go to the university area to
see if we can get you a cheap dorm room rental so you can store your
bags, and then we can go out for lunch and see the city."

---

[3] A copy of this map of New Athens is provided in Appendix 1

"Yes, ma'am," Dylan said while saluting Havana.

The foursome was about to head into the Port Camille subway head house when Marcus pointed into the distance at the East Train Station and asked, "Are those cars driving onto the train?"

Havana looked to where Marcus was pointing. "Yes. We call it 'piggybacking.' If you have an autonomous City Car, or if you rent one, the cars coordinate with the train station's boarding system to go to a designated spot in the double-decker loading platform. When the train arrives, the cars automatically drive onto the train and dock with it. Your car seat is your seat for the ride, and your car charges during your trip. When you reach your destination, the car automatically drives forward onto an opposing double-decker platform, and then you can go on your merry little way."

They continued down the stairs to the subway platform, past some multilevel shelving next to the track with a bunch of weird-looking wheeled boxes on it and past a section of people with bikes. Within two minutes, a subway arrived and they boarded. As they were pulling away from the station Marcus cocked his head and asked, "I don't remember paying to get on.... Is there some sort of fancy wireless payment system that pulls the fare off our phones without asking our consent or something?"

"Subway rides are free," Havana said. "Or rather, they are subsidized with taxes. It helps diversify transportation methods to keep the roads from getting overcrowded."

After a few stops, Havana said, "We could go all the way into Central Station, but let's get off here instead. I always like taking the Inner Ring gondola through Sectors 3 and 4. You'll see why!"

They exited the subway and lugged their baggage onto a glass elevator that took them three stories above ground to the gondola station. In no time, they were gliding over the streets in an air-conditioned, high-speed gondola that had a magnificent view of the business district high-rises and skyscrapers, plus an intermittent view of the lush greenery of Central Park in the background. Several times the gondola passed through the third, fourth, or fifth floor of high-rise buildings, providing a view into the interior workspace of the building.

"Holy shit!" Marcus exclaimed again. "We're going *through* the building! This is crazy!"

"I know!" Havana replied. "I absolutely love taking this ride. I love it even more on weekdays, though, when you get to see the hustle and bustle of all the employees as you go through their floor. Can you imagine working in one of these buildings and having your ride drop you off literally *in* your office?"

As they made their way to the end of the Sector 4 business district, Havana said, "Gondola, we're getting off at the South Avenue stop." The gondola slowed as it crossed over top of South Avenue. The view down the grand street opened up.

"This is one of the major avenues you mentioned?" Dylan asked. "Where are the rest of the lanes? There's only one lane per direction, plus a center turn lane for your commie cars to drive in. That's so stupid! Rush hour must be a bitch here!"

Marcus had been admiring the two rows of narrow, tree-lined linear parks that bracketed the three automobile lanes but now had his attention on the automobile lanes. The avenue was wide enough to fit at least seven full lanes, but the four outer lanes were occupied by the linear parks, plus very wide bike lanes sandwiched between the parks and the buildings.

"Does it look like only having three lanes for cars is causing a problem? Look at how many bicyclists there are versus how many cars there are," Havana said as the gondola diverted away from the main cable and branched off to enter the station.

They were directly over a bike lane, and Marcus saw dozens, possibly hundreds of bicyclists just in the few blocks splayed out in front of him. Probably at least quadruple the number of cars.

"There are a lot more options here than just cars, so we don't need as much space for them," Havana continued. "Plus, being automated, they work in concert, making traffic smoother. Most businesses and schools have staggered start times anyway, so rush hour gets diluted and spread out."

As the gondola entered the station, it came to a stop at a platform, where they exited and took an elevator down to street level, landing at the corner of the University of New Athens's downtown campus. Much like Port Camille, the UNA campus extensively featured pink limestone façades.

Marcus admired the architecture as they walked. The buildings had classical shapes and relatively simple forms, yet they had a grand appearance with coined corners, ornate mouldings and cornices, tall exterior columns, and occasionally statues either serving as columns or carved into the façade and corbelling out to support small canopies projecting off the sides of the building. Marcus was surprised to see that most of the buildings had ornate functioning shutters too.

After passing through an iron gate that had a decoratively sculpted iron banner over it reading "UNA Vida," Marcus turned around and pointed at it. "Why isn't that sign in IPA English?"

"The university is an international institution, so they predominantly use American English and Spanish. It is kind of like how Latin was used in medieval universities because it was a neutral language that people from all over could use. IPA English just hasn't caught on with the rest of the world yet," Havana said.

She continued navigating them through a corner of the campus to the housing department. They breezed through the rental process and were given summer dorm room rentals in the Jefferson Dormitory at reasonably low rates. The layout plan they were given to review indicated that the rooms were of similar size as the rooms in New Miami, plus they each had an attached bathroom, similar to a small hotel room.

"Solitary confinement?" Dylan joked after the housing department employee explained that all dorm rooms were single occupant only.

"You are free to invite people into your room," Havana said. "They just believe that each student needs a safe, quiet space to call their own, where they can be introspective or where students who skew toward the introverted end of the spectrum can recharge their energy levels"—Dylan began making a masturbation hand gesture—"and where everyone can get the proper amount of sleep on their own schedule without the constant interference of a roommate. Sleep is one of the basic human needs at the bottom of Maslow's Hierarchy, after all. And yes, it allows you to masturbate freely without fear of being caught, Dylan," she said with an eye roll.

Dylan balked again at a rule prohibiting amplified entertainment in the rooms, but Havana countered, saying, "There are soundproofed recreation and entertainment rooms on the lower levels that students are welcome to be noisy in."

"So, I have to go hide in a basement dungeon in order to listen to music?" Dylan said.

"You could use headphones for music in your room, but just as you don't shit in the same place you eat, you don't party in the same place you, or others, sleep. Your actions impact others, and it's just plain rude to disrupt people's sleep or peaceful enjoyment of their home. Noise-tolerant environments are rightfully opt-in, not opt-out," Havana said.

Marcus, Dylan, and Kelsey each deposited their bags in their respective rooms, with Havana following Marcus into his room to temporarily leave her bags and to grab a quick hug and smooch while they were briefly alone. As Marcus withdrew from the kiss, he looked Havana in the eyes. "When did you start wearing glasses?" he asked, suddenly noticing the stylish pair she was wearing. "Are they to make you look smarter or more stylish than you actually are?" he joked.

"I swapped out my SEUS sunglasses for my Puerto Paz glasses back at the port. These transition to completely translucent indoors, and they don't work in SEUS," Havana said.

"How could they not work in SEUS?"

"They are e-glasses. They replace phones. They are basically mini-computers that connect to the wi-fi here and that have view screens, a microphone, and speakers on this little projection near the ear," she said, placing her finger on a decorative stub extending from the temple of the glasses. "My bracelet here also doubles as a keyboard and touchpad. I'll show them to you later. We should rejoin Kelsey and Dylan."

After regrouping in a multipurpose room near the lobby that seemed part lounge and part library, Havana suggested that they head out for lunch at Alta, a restaurant at the top of one of the tallest skyscrapers in New Athens that had breathtaking views of the city. She made a reservation on her e-glasses and they headed to South Avenue on foot to enjoy the outdoors after a long night cooped up on the ferry.

Turning onto the avenue, Marcus realized that from the gondola, he had failed to recognize that there were no sidewalks visible from that vantage point. The sidewalks were hidden within the building façades in long, uninterrupted arcades. As they began walking down one, he nearly tripped over Kelsey's feet while admiring intricately sculpted arched ceilings built into the buildings that covered the walkways. He peered through the arches and beyond the bike lane to the grassy, tree-lined strip of park. The sun was strong, but the arcades were completely shaded and relatively cool. They reached an intersection, and more of the street revealed itself.

Marcus pointed up. "Oh, cool, there are bridges between the buildings! I've never seen that before. They're beautiful!"

"Yeah, there are skywalks all over the city. Each neighborhood designs theirs to try to represent the flavor of the area," Havana said. "They form an interconnected web of air-conditioned walkways. On a hot day, if you wanted to, you could walk comfortably around the entire city, never stepping foot outdoors. Usually I prefer the fresh air and the bustle of cafés down here in the arcades, but sometimes when it's really hot, or when I'm in the mood for more peace and quiet, I use the skywalks. There is a system of underground walkways too, but I never use them. Not only because you don't get to enjoy the sun but because they connect to the underground garages and are usually crammed with people and their portable car trunks."

As they waited at the corner for the bike and automobile signals to turn red, Marcus craned his neck around to get a better view of the action on the streets. He had been checking out a row of bicycles stopped at the intersection when the quiet of the street was interrupted by what sounded like a loud version of the binging of a car's door-ajar alarm, and he snapped his head back to see what the commotion was.

Dylan was dancing into the street and then back to the walkway, back into the street, then back onto the walkway.

"What the hell are you doing?" Marcus asked him.

"Testing the commie cars to see if they'll see me and stop."

"And if they don't?"

"Then I guess I'll have a lawsuit to file. I'm sure there's a lawyer every ten feet just like in San Fran."

"Please don't do that," Havana begged. "Both of those cars happened to have people in them. How do you think they felt having the car suddenly slam to a stop? How would you feel if you were in one of those cars drinking a cup of coffee and suddenly the car braked so quickly that you dumped coffee all over yourself?"

"You and your rules." Dylan snorted.

They continued on down the arcaded sidewalk. Eventually the tranquility returned, and the musical back-and-forth chirping of two birds in the trees along the bike paths caught Marcus's attention. It suddenly dawned on him just how quiet the streets were. The majority of the sounds he could hear, other than the birds chirping, were the bustle of the cafés that Havana mentioned loving the sound of, and occasionally the gentle ring of a bicycle bell as one bicyclist passed another. The electric cars drifted by nearly silently and were buffered from the sidewalks by the bike lane and trees. No honking horns like New Miami. *I suppose autonomous cars can't feel anger toward other cars*, Marcus thought, almost chuckling out loud. He didn't even hear any car stereos blaring.

Marcus looked down to observe the source of one of the loudest noises he could identify: the clickity-clacking of Kelsey's boots as she walked. He looked down at his own feet and at the decorative tile floor of the sidewalk. "This sidewalk feels kind of funny. I can't figure it out. It's subtle, but it kind of feels less stiff than I'd expect a tile floor or sidewalk to feel. It's like it's spongy, or my footsteps are dampened or something."

"That's because the sidewalks are Energy Floors," Havana said. "Under the interconnected tiles there is a system of spring-loaded mini-turbines, and every time someone takes a step, it spins the turbines and generates a little electricity that feeds into the electrical system."

As they progressed down the avenue, Marcus noted a pattern in the narrower, winding side streets they crossed. They seemed to alternate in a repeating pattern of three: a one-way eastbound vehicular road with bike lanes each side protected by decorative stone bollards; then a one-way westbound vehicular road with protected bike lanes; followed by a pedestrian-only street filled with public spaces, outdoor restaurant seating, and markets.

Kelsey finally spoke up for a change, but it was only to announce that she really needed to pee again, and she asked whether they could buy a bottle of water at a café so that she could use their bathroom.

"No need," Havana replied. "We can go up to the skywalk at the next intersection. Every building that has a skywalk is required to have a public bathroom along the path through their building. There are public bathrooms everywhere. This skywalk will take us straight to the skyscraper with the restaurant anyway."

While Kelsey used the bathroom, Marcus walked into the adjacent skywalk to continue his inspection of the city. Havana followed him in to admire the view too. After a minute, Marcus said, "I don't see any parked cars."

"The underground garages have interconnected capacity systems that can tell cars where the nearest parking space is. The autonomous cars drop off their passengers and go park themselves. That's where delivery trucks go to make deliveries too. There are distribution nodes all around the city where large train, boat, truck, or airplane cargo gets divvied up and put on small trucks or vans to be delivered in the garages. Then they use electric hand carts to deliver to individual buildings served by the garage."

"What an exotic and fascinating place," Marcus quietly exclaimed.

Havana only smiled in response and continued admiring the view.

Chapter 2: Alta-Vista with a Side of Acrophobia

Upon reaching the restaurant level at the top of the skyscraper, Kelsey announced that she had to pee yet again. She had been getting increasingly agitated as they rode the elevator to the top of the building, grabbing Dylan's hand and nervously shifting her weight to each leg and looking around the elevator like she expected the walls to suddenly fall off.

As she exited the bathroom near the restaurant entrance, some teasing from Dylan about her peanut-sized bladder prompted her to admit that she had a fear of heights, and that her anxiety was making her feel the need to urinate frequently. Havana asked if she wanted to go to a different restaurant at ground level, but Kelsey shook her head, presumably wanting to follow the crowd and do the popular thing as usual.

Dylan was less sympathetic than Havana, teasing Kelsey anew by miming falling off of a pretend ledge and plummeting to his death before suggesting that after a beer she'd be fine. Havana requested a table as far back from the 360-degree panoramic-view windows as they could get, and Dylan and Kelsey immediately ordered beers while Marcus and Havana ordered flavored sparkling water and perused the eclectic menu.

After ordering and each declaring with faux arrogance that their meal would surely win at the obligatory competitive food ordering contest, Marcus and Havana excused themselves to go to one of the observation lounges to look at the city from above.

Marcus looked out the window with the same sense of awe he had while atop the Gateway Arch in St. Louis. It was a beautiful, clear day, and he could see for miles, or for kilometers as he realized a local would say. His eyes traced the dynamic skyline, following the jagged line between metal and air where buildings punctured empty space. The classical architecture he had seen at Port Camille and UNA appeared to be the rule rather than the exception. Simple and efficient but beautiful and with elegant ornamental touches. No collapsing buildings with heaps of Spanish moss like the WUS national capitol, nor row after row of plain, boring boxes interrupted only by the occasional magnificent church like NEUS.

Each neighborhood had similar architecture within it, but he could tell even from this height that the architecture of one neighborhood was different from the architecture of the adjacent neighborhoods. He could see all of the massive Central Park from here, with green trees everywhere looking like a field of broccoli florets from this height. In the center was a large, domed building with gabled wings projecting in the four cardinal directions. He pointed to it. "Is that Central Station?"

"Yes. It is modeled somewhat on the Pantheon in Rome, except with more entrance wings. After lunch we could go for a stroll through the park if you are interested. It will take your mind off of losing competitive food ordering." Havana smirked and reassuringly grabbed his hand. Marcus smiled back, but more for secretly admiring her excitedly compulsive desire to be his tour guide than for anything to do with food.

Marcus continued his aerial survey of the city. His eyes wandered over the rooftops of the lower buildings. Most were a mossy green and brown with beige patterns interspersed. "What's on those roofs?" he asked.

"Most are green roofs with translucent, perforated solar-panel canopies that let water and some sunlight through to the vegetation. Most commercial and public buildings have public roof terraces, and residential buildings have private roof terraces." Havana drew a circle in the air with her finger. "That one over there is one of my favorites to study on. It is so peaceful. Every roof you see has some combination of solar panels, vegetation, and rainwater capture that goes into the non-potable water system. As the rainwater rushes down the collection pipes, it spins small water turbines to generate even more electricity. And see the skyscraper over there? Notice how the metal skin looks white at the top but dark blue at the bottom where it is in shade? It has a color-changing paint that turns white when hot, and a dark color when cooler so that it reflects or absorbs sunlight depending on how hot it is. The windows all have a similar system that changes the polarization of the glass depending on temperature. A lot of these systems were Pippa winners."

After digesting the information and the view for a while, Marcus released Havana's hand and put his arm around her shoulder. "So where does your family live? Do you live with them during the summer, or even during the school year?"

Havana wrapped her arm around Marcus's waist and with the other arm pointed in the distance to the north. "My family lives along North Park, just beyond the Inner Ring. It's about a half mile from the coast. I live with them in the summer but stay in a dorm during the school year."

Marcus turned to face Havana, drew her near to him, and leaned in for a deep kiss. They stood there for a minute embracing and kissing before Marcus sighed. "I suppose we should go back to the table to see what trouble they've gotten themselves into."

When they returned to the table, they could see that Marcus wasn't far off. A waiter was picking up two empty beer glasses after having delivered two new ones.

"Don't go anywhere," Dylan said to him. "We're going to get a third round in a few seconds." Then he proceeded to chug his second beer. Kelsey followed his lead.

"I think two is enough for you this afternoon," the waiter said.

Dylan finished chugging his second beer, smacked the glass back down on the table, belched loudly, and said, "No fuckin' commie is going to tell me what I can or can't do. I want a third. Now bring me a fuckin' third!"

Marcus angrily slammed his fist down on the table and through gritted teeth said, "Dylan, you're embarrassing us and yourself. Shut the fuck up!"

Dylan looked at Marcus with a quizzical look on his face, like he was surprised that Marcus was angry at him, and like he was teetering on the edge of a decision between civilized friendship and rebellious chaos.

Marcus held his hand out, palms down, in a gesture of reassurance and spoke more calmly. "Let me handle this. I'll get you a third beer." Marcus stood up and, attempting to look calm and casual, chased down their waiter, who had already begun walking toward the kitchen. He caught the waiter's attention and apologized, and then asked if the restaurant had any non-alcoholic beer, which they did. He ordered a round for the whole table and made his way back, texting Havana "Ordered non-alcoholic beer" as he walked so that she would be in on the ruse.

As he sat down, he could see Havana tapping a response on her bracelet. His phone chirped with a new text alert, but Dylan and Kelsey's phones chirped too. *Shit! Did I accidentally respond to a group text and send that text to Dylan and Kelsey too? Or did Havana forward it to them and rat me out?* he thought. He looked down and saw a text:

"Puerto Paz Department of Immigration requests a meeting to discuss the duration of your stay. Please bring all members of your travel party to the meeting. Will 16:00 on Monday accommodate your schedule?"

Marcus was relieved that he hadn't accidentally texted about the beer to Dylan and Kelsey, but this text from the Department of Immigration didn't put him much more at ease. Just then, Havana's reply regarding the non-alcoholic beer arrived: "Pragmatic, but more deception? I'll go along, but you really need to come clean with D on things."

Dylan read the immigration text and whined, "What the fuck? Why the hell do we have to meet with the fucking commies? I just want to kick back on the beach and party a little. Why can't they just leave me the fuck alone? They're probably going to assign us commie minders to follow us around or something."

Marcus showed Havana the immigration text. "Maybe the waiter told them how awful you just treated him," he said to Dylan coldly. "And maybe now they're going to ask us to stay for a shorter duration because they don't want tourists who are assholes." He paused and looked at Havana. "Sorry. *They are*, not they're."

Havana didn't respond to Marcus's IPA American English self-correction, and she didn't look amused with the situation. She closed her eyes briefly and took a deep breath in through her nose and out through her mouth.

Their food arrived, and the rest of the meal felt awkward. Kelsey didn't speak at all and pecked at her food a little, mostly stirring it around on her plate. Havana would reply to questions but hardly initiated any conversation. Marcus felt like he had to walk on eggshells with Dylan, trying to make it clear that he didn't condone the poor treatment of restaurant staff or getting drunk at one p.m. in one of the classiest restaurants he had ever dined in, while simultaneously preventing Dylan from feeling ostracized. At one point he caught himself mindlessly commenting on how beautiful the weather was, like he was dining with a bunch of strangers and needed some small talk to get a conversation going. Dylan kept looking over at Marcus with a look on his face like he was still deciding whether he wanted to make Marcus happy and conform to his standards of behavior or just let loose with an attitude of "fuck everyone and their stupid rules."

After a while Marcus started avoiding eye contact with Dylan. He tried to get some conversation going again, suggesting that they each put a portion of their meal on a side plate and pass them around so that everyone could sample a little of everyone else's meal. It was the judgment phase of competitive food ordering, except that he stopped short of suggesting it be a contest. Now did not feel like a good time for a competition or anything that could trigger an argument. The others obliged, and it did instigate some small talk about what people liked or didn't like, and it got Kelsey to stop playing with her food and actually insert some of it into her mouth, but the mood at the table still felt relatively tense.

"What is this?" Marcus asked when the side plate with a sample of Havana's meal reached him.

"Vegetable Pad Thai," Havana said.

"I've never even heard of it before," Marcus said while cautiously sticking a fork into the noodles. He took a bite and discovered that it was delicious, but he maintained a poker face so as not to influence any potential judges should the food sampling eventually evolve into a round-robin competitive food ordering contest. "I noticed on the menu that there were only a few meat-based dishes and most things were vegetarian. Does Puerto Paz have menu rules like WUS, where a certain percentage of the menu has to be vegetarian?"

"It isn't mandated, but the government uses tax incentives to encourage it. They encourage a diet high in vegetables and relatively low in meat, and they subsidize a lot of vegetable farmers to maintain low prices for healthier foods. They also use carrot-and-stick incentives and penalties to ensure that neighborhoods and regions have plentiful access to healthy foods, especially healthy fast foods, so that no particular area turns into a healthy food desert."

"A man can't be a man and just be free to eat a fuckin' cheeseburger anymore," Dylan muttered. "You remember the cheeseburgers at Fonzarelli's, MC? Those were the best. Nothing like wolfing down a cheeseburger with the team after a big win."

"Well, actually, there are plenty of places to get cheeseburgers," Havana objected. "But the government acknowledges the fact that the environment people are placed in heavily influences their decisions. There have been hundreds of studies that show that our choices aren't always as free as we think they are. What you eat at any given moment when you are out and about in New Miami, for example, is influenced by all sorts of things, like convenience and availability, marketing, familiarity, and cost. They all influence what restaurant you choose, and then you get in that restaurant, and your choices are influenced by things like plate size or the sequence of foods in a buffet line or whether they even have healthy options on the menu at all. In New Miami, almost every restaurant served nothing but junk food. A little bit of government influence in making sure that there are plenty of healthy options makes a huge difference in the health of an entire population. Physical health affects mental and psychological health, so it is paramount that a society be structured to maximize the opportunities to make healthy choices."

Havana had already lost Dylan's attention, so she turned to Marcus to finish her thoughts. "There are all sorts of ways that the government subtly nudges the environment to lead to a healthier society, creating conditions where everyone has enough time, money, and opportunity to eat a healthy diet, get sufficient sleep, get sufficient exercise, and socialize with other people, and I, for one, appreciate it. And I appreciate it even more now that I've experienced living in New Miami."

As lunch wound down, Havana suggested the walk in Central Park that she was craving, but in an attempt to appease Dylan, she also added an alternative offer to show everyone the east beaches. Dylan and Kelsey both wanted to go to the beaches, but Marcus wanted to go to Central Park, so he suggested that they go back to the dorm for Dylan and Kelsey to grab their beach gear and then have Havana direct them on how to get to the beaches before he and Havana diverted to Central Park. Everyone seemed content with this plan, so they paid their bill. Marcus guiltily tried to leave a sizeable cash tip for the misfortunate waiter, but Havana picked up most of it and handed it back to him. "Tipping isn't customary here. Waiters are paid living wages and are expected to do their jobs just like the workers in any other industry. You can leave a little to acknowledge what a difficult table we were, but our waiter isn't trying to make a living off of tips or anything."

Half an hour later, Marcus and Havana were walking alone through Central Park while Dylan and Kelsey were on a train to Playa Nueva. Marcus clasped Havana's hand in a non-verbal plea to reconnect after the anxious lunch. She obliged but said, "I don't want to be a nag, but you really ought to come clean with Dylan about why you are here in Puerto Paz."

Marcus sighed. "Listen. No matter when I tell him, it will instigate a tantrum. I could have told him I was coming here to see if I wanted to live here while we were back in New Miami, but he would have thrown a tantrum then, he would have refused to come here, and he might have even talked me out of coming here too. I could tell him now, but I still haven't even decided whether I want to live here, so I'd be setting off a tantrum that might be for no good reason if I decide not to live here. The way I see it, I'm better off not telling him until I know for sure I want to live here and my options are clear. And who knows, maybe if he gets to know Puerto Paz without the pressure of feeling like he's making a decision to permanently move here, then the idea of living here will actually start to grow on him. You know him, he's a rebel without a clue. If you tell him he should move here, he'll say no just to spite you. I think waiting really is the best option, both for me and for him."

Havana frowned but nodded. "I guess. What you are saying feels wrong, but I see your logic. But it seems like the logic of a military officer trying to strategize and outwit an enemy rather than a friend trying to help another friend. You need to reach out to him more. His antics might be a reaction to stressors in his life."

"I think his antics are a symptom of 'Ares' getting too big for his britches," Marcus countered. "Ever since he knocked out Apollo, he's acted like he's some sort of god. That punch was probably the worst thing that could have happened for him. His ego has gorged on the worship of his new frat bros, and now he thinks we're all his minions. He's being such a dick that I'm not really feeling much desire to be around him."

"Maybe it is ego, but I was starting to get the impression that he feels jealous of our relationship," Havana said. "Think about it. You probably mean the world to him. He has no mother, practically no father. The frat boys back in New Miami don't qualify as true friends. They will lose interest in him the second another alpha male steps in and dethrones him. You are it for him. Then you meet me, and you start spending all your time with me instead of him?"

"I just...I don't know," said Marcus. "If he thinks the world of me, then why is he constantly badmouthing everything and everyone I like? I don't really want to reach out to him until he stops. Plus, all he wants to do is get drunk at bars. I'd rather explore the city."

"The badmouthing and drinking are part of the symptoms. Emotionally, he's in rough shape, and you are in better shape. You need to be the bigger person who makes the first effort to bridge the gap, and you need to work on your gentle confrontation skills too."

Marcus thought for a moment. "Huh. Maybe you're right. He did say something weird to me at Port Camille after you left about how it was the first time in a long while that he and I had been together without you. I have no idea where to even begin with him right now, though."

"Maybe we should try more foursome outings," Havana suggested. "So he can see that I'm not a threat to him and that we can all be friends."

"You see how well that turned out at lunch today?" Marcus said.

"True. Well, how about this? I kind of feel like I've been neglecting my friendship with Kelsey. Why don't Kelsey and I have a ladies' night soon, and you and Dylan have a guys' night at the same time, so that you can reconnect with him? After Kelsey's near acrophobia-induced nervous breakdown, I've been thinking about ways to discreetly recommend my therapist to her."

"You see a therapist? Like a shrink therapist?" Marcus asked, stunned. "You don't seem crazy to me."

"After spending most of the summer in New Miami, I definitely will need to see my therapist! But on a more serious note, yeah, most people here do see therapists. It's quite normal. Most people can't see their own faults and limitations, they have to be revealed to them through someone else's eyes, so therapists help us to see the things that we can't see ourselves, the things we hide from ourselves and from our friends. The human brain has defense mechanisms to prevent it from seeing truths. Of course I see a therapist, and you should too. Everyone should."

"I don't know," Marcus said. "I thought shrinks were for people messed up in the head. Mental patients."

"Well, I think it would help Kelsey with her fear of heights, and once she gets her foot in the door, it could lead to help with her anxiety and self-esteem issues. The SEUS culture has really done a number on her."

They continued to meander in the general direction of Central Station. Marcus's attention was seized as they walked past some athletic fields where he saw a group of elementary school kids playing a pickup game of touch football until Havana returned to her tour guide duties. "Did you know that New York City used to have a big park in the middle of it called Central Park?" she asked. "The city planners named this park after it, sort of in memoriam."

"No!" Marcus responded. "Was it as big as this one?"

"I think so. Similar in size, I think, but rectangular instead of circular. After the partitioning, EUS sold it off piece by piece to developers though. Sad. This is one of my favorite places in the city. I imagine New York must have been so much nicer before they developed it."

"Yeah, and before the drug wars turned so much of it into a battleground. I've never actually stepped foot in New York City. Heard too many horror stories."

Havana's glasses beeped. "Ooh, a flash poll. Can we sit down on the bench over there for a minute? I have my Puerto Paz account set to notify me of flash polls and news on topics I care most about, and there is a poll going on right now about intergenerational off-campus housing that mixes students, especially students in the medical fields, with senior citizens, and I really want to respond to it."

Marcus agreed, and they sat down. Havana pulled her bracelet off of her arm and squeezed the end, causing it to flatten and expand into a nearly full-sized keyboard that she placed on her lap and began swiping and tapping.

"Nifty," Marcus said.

"After I'm done, I'll let you give it a try."

After glancing around the park and noticing that pretty much everyone in Puerto Paz seemed to wear glasses, Marcus returned his attention to the kids playing football. Realizing Havana was going to be a few minutes, he trotted over to the kids and offered their quarterback some tips on throwing mechanics. After his coaching session concluded, he saw that Havana had her bracelet back on her arm and was smiling at him, so he rejoined her on the bench.

"That was sweet what you did there," she said with a look that made Marcus think that maybe she had started to forgive him for the lunch scene. "Want to try out my glasses?" she asked.

"Sure. I think. Suddenly I'm reminded of an episode of *Star Trek TNG* where the crew is duped into getting addicted to a game on a glasses-like visual input device. These won't stimulate my addictive pleasure centers, will they?"

"Oh, shut up, Wesley!" Havana joked, riffing on a line from *Star Trek* loosely related to that episode.

Havana handed Marcus the glasses and showed him how they worked, using his choice of either verbal commands or left winks and right eye winks to control input without the bracelet keyboard, before handing him the keyboard to use as touchpad input.

"All this winking must lead to a lot of confusion about whether someone looking in your direction is flirting with you!" Marcus said.

"Actually, there is a subtle pinky extension gesture that is used to discreetly express interest in someone."

A message popped up on the projection view screen thanking Havana for having responded to the poll she had taken. "So, not to sound like Dylan or anything, but with polls like the one you were taking, does the government track your every response, maintaining a database of your opinions that they can use against you?"

"There is an option to respond to polls anonymously, but anonymous responses get weighted less in the factored survey results. They always publish the results both factored and unfactored, but hardly anyone pays any attention to the unfactored results. There are basically four ways to respond: anonymously, semi-anonymously, publicly, or as a public expert. The more public your response is, the higher impact it will have on the factored results. The semi-anonymous way is from your authenticated account, but your personal info is hidden in the response, and the only way to find out it was you is through a court order. If you respond publicly, then everyone can see it was you, but you'll have a bigger impact on the factored results. For the public expert option, you have to register and get approved as an expert on a particular subject, so that for example, a doctor could weigh in on a topic about public health. Expert opinions tend to be weighted the highest in factored results.

"Another variable that affects the factored results is your 'strength of conviction' response. If you vote that you feel strongly about your response, it will have a bigger impact than if you feel weakly about it. The government also uses data about which privacy option the general population is using most to gauge the level of trust in the government and fellow citizens. You can't really have a healthy society unless people trust one another, so on the rare occasion that the government starts seeing data indicating trust levels are on the decline, they start working to figure out why and how to rebuild that trust."

Havana noted the time and announced that she should probably call it a day and go see her family for the first time in several months. She paused for a minute before asking, "I don't want to make you feel pressured either way, because I know some guys think meeting a girlfriend's family means taking a relationship to a whole different level that they aren't ready for, but I'm sure you could join us for dinner if you wanted."

"I would love to meet your family during my stay here, but not tonight," Marcus responded. "I think I've had enough excitement and stimulation for one day, and I could use some alone time to recharge."

She nodded, and they got up from the bench and experienced one last burst of crowded stimulation in the cavernous and busy Central Station to catch a subway back to the University district. Havana and Marcus embraced and kissed passionately for several minutes in his dorm room before she collected her baggage and went on her way to reunite with her family.

Marcus, pleased to find that the room was in considerably better condition and better appointed than the dorm in New Miami, unpacked his bag and put everything neatly away in its proper location. He lay down on his bed and closed his eyes, admiring the peaceful silence. No music blasting. No shouting. No cigarette smoke. They even had engineered the doors to close and lock silently. He drifted off to sleep for a late-afternoon nap, feeling content.

Chapter 3: Dr. Nigel Goodall, PhD

Marcus woke up Monday morning with his mind racing about that afternoon's meeting at the Department of Immigration. A jog in Central Park, which seemed to be a popular idea with the locals, followed by a shower and lunch, helped calm his mind a bit.

Later that afternoon, annoyed that he was unable to find or get ahold of Dylan or Kelsey, Marcus left the dorm solo, wearing his only set of good clothes—the same clothes he had worn on his first dates with Simone and Havana.

As he walked into the main lobby of the Department of Immigration, he felt his cell phone vibrate. It was Dylan saying, "Be there in ten. Train noisy."

Thank God, he thought.

At the reception desk, a slender young woman, who looked like she might have been of Indian descent and was either college age or recently graduated, stood up to greet him. She was wearing a white polo shirt with a black Puerto Paz symbol on the left chest, and when she stood up, Marcus noted that her pants seemed almost too dressy to go with a polo shirt.

"Hello, I'm Priya. You are Marcus, correct?"

Marcus confirmed his identity while mentally admonishing himself for having assumed the young woman would have an Indian accent.

"You will be meeting with Assistant Director Goodall today. Is the rest of your travel party arriving separately?"

"Yes," Marcus replied. "I just got a text from Dylan that they should be here in about ten minutes."

"Excellent. Unfortunately, the assistant director is running a bit late. There are less than two weeks until the universities begin autumn trimester, so this is always a busy time of year for our department with the influx of foreign students and professors. Our morning meetings went a bit long, and we are just starting to get back on schedule. Would you mind waiting in his office? I think he will be with you in about fifteen minutes."

"Sure, no problem," Marcus said.

"Excellent. Right this way, please," Priya said as she led Marcus to the assistant director's office. There she showed him the rack of literature about Puerto Paz, mentioned the free New Athens Wi-Fi system, and welcomed him to any snacks or beverages from the mini-bar. For coffee or tea she noted two ways to start the electric kettle: One by pressing the button right there on the kettle, and the other, the way that she said always brought a smile to the assistant director's face, by pulling the lever by the door.

The young woman departed, leaving Marcus alone in the office. Marcus began wandering around the room to keep himself amused as he waited. The first item on his agenda was to see what the deal was with the lever near the door that supposedly started the electric kettle from a fifteen-foot distance. When he examined it, he saw that it connected to a series of small pulleys and levers, on top of which a small round marble was perched. If the lever were pulled, it would trigger the marble to rise up and be thrust onto a wooden ramp. The wooden ramp morphed into an intricately carved wood installation on the wall that at first glance he had assumed was a large piece of carved wood artwork hanging on the wall. Upon closer inspection, though, he realized it was an elaborate Rube Goldberg contraption. He walked to the other end of the wall where a spring-loaded mini gavel was attached to the wooden installation, ready to swing into action to strike the on button of the kettle.

Next to the kettle, a tall, upside-down J-shaped faucet sprouted from a small stainless-steel sink. Below the sink was a foot pedal sticking out from the face of the cabinet. Curiosity got the best of him, as he couldn't figure out what the pedal was for, so he stepped on it. Nothing happened. He checked the clock on his phone and then continued looking around. Next to the sink, a few pieces of tropical fruit he didn't recognize were arranged in a bowl. Despite Priya's invitation, somehow he never felt comfortable taking food or drink from a stranger. It wasn't that he worried it would be tainted or poisoned, or a matter of distrust, but rather a feeling that taking it would somehow be rude.

He continued past a window to a wall that had the assistant director's diplomas and credentials. He looked at one that read "Tufts University, School of Arts and Sciences. Be it known that Nigel Goodall, having satisfied in full the requirements for the degree of Doctor of Psychology…"

Just then, Priya reentered the room with Dylan close behind her.

Priya began her spiel about snacks and literature for Dylan's sake, but as soon as she had explained the coffee options, Dylan just turned his back on her, started walking toward the kitchenette, and put his hand up. "Yeah, yeah, yeah. I got it."

Priya terminated her speech, did an about-face, and walked back out the door, seemingly unfazed by Dylan's rudeness. Dylan began trying to figure out how a French press worked.

Marcus said hello, which garnered a grunt of "hey" in return. "Know how to use this stupid thing?" Dylan asked.

Marcus, having seen one of the tribe people in Wyoming use one during one of his dishwashing stints, talked Dylan through the process. Dylan grunted and began following Marcus's instructions. As Dylan fumbled with the press, Marcus asked him to hold off on starting the electric kettle. He went to the door and pulled the lever, initiating the descent of the marble down the wooden ramp of the Rube Goldberg machine. After picking up speed, the marble did a full 360-degree loop within one of the decorative arms of the sculpture, and then hopped over a gap before continuing on down another ramp.

After several minutes and multiple complex maneuvers, the marble reached the end of the sculpture, fell down a shaft, and hit a platform that triggered the spring-loaded hammer that swung around and hit the on button of the kettle, which shut the kettle off because Dylan had gotten impatient during the two-minute fiasco and had already pressed the button himself. Dylan hit the button again to turn it back on and completed assembling his cup of coffee, and a couple of minutes later he collapsed into one of the comfortable chairs in front of the assistant director's desk, blowing steam off the top of the cup.

Marcus looked at him to try to get a read on his mood before sitting down in the chair next to him. He was wearing khaki cargo shorts, a navy-blue New York Yankees T-shirt, and a white pinstriped Yankees baseball cap that was pulled down low to obscure his eyes.

"You look like shit," Marcus said. "And where's Kelsey?"

"I feel like shit too. Kelsey's sick. She wasn't feeling well enough to come."

"Let me guess, brown-bottle flu?"

Dylan smiled wryly. "We had some fun last night. We didn't go to bed until four a.m., and I only got up a couple of hours ago. She can't keep up with me, though."

"Did you even make it back to the dorms? I knocked on your doors before I left, and no one answered."

"Nah, fuck the dorms. We rented a hotel room on Playa Nueva next to where the action is."

The boys' conversation was interrupted as a mostly bald Caucasian man in his late fifties entered the room, strode confidently to the desk, and put down a computer tablet and some papers. He was dressed similar to Priya, with dressy black pants and a red polo shirt tucked into his pants, a black Puerto Paz symbol on the left chest. He took off his glasses, set them down on a pad on his desk, and looked up with a smile that was closed-mouth yet big enough to cause his eyes to squint before extending his arm toward Marcus for a handshake.

"Hello. Welcome to Puerto Paz. Sorry for the delay. My schedule has been out of control today. You are my last appointment of the day, though, so I am all yours now."

Marcus was once again surprised by the accent coming from someone within this building. This time it was the assistant director's British accent, emphasized by his pronunciation of the word "schedule" that sounded like "shed jewel." The man turned to shake Dylan's hand, but Dylan remained in his chair and just waved at him.

"Very well. Nice to meet you both. I'm Nigel. You must be Marcus and Dylan, correct?"

"Yes," Marcus replied. "Do you want us to call you Nigel? The diploma over there says you are 'Doctor' Nigel Goodall, PhD in psychology."

"Yes, Nigel is good. I'm not a big fan of using titles. I find it builds walls of formality that hinders communication and makes people feel like I think they are inferior."

"You're a shrink?" Dylan scoffed. "Am I here for you to probe my mind to try to learn EUS secrets or something? I'm not a spy, you know."

Nigel cocked his head and wrinkled his brow while looking at Dylan. "I don't think you are a spy. And I'm not here in the capacity of a psychologist. I used to be a clinical psychologist in a past career, but I have since moved on to this job at Immigration."

"Tufts is in NEUS, isn't it?" Marcus asked, referring again to Nigel's diploma.

"It is indeed. Just north of Boston. I went to university there, and the partitioning of the United States was happening essentially *as* I was receiving my doctorate." Nigel paused, looked down at the coffee cup in Dylan's hands and then up at the Rube Goldberg art installation on the wall and smiled. "I see you've met Borat!" he said, gesturing at the wood artwork on the wall. "Borat the Bureaucrat is what I named my Rube Goldberg machine. It was carved by Eleanor, my best friend from university. She majored in structural engineering, and as her career progressed, she became somewhat of an expert in wood design, and she took up a hobby of wood carving and Japanese wood joinery techniques. She gave me this masterpiece as a housewarming gift when I moved here to New Athens some fifteen…or is it twenty years ago now? Good lord, time flies."

"So, you lived in NEUS for what, about fifteen years before you moved here?" Marcus asked.

"No, I was only in NEUS after the partitioning for a few months. After Tufts and the partitioning, Eleanor and I were both desperate to leave the newly formed EUS, so we moved to San Francisco and were roommates for a few years. I'm sure we were better off in San Fran than we would have been had we stayed in EUS, but Eleanor used to complain bitterly about how ridiculously complex the building codes were getting there. Things like six-hour-long calculations required by the newer codes that resulted in the same values as the simple table lookups from the older codes.

"We both became increasingly frustrated with the bureaucracies of WUS over the years, and when I moved to Puerto Paz, she gave me this gift to remind me to not let my actions become wildly bureaucratic or cumbersome and to maintain simplicity and efficiency. To 'Keep It Simple, Stupid.' No point in making a convoluted system requiring all these unnecessary maneuvers and processes to achieve an uncomplicated result when you could simply walk over and press the damned button and save everyone time and aggravation."

Marcus looked over at Dylan, who had turned to look at him. Dylan had a raised eyebrow that seemed to wordlessly communicate an "I told you so" about the time wasted running the Rube Goldberg machine when he was making his coffee.

Nigel continued. "It is a much-needed reminder too, because here in Puerto Paz we tend to skew towards the order-liberal side of the spectrum, like WUS, and we need to be reminded not to let ourselves get carried away with our bureaucratic tendencies. We strive to curb the extremism of places like WUS. Balance is key, though, as it is possible to oversimplify things. It is like trying to calculate the volume of Dylan's coffee mug. Use pi calculated to one digit and you'll underestimate the volume significantly, but calculate pi to fifty digits, and you are just wasting your time. Three to five digits is typically sufficient."

"We made Rube Goldberg machines from a kit in my AP Physics class last year," Marcus said. "They were nowhere near as beautiful and intricate as Borat here, but our teacher made us use physics equations to predict how we needed to assemble the pieces in order for the machine to deliver a mini-cannonball to an enemy target. I got a big kick out of Borat. It is a beautiful work of art too."

Nigel nodded. "Thank you."

"So, your time living in NEUS was before it became NEUS," Marcus said. "What was it like back then? Did you like it? Did my history books get it right that it was all the liberal terrorists' fault that the United States partitioned?"

"Hah! I highly doubt your text books got it right. NEUS is notorious for revisionist history. The liberal terrorism was awful, but there was a lot that preceded their formation that set the path to partitioning, and almost to civil war, in motion. Not to excuse their violence, but in my opinion, the liberal terrorists were just reacting to horrible things that the conservatives started. The liberals tolerated feeling helplessly oppressed for a long time before they resorted to violence. One person's terrorist is another person's freedom fighter."

"So, what was the lead up to the terrorism? What was life there like before the terrorism, and what changed?"

"It was all dopamine and no serotonin. Everyone was chasing that next high. They were primed for a split into extremist factions. The media was more interested in ratings and advertising than in the truth so they were always trying to manufacture controversy or focus on sensationalist stories. Same with politicians. All emotion, no intellect, and everything getting more extremist. The way that the United States election system was set up, naturally leading to a polarized duopoly, was what really did them in though."

Nigel paused, pointed up at his diplomas, and then continued. "On a personal level, I've always felt that my time at Tufts was a sort of microcosm of the problems since Tufts straddled two cities that went in opposite extremes until the partitioning. One half of campus was in Somerville, where they had enforcement officers everywhere handing out fines for the most ridiculous things, and the other half was in Medford, which was the Wild Wild West by comparison and lacked some of the most basic city services. In my mind, it was like Somerville during the time of the USA was the precursor to WUS's Gestapo, and Medford during the time of the USA was the precursor to SEUS's lawless libertarian chaos."

"But what about the terrorists? It sounds like maybe tensions were high, but that doesn't mean you can start setting off bombs," Marcus said.

"Yeah. The liberal terrorists were what set things off," Dylan agreed.

"There was a tremendous amount of political animosity in the country leading up to the partitioning, and we were very lucky that it didn't turn into an all-out civil war. It was definitely not all the liberals' fault, though. There was plenty of blame to go around, but if I had to pick one party to fault, I would definitely say the Republicans deserved more blame. They were first to develop a negative media system of lying, vitriolic extremist radio hosts, then later they brought that same lying vitriol to television. They were the first to abandon the concept of compromise and to threaten filibusters and entire government shutdowns over every issue that came before Congress when in the minority, and to bully their agenda through when in the majority. They were the ones who tried to subvert democracy by suppressing the vote and rigging elections.

"There were at least a dozen assassinations of liberal leaders preceding the first liberal bombs, but they were committed with guns, and everyone had already become so desensitized to gun violence that it hardly even registered as news. And every time there was a shooting it would somehow get chalked up to a single, mentally ill lone wolf. Bombs were often associated with groups rather than individuals, and they resonated in the news cycle due to their infrequent occurrences and the scariness of a remote, faceless attacker. Everything liberals did to push things toward their extremist side and away from a rational centrist attitude was a reaction to negative and extremist actions the Republicans did first. Conservatives set the pendulum in motion."

"Bullshit," Dylan said, his good hand slapping the armrest. He began gesticulating wildly, the same way he had at the San Francisco beach. "The reason the country split goes back to when the presidential election ended in an electoral tie, and the Democratic senate put their candidate in office even though he lost the popular vote." He punctuated the end of his sentence with another thump on the armrest. Marcus briefly rubbed his temples in preparation for the possible onset of a headache if the thumping continued.

"Yes, that did happen, and it demonstrated less than morally correct behavior, but it was less reprehensible than several years earlier, when the Democratic candidate won the popular vote and the electoral tally came down to who won Florida, and the conservative Supreme Court intervened to prevent a full recount despite anomalies, allowing the Republican to win even though a later recount revealed that the Democrat had indeed won. It was also preceded by the Republican congress refusing to fill Supreme Court vacancies for several years while there were Democratic presidents. You might be able to convince me that in the end the blame should be spread equally, but you could never convince me that the Republicans didn't start the atrocious behavior first."

Dylan huffed in disgust but seemed to have run out of historical data to continue his argument. "So why are we here?" he asked. "The text said something about discussing the length of our stay. It didn't say anything about criticizing our homeland."

"Right," Nigel said, his tone changing from congenial to more businesslike. "I have gotten us a bit diverted from the main purpose of bringing you here. The reason we have asked you here is primarily to clarify your duration of stay, since on your Customs and Immigration questionnaire one of you selected that you were uncertain whether you would be staying here longer than two months, while the other two selected durations of less than two months.

"First, typically groups of people traveling together all select the same duration, so we want to clarify whether one of you is indeed potentially staying longer than the two-month limit for traveling without a visa, or whether that was an error. Second, if one or more of you does plan to be here longer than two months, we wanted to provide you with the information you will need to apply for either a visa or for citizenship, whichever the case may be. Third, even if there was an error, since you are here anyway, we wanted to welcome you and provide you with any resources or information you may need about Puerto Paz. When traveling in a foreign country, it is always best to know as much as you can about that country's culture and laws, for example, their culture and laws regarding public drunkenness." Nigel looked directly at Dylan during his last sentence before continuing. "Lastly, we wanted the whole travel party here together because we wanted you to feel relaxed and at ease with us, and you are more likely to feel that way in the Immigration Department office in a foreign land when you are with people you know and trust than if you were meeting with us alone."

"Well, none of us is staying here longer than two weeks, much less two months," Dylan said. "We're just here on vacation before the fall semester at New Miami starts. Problem solved."

"Well, Marcus," Nigel said, "since you were the one who marked 'uncertain' on the questionnaire, I'd like to make sure that you concur."

At this point, both Dylan and Nigel were looking at Marcus, waiting for a response. Marcus didn't want to look at either of them, but he knew lack of eye contact would be a dead giveaway that he had doubt. He looked at Nigel and sheepishly shrugged his shoulders. "I was filling out the questionnaire after a thirteen-hour ferry ride and was a bit discombobulated. I must have checked the 'uncertain' box by accident."

Nigel looked at Marcus for a couple of seconds. Marcus felt like Nigel was looking through him to his soul. Marcus momentarily looked up at the diploma on the side wall before forcing himself to reconnect eye contact with Nigel.

Nigel turned to Dylan. "All right, then. I guess now that we have heard what you have to say regarding the issue of your duration of stay, we can move on to providing you with whatever information you may desire. Have you both downloaded the Puerto Paz app to your phones?"

"Is the app for tracking and controlling us?" Dylan asked. "The technological replacements for commie minders following us around telling us what we can or cannot do? Aren't you going to just force the app onto our phones the way you forced my phone number out?"

"First, we are not communists," said Nigel. "In fact, I would say we are more democratic than EUS is. Less capitalist, but more democratic. We have plucked the best ideas from various different historical governments, including some from communism, to form a better society and government, but we are certainly not communists in the way people from EUS characterize us.

"Second, there is a lot of useful information in the app, as well as ways to get assistance should you need it. We are in hurricane season, and the app can provide emergency info about storms, shelter, and aid. Two-way communication, or at least the opportunity for it, is of paramount importance for the Puerto Paz government and its citizens, and we like to extend that courtesy to guests. If you don't want to download the app, that's fine, but at least let me give you some printed literature that outlines the most critical info you might need, along with some other interesting bedtime reading about Puerto Paz."

As Nigel stood up and walked to the rack near the door, Dylan turned to Marcus with a look that said, *What the fuck, dude? You're the reason why I'm wasting my time here?* Marcus just raised his palms up and shrugged his shoulders.

Nigel returned to his desk. He put all of the pamphlets he had selected in a pile in front of him on the desk, then, like a casino dealer distributing cards for a game of poker, began picking up pamphlets from the pile and placing them in two collated stacks at the edge of the desk closest to the boys. "Here is a pamphlet for each of you describing the history of Puerto Paz. Here is a pamphlet with emergency and other important contact info. And here is a primer.

"The primer contains invaluable information for understanding the core philosophies of Puerto Paz, our culture, our laws, and the structure of our government. Probably the two most important concepts in the primer are, one, finding balance between extremes, or in other words moderation of quantity but not of quality, and two, overcoming irrational fears and the tribal mentality."

"You have to live to the extreme to be a winner," Dylan interjected. "Moderation leads to mediocrity."

"I disagree," Nigel replied. "I'll give you an example. I do triathlons. If I were training for an Ironman Triathlon, the two extremes in training for it are: hardly doing any preparation at all and practically doing an Ironman every day during training in preparation. Both will result in poor performance, or possibly in no performance at all at the race. Lack of preparation will result in my muscles being unable to cope with the demands during the race. But the other extreme is overtraining, which will almost guarantee injury, illness, and fatigue. If I overtrain, chances are I won't even reach the starting line. The best chance of success is to find a balance between training and recovery. It involves not just quality work but intelligent work that avoids an excess of quantity. There is an endless list of examples I could give demonstrating situations where balance or moderation lead to healthier, happier outcomes than extremism."

"What about taking cyanide pills? You can't really do that in moderation and be healthier than the extreme of not doing it at all," Marcus said.

"As with any rule, there are always exceptions. There are some situations where moderation would be bad and extremism good. You are correct that you can't take cyanide pills in moderation because it is too dangerous. The exceptions to the rule often happen when one is faced with a dangerous crisis situation, like global climate change or the rise to power of a genocidal Hitler.

Occasionally we'll find other exceptions, such as transportation networks, that just won't work well enough unless we build it to its maximum potential. It is critical to be able to correctly identify these exceptions, though, because the tendency throughout history has been for people to slide down the slippery slope of exceptions and start seeing *everything* as a dangerous crisis situation requiring extremist response."

"So, you said you do triathlons?" Marcus asked. "Do you swim in the ocean? I've been dying to go for a swim in the ocean, but in San Francisco it was prohibited, and in New Miami the water was too polluted. My girlfriend said here would be a good place for swimming in the ocean."

"My triathlon team and I do swim in the ocean," said Nigel, smiling. "In fact, tomorrow morning we have a swim scheduled before work. You are welcome to join us if you would like."

"I don't know if I'd be able to keep up with serious triathletes."

"Oh, don't worry about that! We have a mix of abilities and speeds on the team, and I myself am not terribly fast."

"Sounds good," Marcus said. "Text me the when and where, and I'll be there."

"So, where was I?" Nigel continued. "Oh, yes, that's right. The primer. In Puerto Paz, we have civics classes as part of the curriculum from early in elementary school through college. Typically, citizens who are born and raised here, or immigrants who move here at a fairly young age, learn everything that is in this primer as a part of those classes. The classes go far beyond just what is in this primer, into things like life skills including financial planning, career planning, stress management, overcoming the natural tendencies for fear and a tribal mentality that can be detrimental to society, et cetera.

"For people considering applying for citizenship at an older age, in addition to personality testing that they are required to go through to assure that they aren't badly incompatible with our society and vice versa, there are intensive catch-up civics classes that are required for citizenship. The path to citizenship is actually fairly easy once you've gotten through the personality testing and classes. The primer is sort of a summary or syllabus for those classes, and it can also serve as a good introduction to local rules and customs for foreigners even just visiting the country."

"So you brainwash kids from a young age with commie propaganda. Got it," muttered Dylan, interrupting Nigel as he grabbed his stack of pamphlets. "Whatever. So, we have your pamphlets, we're only staying two weeks, you're not assigning us minders, and you understand that we're not spies trying to sell your secrets to the EUS government. Does that mean we can go now and get back to partying on the beach?"

Marcus looked at Dylan with his brow furled. This time it was Dylan's turn to lift his palms up and shrug his shoulders at Marcus.

"Listen," said Marcus, "there is plenty of time to party on the beach. Can you give me just ten minutes or so to hear what Nigel has to say? I'd like to be able to surprise Havana with some knowledge about her homeland."

Dylan sighed an exasperated "fiiine" and slumped back in his chair, pulling his Yankees cap even lower down his forehead.

Nigel began a rebuttal of Dylan's brainwashing comment. "First, for any society to function in a healthy, cohesive manner, there needs to be communication between the society as a whole and the individual. There needs to be clear communication of what the expectations of behavior are, and why the rules have been made the way they are. The civics classes are part of that communication. One of my frustrations while living in the former United States was that there would be laws and rules with no corresponding explanation of *why* those rules were enacted, nor was there a description of their intent. People wouldn't understand why a rule existed, if they even knew the rule existed at all among the thousands upon thousands of ultra-specific rules buried in thick codes, which is a whole other can of worms that I won't open now, and so they would ignore the rules they didn't understand or that they thought weren't important.

"Second, I would consider the work we do to help individuals overcome irrational fears and tribal mentalities as *un*brainwashing rather than brainwashing. It helps people to stand as strong, independent individuals rather than fear-driven sheep just following the herd off a cliff. Libertarian groups like SEUS, where there are no rules or order, inevitably devolve into classes of bullies and abused slaves."

"Why would the abused slaves allow themselves to be

enslaved?" Marcus asked.

"A combination of fear and adaptation. Humans develop coping mechanisms to help them adapt to their surroundings, and once they have acclimated, if their perspective isn't challenged from time to time, then it becomes difficult for them to see things from a different viewpoint.

"If you come from a lifetime of libertarian lawlessness, then you will adapt to it and think *that* lifestyle is normal, and that a more ordered lifestyle is oppressive. If you come from a lifetime of order-liberal society, then you will think *that* is normal, and you'll find the freedom-conservative, libertarian lifestyle chaotic and uncivilized. So, you can either feel perfectly normal in a more ordered but balanced society that functions in a healthy manner, or you can feel perfectly normal in a chaotic society that is dysfunctional and unhealthy.

"The ideal society, and the one that data shows is the healthiest and most successful, is balanced somewhere in the middle. An extreme lack of order is chaos, and an extreme overabundance of order turns into control. We seek a balance between them."

"What do you mean when you talk about 'tribal mentality,' though?" asked Marcus. "Are you saying it's bad to be a part of a group? Isn't your triathlon team your version of a tribe?"

"No, it is definitely not bad to be a part of a group! The interconnection of belonging to a group is critical to human well-being. Studies have shown that solitary confinement of humans is devastating to their health."

"It sounds like you're trying to have your cake and eat it too. Like you're saying groups are bad one minute and good the next," Marcus said.

"Again, it is a matter of balance. Group connections are necessary, but those connections can become a problem when it is taken to an extreme, when loyalties become excessively strong. With my tri team, it is about finding the middle ground and not becoming excessively loyal to a teammate just because they are a member of my in-group, such as covering for them if they cheat during a race, or rejecting those not on my team just because they are not a member of my in-group." Nigel paused and thought for a moment before looking at Dylan's Yankees cap and shirt. "Like rabid Yankees fans' reactions to rabid Red Sox fans."

"Die, Red Sucks, die!" Dylan nearly shouted while pumping his fist in the air.

"That is precisely the tribal mentality I'm speaking of. When I lived in the Boston area, I remember the occasional report of a fan of one team getting into a fight with a fan of the other team, and sometimes there was even a murder. I was astounded. A murder! Over baseball team loyalties! It's just a silly game meant to entertain and pass the time. How on earth could anyone allow their support for their team to get to the point where they are taking the life of another human being?

"Two other realms in which you see a lot of tribal mentality causing problems are religion and politics. Throughout history, there has been a tremendous amount of ostracism of, or even murder of, people who didn't conform to another group's religious or political beliefs. Terrorism typically comes down to either religious or political extremism. The kind of tribal mentality I refer to is when love of country turns into a national narcissism and an attitude that every other country is inferior, or worse yet, an enemy. Or when love of a religious group causes the same changes in attitude toward other religious groups. You see the results of tribal mentality in misguided loyalties to mobsters or gangs too. It is an excessive loyalty that results in damage to society, and I think it often stems from operating too much out of emotion, especially fear, and too little out of rationality and intelligence."

"But how do you maintain group cohesion without absolute loyalty?" Marcus asked.

"It is about avoiding a level of loyalty where you begin to see outsiders as 'others.' You have to be capable of introspection, examination, and consideration of the viewpoint of a complete stranger in order to overcome the tribal mentality while maintaining healthy group connections. It is why as part of our civics classes, we provide virtual-reality empathy-emersion games to realistically give the sensation of being in someone else's shoes for a while.

"It is also critical that you not allow irrational fears to paralyze your relationships, as irrational fear is detrimental to a healthy society. You have to have an attitude of collaboration more so than competition, and you can't do that when fear—such as fear of not having a romantic or sexual partner, fear of not having a job and making a living, fear of not getting needed resources, fear of not being liked, or fear of failure—is clouding your judgment. It is why, as a part of our civics classes, we teach cognitive behavioral therapy techniques to help people overcome their fears when they become irrational and unhealthy. It is also why we consider part of the government's function to be making sure everyone's most basic needs, such as food, shelter, and safety, are all met, so that we don't have a society full of people operating in fear of just trying to survive."

"Dude," Dylan said, "you have to have competition. You can't just have a kumbaya, let's all get along, nanny-state society. Competition is what motivates people. You even said it motivates you to exercise. That's just life. We compete, and there are winners and there are losers, and tough shit for the losers. All government does is just fuck things up, especially pie-in-the-sky liberal governments that are disconnected from reality. They try too hard to keep life from being unfair, but it isn't something anyone can control. Life just *is* unfair, and the less government the better."

"On a personal level," said Nigel, "it isn't competing versus other triathletes that motivates me. I couldn't care less whether I come in first place or last place—what matters to me is how I do relative to my personal bests. I would rather have the fastest times of my life and come in last place than to have times considerably slower than my personal bests while winning the race. In the manner in which you describe competition, as being 'me versus them,' it does not motivate me one bit.

"Honestly, though, not even my race times mean that much to me. I do triathlon races more to stay physically fit because physical health affects every aspect of one's life. Being on a triathlon team, in addition to the fun and social components it adds to my life, provides a sense of obligation that keeps me from skipping workouts when I'm tired. Signing up for races helps keep me motivated to exercise too, as I know that if I don't train regularly, then I'll be miserable during the race.

"Getting back to the global level, though, I agree that liberals can veer too far off in the direction of idealism and develop pie-in-the-sky ideas, but so can conservatives. Do you think that NEUS's idealistic attempts at the war on drugs, immigration, or abstinence and abortion control are realistic or effective? Or that SEUS's dogmatic ideology of the invisible hand of the market solving all problems without any regulatory interventions, or their belief that a person's monetary wealth is all that determines their worth as a human being, are reasonable? Of course they are not! There has to be a balance between idealism and pragmatism.

"As for the issue of fairness of life, yes, life can be unfair. It is unfair when a tornado randomly selects your house to destroy, but for human-caused unfairness, it is our duty and moral obligation to make society as fair as possible. As for competition, we recognize that the reality is that there will be a mix of competition and collaboration. We are not so naïve as to think that our society will be 100% collaboration, but we still strive to emphasize it. Just as an automobile is greater than the sum of its parts, so too is a collaborative society. The problem with competition is that it tends to generate the unhealthy 'us versus them' tribal attitude that I was just speaking of, and it ends up sabotaging groups. I can show you dozens of studies showing that collaboration is superior to, and healthier than, competition, but we do accept that in reality there will be some sort of hybrid of the two, and that what matters is finding a healthy balance and continually working to make sure that the competition is healthy rather than destructive."

Dylan folded his arms and sneered. "The only thing governments do is get corrupt. The weaker they are, the better."

"Governments are necessary to protect the commons and to serve as an impartial arbiter for difficult decisions where a large population will have one opinion, and another large population will have a differing opinion. Someone has to step in and decide what is fair and in the best interest of society as a whole. It is like the referee in a basketball game. Ever play in a pickup game of basketball without a referee? The game inevitably ends up suffering because some players constantly claim fouls that clearly are not legitimate, while other hard fouls go unenforced. Often it devolves into intimidation, bullying, and cronyism as to which fouls are enforced. The game is much more enjoyable when it is fairly refereed. Laissez-faire systems always fail. Some bare minimum of law and order is necessary for a culture of fairness to thrive."

"Yes," Marcus interjected, "but I've also seen basketball games where the referees were awful, and they skewed the results of the game."

Dylan excitedly pointed at Marcus in agreement, then smacked his hand back down on the armrest.

"True," Nigel said. "You do need well-trained, rational referees who aren't extremists."

"What are the commons you were talking about?" Marcus asked.

"Yes. The other major task for governments I mentioned was protecting the commons," Nigel continued. "When it comes to protecting the commons, I mean shared resources like open spaces, park lands, and other land uses—air quality, water quality, massive civil engineering works like water and sewer, and transportation networks. Without sufficient government regulation of these shared resources, corporations have proven time and time again that they cannot control themselves, and if left to their own devices, they will form monopolies and consume every resource, harm society, and decimate the planet. Their motivation is profit, and being environmentally friendly isn't profitable. There *has* to be a watchdog, a police force, that protects society from being pillaged by its own industries. A good government is responsible for making sure resources are protected and used in a healthy and fair manner. It is the referee of society."

"But you just agreed that referees can become corrupt, right?" Marcus asked.

Dylan sat forward in his chair. "Yeah! Marcus knows what I'm talking about! You tell him, MC!"

Nigel smiled. "Governments *can* become corrupt, but so can any group. Corruption can happen wherever two or more people attempt to form a group. Corruption could even happen between the two of you boys. It happens in private corporations, where the primary objective is to make money, far more frequently than in governments, where the objective is fairness and justice. Well, at least it happens less frequently in governments that have restricted private financial investment in political elections.

"I could list hundreds of cases in which EUS or, prior to the partitioning, USA corporations were corrupt, immoral, and illegal. Enron reporting false profits, Wells Fargo fleecing their customers with fake accounts in their names, Wall Street banks that caused an economic recession due to risky and likely unethical behavior. The tobacco and sugar industries falsifying or hiding health data, coal mines falsifying or ignoring safety procedures, investment firms pushing investments on their client that benefit the firm rather than the investor. Literally hundreds upon hundreds of examples. But it can also happen in condo associations or book clubs too. It can happen in Girl Scout troops, charities, and churches, and in fact, it has happened in many groups like that. No group of people is perfectly safe from the possibility of corruption, but personally I am much more trusting of the groups whose motivations, their primary reason for existing, isn't profit. Therefore, I find governments and unions much more trustworthy than private corporations.

"One of the primary methods for preventing corruption is checks and balances. That is why here, as you'll read in the primer, we have large similarly influential groups of people that counter the power of other large groups. The government, the consumer and employee unions, and the corporations all balance each other out and fight to maintain fairness for all. The idea of checks and balances is one that the founding fathers of the United States definitely got right. Everyone needs to feel a sense of accountability and obligation to someone else."

"Sounds like competition to me," Dylan said.

"Yes and no. Having equally powerful opposing forces actually encourages collaboration. It is when those forces are imbalanced that collaboration tends to break down," Nigel said.

"Do you think corruption is the result of people being inherently bad?" Marcus asked. "What about a sense of accountability to God preventing corruption? Couldn't Christianity influence whether people are good or bad and serve as a check against corruption?"

"My experience has been that religious people do not have a monopoly on morals. I could rattle off a long list of immoral acts Christians have committed throughout history, or even just throughout my own life. I have met far too many atheists and agnostics with hearts of gold, and far too many Christians who behave immorally, to believe that non-Christians are morally inferior or more susceptible to corruption," Nigel responded.

"A godless commie would think that," Dylan muttered almost

inaudibly.

"I don't think the issue of whether people are inherently good or bad is a black-and-white issue, though," Nigel continued. "What I have found is that people are inherently somewhere between good and bad, and how they behave at any given moment is highly dependent on circumstances and environment, much more so than they'd care to admit. A person who is normally good might act bad in the wrong situation, and vice versa. Momentum is often underappreciated too. Good habits tend to beget good habits, and bad habits tend to beget bad habits, so often people who seem chronically bad are people who have gotten trapped in a cycle of misfortune and bad decisions or were raised in a bad environment.

"Data also suggests that where bad things happen, it is typically a result of just a handful of bad actors. For example, in areas of high crime, it typically boils down to just a half dozen to a dozen people, typically young men, who are at the root of nearly all of the crime. You remove just those few bad actors, and suddenly the crime mostly goes away, but then the challenge becomes trying to rehabilitate troublemakers. It is much easier to catch bad situations at a young age and guide young children toward a path of good habits than it is to rehabilitate someone older who has gotten themselves trapped in a cycle of unhealthy decisions."

"So, you sit all high and mighty in your throne selecting who stays and who goes?" Dylan asked argumentatively. "Do you conservative-haters just pluck out all of the conservatives and put them in prison for being 'bad actors' or something?"

"No. Being conservative is not a crime. In fact, we value conservatives. They provide checks and balances to the more dominant order-liberal values. We depend on conservatives to speak up when the pendulum starts swinging too hard to the order-liberal side and the order starts getting oppressive, so that we can reevaluate what we are doing and see if there is a way to simplify things. A problem we have, though, is that conservatives are more prone to irrational fears than liberals, and they are especially fearful of change and non-homogeneous culture.

"Studies show that the parts of the brain that detect threats are more active in conservatives, whereas in liberals the parts of the brain that detect nuance and complexity are more active. This results in liberals seeing things as shades of gray, whereas conservatives see things more black and white and are prone to crying wolf in terms of what is or isn't a valid threat. In their defense, sometimes there is a legitimate threat, and the liberals don't see it until the conservatives point it out, but in general, fear of change retards progress. Businesses that fear change tend to fail. So do societies. They stagnate and then get overtaken by groups that do change and take risks."

"Not everything that's shiny and new is good just because it's shiny and new though," said Marcus. "You can't just change for the sake of change."

"I would agree with that, actually," Nigel confirmed. "But getting back to the conservative role here, as I've said, Puerto Paz identifies as an order-liberal-leaning society, and we tend to not be afraid of change or of taking risks, but we value trusting and respecting one another, or at least *starting* from a position of trust and respect until the person we are dealing with proves otherwise. We see benefit from having a diverse opinion base, including conservative opinions. Once again, it boils down to maintaining balance between extremes. A country is best when there is diversity of opinions, and when those opinions meld together into something in the center. Bubbles of extremism lead to extremist leaders, which leads to everything going haywire."

"Trust is important. I think in EUS, or at least in NEUS, they tend to be distrustful because they believe everyone is inherently bad," said Marcus. "It's the reverse of what you just said. Don't trust anyone until they've proven they deserve to be trusted."

"I think you are mostly correct," Nigel responded. "And I think it also can become a bit of a self-fulfilling prophecy. If people are repeatedly told that they are inherently bad or untrustworthy, then they start to believe it, and they start to behave badly. And if you believe the only thing stopping people from behaving badly is religion, then you'll distrust anyone who isn't religious, or even of your particular brand of religion. Without a minimum level of trust in one another, you can't have a functioning society, and it will result in people behaving selfishly and badly.

"Similarly, when you have libertarians running the government, and they believe that government is inherently corrupt and unworthy of trust, then they will destroy all the good things the government does, and you'll end up with everyone thinking the government is useless because of what the libertarians did to it. It will inevitably devolve into monopolies and robber barons that enslave the rest of the population and view humans as expendable, and all of the freedom will end up in the hands of a few wealthy elites.

"Excessive corporate power is, in fact, why the founders of our country set up the Consumer Union and Workers Union as a part of the government as a check against corporate power. Losing one unhappy, abused employee might seem insignificant to an employer, but the threat of losing hundreds or thousands of employees gives employees some bargaining power. Similarly with the Consumer Union, having one customer blacklist your product is insignificant, but having thousand joined together in solidarity to blacklist your product could cripple your business."

Marcus noticed some movement out of the corner of his eye in Dylan's direction. He looked to his left and saw Dylan had his elbow perched on the arm of the chair, with his forearm vertical, and he was repeatedly making a clamping motion with his hand as if he was operating the mouth of an imaginary sock puppet. It was the "talky, talky, talky, no more talky" gesture from an old Adam Sandler movie that meant Dylan was tired of the conversation. Marcus ignored his nonverbal request to end the conversation and continued. "So it seems like a lot of what Puerto Paz does is an attempt to make life fair."

"Indeed," Nigel replied. "There are several basic human morals, and fairness is one of the most important of them. The only moral I might value more highly is compassion. Everyone cares about fairness. We want someone who works harder to receive more compensation than a slacker, but there is a certain base level at which care and compassion have to be the starting point. Only once someone's basic human needs are met—those needs that form the foundation of Maslow's hierarchy, which you will read about in the primer—can the fairness morality kick in. That is the lower boundary of fairness. There is an upper boundary to fairness too, where people are being overcompensated, not acknowledging all the support they get to achieve that success, and taking more than their fair share, resulting in harm to society."

"That's what the quote on the Michael Debroux statue at Port Camille was talking about, right?" Marcus asked.

"Indeed. This is also what is happening in SEUS now, where thousands of people are literally starving to death while a few elites hoard all of the resources and set their own salaries at millions of dollars. It turns into a freeloader issue, where the rich and powerful are determining excessively high compensation for themselves and monopolizing resources because they *can*, rather than because they deserve it. At a certain point, it stops being meritocracy and starts being greed. Conservatives and liberals are often looking at two sides of the same fairness coin, both concerned with freeloaders. Freeloaders not working hard enough on one end of the spectrum versus freeloaders who have power and greed and take more than their fair share on the other end of the spectrum. A battle between sloth and greed."

Nigel sat up in his chair and looked at the clock on his bracelet. "Well, then. I feel like I've just given you an entire civics class in the last half hour."

Dylan, proving that he was still awake, grumbled, "Yeah. I thought you said your shed-jewel was busy."

"It is, but this sort of meeting is important to me, and I wanted to afford you the courtesy of answering any questions you might have. And besides, all I have left tonight is some paperwork that I'm not looking forward to, and our chat has been a welcomed procrastination." Nigel turned to Marcus, completely ignoring Dylan, who clearly just wanted the conversation over with. "Are there any more questions you have, Marcus?"

"Yeah," Marcus said, noticing Dylan face-palming out of the corner of his eye. "What does that foot pedal under the sink in your little kitchen do?" he asked, finally scratching the mental itch that had been bugging him since his solo tour of the room.

Nigel turned around to confirm what Marcus was referring to. "That controls the water coming out of the tap. It is useful for minimizing water usage while washing dishes." He stood up and walked over to it to demonstrate as he spoke, and Marcus stood up to see over Nigel's desk.

"You have to turn the water on with the handles first, and once it is on, you can engage the foot pedal by stepping on it. Then you can nudge it left or right and stand there with your foot blocking it from returning to center when you want water flowing, and shift your foot away when you don't. It relocks when you turn the handles to off, or when you step on it again. We found that without the foot pedal, people washing dishes find it too cumbersome to manipulate handles to turn water on and off while they are trying to hold dishes, sponges, and soap bottles in their hands, so they waste a lot of water."

Nigel walked over to the boys and extended his hand to Marcus for a farewell handshake. "It has been a pleasure meeting you. I will text you later tonight about the swim. If either of you has any questions, please feel free to contact me. Enjoy your stay, and have a good night."

Chapter 4: Parental Apprehension

"That was fucking brutal! That guy never shuts up! And I gave you way more than ten minutes. Jesus, you kept asking question after question," Dylan said as the boys headed toward the exit.

"Well, I wanted to hear what he had to say. This place is unlike any place we've been before, and I was curious. You lived, and maybe you learned something new."

"Whatever I learned, I'm going to forget after I kill those brain cells on Playa Nueva tonight," Dylan said as he pitched Nigel's literature in a garbage can. "You want to come party with me? Kelsey might need to sit this one out, so it could be just you and me like the good ol' days. We can do some shots of 'teh-kill-ya.'"

"Dude. Don't waste these. Someone else could use them," Marcus said as he fished the literature out of the garbage. "And I can't join you tonight. I have dinner plans with Havana, and I need to get to bed early for my swim tomorrow morning. Besides, we never used to booze it up in the 'good ol' days.' How'd you get your hands on tequila anyway?"

"Don't ask. You don't want to know. You do realize we're on vacation, though, don't you? In less than two weeks, we'll be back in boring classrooms in New Miami, and if my hand heals quickly, it won't be long until I'm working my ass off on the football field. Now is the time to let loose and party and have fun!"

"I'm having fun. There is a lot to explore here. It's so...different," Marcus said.

"Whatevs. I'm gonna catch a train back to the beach and check on Kelsey. Catch you later."

The two boys went their separate ways, with Dylan heading back to the beach area and Marcus headed back to his dorm room to recharge, feeling like he had spent all of his social energy for the day and needing to be introverted for a while before dinner with Havana.

Back at the dorm room, he lay down and started looking at the literature Nigel had given him. Most of the information in the history pamphlet he already knew from the San Francisco City Hall exhibit or from Havana. It was the primer that had him most curious at the moment, given the topics of discussion with Nigel. He opened the small booklet to the first page and began reading.[4]

A while later, Marcus's cell phone chirped, knocking him out of his state of concentration. It was Havana asking whether he was on his way. He looked at the clock and realized he was late.

"Sorry," he texted back. "Got caught up reading the Puerto Paz primer."

"We are going to lose our reservation," Havana replied. "Dinner at my house, okay?"

Marcus responded that he was fine with that and hustled out of the dorm, still wearing his one good outfit.

He speed-walked to the South Avenue stop, occasionally cursing under his breath, and hopped on a subway that went to the North Park stop nearest Havana's home. *Shit!* he thought. *Meeting a girlfriend's parents is nerve-wracking enough, especially when they're white, but add to it tardiness and a missed dinner reservation? And my unfamiliarity with local customs isn't exactly going to help me either. God, I hope I don't fuck this up.*

From the stop, he walked in the shade under the canopy of trees lining the road, their branches arching over the street. Upon arrival at Havana's family's stucco and clay tile roofed house, Marcus rang the doorbell. A dog began barking, and Marcus could hear the pitter patter of small paws approaching the door and then dancing around waiting for it to open. *I think I'm more anxious about what's on the other side of that door than you are, little buddy,* Marcus thought.

Havana and both of her parents, clad in casual shorts and T-shirts, opened the door and greeted him together, offered hugs, and invited him in, partially alleviating Marcus's anxiety.

"Sorry I'm late," Marcus said as he kneeled down and extended a hand for the dog to sniff.

---

[4] Appendix 2 at the back of the book contains a copy of the *Primer on Puerto Paz Politics and Philosophies* that Marcus is reading.

"You are shattering my stereotypes of NEUS people already," Havana's father said with the corners of his lips curling slightly. "I had assumed they were all a very time-minded people. A very time-minded people indeed."

Marcus looked at Havana apprehensively, but she was looking down at the dog. He turned back to her father. "Yes, sir, Mr. Lamarr. Usually I'm much more punctual. I got caught up reading the primer that the assistant director of Immigration gave me."

Mrs. Lamarr lightly slapped her husband on the chest. "Maybe you should let me do the talking if you are in the mood for teasing, Steinbeck." She turned her attention back to Marcus and put her hand on his shoulder. "It is a pleasure to meet you, Marcus. You can call us by our first names. I'm Irene. Welcome to our home."

"Thank you, Irene. Steinbeck," Marcus said, dipping his head in a mini-bow, first at Havana's mom, then at her dad.

The whole family burst out laughing. Marcus scanned their faces, trying to figure out why they were laughing at him.

"My dad's name is Gordon," Havana said. "My mom was just teasing him, calling him Steinbeck because he was riffing on a quote from a book by John Steinbeck. Marcus, meet Gordon Graham, Irene Lamarr, and down here is Leonardo, or Leo for short. Mom and Dad, Marcus."

Havana's parents returned to their meal-prep duties in the kitchen, while Havana and Leo began showing Marcus around their home.

"You look very formal," Havana said. She smiled and gestured for him to walk from the foyer to the living room.

"I had wanted to make a good first impression," he said. "Not sure I succeeded," he muttered quietly to himself has he walked ahead of Havana.

"Sorry, I didn't catch that last part," Havana said.

"Nothing."

"I could throw on something nicer if you feel out of place."

"I'm fine," Marcus said.

Havana began her tour. The interior furnishings were pleasant and classical but functional. The home was fairly tidy, with occasional small pockets of clutter. Neither a stifling museum of a home, nor the cluttered chaos of a hoarder. The artwork was what really captured Marcus's attention though. A couple of impressionist and Art Nouveau paintings, but mostly beautiful photographs of architecture. Marcus asked Havana about them, and she said they were photos her family had taken in Europe. A photo of the lobby of a cathedral in Siracusa, Italy, taken by her dad. One of a motor scooter in the traboules of Lyon, France, taken by her mother. And one zoomed in on a Greek column capital with a church tower rising up behind it, taken by Havana herself at Diocletian's Palace in Split, Croatia. "I'd love to see these places in person someday," Marcus remarked.

He continued surveying, looking for anything that reminded him of his own family's home. He did find some family photos interspersed among the décor on end tables and shelving. "Everyone is smiling," he said and chuckled while inspecting a few photos more closely. *I can't believe I botched her dad's name. And was his last name different than Havana's? Did I botch both his first and last names? Great impression*, he thought as he looked at Havana's dad in a photo.

They walked past the study, where Marcus pointed to some antique-looking nautical instruments and scientific tools displayed around the room. "Are those real? Is your dad into sailing or something?"

"They are a mix of real historical equipment and modern reproductions, and they are actually my mom's," Havana said. "She's a marine biologist, and she loves all things ocean-related."

After Havana finished her obligatory tour guide duties, she asked Marcus whether he could help her sous chef for her parents since they were having to unexpectedly cook a larger meal. As they walked into the kitchen, Gordon looked up and nodded, then turned to Irene.

"It's getting a bit dark in here," Gordon said.

Marcus froze and perked up his ears, bracing himself emotionally for confirmation that it was a veiled racist comment, but then Irene opened the shutters on the kitchen window, flooding the room with evening daylight.

Marcus silently exhaled in relief as Gordon thanked Irene.

"Can you get the turmeric from the pantry?" Irene asked Havana.

Havana opened a closet door, and Marcus peeked in behind her, watching as she said "turmeric" out loud, and a small LED on the surface of one of the dozens of identical plastic containers lit up, and she grabbed it.

"Where are the labels?" Marcus asked as he looked around at the other perfectly ordered shelves filled with several sizes of similarly designed plastic bins filled with grains, legumes, spices, and other dry foods.

"Most foods are sold in bulk," Havana said. "All grocery stores and farmer's markets use the same few styles of nestable containers, and when you put your container in the loader, it automatically programs the little electronic chip in them with what's being put in it. Restaurants use the same containers for leftovers too. Every once in a while we set out a stack of empties to be collected for sanitizing and reuse. It cuts down on wasteful packaging."

"The organization of the containers and their different colored contents makes it look almost like artwork," Marcus said.

"The containers are actually Pippa winners," Havana replied. "They are made of a bioplastic that is stable until you immerse it in a reactive agent, then it becomes compostable. There are other low-tech efficiency innovations in this room too, some Pippa-winning, like the refrigerator and oven that passively vent to the exterior of the house on hot days, and to the interior on the rare cold day, along with simple things like the shutters that prevent solar heat-gain and double as protection against flying debris during hurricanes."

Havana handed the turmeric to her mother and asked her what they were making for dinner.

"Chana masala with a side of baby spinach sautéed in olive oil and garlic," Irene responded. "Except that we are low on rice, so we are improvising a pasta version of the main dish. Can you two chop some garlic, onion, and tomatoes?"

"So, did I really mess up your dinner plans?" Marcus asked Havana's parents apologetically as he began peeling the garlic.

"Don't worry about it," Irene assured him. "Usually on Sunday nights we cook a couple of meals and freeze them for reheating and eating during the work week. All this does is change which night we eat our premade meals on."

"So Sunday night meal prep is sort of a tradition in your

household? Do you have any other traditions? Like a family game night?"

Gordon chuckled, but it was Irene who responded. "People in Puerto Paz often cringe a little at the word 'tradition.'"

"Speak for yourself, dear," Gordon said.

"Well, *most* people cringe at that word. We tend to have high levels of skepticism about anything with that label. Traditions often try to normalize behaviors that aren't healthy for society, so we try to always evaluate traditions to determine whether they serve a good purpose. I guess you could call our Sunday night dinners a tradition of sorts, though."

"And we have the tradition of one holiday per month," said Gordon. "And we have bi-annual neighborhood parties at the neighborhood community center that is sort of a tradition to keep the communication lines among neighbors open. And the coin flip at the hospital with the winner getting to pass along their last name and loser choosing their baby's first name."

"Oh, I don't know if the coin flip counts as a tradition though, since it is really only a last resort if the parents haven't decided the names in advance," Irene said. "And the rest of the traditions you named all have very good reasons behind them."

"That's nice that you live in an area that can afford a community center," Marcus said.

"All neighborhoods have community centers," Havana said. "They are required so that the residents have a soundproofed place to host parties or to play loud music. Most residential areas have strict noise ordinances for the same reasons we discussed at the dorms."

"I'll bet Dylan would object to that," Marcus said.

"There are some noise-permissive areas he could live in if that's what he wanted," Havana said. "The city has a mix of lifestyle zones that vary in rules. Once a year, citizens are encouraged to take a survey, and the government tries to match zones with different personalities to give people a chance to live in a zone that is most compatible for them. It is imperfect, but better than just random chaos with things like loud musicians living next to peaceful introverts."

"After the New Miami dorm experience, I can understand the

need for a quiet place to sleep, but what does having similar personalities grouped together do to diversity?" Marcus asked.

"There is an understanding here, regardless of zone preferences, that a peaceful home life is critical to health, and that it's not okay to do things that negatively impact other people's lives without their consent. Typically we like to alternate between a restful, peaceful, comfortable state at home and an active, explorative, challenging state outside of home. Outside the comfort of home is where diversity really blossoms."

"Speaking of diversity and traditions, we don't get a lot of visitors from NEUS here," Gordon began. "My understanding is that they tend to be a bit insular and xenophobic. You are actually the first person from NEUS we've ever hosted in our house. Are traditions something you value highly in NEUS?"

"I think so," Marcus said. "I've always liked our Thanksgiving and Christmas meal traditions. And when the college football conferences in EUS split up to segregate north from south, I guess I missed some of the traditional rivalry games that disappeared. I never did get used to the new conferences."

"Ah, a fellow football fan! Irene and I both play in recreational football leagues," Gordon said.

"He means gridiron, Dad," said Havana.

"Ah, yes. Very aggressive and combative sport."

Marcus stopped dicing garlic and looked over at Havana but failed to catch her eye.

"You know, there is a story I remember my parents telling me that helped me understand people like Irene's views on traditions," Gordon resumed. "They said that there was once a couple cooking a Christmas roast and that the husband, as he always did, chopped off and discarded the end of the roast before sticking it in the pan. The wife, having witnessed him do this year after year, finally asked him why he chopped off and wasted the end. He paused and said, because that was what my mother always did. The wife asked why his mother did it, and the husband didn't know, so they called his mother and asked. She said that it was because it was what her mother always did. They called the husband's grandmother to ask her why. She responded: 'Because my oven and roast pan were too small to fit the whole roast in.'" Gordon chuckled.

"Speaking of large cooking vessels, could you get out the large wok, dear?" Irene said with the lack of enthusiasm for Gordon's story of someone who had heard it a million times before.

Marcus and Havana delivered the chopped ingredients to Irene and headed into the dining room to set the table.

Marcus turned to Havana. "So does your dad think I'm not good enough for you? It felt like he was judging me with the comments about NEUS people and football being combative."

"Oh, don't worry. He's just curious about NEUS. He means no harm, and both of my parents have always had an attitude of the only criteria for my boyfriends being that they make me happy." She placed the final glass on the table. "Have a seat. I'll help my parents bring the food in."

Marcus sat down briefly until he felt a damp pressure against his hand and looked down to see Leo looking for attention. He got out of his chair and kneeled on the floor to pet him. Havana and her parents entered the room.

Gordon smiled. "You can always tell a lot about a person by how they interact with animals."

"We are all animals, humans and all," Irene said.

"That's my little marine biologist for you," Gordon said.

Minutes later, they were all seated, serving themselves dinner. Marcus raised a forkful of the main dish to his nose and sniffed the spicy curry.

"Everything okay?" Irene asked.

"Yeah. I've just never had Indian food before," Marcus said. "It smells…"

"Unfamiliar?" Havana asked.

"Yeah."

"Try a bite. If you don't like it, we have some frozen meals we could heat up in a hurry," Havana suggested.

Marcus took a small bite and let it sit on his tongue for a moment before chewing and swallowing. He raised his eyebrows and took another, larger bite. "This is really good!" he said.

A few bites later, Havana asked, "So how did the meeting at Immigration go?"

"Good. Except Dylan is still being a…he's still being rude. And Kelsey was too hungover to even show up."

"Ugh. I need to spend some time with her and give her a break from the Dylan drinkfest."

"Yeah. I don't know why he feels he has to do that nonstop. Nigel was pretty cool, though. I'm actually going swimming in the ocean with him tomorrow morning."

"Awesome! Can I come with, if the timing works? I start my two weeks of shadowing doctors tomorrow, but if it is early enough, I could swim before going to the doctor's office."

"Nigel seemed to have an attitude of 'the more the merrier.' I suspect he'd be fine with that. I'll text him later."

A few bites later, Gordon spoke up. "I was honored that the reason you were late is that you were learning more about our country," he said. "What did you think about the primer?"

Marcus thought for a moment. "It was a lot to digest in one short sitting. I need to dig into parts of it more. Some things, like the election process and the consumer and worker unions are a lot different than back home, and I haven't had time to really figure them out yet."

"Don't worry," Irene said. "We could all spend lifetimes pondering political and social variables and still not feel like we have our minds fully wrapped around everything."

Gordon raised a finger. "Out of everything in the primer, though, I think we could all agree that the election systems Puerto Paz developed in its infancy were the single most critical thing we did to not only differentiate ourselves from our EUS and WUS roots, but to improve our system of government. Trust is so important, and if you don't have confidence in the system of elections, then trust in the government collapses. A lot of the kinks were worked out in the *Renaissancity* game in reaction to problems people were encountering in the USA, and later in WUS and EUS."

"That's my little software programmer, always plugging the role of the *Renaissancity* game!" Irene said, followed by a playful smirk. "I would tend to agree, though. Leading up to the partitioning of the USA, they were finding that congresspeople were spending more than half of their time fundraising for elections rather than governing. Entire states were being misrepresented by extremist whackjob representatives because the districts were gerrymandered in a way that made it impossible for one party to lose, effectively creating a monopoly.

"Their entire government was reduced to a binary yes-or-no two-party system because of the winner-takes-all, plurality voting system. There was no opportunity to vote for an alternate party candidate because doing so was essentially equivalent to handing your vote to the major party candidate you disliked most. In fact, I would say that implementing instant runoff voting here, perhaps along with making all elections publicly funded, was the most fundamentally critical change we made versus the way things had been done in the United States. It allowed for a more accurate expression of voter will."

"And setting up district boundaries based on a combination of physical landscape boundaries and geometric algorithms, rather than on the whims of political operatives, were also extremely important to making elections fair, and it was a truer representation of the people's desires," Gordon said. He made a slight bowing gesture and said, "Again, on behalf of all software programmers, you are welcome," eliciting a chuckle from Irene and Havana.

"I read that you make voting day a public holiday, which I found simple yet remarkable," Marcus said. "Back in New Rochelle, when my older brother came of legal voting age, I asked him who he voted for in an election, and he said he hadn't voted at all because he didn't have time that day to vote."

"Awful," Irene said. "It is the responsibility of democracies to make elections as fair and representative as possible, and how can you have that if the people cannot vote?"

"Speaking of fairness," said Marcus, "Nigel mentioned needing a base level of compassion before a fairness morality kicks in. Something about assuring that people have their most basic needs met before you start worrying about whether people who work harder or smarter earn more than those who don't work as hard. It seems to tie in with the Maslow's Hierarchy chart that was in the primer, but I wasn't sure what the purpose of the chart is."

"Basically, it is a very simplistic model, developed over a century ago, to represent basic human needs and wants in a prioritized manner," Havana said.

"Sometimes it can be overly simplistic," said Irene, "and the expectation is not necessarily that people will proceed linearly up from the base levels to the top levels, but it is useful in prioritizing government policy decisions nonetheless, and it aids in guiding societal and individual development."

"At the base of the pyramid are basic human survival needs," Havana continued. "Things like food, water, safety, and medical services. They result in the highest priorities of the government being things like agriculture, water and sewer systems, environmental protections, and police, fire, and hospital services."

"The commons," Marcus said.

"Some of them are," Havana confirmed. "We do attempt to balance things out and 'walk and chew gum at the same time,' in that we attempt to address higher levels of the Hierarchy simultaneously with lower levels, but by identifying the lower levels as higher priority, it helps keep our policies in line with our core philosophies. Our objective is to get as many people as we can to as high of levels in the Hierarchy as possible."

"A chain is only as strong as its weakest link, and similarly a society is only as successful as its most struggling citizens," Irene said.

"Not to get all Dylan on you, but doesn't a government providing too much service to citizens make them dependent and unable or unwilling to work hard for themselves? Doesn't it turn it into a nanny state?" Marcus asked.

"First, our government is highly active in making sure the lowest levels of the Hierarchy are achieved by all, but in the higher levels, the government plays a much reduced role and mostly only offers systems of incentives or disincentives to try to shape healthy behaviors," Havana said. "Second, healthy people typically have a desire to be productive members of society. They don't *want* to be a drain on society. If you have a society full of healthy people making healthy decisions, that tends not to be a problem."

Gordon raised three fingers. "And third, I would add, we are vigilant about abusers of the system and have procedures for addressing them."

"Abusers are rare, though," Irene added. "And if we are going to err, I would rather we erred on the side of compassion and have a few societal leeches than to err on the side of fairness and have decent people unable to survive because they fell into bad circumstances."

Gordon tilted his head. "You know, I hadn't thought about this before, but I'm realizing that I think conservative-leaning people tend to gravitate toward careers involving the base levels of the hierarchy. Jobs like police, fire fighters, and farmers."

"Doctors provide base-level service too, and I think they tend to be more liberal-leaning on average though, so it isn't like the conservative-leaners have a monopoly on the base levels of the hierarchy," Havana said.

"And people who work for the government in environmental protection can be considered as offering base-level services, and they tend to skew more liberal too," Irene added.

"I guess you are right," Gordon acknowledged.

"Maybe conservatives do gravitate toward security careers, though," Marcus said. "Nigel said that conservatives are better at detecting threats, whereas liberals are better at detecting nuance."

"The conservatives are a security-minded people. A security-minded people, indeed," Havana said as she pursed her lips to one side of her mouth and looked sideways at her dad out of the corner of her eye.

Gordon chuckled. "Well, the part of my brain that detects nuance is at least active enough to detect that I'm being teased."

"Speaking of security…" Marcus began. "I was kind of surprised by the level of security at Port Camille, and by what Nigel was saying about immigration requirements here. For a society that stresses balance, they seem so…" Marcus paused, trying to find the right words.

"Harsh?" Irene asked as she reached for a slice of bread on a tray and then began to saucer the last remnants of her meal.

Marcus nodded. "It seems rather insular and xenophobic," he said, raising an eyebrow at Gordon.

Gordon guffawed briefly, raising his hand to cover his mouth for a moment before struggling to swallow his food. "I think Irene here would tend to agree with you."

Irene nodded. "Immigration policy was a subject of great debate during the formation of Puerto Paz. We do tend to be liberal-leaning on average, but security tends to be a high priority for the conservative-leaners, and we found that it was a good way to compromise with them. The liberal-leaners conceded that it does no one any good to let someone rebellious, who wants to upset the system, into our society. It does neither the country, nor that person, any good."

"There needs to be some basic level of compatibility between our society and the people we let into it," Gordon said. "We are open and have free exchange of cultures when it comes to short-term visits, but more restrictive when it comes to moving here permanently. There has to be a social contract that everyone buys into and is bound to. It is best when that contract is relatively loose, though…. Like a romantic relationship. You don't want your significant other to be excessively controlling and overbearing on one hand, but on the other hand you want them to be compatible with you and not violate your trust or violate the 'rules' of romantic relationships that are there to prevent harm. If it is too loose, then it loses all cohesion and meaning."

Irene nodded again. "But there are limits to just how much liberal-leaners will sacrifice in the name of security. We compromise to give them a lot of what they want for security and immigration, but we consider it our duty to put our foot down if it gets too extreme and starts to harm our society. And when it comes to crime and punishment, except in extreme cases, we insist on the more liberal approach of rehabilitation for offenders rather than the 'lock them up and throw away the key' retribution approach favored in more conservative cultures."

"Compromising with conservatives on security is kind of like your favorite show, *Star Trek: The Next Generation*," Havana said.

Gordon's eyes got wide. "TNG is your favorite too?" he exclaimed. "I love that show! Half the reason I got into the computer programming field is because I wanted to program a real-life android like Data. If there is a heaven, I'm sure there will be infinite new episodes of TNG there!"

Marcus and Gordon exchanged a knowing nod as Havana continued. "You would think that Worf, who comes from a very combative, warrior-minded Klingon culture, wouldn't fit in with the Federation's more pacifist way of life, right? But they made it work by putting Worf in charge of the thing he cares about most: security. But Captain Picard and Riker can, and do, overrule Worf when Worf is getting too extreme. That's kind of how it is here in Puerto Paz with conservative-leaners like my dad. Puerto Paz, like the Federation, takes diverse personalities and opinions, people with differing strengths and weaknesses, and it finds a way to moderate those differences and work together as a cohesive, collaborative unit. It is a give and take between the individual and society, where the society adapts to the individual's personality some, but so too does the individual adapt to the society some."

Gordon groaned and turned to Irene. "So I've gone from Steinbeck to Klingon now. I think I have devolved." He put his utensils on his plate and started gathering his dishes. "It looks like it is time for me to tuck my tail and retreat into the kitchen." With dishes in hand, he leaned over and kissed Havana on the top of the head on his way out. Irene and Havana began gathering their dishes and standing up, so Marcus followed their lead and they all headed to the kitchen.

"I always saw Captain Picard as the key ingredient in the mix on *Star Trek*," Marcus said as they entered the kitchen. "They worked well because Picard was a strong leader, and the crew was loyal to him."

"Captain Picard was important," Gordon acknowledged as Havana deposited some dishes and then headed back toward the dining room. "He was a good leader, but he wasn't perfect. He was good because he had an *alta-vista*, and he respected and valued all opinions and weighed them all to find diplomatic and appropriate solutions. Loyalty is a two-way street, though, and the crew was only loyal so long as the captain was making reasonable demands. There were a couple of episodes where they rightfully discussed or attempted mutiny, either against Picard or other Federation leaders," Gordon said before he disappeared into the pantry.

"And individuals play a big role too," Irene said. "The captain can't make everything happen. The crew has to perform their unique specialties while simultaneously seeing that their job and perspective is just one small part of a bigger picture. The captain is just the person who sees and communicates that full picture more clearly."

Havana returned to the kitchen with more dishes, and Marcus began dishwashing duties by turning on the faucet and releasing the foot pedal to confirm that he was operating the pedal correctly.

"Wait a second before you start washing," Havana said. "Hey, Mom, is the chana safe for Leo?"

"It has garlic and onion, which are toxic for dogs except in very small quantities," her mother said. "I'd say only let him have a little of the leftover plain pasta and bread."

Havana grabbed a couple of fully saucered dinner plates, set some plain pasta on one and a piece of uneaten bread crust on the other, and put them down on the floor for an eager Leo to lick clean.

"Eww!" Marcus shouted as he wrinkled his nose. "You eat off of plates that the dog has licked? That's disgusting!"

Havana's eyebrows pinched together and raised. "They get washed before we eat off of them. The dishwasher completely sanitizes them."

"I still say it's gross."

Havana shook her head. "Would it make you feel better to double-wash them, first by hand, then by dishwasher?" Marcus nodded, and Havana began handing him the dishes after Leo had finished licking them clean.

Marcus, nose still wrinkled, nudged the foot pedal again and began scrubbing and rinsing, then stacking the hand-washed dishes on top of the counter next to the dishwasher. Havana then took them, bent over, and inserted them into the bottom rack of the dishwasher. Marcus began washing the pots, pans, and serving dishes that Irene and Gordon handed to him while they finished putting away the leftovers. The wrinkle of his nose disappeared as he took a few glances over to admire Havana's butt each time she bent over. He quickly turned his head back toward the sink whenever Havana leaned up to grab more dishes off the counter.

Havana stood up and put her hand on his bicep. Marcus looked over at her and saw a sly smile on her face. "I'm impressed that you know how to use the foot pedal, but if you keep focusing on my butt instead of the dishes, then you'll end up wasting as much water as if you hadn't been using the pedal," she said, before patting him on the butt and then leaning in and giving him a quick kiss on the lips.

As the kitchen returned to its pre-dinner state of cleanliness, Gordon suggested a night cap in the living room since it was a special occasion. The foursome, plus Leo, meandered to the living room, and everyone except Gordon got comfortable on the furniture. Gordon opened a cabinet.

"Everyone okay with Scottish whisky?" he asked.

Irene and Havana approved, so Marcus shrugged his shoulders and consented. Gordon placed four lowball glasses on a decorative serving tray. "Have you ever had Scottish whisky before, Marcus?" Gordon asked.

"No. The only alcohol I've had before is beer. Isn't hard liquor still illegal for me here?"

"Without adult supervision, yes, but in a family setting like this, it is okay. The intent of the law is to prevent binge-drinking intoxication, and we won't be having much here." Gordon reached into the liquor cabinet. "Since it is your first Scottish whisky experience, I think we'll go with a nice, smooth Highland with a caramel palate." Gordon pulled a bottle out and began pouring, then delivered the serving tray to the coffee table in front of the family. "For your nosing pleasure. I'll be back with the water in a moment."

Marcus followed Irene and Havana's lead and inserted his nose into the glass and inhaled. Unlike the ladies, he then took a sip and struggled to swallow the liquid. His tongue felt numb, and then it was as if his throat were on fire. He coughed. Havana giggled.

"You should wait for Gordon to return with the water," Irene said. "Typically we add some water to the whisky to moderate the harshness and to open up the flavors."

Gordon returned with another lowball glass with water and an eyedropper in it, set it down, and one by one everyone sprinkled a little water into their glass, swirled it gently, then took a small sip.

"Better?" Irene asked.

Marcus nodded.

"Mmm. You know what would pair well with this?" Havana asked the group. "Some dark chocolate."

"Definitely!" Irene agreed. "Let's go get some." The two ladies stood up and headed toward the kitchen, leaving Marcus alone with Havana's father. Marcus looked intently down at his whisky, uncertain what to say.

Gordon broke the silence. "I want to apologize if comments I made earlier made you feel uncomfortable. I want you to know you are absolutely welcome here. It has been ages since I've dated or had to meet a girlfriend's parents, and I had forgotten how stressful it can be."

"Thank you," Marcus said.

"That being said…with the ladies out of the room, would it be okay if I put you on the spot one more time with a riddle of sorts? The reason I ask is that you actually remind me a lot of myself when I was younger. You come from a more conservative culture, and I tend to lean more conservative too. There are other stories and riddles, beyond the Christmas roast story, that I learned in my youth that helped me 'see the light' of other views, and I'm curious whether you'll respond to this particular riddle the same way I did when I first heard it."

Marcus nodded, thankful that after his third sip of whisky he could already feel a mellowing of his nervous system. "I'll give it a shot."

Gordon began. "Is it easier to see a building in the distance, say across a body of water, on a bright and sunny day, or when it is cloudy and overcast?"

Marcus looked for an answer in his whisky glass for a moment. He wanted to respond quickly and confidently but had to pause to weigh the options. His immediate instinct was that of course you would see better in bright sunlight than the dimmer light of an overcast day, but it felt like a trap. Riddles were always trick questions. He tried to find a logical explanation for how it would be easier to see on an overcast day but failed, and it felt like enough time had elapsed that he owed an immediate answer. "Sunny," he blurted out.

"I'll preface the answer by saying that I mentioned earlier that *Star Trek* was half the reason I got into computer programming," Gordon said. "The other half is that I tend to gravitate toward things that have nice, clear, binary answers…things that are yes or no, black or white. I think to some degree most humans share that desire for things to be black and white. We crave simplicity and order. We want desperately to see patterns among chaos and randomness. We make connections that aren't there to make the world seem simpler. The problem is that life often isn't that simple. There are shades of gray, and the more you see those shades of gray, the more you can empathize with people who have different opinions than yours."

He paused and swirled his whisky before taking another sip. "The answer to the riddle is that it depends on the specifics of the situation. If it is early or late in the day, and the sun is low, and you are looking in the general direction of the sun, then the building will be a backlit silhouette that is harder to see than if there were clouds filtering the sunlight and bouncing the light around to create a more uniformly lit building. If the sun is high in the sky or behind you, then it will be easier to see it when it is sunny. Sometimes it is easier to see a building in the distance when it is sunny, other times when it is cloudy."

"I see," said Marcus.

"Good for you for mulling it over a bit before answering, though. It is a sign that you like to think carefully and weigh options before you answer. That's better than I did when I was first asked the question. I just blurted out 'sunny' immediately without even pausing to think about it."

"I only paused to think because I sensed a trick question, though," Marcus said sheepishly.

"Ahh, yes. The hyperactive amygdala. I know it well," Gordon said through a chuckle.

Havana and Irene returned with a tray of chocolates. The foursome enjoyed their whisky and noshed on chocolates, and the conversation turned to which modern Puerto Paz TV shows were good enough to be in the same league as *Star Trek*. Between the sedating effect of the whisky, the chocolate-induced rush of endorphins, and Marcus not being familiar with any of the TV shows they were discussing, he gradually tuned out of the conversation and just enjoyed the background buzzing of friendly voices as he sank down into the chair and rested his head on it.

A clock began chiming softly, awakening Marcus from his hypnosis. Noticing that it was a lot of chimes, he snapped upright in his seat and pulled his phone out of his pocket. It was eleven. He saw that he had missed a text from Nigel explaining the when and where of meeting for swimming the next morning and texted back that Havana was planning on coming too.

"I should really be going. The swim is pretty early tomorrow," he announced.

"You could stay here tonight if you wanted," Irene suggested.

"My swimsuit is back at the dorm," Marcus said, still feeling uncertain about the taboo of spending the night at the house of his girlfriend's parents.

"If only we had more time. I could tell you about the different species of sea life you are likely to encounter tomorrow morning," Irene said.

They stood up together, and Gordon and Irene walked over to Marcus and gave him a hug and expressed how pleased they were that Havana was dating such an outstanding young gentleman, prompting Marcus to smile at Havana with a mix of pleasure and embarrassment. Gordon rescued the moment from getting too serious by raising a hand like he was motioning for Marcus to stop, then split his ring finger and middle finger apart into a Vulcan greeting gesture. "Live long and prosper."

Havana walked Marcus to the door, where Marcus shared the swim information and noted that Nigel had added an invitation to treat him to breakfast after the swim. Havana said that she wouldn't have time to join them for breakfast but that she looked forward to the swim. They kissed goodnight, and Marcus headed back to his dorm room for a late bedtime.

Chapter 5: Bilateral Breathing

Tuesday morning, Marcus hopped on the subway to Central Station, then transferred to the line that headed northeast, under the major shopping avenue, and took it to the end of the line and walked across the northern boardwalk. He paused briefly at the edge of the boardwalk. To his left and right he saw an endless tree-lined tile path, and ahead of him a small pebbly beach leading out into a vast expanse of blue sea.

He exhaled and felt his shoulders release and sink before he deeply inhaled the briny ocean breeze. He looked off to the right, where he spotted the blue bath house where Havana, Nigel, and a dozen other people from Nigel's triathlon team were already gathered. He returned his gaze to the sea as he walked the final paces to the group and watched the nearly glassy smooth water away from shore transition to steady ripples nibbling at the coastline.

Nigel greeted him with the same big, eye-squinting, but mouth closed smile and a hand shake that he had greeted him with the previous day in his office. Marcus gave Havana a quick kiss and then followed Nigel into the bathhouse to be shown where to change and where the lockers were to put his dry land clothes. Nigel also handed him a towel, a bright orange swim cap, goggles, and an emergency flotation buoy hooked to a belt.

After Marcus had changed and rejoined the group, Nigel introduced him to everyone. Marcus quickly got lost in all of the new names.

"I'm proud to say we are a very diverse group," Nigel said. "We have a delivery person, a hair stylist, a farmer, a waitress, an administrative assistant, a CEO, an engineer, and an actor, to name a few. Diversity like this keeps us from living in a bubble of similarity where we might start to see anyone not like ourselves more for our differences than for our similarities. It is the antidote to prejudice. Mileva and I met on our Diversity Day holiday, in fact, and have had some wonderful chats about how the immigration policies I work on impact her farm business."

"Are we going to yap, or are we going to swim, my friend," Mileva said, giving Nigel a gentle elbow to the ribs.

"I digress, as usual. To the water we go," Nigel said. "So, open-water swimming. Are you able to bilateral breathe?" Nigel asked as they walked toward the sea.

"You mean breathe to either side? I definitely prefer breathing to the right, but I think I can probably breathe to the left too," Marcus said.

"You might find that sometimes either the sun or waves will be on one side, and it can be advantageous to breathe to one side on the way out and to the opposite on the way back, but if you can, it helps reduce neck strain to breathe on alternating sides."

He squinted as he looked out to sea, then continued. "Another critical skill for open-water swimming is sighting. Every six to twelve strokes or so you'll need to bob your head up a little mid-stroke so that your goggles break the surface of the water and you can see forward, spot a fixed object on shore that you've chosen in advance as a marker to navigate relative to, and then duck your head back down to complete the stroke in one fluid motion." Nigel bent over and moved his arms like he was swimming and demonstrated what he was referring to, looking up briefly as he rotated his arms.

"Lastly, if you feel a rip current pulling you away from shore, continue swimming parallel to shore until you've broken free from it, and only then should you worry about trying to swim back towards shore. Trying to swim into it is usually futile, and it will leave you exhausted and no closer to shore."

As they walked the narrow, pebbly shore to the water, Nigel pointed into the distance and continued to explain that they would be sighting off of the reconstructed Castillo de San Salvador de La Punta that was about a mile to the east, per his estimated conversion from kilometers. Many of the swimmers would be swimming all the way to the castle and back, but there was a yellow bathhouse on shore about halfway there where he, Havana, and a couple of other swimmers planned to stop when they were even with it and turn around to keep it to a one-mile-round-trip swim. Nigel wanted Marcus to turn around there with them, given his lack of recent swimming.

Marcus held a hand to his forehead like was saluting, trying to shield his eyes from the sun so he could spot the castle. *Sure enough,* he thought, *it is just a silhouette.*

As they waded into the warm, clear water, Marcus turned to Havana to give her a little good-natured teasing, thinking he would say something like he was going to beat her at swimming the same way he always beat her at food ordering. Havana had just put her yellow swim cap on, and he ended up bursting out laughing. "You look like a cone-headed alien!" He giggled. "I'm sorry. It just caught me by surprise. With your hair all pushed up into the cap, it makes a cone shape."

Havana just stuck her tongue out at him and made a goofy face.

"Ready, everyone?" asked one of the women in the group. She pressed a button on her watch and dove under the water. A chorus of beeps followed as others pressed start buttons on their watches too, and then in groups of three or four, people dove under the water, resurfaced, and began swimming toward the castle.

Marcus dove in to follow. He felt so elated and jubilant to finally be in the ocean that he had difficulty controlling his initial pace. He nearly sprinted away from the starting spot, breathing to the right every fourth stroke, then after a minute he increased his rate of breathing to every other stroke as his body attempted to transition from anaerobic to aerobic activity and began demanding more oxygen.

He poked his head up to sight and was surprised to discover that most of the group was still ahead of him. In fact, most of the swimmers had increased the distance between him. *This isn't a race. This isn't a race. Who cares if I'm slower than them?* he reminded himself.

He slowed down a little and decided to try breathing to the left a few times. The first try ended with a trachea full of water. He stopped swimming and began coughing while treading water. He heard the ghost of his sister's voice matter-of-factly explaining that people weren't allowed to swim in the ocean in San Francisco because they might drown.

The only two people who had been behind him at this point caught up to him, and one of the guys, a man likely older than Nigel, stopped to ask him if he was okay. Marcus gave him a thumbs-up, coughed out the last of the salty water, and put his head back in the water and began swimming, a bit more slowly and more deliberately. A few more rounds of breathing to the right only, and then he tried to his left again, putting a little extra into his body rotation as he breathed. This time he inhaled all air.

He plodded on, trying to maintain a pace slower than he normally would go in order to match the two slowest swimmers. The salinity of the water helped buoy his dense, muscular body, making the effort to stay afloat considerably less strenuous than during the swim at the Wyoming lake. As he continued sighting, he would occasionally keep his head out of the water for a full stroke to take an extra-long peek to see whether he could find Havana's yellow cap and emergency buoy, but he had difficulty spotting her.

After a while he stopped bothering to look for her and just looked down as he swam. With the water so clear, he could see all the way to the bottom. A small school of fish with light-blue stripes down their bodies darted diagonally across his path. He felt his heart rate pick up, and he had to increase his rate of breathing to compensate. It was the first time in his life he'd observed fish in their natural environment.

The underwater scenery was exhilarating, as was the alternating scenery of the coast and the wide-open sea during his brief glimpses above water. The only sounds were the muffled gurgle of water rushing past his head mixed with the steady, rhythmic whoosh of one hand entering the water followed by the other hand, and the gentle, faraway drumbeat of his kick. He settled into a bilateral breathing pattern of every third stroke. Nothing mattered at this moment other than keeping a steady kick and the steady windmill of his arms. The stresses of figuring out what he wanted to do with his life, where he wanted to live, and who would be there with him dissolved into the warm water.

Realizing that he hadn't lifted his head to sight in at least twenty strokes snapped him temporarily out of his trance, but he only required a minor course correction, and he realized they were getting fairly close to the yellow bathhouse. A few minutes later and he could see Nigel, Havana, and another swimmer up ahead treading water, waiting for him and the two other slowest swimmers.

He was glad he hadn't teased her about beating her in swimming and wondered whether she would tease him given that she was clearly much faster than he was. They reached the turnaround point, and he realized that they were in shallow enough water that they were standing on the bottom rather than treading. He walked over to Havana, and she gave him a hug and a kiss and asked him how he was doing.

"This is awesome!" he panted as he regained his breath. "Wow, you're a really good swimmer."

"I used to swim competitively," Havana said. "Now I'm more about volleyball, yoga, and running, but I cross-train to keep my muscles balanced and healthy, and I do the occasional triathlon. You're not so bad yourself, especially given that you haven't been in good swimming shape for years."

"Yeah, I was a bit surprised by just how much slower I am than some of the older people here," Marcus said.

"Given how physically strong you are, I suspect the reason you aren't as fast as you hoped has to do with body position and technique. You're probably trying to muscle your way through the stroke, and your position is creating a lot of drag, so you end up fighting yourself. Maybe we'll get a chance to swim together sometime, just the two of us, and we can work on that. That will have to be another day, though. When we get back to the blue bathhouse, I will probably have to make this a splash and dash and get myself dressed and to the doctor's office on time. If I don't see you before I leave then I'll text later to see if we can get together toward the end of the day."

They kissed goodbye just in case, and a smaller chorus of watch beeps signaled the start of the return leg.

The currents had apparently been flowing with them on the first leg, and the return leg was a struggle. Marcus could feel himself getting rather fatigued toward the end. He was relieved they hadn't swum all the way to the castle, and when he reached the blue bathhouse, he found that Havana was long gone. He rinsed off in the outdoor showers, changed inside the bathhouse, and met with Nigel to go to breakfast.

Chapter 6: de Grasse Café

Nigel led them up to the northern boardwalk, and they walked a half mile uphill along the coastal pedestrian path to a restaurant at a large, rocky cliffside that overlooked the sea. Ahead of them Marcus could see the yellow bathhouse, and with the sun a little higher in the sky, he could see the castle more clearly in the distance.

On the inland side of the boardwalk stood a small building only large enough for a kitchen and a few tables. On the sea side of the boardwalk, large blue and yellow umbrellas capped tables on a terrace that hugged the cliff's edge. They sat down at a table alongside the railing that guarded the terrace.

Marcus briefly stood back up and peered over the railing to confirm what he had caught a glimpse of during the swim. At the center of the terrace, a gap in the railing led to a rock staircase that had been carved into the side of the cliff. The staircase wound its way down to several lower terraces that clung to the sides of the cliff and also had café tables. A waiter popped into his view below, seeming to walk straight out of solid rock and onto one of the lower terraces. There had to be some sort of tunnel through the cliff that went under the boardwalk and connected to the restaurant building. Another rock staircase less than a football-field distance away connected to the yellow bathhouse. Teenagers were hanging out on little natural plateaus in the cliff alongside the stairs, with an occasional jumper leaping off the plateau and into the sea below.

Marcus picked up a menu that said "de Grasse Café" on the cover. His body had the wonderful warm, glowing sensation generated by a good workout, but having just swum a mile on an empty stomach, he was famished.

Nigel spent a minute having a friendly chat with the waiter, giving Marcus the impression that maybe they were friends. Marcus instinctively pulled his phone out of his pocket to occupy his mind during the moment of inactivity. He saw that he had missed a text from Dylan during the swim. It was a photo of him and Kelsey chugging beers at a bar, surrounded by several people, some of whom he recognized as the Australians from the Port Camille map a few days earlier.

"You're up this early?" Marcus texted back.

"Kelsey woke me up to go barf. Getting room service then going back to bed soon."

Marcus lifted his phone up and took a photo of the view from the café tables and texted it to Dylan with a note: "Had a great swim. Incredible view. Nigel treating for breakfast."

Dylan wrote back: "Enjoy your date with your new boyfriend."

"And you with your new Australian boyfriends," Marcus responded.

"There are Aussie chicks here too, fag."

Marcus shook his head and stuck his phone back in his pocket.

"God, this is beautiful!" Marcus exclaimed, continuing to survey the scenery after the waiter had returned to the kitchen. "Thank you so much for inviting me out with your team. I had been dying to swim in the ocean!"

"My pleasure," Nigel responded. "It was great to have you and Havana along."

The two of them sat there for a few minutes, alternating between talking about the swim and admiring the view before Nigel changed the conversation to Marcus's experiences in New Athens so far. As Marcus was describing the walk in Central Park with Havana, he remembered the diploma on Nigel's office wall.

"You used to be a psychologist, right? Tell me, is it normal for mentally healthy people to see psychologists? I thought they were just for people who weren't right in the head."

"Here it is normal," Nigel said. "We seek the truth, and sometimes it takes someone else to help us find the truth within ourselves."

Their food arrived, and Nigel thanked the waiter. Marcus was ravenous but made every effort to eat like a civilized human and not just inhale his meal. Clearly Nigel was hungry too, as for the first several bites of the meal, the conversation halted, and the two of them focused their full attention on eating. Nigel picked the conversation back up a few minutes later, asking Marcus his reasons for running away from home and his experiences throughout his travels. Marcus relayed the ever-expanding story of his journey once more.

The meal was beginning to wind down as Marcus concluded his tale, and he knew that soon Nigel would need to go to work. He looked down at his plate and saucered a last glob of melted cheese with a piece of toast. After chewing for a few seconds, without looking up, he said, "So, when I was in San Francisco staying with my sister, I started the process of collecting all of the paperwork needed to transfer into high school there. It would have been a more than year-long process to complete the transfer because of all the bureaucracy. When we went to New Miami, they accepted us into the university immediately, no questions asked. All they cared about was whether we had money for tuition and housing. What is that process like here in Puerto Paz?"

"Under the age of eighteen years it can be a little tricky, especially if they aren't moving here with a legal guardian. In some situations, there may be a case for emancipation, where they are effectively declared an adult and are in charge of their own affairs, although they are assigned a mentor until the age of eighteen. In that case, the applicant would go through academic testing to see whether they went into university or continued high school.

"The overall process is like most things when compared to Urban WUS and SEUS. It is considerably faster and less complex than Urban WUS but more formal and involved than SEUS. The emancipation process would include an expedited consultation at the beginning that could get the applicant into school while the longer, official review process continued. Applying for citizenship simultaneously is highly recommended and can help the chances of a smooth transition to life in Puerto Paz."

"If someone from EUS under the age of eighteen were emancipated and moved here, where would they live?" asked Marcus. "Especially if they continued in high school rather than going straight into college?"

"Assuming they made it through the immigration process and were found compatible with our society, they would have several options. We do sometimes put young adults, especially ones who have demonstrated higher levels of maturity, into college dormitories. We find it often works well to mix ages and to have natural mentor and mentee relationships develop between peers of different ages. Other times they are given the option to live with their assigned adult mentors until they turn eighteen. Whatever the situation, we find a suitable accommodation. Usually the accommodation includes a living stipend with the understanding that a student can't, and shouldn't, work full time, but it assumes some small level of part-time work or disappearing low-interest loans or grants."

"So, with all this talk of Puerto Paz valuing moderation, what is the likelihood that someone with a more extreme personality would be accepted here?" Marcus asked.

"It isn't completely out of the question," Nigel responded. "If they have a strong level of respect for others and they are careful to not let their actions or extreme views be a detriment to the lives of the people around them, and they have other qualities that we value, then it is still a possibility they'd be found sufficiently compatible. We wouldn't want to turn away the next Einstein for being a workaholic, despite our belief that it is better if the average person here is not a workaholic."

"What would happen if they were found incompatible with the society?"

"They would be extradited back to their home country."

"What if they had nowhere else to return to? What if they couldn't go back to EUS, or refused to go back there?"

"We would first try to find a country that had a culture more compatible with their personality, and we would essentially shop them around to those countries. If that failed, then the place of last resort is always Isla de Juventud, an island not far from Puerto Paz's mainland that is technically a part of Puerto Paz. There are no laws there except that inhabitants aren't allowed to leave unless they are traveling to somewhere that has consented to accept them. It is sort of along the lines of how Australia was originally a penal colony for Great Britain."

"Hmmm. And if I was found compatible, what would life be like? What about football? A guy from Puerto Paz who I met on the flight to New Miami told me football, or I guess you call it gridiron, is different than in the EUS, but would I be able to play? Or would track and field be an option?"

Nigel paused briefly, and the corners of this lips turned up into a gentle, subtle smile. "Both could be options. Gridiron isn't as popular here as it is in the EUS, nor is it as high paying for professionals, but it is an option. The high schools have teams and leagues, but we have had to combine college and professional gridiron players to make two professional teams that compete in the Caribbean Gridiron League. Track and field is extremely popular with the high school and college students. Our country goes nuts for the Summer Olympics, and track and swimming are always the favorites."

"The guy on the airplane said the rules for gridiron are a bit different."

"Indeed they are," Nigel said. He cocked his head to the side. "The mention of gridiron on the heels of our conversation yesterday about government and politics reminds me that I have always found it extremely fascinating how EUS, a country known for its kneejerk negative reactions to socialism, has such socialist sports leagues. They have all sorts of systems designed to promote parity: drafts instead of unrestrained recruiting, salary caps, trade restrictions, profit redistribution, player unions to fight for fair wages and treatment, referees to enforce rules of fairness.... It always amazes me how the citizens of EUS can be so strongly in favor of those systems in sports, yet in real life they are content to just let unregulated capitalism run roughshod over their society."

Marcus chuckled. "I guess I've never looked at pro sports that way before. It is kinda socialist. But if that's considered socialist, then isn't Puerto Paz socialist too? How do you justify your claim that you're not communists?"

"Communism and socialism are not the same thing. As I've said, we are not communists. The government does not control everything. It gets a bit complicated as political and economic terminology begins to mix. Economically we are a hybrid between socialism and capitalism. We call it symbiotic capitalism. Politically I would call us a social democracy."

"I'm not sure I understand the nuances. How is it different than

EUS or WUS?" Marcus asked.

"Our system is still highly democratic. We have elected representatives, and many issues are either heavily influenced by polling or decided directly by public referenda. When comparing Puerto Paz to WUS and EUS, what the politics boils down to is that the former USA fractured into four political extremes. First it split liberal versus conservative, resulting from a battle between equality-based collaborative collectivism versus a competitive hierarchical caste system.

"Then each of those split again into freedom versus order, resulting from a battle between individual control versus group control. You have the order conservatives in NEUS, who have a centrally regulated caste system based on race, religion, gender, or other tribal criteria. You have the freedom conservatives in SEUS, who have an unregulated caste system based mostly on wealth. You have the order liberals in Urban WUS, who believe everyone is equal and that it takes a village to raise a child but that it is best accomplished via government control. You have the freedom liberals in Rural WUS, who also believe everyone is equal and that it takes a village to raise a child but that it is best accomplished via a disorganized hodgepodge of individual choices.

"In Puerto Paz, we try to find the center of that matrix and lean slightly to the left of center. We value freedom, but within boundaries of order...freedom up to the point where it starts to harm society. The boundaries are there to protect citizens from some, but not all, harm. Reasonable people can disagree on the exact location of those boundaries, but with an attitude of non-extremism, those disagreements are over relatively small degrees of differences, and not getting one's exact desires in where the boundaries are placed isn't as big of a deal.

"Economically we attempt to find a middle balance point between unregulated free markets and government or collective control of everything. Anyone is free to run a business, but it has to be run within the boundaries of fairness and ethics that are democratically decided by the population as a whole. Salaries, however, are regulated, and income gets redistributed to account for the power grab that inevitably happens when small groups control the flow of money."

"Didn't the Soviet Union try to control markets and money and end up proving it is impossible?" Marcus asked.

"They failed in large part due to corruption and a lack of checks and balances. Our system also preserves the motivation of earning more by working harder or smarter, just not to the extreme of a culture like SEUS's. Our system isn't perfect, none ever is, but it is a drastic improvement, and we can't let perfection be the enemy of good. Mechanically the biggest difference is that they tried to control the market, whereas we let the market operate, within boundaries, and we moderate the flow of money mostly via taxes, and we use public polling to help decide what fair salaries and profit levels are versus what is gouging."

Marcus found himself playing devil's advocate. "Shouldn't people be able to keep what they earn?"

Nigel peeked at his watch. "First, taxes are necessary to fund the commons and institutions of public good, such as police, fire rescue, and public education. We try to find the balance between sufficiently funding the commons and impoverishing hardworking people. It is probably the biggest source of argument in our country: where that balance point is. One side occasionally has to be reminded of all the great things their taxes pay for, and the other side has to occasionally be reminded of the financial impact those taxes have on peoples' lives. With a less drastic income gap between our richest and our poorest, though, everyone is feeling a similar level of 'pain' from taxes, so reminders of the impact of taxes are rarely needed.

"Second, you have to define what *earned* means. Are people being paid what they *deserve*? Consider the issue of jobs in an industry that can produce things in bulk, versus those that can't. For example, an actor can make a single movie in just a few months' time, but that movie can sell millions of copies over decades at a price affordable to those purchasing it, generating a large volume of money through those bulk sales. An architect, conversely, can only work on a couple of buildings at a time, and typically each design is a custom, unrepeatable, one-of-a-kind design that generates no royalties. The architect gets paid only once, and it still needs to be designed at a price that the client can afford, so the architect, even if they are the most talented architect in the world, can't just jack up the prices to millions of dollars to make a salary comparable to the actor. So, is it fair for a hardworking, talented architect to make relative peanuts while an actor rakes in millions? Especially when you consider the relative importance of what they are doing for society? I mean, shelter is a *need*, but entertainment is really only a *want*.

"To our people that demonstrates unfairness, and unfairness like that should be corrected in order to make a better society. So, we let the market operate relatively freely, but then we use taxes to cap incomes at the high end and offer reverse income taxes at the low end to nudge income towards a more balanced and fair state."

"How do you make sure the taxes are fair, though?" Marcus asked.

"The conversion from raw salary to regulated salary is fairly simple. Occupations are categorized into ranks by importance to society. These ranks are regularly adjusted by weighted popular voting. The ranks determine basic salary minimums and maximums. Your employer then determines performance-based bonus-level factors so that better-performing and harder-working employees still make more money than employees who don't perform as well. The end result is that those who work harder make more, and those who lack power don't get screwed by those with power."

Nigel paused the conversation as he spoke to his e-glasses to pay the bill. He then looked at Marcus. "Well, Marcus. You have shown a lot of interest in Puerto Paz, above and beyond that of a dutiful boyfriend learning about his girlfriend's culture, and now you have asked several questions related to the process involved in you moving here and possibly becoming a citizen. This is all on top of a feeling I got back at my office that you weren't comfortable exploring some of these issues in the presence of Dylan. I have to ask: Are you sure it was an accident when you selected the answer at Port Camille indicating that you were uncertain whether you'd be staying here longer than two months?"

Heat rushed to Marcus's face. No more dancing gingerly around the subject; it was time to come clean. "It wasn't an accident," Marcus confessed. "But I don't know how long I want to stay here. I wasn't sure how to answer the question. Technically I'm just here for a two-week vacation, and when it's over I go back to New Miami, but I'm using these two weeks to get a feel for whether I might want to move here. I'm testing the waters, so to speak. I know Havana would love it if I did, and so far I've found everything here amazing, but I feel torn. I can't abandon Dylan, and I think he wants to go back to New Miami to play football, and I feel obligated to stick to that plan."

"Why do you feel like you would be abandoning Dylan if you chose Puerto Paz and he chose New Miami?" Nigel asked.

"NEUS men are loyal. They don't ditch their best friend. I can't do that to him. We've been best friends for over a decade. I can't just desert him like that. Besides, if I left him to fend for himself, I think he'd blow all his money and end up homeless and overdosing on drugs within a few months. Someone has to watch out for him. He's had a rough life."

"You said that 'NEUS men are loyal.' I don't mean to sound insensitive, but do you still consider yourself a 'NEUS man'? Clearly you were unhappy enough with the NEUS culture to run away from home. Is loyalty, perhaps even an extremist version of loyalty that does harm to yourself, a part of that culture that you admire? Or is it something you feel programmed into you, and you have to obey it even if you think it is incorrect?"

Marcus shrugged. "I don't know. Maybe a bit of both? I mean, I wouldn't want my best friend to ditch me at the drop of a hat, but at the same time, I don't want to go back to New Miami. I hate it there. And so far I have liked it here. And I want my relationship with Havana to continue to grow, and I don't know if that would be possible in a long-distance relationship."

"If you told Dylan you were moving here and explained all the reasons why, but he still said he wanted to go back to New Miami, would you consider your going your own separate way as 'ditching him at the drop of a hat,' as you said? Don't your desires and your happiness factor into the decision?"

"I don't know. I'm not even sure I know what I want yet. There are pros and cons to both staying here and going back to New Miami."

"What would be the perfect scenario in your mind? The result that you would find most satisfying?"

"I guess if I could talk Dylan into moving here to Puerto Paz. He could get the psychological help he needs. We could both play football, or at least a sort of tamer version of football. I could get back on track for a career in engineering. I could be in a culture and society that I like way better than any of the other ones I've been in this entire summer. I could see Havana every day."

"Does Dylan not know your desires? How you dislike New Miami?"

"I think he knows I'm not fond of New Miami, but we haven't really discussed the possibility of moving here. I've been kicking the can down the road on that conversation until I know for sure what I really want because I know he'll react badly. He's rebellious. Sometimes he's rebellious just to prove a point, even when he knows he's wrong. You mentioned negative kneejerk reactions of EUS people to socialism, and that's Dylan's attitude toward Puerto Paz in a nutshell. I've been hoping that while he's here he'll see what a great place it is and get over those kneejerk reactions, but I'm not confident that his mind will change. We had a plan to go to New Miami, and I'm sure he would try to hold me to it."

"Hmm, I see," said Nigel. "I do think openness and honesty is the best policy. If he's as good of a friend as you say he is, he'll be understanding, even if he's simultaneously disappointed. I do think that you need to hold him to the same standard that you hold yourself to. If it is disloyal for you to not join him in New Miami, then it should be equally disloyal of him to not join you if you want to stay in Puerto Paz. Either that or neither of you should be considered disloyal for following your hearts. From what you've told me so far, it sounds like there never was much of a plan. Your whole journey since you decided to run away from home has been rather spontaneous. If there was a plan, it was to stay with your sister in San Francisco, but that plan didn't work out, so you moved on to a new idea. You gave that idea a shot, but now you've learned that you don't like New Miami, and you have an even newer idea. If it is okay for Dylan to amend the San Francisco plan, then why wouldn't it also be okay for you to amend the New Miami plan?"

Marcus sighed. He thought Nigel was correct in theory, but he was having trouble reconciling theory with practice. In practice he knew that Dylan was too stubborn and rebellious to be open and honest with about this issue, and the loyalty explanation Nigel gave made sense logically, but it just didn't *feel* right.

"Listen," Nigel began again, "I understand teenage

rebelliousness. I went through a rebellious phase myself at around the age of thirteen. It took me at least a decade to figure out why I became so rebellious for a few years, not realizing for the longest time that it was triggered by being bullied between the ages of eleven and twelve. I rebelled because I wanted people to think I was tough, and I wanted people to think I was tough so that they wouldn't bully me."

"You seem like a decent person now. What got you to snap out of that? Marcus asked.

"It was the combination of a safe environment, plus one teacher who went above and beyond the call of duty and was unwaveringly kind and compassionate towards me, even in the face of me being a complete asshole to him. The safe environment came about when the troublesome kids were moved to a different wing of the school for remedial classes, allowing me to let go of my fear. So in that vein, I agree with you that Puerto Paz is the best place for Dylan. It is a much safer environment than New Miami, and he can get the therapeutic help he needs to overcome his fears.

"The trouble is that he is already seventeen years old, and the older a troubled person is, the harder it is to reach them and to help them change. What I don't think you should do, though, is tie your future to his. Reach out to him, yes. Try to help him, yes. A little bit of compassion at the right time can positively change someone's life forever. It is our moral obligation to reach out to help one another, but that person you are trying to help has to choose to accept your help. You can only lead a horse to water. If he rejects your help, you have to do what is best for you and let him go. There are limits to loyalty, and you can't just follow someone blindly no matter what they do. You have to find that healthy balance between reaching out and letting go. Relationships are a delicate balance between challenging your partner or friend to be a better person and letting them be who they are."

Marcus still wasn't sure what to think. He would need to mull things over more. His mind kept replaying the aftermath of the fight at the frat party in New Miami, reviving the feeling of how it had bothered him how disloyal Apollo's frat brothers had been when Dylan knocked him out, not to mention how loyal Dylan had been to Marcus by stepping in to punch Apollo. Nigel looked at his watch and then back up at Marcus.

"Here is what I would recommend," Nigel said. "I would recommend you go through the pre-immigration testing just to see about your compatibility with Puerto Paz's culture. Based on what I know of you so far, I think you'll easily find a high level of compatibility with our culture, but if you happen to test as incompatible, then maybe that will make the decision to stay in New Miami easier. If you test as compatible, it doesn't mean you are locked into moving here; it just means your options are open, and you can still wait to make your decision later. Even if you decided to stay in New Miami, I presume you might want to visit Havana here on a fairly regular basis since it is just a ferry ride away, so having gone through the pre-immigration testing now would expedite getting the credentials you would need in the future to visit Puerto Paz that frequently. We do have limits on cumulative visits in a short period of time, so visas are needed if you want to visit frequently.

"I would also recommend you tell Dylan about the options you are weighing. Remind him that he is an important part of your life and that you are hoping he will join you if you decide you want to move here. I would recommend he go through the compatibility testing too. I suspect he is more likely to be found incompatible, but we don't like to split up close friends, so we would likely try to come up with a way to get you both citizenship as a pair. It would likely involve mandatory psychotherapy for Dylan, though."

Nigel looked at his watch again. "I'm sorry," he said. "We have flex time at work, but I'm beginning to push the boundaries of that flex, and I really must be departing. You have my number, so please text or call me anytime if you'd like to explore these options more, or if you have any questions."

Marcus thanked him again for getting him in the ocean and for treating him to breakfast before Nigel speed-walked away toward the nearby gondola station. Marcus meandered over to the yellow bathhouse and watched the cliff-jumping teens from closer range.

After a few minutes he pulled out his phone. He was toying with the idea of texting or calling Dylan to invite him to hang out together someplace where he could tell him about his thoughts on the possibility of moving to Puerto Paz. Maybe someplace on the beach that served beer where they could knock back a drink or two to make the conversation a little easier. He looked down at his phone several times between teen jumps, with his texting app opened to his last conversation with Dylan, but he couldn't bring himself to send a message. He put his phone down for a minute, watched another cliff jumper, then picked it back up and started browsing the internet. He found himself instinctively returning to his favorite distraction from back home in New Rochelle: a NEUS sports news website.

The Yankees were in first place in the six-team American League and were about to start a cross-town series against the Mets, who were in first place in the seven-team National League. Ohio State's first football game of the season was in a little over a week, and their star running back had twisted his ankle in practice and was questionable for the game. He grabbed his Ohio State keychain out of his pocket and began alternating between rubbing it while reading and clasping it as he scrolled through the story on his phone.

News from home led him to think of family. He began to wonder how his mom was doing, or even what she was doing, alone in an empty house all day waiting for his grumpy dad to get home. She defined herself as a stay-at-home mom, and her first and third "projects"—Sharon and himself—were likely considered failures, at least in his dad's eyes. Now came premature retirement with the task of finding new things to fuss over.

He imagined that she was probably redoubling the level of long-distance attention devoted to his brother, Saul, her one and only success. He smiled as he daydreamed of her sending care packages for his dad to deliver to Saul on a daily basis at West Point. He remembered how she would pray while baking, and he imagined her trying to bake prayers into the treats she was making for his brother. He thought again about his mom's last words to him the night he ran away, about how she sensed that he wasn't at peace and that he should pray on things.

He suddenly snapped back to reality, picked up his phone, and texted Dylan. "Want to grab some beers at the beach this afternoon?" Dylan didn't respond. *Probably back asleep again,* Marcus thought, almost relieved. He didn't really want a reply yet. He needed more time to think about what he wanted to say to Dylan, and how best to say it. He watched the cliff jumpers and admired the view a while longer before heading back to his dorm room, feeling drowsy.

Chapter 7: Playa Nueva Con Un Viejo Amigo

"Fuck yeah! About time you took the stick out of your ass and came out to the beach to kill some brain cells. You've been absent from Fun 101 for three classes in a row. Truancy penalty is chugging a beer for every day you missed."

Marcus couldn't decide whether he wanted to laugh or shake his head after reading Dylan's text response to his suggestion of getting together at the beach. He dragged himself out of bed, having nearly fallen asleep until the alert from Dylan's text had startled him into reopening his eyes.

At noon he stumbled out of the pleasant climate of the dorm building and into the sweltering heat to head to Playa Nueva. A few minutes later, he was sitting on the train in the air-conditioned comfort of the New Athens public transportation system, mulling over his upcoming conversation with Dylan.

He thought about what Nigel and Havana had said about how he should come clean with Dylan right away and tell him he was considering moving to Puerto Paz, but they didn't know Dylan as well as he did. *Sure, if Dylan were as psychologically healthy as Nigel and Havana are, and probably as healthy as everyone they know, then it would make total sense to be honest and upfront. But with Dylan, given his kneejerk rebellious responses you just can't do that,* Marcus thought.

Marcus considered what Nigel had said about how a safe environment along with a compassionate mentor had led him back to a healthier path when he was a young teen. *Is there a way for me to be like Nigel's compassionate mentor while still not revealing my desires just yet? And perhaps the bigger question is whether I even know for sure what I desire yet. American football has been my life...am I really ready to give up football as I know it?*

The train's loudspeakers gave a gentle chime before a prerecorded announcement played, indicating the Playa Nueva stop. Marcus got out and paused for a minute to watch the computer-choreographed dance of the piggybacking cars getting on and off the end of the train. He pulled his phone out and texted Dylan that he was at the station and asked where to go to meet him from there. Dylan texted back with the name of the bar on the west end of the beach, where he said he already had a one-beer-to-none advantage over Marcus and that Marcus had some catching up to do.

Good, thought Marcus. As long as Dylan stayed in the happily tipsy, buzzed zone but did not cross the line into the angry-drunk zone like his dad, he would be much easier to deal with. Marcus could nurse a beer without losing too much of his faculties, and so long as Kelsey wasn't a problem, he might be able to pull off talking Dylan into doing the pre-immigration testing with him.

Marcus walked into the bar. An easy-listening song with lyrics about a woman being to blame was playing, but at a volume still low enough to have a conversation. The place was spotlessly clean. It had a party vibe, but it was muted by the healthy Puerto Paz sensibility. It was probably the most frat-like place in all of Puerto Paz though, and of course this was where Dylan had chosen to spend his time. Marcus spotted Dylan but didn't see Kelsey with him. Dylan stood up to greet him, and they exchanged the traditional double slap on the shoulder.

"Is Kelsey here?" Marcus asked.

"Nah. She's been such a lightweight lately. She can't keep up. Constantly wanting to call it a night early, too hungover to do anything until after four p.m. She's kinda getting on my nerves. I need to hang with people who can party. It's about fucking time you showed up here. Least you'll be able to keep up with me."

"Well, you do realize she weighs next to nothing, right? She's practically anorexic. Of course she's not going to be able to match you drink for drink."

"College is all about training for moments like these, when you are on vacation, don't have classes, beer and wine are plentiful. You've got to train for this moment, man, and Kelsey is acting like an amateur, dude."

"Be careful with her, D. She's delicate. Don't break her."

"Whatevs. Let's get you a beer, man. Gotta get you anesthetized to pull that stick out!"

Marcus rolled his eyes. "I don't want to drink *too* much. I have plans with Havana later," he said.

"If you get too tipsy, you can always get a hotel room here or crash in our room. I'm sure Havana could live without you for one night for a change."

Dylan caught the bartender's attention and ordered a beer for Marcus while Marcus looked out of the open-air end of the room, which had a view out onto a beach that faded gently into the ocean. It was nearly as beautiful of a view as from the cliffs during his breakfast with Nigel that morning. He blinked his eyes clear a few times as he returned his attention from the bright exterior to the shaded interior, then looked up at the ceiling fans, identifying them as the source of the air stream tickling the hairs on his arms. Marcus began to engage Dylan in small talk about how beautiful the weather was and how great the scenery was everywhere. It transitioned into asking Dylan what parts of the city he had seen so far.

"I've seen this bar. I've seen the bar next door. I've seen the bar across the street, and the nightclub next to it, and my hotel a few doors down from that."

"That's it? You haven't gone and explored the city? Not even once?" Marcus asked. "Did you see the photo I sent you from the cliffside café overlooking the sea after my swim? The cliff jumpers there? You haven't even been to Central Park?"

Dylan looked at Marcus blankly. "None of that is on the Fun 101 syllabus, dude. Except maybe the cliff jumping."

"You gotta get out more, man. There's so much more to see. This place has fascinating things everywhere," Marcus said.

They sat there in silence for a minute. Marcus felt like he had run out of things to say, so finally he filled the void by asking Dylan whether he had seen that the Yankees and Mets were about to play each other with both as league leaders. Talk of NEUS sports got Dylan sidetracked into reminiscing about the best moments of their high school football careers together, and then about the prospects of becoming football studs on campus at New Miami.

"Dude, I cannot wait until my hand fully heals. We gotta talk to

Coach about the trick field-goal play we drew up last year. It would be so awesome! You and me winning a big game together!"

"I don't think Coach likes me much. He hasn't even given me the contract he promised. And the feeling is mutual."

"Doesn't matter whether you and Coach like each other or not, just whether we win," Dylan said. "And after football season begins party season. I'm a god at Alpha Sigs now. I'll hook you up. Stick with me, and I'll get you into all the good parties, and you can have any sorority babe you want."

"I already have the sorority babe I want," Marcus said.

"When the cat's away, the mice will play."

After another lull in the conversation, and after getting nearly to the bottom of his beer, Marcus worked up the nerve to pivot the conversation to the topic of pre-immigration testing. "So, Havana has been talking to me about how we're going to make our relationship work long distance while she's here and I'm in New Miami. She's been really pressuring me to go through this pre-immigration testing stuff. She said I'd need to do it in order to get the visas and stuff I'd need to visit her frequently. I know she doesn't really like New Miami all that much, so I'd probably be the one doing most of the traveling to here to visit her. I was thinking it would be good if you and Kelsey went through the testing with me. Kelsey and Havana are good friends, so I'm sure Kelsey will want to come here on the ferry from time to time. This place is like a tropical paradise, and I'm sure Kelsey likes the beaches without the New Miami stench, and you like it here, right? I mean, how awesome is it that we can sit here and drink a beer without having to sneak it? I'm sure you'd want to join us here from time to time. Even if you did the pre-immigration testing, it doesn't lock you into anything. Neither of us would have to come here again if we didn't want to; it just gives us options. I'm not even sure I need the visa, but I figure it's harmless to try. So, you in?"

Dylan rolled his eyes. "Man, you are really obsessed with getting that nookie, aren't you? Just this one particular nookie too. She's got you whipped! Does she have some sort of magical poontang or something? You know there are plenty of hot chicks in New Miami, right?"

"Maybe she's *the one,* though."

"Seriously, dude? First of all, there's no such thing as 'the one.' There's only the thousands that need seducing. You gotta play the field, man. Second, at age seventeen, you think you've found the one woman in the world who can make you give up chasing skirt for the rest of your life?"

"Maybe. I don't know. She's smart, funny, beautiful, kind. She has it all."

Dylan closed his eyes and shook his head. "Man, if you gotta do this testing shit to get you some pussy, fine. I'll make you a deal. You get a second beer right now and chug it, and I'll go through that bullshit with you. Just don't forget, though: bros before hos."

"Right." Marcus took one last big swig of his beer to finish it off, feeling simultaneously elated that Dylan had just agreed to go through the pre-immigration testing with him, yet nervous about his comment suggesting that he should prioritize Dylan ahead of Havana. Dylan flagged down the waitress for another beer for each of them, and Marcus relented against his better judgment and guzzled his while Dylan chanted, "Chug! Chug! Chug!"

"You know," Dylan said, "before today, I was starting to suspect that Havana was making you soft. You chugged your second beer, though, so maybe I was wrong. I can't tell yet for sure. I need another test to see if she's turning you soft. You and me, out on the beach. Line of scrimmage blocking drill. You push me off the line three out of five times, and I'll believe you haven't gone soft."

The impulse-control center of Marcus's brain was feeling as numb as the end of his nose. "Dude," he said, tipsily, "you couldn't push me off the line even once in ten tries."

"Oh, we're on!" Dylan said as he got to his feet and headed toward the open-air end of the bar to the beach.

Marcus followed him out. He squinted and shielded his eyes as they walked onto the glistening beach. Dylan turned his back to the ocean and dragged his heel through the sand to create a line of scrimmage. He took his position on one side of the line and got into a three-point lineman's stance. Marcus took his position opposite Dylan and got down into a four-point stance with both hands on the hot sand.

"Down, set, hut-hut, hike!" Dylan grunted, and both boys leapt up and engaged in a sumo-like shoving contest to try to push the other back from the line. Marcus easily stood his ground and forced Dylan to backpedal and fall on his ass. He walked over, bent down, and offered a hand to help him up. Dylan rejected Marcus's hand and got up on his own. They lined up again.

"Down, set, hut-hut, hike!" Dylan tried a juke move before engaging Marcus low, but Marcus still held his ground, muscled Dylan into a higher position, and shoved him backward.

They went a third time. This time Marcus blasted off the line, lifted Dylan up off the beach, and let go of him, letting his forward momentum dump Dylan backward and onto his ass again. Dylan grunted as his body hit the beach. Marcus went over again to offer a hand. Dylan grabbed his arm with his good hand and used a leg to trip him while he pulled at Marcus's arm to get Marcus tumbling forward and down onto the beach. Dylan rolled over and pounced on Marcus's back.

"Unsportsmanlike conduct. Tripping and late hit. Fifteen-yard penalty!" Marcus shouted.

"Oh, yeah? Would it be a holding penalty on top of it if I put you in a rear-naked choke?" Dylan asked as he started threading his forearm under Marcus's neck to put him in the choke.

Marcus ducked his chin down tight to his chest to protect his neck and rolled the two of them over, both on their backs with Marcus lying on top of him. He grabbed Dylan's cast and left wrist and bench-pressed Dylan's arms away from his own body, then wriggled his body to rotate over top of Dylan's body and landed face down on top of him, his full body weight pinning Dylan down. He scrambled up into the full-mount position, straddling Dylan's abdomen with his thighs, tucking his ankles under Dylan's hamstrings, and pushing down on Dylan's shoulders with his hands.

"Did you forget that I'm my dad's little cadet and he's been training me in hand-to-hand combat practically since I was born?" Marcus asked tauntingly.

Dylan squirmed a bit, trying to get free, but he was already panting heavily from the exertion, and Marcus could see it on his face that even in his inebriated state, Dylan knew he was helpless under Marcus's physically superior strength and dominant position.

"What I forgot is that you like to straddle men like a homo," Dylan said.

"Of course you get all homophobic as soon as you start losing. You pin me and it's 'cause you're strong and manly. I pin you, and I'm a homo. I'm not letting you up until you submit."

"I submit," Dylan relented as the bar owner walked up to them to confirm that everything was okay.

"Yeah," Marcus said to the bar owner. "We're just goofing around. We're done now though."

The two boys got up, brushed as much of the sand off themselves as they could, and walked back into the bar to order some nachos and to get another beer.

An hour later, as Marcus was checking his phone to see how late it was getting and whether he'd missed a text from Havana saying she was done shadowing for the day, Kelsey meandered in. She looked fully made up and like she was going to a frat party, but there was only so much makeup could do to hide the bags under her eyes from several nights in a row of heavy drinking. He filled her in on the plan to go through pre-immigration testing to allow them to visit Havana whenever they wanted. Kelsey seemed apathetic but agreed to the testing, undoubtedly because it was what the crowd was doing. Marcus hadn't received a text from Havana yet, but he saw Kelsey's presence as his opportunity to tag out, and he said his goodbyes, offering the excuse that he had dinner plans with Havana and that she would be going off-duty at the hospital any minute.

As he was walking away, Kelsey called out to him. "Hey, Marcus? When you see Havana, tell her I, like, lost my phone last night, but that I'm a yes for ladies' night tomorrow night and a musical at the theater sounds great?"

Marcus signaled a thumbs-up and turned back toward the door. He heard Dylan first shout, "Gay!" followed by a whiny, "Wait, now she's trying to pry you away from me too? What the hell?"

Marcus passed three men on the way out. He heard a thick Australian accent as one of them teasingly shouted, "Dylan, you alcoholic bum! Have you even moved from that seat since last night?"

"Liam, you wanker! I see your beauty rest did you no good!" Dylan cheerily shouted back.

The door closed. Marcus wasn't sure, but he thought Dylan might have called his name. He kept walking.

Chapter 8: Garden of Eden

The stimulation of people-watching on the train and subway temporarily boosted Marcus's energy levels, but back in his dorm room, his multiple beers with Dylan on top of the early-morning exercise caught up with him. He lay in bed, closed his eyes, and drifted off, but a mere fifteen minutes later he awoke to the sound of his phone ringing. The caller ID came up as Havana. He groggily answered. It was four p.m., and Havana said she'd be leaving the doctor's office soon and wanted to know whether Marcus would meet her in Central Park. Something about craving fresh fruit. Marcus said yes, not even sure of what he was saying yes to, and only truly cognizing the where and when of meeting her. Everything else was a bit fuzzy.

Thirty minutes later, he was walking hand-in-hand with Havana in the northeastern section of Central Park. She walked them to a garden area that had vegetables planted under a partial canopy of fruit trees, shielding them from much of the scorching Caribbean sun. Havana walked up to one of the trees and plucked a piece of fruit that Marcus didn't recognize.

"What is that? Are you allowed to just walk up and take it?" he asked.

"It is guava. They are delicious. I like oranges even better, but they are out of season. And yes, it is okay to just pick one and eat it. They are public gardens, and the fruit is for anyone who wants it."

Marcus started heading to a piece of fruit that looked ripe but hesitated before picking it. He turned to Havana. "This isn't like the Garden of Eden or anything, is it? I'm not going to get kicked out of paradise for eating this, am I?"

Havana laughed, squirting guava juice on her chin. "No, silly. You get to stay even if you eat the fruit."

"Good. Because this place is really growing on me. Nigel encouraged me to do the pre-immigration personality testing this morning, and this afternoon I talked Dylan and Kelsey into doing it with me. Even if I don't move here permanently, he said it would help get the visas I need for frequent visits."

Havana wiped the guava juice off her face and went up on her tippy toes to give Marcus a peck on the cheek. "I love that idea," she said.

The guava only stimulated Marcus's appetite. He mentioned his hunger to Havana, and they agreed to hunt for a restaurant

"Oh, I almost forgot. Kelsey said she lost her phone, but she's on for girls' night tomorrow." Marcus shook his head. "I don't know why you hang out with her. She is so anxiety-riddled, needy, and annoying."

Havana gave Marcus a disapproving look. "She's better in one-on-one situations. It is when she's in crowds, or especially around guys, that her anxiety levels start climbing. Her abuse of the word 'literally' might chafe my eardrums, but I do consider her a friend. Besides, I could say the same about not understanding why you hang with Dylan, but I've done nothing but encourage you to hang out with him...and you aren't exactly Mr. Serenity yourself."

Marcus shrugged. Havana reached out for his hand and clasped it. As they walked hand-in-hand toward the edge of Central Park, in the general direction of an area where Havana had said they would find a diverse array of restaurants, the brick path they were walking along split into multiple paths that each led down a series of tree-lined alleys. Each alley had a pair of paths sandwiching a center strip of manicured flower gardens interrupted by a repeating series of stone obelisk monuments. Under the canopy of the trees, a sea of tan polka dots sprouted from the green grass. As Marcus approached, he determined that it was a field of mushrooms. He turned toward the center of the path and noticed that each of the stone obelisks had a few dozen names carved on them.

"Is this a war memorial or something?" he asked.

"It is a mushroom burial garden. It is like a cemetery, except the people in this garden are put in a mushroom spore suit, and they naturally decay and turn into fertilizer for the gardens."

Marcus gasped while releasing her hand. "That's disgusting!" he nearly shouted.

"What's disgusting about it?"

"It's desecrating the dead. It's gross."

"I don't think it is gross," Havana said. "I think it is beautiful. Instead of being pumped full of toxic chemicals and then buried in a lacquered box that leeches out contaminants, the people here transform into food for plants. Their cells become part of another living organism. When I die, if my body isn't donated to science and used for medical-student dissections, then I hope to be buried in a mushroom spore suit here. After donating any organs I can to medical patients, of course."

"But it is so disrespectful of the dead. It is un-Christian," Marcus objected.

"How so? It is a natural process that acknowledges the life-death cycle. Personally, I think Christian burials demonstrate a denial of that cycle. It's like they want their dead to be frozen in time, never acknowledging what should happen to the body next. I, for one, want my death to be active and positive. I don't want my body to sit there passively polluting the ground. I want it to be recycled into new life. And even if it were un-Christian, what if the people buried here weren't Christians?"

"Maybe Dylan was right about you all being godless commies."

Havana looked at him with an eyebrow raised. "Seriously?" she asked.

"Sorry. I don't know why I said that. I'm hungry. I can't think straight when I'm hungry."

"We will get you food soon enough, but for the record, Puerto Paz is neither godless nor communist. Regarding our burial rituals, though, even from a Christian perspective, the Bible says 'dust we are, and to dust we shall return,' does it not? So why would mushroom-suit burials be desecrating the dead? I'm a bit surprised by your reaction to it. I thought part of what you hated about NEUS was how they crammed religion down your throat. Do you consider yourself Christian?"

"I did hate people trying to control my religious activities, but yes, I do consider myself Christian. Aren't you?" Marcus asked. "I mean, you seem to know your Bible verses, and...I always just assumed..."

"No. I consider myself spiritual, but not religious. I believe in the existence of *something*, a force, a being, I'm not sure what. It doesn't seem to like to clearly reveal itself, and as a result I distrust anyone who claims to know its will. Part of our curriculum in school, though, was a Fundamentals of World Religions class. It started from a more historical and anthropological perspective, then moved into what each religion believes and both the good things and bad things that have been done in that religion's name and the impact of extremist wings of religions on society."

Marcus briefly turned around to see how far they were from Central Station and found himself blinded by sunlight. "So you know a lot about Christianity, yet you reject its teachings?" Marcus asked.

"I believe some of the philosophical teachings found in the Bible, like 'do unto others as you'd have others do unto you,' but I don't think those teaching belong exclusively to religion. Personally, I find a lot of faults with organized religion in general. There are issues with the way the major religions started as oral storytelling." Havana paused at one of the obelisks and went up to it and skimmed her fingers across one of the names. Marcus briefly looked where her hand had touched and saw the dates "2035–2047" inscribed in the stone before he turned his attention back to the direction of the restaurants.

"As a child, did you ever play a game of 'telephone,' where you whispered a paragraph into the ear of the person next to you, then they passed that paragraph on around a circle until it got to the last person, and they tried to repeat the original statement but ended up absolutely butchering it?" Havana asked without pausing for an answer. "The start of the major religions was like that, except that the game went on for decades in the case of the New Testament, and for centuries in the case of the Old Testament, before anything was written down."

She began walking again as she talked. "Plus, you don't really know who the story originated with. You don't know if it originated with a trustworthy source or a Charles Manson-like lunatic, and there isn't enough accurate historical data to fact-check them. It was typically written by men centuries before the scientific method was developed, when humankind had little understanding of the world around them, and they were prone to associate things they witnessed to magic. That garbled message, combined with the motivation of kings and churches throughout history to cherry-pick which stories were kept and which were rejected, to shape religion and to use it to control their subjects, casts organized religion in a very dubious light in my opinion."

Marcus looked at the ground as he walked, noticing the long shadows the obelisks cast. They reminded him of sundials, pointing them in the general direction of the restaurants. He felt his stomach gurgle. "I've found some of the things I've been taught a bit fantastical, but you have to have faith in something, right? Otherwise you are just spiritually empty."

"I certainly don't feel 'empty.' I think people believe in fantastical things because they want so desperately for them to be true. Life is too scary for them without that security blanket, so people cling to it out of desperation. Plus, a lot of parts of religion seem to conveniently confirm that the believers are special snowflakes...like that only *they* get to go to Heaven because they are special...or that *they* are superior to, and have dominion over, the rest of the animal kingdom, despite it being demonstrably true that we are not that different from other animals on this planet."

"But what about the sense of community? Churches back home are the fabric of society," Marcus said, now looking up and staring intently at the one building in the entertainment district ahead that could be seen poking above the park's perimeter trees.

"And you think church is the only place to find a sense of community?"

Marcus stopped dead in his tracks and raised his hands up into a half 'Jesus-on-the-cross' position. "So, you're saying that someone like my mom, who sure seems to find her religion reassuring and has no doubts that what she believes is truth, is just living in a useless fantasy world? That the vast majority of the world is wrong?"

"If ninety percent of the world said it was a good idea to jump off a bridge, it doesn't mean that I would do it. Everyone thinks that theirs is the right religion simply because it is theirs, because it is their tribe. There is no proof that they are right. The only way a correct religion could be determined is if God came down and publicly said 'this religion is the only true religion,' which is ultimately why religious debates are futile."

As Marcus opened his mouth to speak, he felt a slight numbness in his teeth as he released them from a grinding clamp. "Somehow I get the impression that a little thing like futility isn't going to stop you from continuing to express your opinions on it," he said before clenching his jaw again. *Jesus, I probably look like Reverend Wegener right now with my jaw locked like this*, he thought.

"Well, some of the things I've witnessed about religion while abroad are absolutely ridiculous. Some sects have gotten so extremist and perverted in their beliefs that I swear that if the second coming of Jesus happened, they would claim that Jesus was the Antichrist rather than the Savior. The fanaticism of prayer rituals I have witnessed has been a bit shocking too. I mean, if you were God, and you had created the universe, would you want all the people you created groveling and kissing your ass? Or would you want them living their life and exploring the world you created? Learning...inventing? Would you want them fighting over you, their god, because they disagree about who knows your will best? It is like if you had a child, would you want that child to spend each day shut in the house doing nothing interesting and spending half the day sucking up to you? No! You'd want them to learn, grow, explore, create! You'd want them to make things that you could hang on the fridge. Do interesting things that you could tell stories about."

Havana started chuckling.

"What's so funny?" Marcus asked.

"I said 'groveling.' 'Oh, don't grovel! If there's one thing I can't stand, it's people groveling!'"

Marcus just looked straight ahead, his jaw still clenched.

"Get it?" Havana asked. "You said *The Holy Grail* was your favorite movie, didn't you? It's a quote..."

"I got it," Marcus said curtly.

They continued walking in silence. A few blocks later, they were in the heart of the theater district, reviewing the menus posted outside of restaurants. Walking past a couple of theaters, Havana asked Marcus if he had ever been to a theater to see a live play or musical before. He shook his head, and she suggested they try to see one during his remaining time in Puerto Paz. Her expression changed from compassion to smirking. "*Jesus Christ Superstar* might be playing down the street."

Marcus responded with a look of disgust.

"Sorry. I guess that wasn't as funny as it sounded in my head. I was just trying to lighten the mood," she said.

After stopping to read the menus outside of three different restaurants, Havana asked him if any menu had caught his fancy yet, to which he replied that he had only been looking at the menus to humor her, and that he was so hungry that he'd be happy to just walk into the closest restaurant and randomly point at the menu and shove whatever was delivered into his mouth.

"How about Cuban?" Havana asked.

"Is it food? Can I eat it?" Marcus asked.

"Wow. You are in quite the mood." They entered the Cuban restaurant, sat down, and began perusing the menu. "The Cuban sandwich is quick and makes a good entry-level Cuban experience—"

Marcus slammed his menu down on the table.

"What?" a wide-eyed Havana asked.

"Please tell me that 'fried crickets' is just a silly name for something, and not *actual* fried insects."

"They are fried insects."

"I'm not eating here."

"Oh, come on, Marcus. You don't have to order them."

"I'm not eating here."

"You are being ridiculous. You don't have to eat them, and even if you did, insects are healthier than most other animal-based proteins, and they are a more environmentally friendly food-source too. They are cleaned and cooked. Don't tell me you are so puritanical that you are scared of eating insects."

Marcus stood up and started heading for the exit.

"Fine," Havana grunted as she stood up to follow him. She muttered something mostly unintelligible, but Marcus thought he heard the words "cerebral atrophy" as he walked away.

Marcus walked out the door, turned, saw a sign for an Irish restaurant next door, and walked in, Havana trailing him. He took a seat at a dark mahogany table next to an unlit stone fireplace and hid his face, along with a stealthy middle finger, behind a menu.

"Oh, here's the cheeseburger Dylan was worried he wouldn't be able to find in New Athens. I think I'll get that."

"As you wish," Havana said, shaking her head.

After they ordered, Marcus gently massaged the muscles behind his jaw while staring intently at a TV screen that was showing a local baseball game. Their meals arrived, and he closed his eyes and bowed his head to say a prayer. He opened his eyes and saw Havana looking at him, but she said nothing. Halfway through his cheeseburger, Marcus could feel his sense of hunger beginning to dissipate.

"Feeling better? How is it?" Havana asked.

"I think so. It's good."

"So, is attending your first play or musical something you'd be interested in while here in New Athens?"

"Maybe," Marcus said as he shrugged, his gaze still fixed on the baseball game.

"We could make it a date, if you want," Havana suggested. "I'm not sure which one you would be most likely to enjoy, though."

"I dunno," Marcus said.

"Are you okay?" Havana asked.

"I'm fine. Are there any you would recommend, or that you are dying to see?" Marcus asked.

Havana looked at him for a moment before taking another bite of her veggie burger and chewed while looking at him some more. "Well, I'm partial to the classics, but I think I've seen all the classics currently playing. I tend not to like more modern, avant-garde productions. I think if I were to pick one now, I'd probably just go with whatever is playing at the most aesthetically pleasing theater, just because I love the ambiance of a beautiful theater."

"Yeah, I suspect I wouldn't care for modern either."

Marcus ate the rest of his meal quickly, and the conversation tapered off.

After dinner, the couple returned to Marcus's dormitory. On the way to his room, they passed the public lounge. Marcus looked over and spotted the bookshelves full of books meant for residents to borrow as they pleased. He silently diverted his path to investigate.

"Where are…?" Havana said as she stopped and turned to follow him.

"A book might be a nice way to pass the time tonight," Marcus said as he arrived at the shelves and began reviewing the selection.

"I guess," Havana said. She began examining the selection with him. After a minute she pulled one forward to the edge of the shelf and pointed at it. "This is the one my dad was riffing on last night. *The Moon is Down*. It is one of my favorites."

Marcus nodded, then kept looking around. None of the titles were familiar, and he had no idea which book to select. He found himself at the book Havana had pulled forward, creating a bump in the otherwise orderly row of books that all had their spines in a uniform plane. He pushed it back in to restore order. Then changed his mind and pulled it out completely and began reading the back cover.

> *Occupied by enemy troops, a small,*
> *peaceable town comes face-to-face with evil*
> *imposed from the outside—and betrayal born*
> *within the close-knit community…*

He clutched the book at his side and looked at Havana, who now had three different books pulled forward to the edge of the shelf, creating three new punctures in the plane. She was looking from one to the next.

"You ready?" he asked. She grabbed one and pushed the other two back into alignment. They headed to his room where they began the evening lying side-by-side in his bed, reading.

An hour later, Havana closed her book, put it down, and rolled over on top of Marcus, straddling him. She began to peel his shirt up, but Marcus continued to hold his book on his chest, blocking her from lifting his shirt any higher.

"I'm really into this book now," Marcus protested.

Havana slumped down onto his side, pinning his arm against his rib cage before rolling over onto her back and picking up her book again. Ten minutes later, she put her book back down and ripped off her own shirt and bra, grabbed Marcus's book out of his hands, and tossed it onto the bed next to hers before straddling him again. Marcus submitted. They kissed.

"You seem so tense," Havana said. "Even your lips seem rigid. Maybe a full release will help." She had a sultry smile, and her eyebrows danced with innuendo. She slid down his torso, pulling his pants and underwear down. Her head began bobbing slowly like she was nodding "yes," but Marcus's body was saying "no."

After a few minutes, Havana climbed back up his torso. "Well, maybe tonight's not the night for you, but it still can be for me?" She rolled onto her back, pulled her own shorts and underwear off, spread her legs, and looked over at Marcus expectantly. He obeyed.

A short while later, Marcus had returned from the foot of the bed and was on his back again. Havana was drifting off to sleep with her head on his shoulder. Marcus lay there wide awake. He carefully picked up his book and rolled Havana off of his arm and onto her back. He read some more. And some more. He finished his book and set it aside. He found the book Havana had picked out—a compendium of novels by George Orwell—lying in the bedsheets and began reading that. He stayed awake for hours, reading *Animal Farm* and *1984*. His pants were lying on the floor next to the bed. He pulled his keys out of the pocket and rubbed his keychain as he continued reading Havana's book. He looked over at the clock on the wall and watched the digits change to 02:00.

Chapter 9: Big TenT

Havana's e-glasses alarm woke them up early Wednesday morning so that she could head off to her doctor shadowing. "Looks like someone's gonna get caught wearing the same clothes as yesterday, and everyone will know where you've been," Marcus teased. "Maybe tonight you'll have to sleep at your place so that you have a fresh outfit to wear to work."

Havana stuck out her tongue. "First of all, the doctor I'm shadowing is at the hospital today, so I'll be changing into hospital scrubs, and no one will know the difference. Second, sex and sleepovers aren't considered dirty or taboo here, so no one would care anyway."

Marcus walked Havana to the dorm's front door and said goodbye.

"Aren't you forgetting something?" Havana asked before closing her eyes and puckering her lips.

Marcus kissed her. Havana opened her eyes and touched his arm. "Are you sure you are okay?" she asked. "You seemed off last night, and it seems to be continuing this morning. Anything you want to talk about?"

"I'm fine. I'm just tired. I didn't sleep that well."

"Okay. I have to run, and tonight is supposed to be ladies' night, but if you change your mind and want to talk about anything, I can cancel with Kelsey."

"I'm fine."

Marcus returned to his room alone, lay back down in bed, and continued reading. Hunger drove him down to the cafeteria, where he read while eating. He returned to his room and read until he fell asleep for several hours. He awoke feeling hungry again and repeated his book breakfast with literature lunch.

Dylan texted during lunch, asking whether he wanted to bar hop on the beach with him that night while the girls were out abandoning them. Marcus texted back: "Feeling introverted. Will probably just spend the day reading and go to bed early. Besides, we just did the bar thing. If I did anything social today, I'd want to do something other than bars, and closer to the dorm."

After returning to his room and resuming *1984*, he drifted off to sleep again. He awoke an hour later, picked up where he had left off, and laughed at the irony of having fallen asleep at nearly exactly the same point in the book that the character Julia had fallen asleep while the character Winston read to her. Finally, he finished the last of the books he had. He searched his room for more reading material but only found some pamphlets introducing new students to campus life at UNA and the literature Nigel had given him at their meeting. He spread them on his bed, opening a couple, but couldn't find the will to read beyond the first paragraph of anything.

Marcus walked back downstairs to the lounge to refill the voids on the shelf and to consider another book. He hadn't been paying close attention to where exactly Havana had found the books the previous night. He paced back and forth along the row of shelving, trying to find their proper places. As he searched, he heard a feminine voice call his name.

"Marcus! You look lost!"

Marcus looked around for the source of the voice. A group of about a dozen people were sitting on couches and chairs in a darkened corner of the lounge in front of a bright screen that said, "Press play to begin." He struggled to make out the shadowy faces in the backlit seating area. One of the figures stood and approached, her features clarifying the closer she got.

"Priya!" Marcus said, finally overcoming the struggle to identify her out of the only context that he knew her from. At the Department of Immigration, she had been dressed more formally than her current shorts and T-shirt, and her hair was now released from its bun and hung down past her shoulders.

"Need any help? You look lost," she reiterated.

"I finished these books, and I'm just trying to remember where on the shelf I got them from last night before I start looking for a new one."

"There is a spot down at the end where you can return books, and the staff will figure out where to put them if you want." Marcus shrugged and followed her suggestion. "We were about to start a movie if you'd like to join us instead."

"I don't know. I'm not feeling terribly social today. Sometimes I get in introverted moods."

"That's fine. Just thought you might want a break from binge-reading. That's an awful lot of dystopia to be digesting in such a short time! Plus, you don't really have to be social while watching a movie. It is kind of the best of both worlds, where you can enjoy the comfort of being around people while not needing to talk to anyone. Want any suggestions on a next book? Maybe some lighter reading for a change of pace?"

Marcus nodded. "Do you go to school here at UNA?"

"Yes, during the school year. I stayed in the dorm this summer to be close to my internship at Immigration. My family lives pretty far away."

Marcus nodded. "So what movie are you watching? Is it a recent release? Made here in Puerto Paz?"

Priya went on to describe the blended action-drama-comedy, that she was pretty sure was a locally made movie released within the last year.

"Sounds intriguing," he said. "Maybe I will join you."

He followed Priya over to the seating area where the group had just started the opening credits and sat in a still-warm recliner while Priya joined her friends on a couch. He sank back and immersed himself in the alternate reality on the screen.

Two hours later, the movie ended and the lights were turned back on. The bespectacled group started chatting amongst themselves about the movie, but a young woman, possibly of Latin American descent, turned around and noticed Marcus. "Hi! I'm Marie. What's your name?"

Marcus introduced himself, and more people began to notice the new guy in their midst. Marcus got lost in a sea of new names as Priya introduced him to everyone else.

"Anyone up for dinner?" Marie asked the group.

A young white guy, who had the relatively muscular body of a decathlete, excitedly waved his arms and said, "Ooh, ooh! It's feijoada night at my family's restaurant out in Carver! We should all go there!"

Marcus sat back and listened to the group chatter about who did and who didn't have conflicting appointments and whether Carver was too far away. After three of the thirteen people begged off, the remaining ten seemed to come to a consensus that they liked the idea but that they would have to leave soon in order to return at a reasonable hour. Priya turned to Marcus and asked him if he wanted to join them.

"What is fey-zhoewada?" Marcus asked.

"It is a stew of sorts. Portuguese in origin, but I think Nikola's family does a Brazilian variety."

Marcus shrugged. "I'm all alone tonight. I guess I might as well join you."

"We're eleven," Priya announced to the group. "Vans seat twelve, right? We're taking a City Van I assume?"

The group discussed logistics briefly before Nikola ordered a van. Five minutes later, they were boarding a capsule-shaped white van. Marcus headed to the front where he intended to sit in a solo front passenger seat, but he was surprised to discover that seating was two rows of six seats along the sides of the van that all faced sideways toward a middle aisle. He had completely forgotten that this would be an autonomous vehicle, and he hadn't realized it meant that the seating might be arranged differently. He sat at the front end next to Priya anyway.

The conversation that had started up after the movie continued seamlessly into the van, but Marcus spent the first five minutes of the ride with his gaze glued to the front of the vehicle, marveling at the driverless operation. He alternated between monitoring the route map, sensor data, and other vehicle status info displayed on a computer screen above the front window and looking out the window, comparing reality to virtual reality.

"What's up with the road?" he asked Priya as they glided down one of the main avenues. "Those lines painted on the road look funny."

"They are bioluminescent solar collectors built into the road that also act as guides for the autonomous vehicles and provide surface light."

Marcus turned his attention back to the interior.

"So, Marcus, what did you think of the movie?" Marie asked from across the aisle.

"It was pretty good. No *Monty Python* or anything, but I laughed a few times."

Several people laughed at his comment. One person commented, "Nothing ever will be as funny as *Monty Python*."

"It was nice to finally see something fresh and new, though," Marcus continued.

"Marcus is from NEUS," Priya clarified for the group. "You don't get new releases there, do you?"

Marcus shook his head.

"Not every day we get to meet someone from NEUS!" Marie said.

"Are all of you from here?" Marcus asked.

"Nasir is from Iraq," Marie said, pointing to a young man a few seats down from her. "But I think everyone else is from Puerto Paz." Marie's finger began scanning the rows as she continued. "Pierre, Linus, Katherine, Malala, and I are all from New Athens. Priya and Niels are from DaVinci. Gertrude is from Noether, and Nikola is from Carver, where we are headed now."

Priya leaned over to more privately say, "DaVinci is Puerto Paz's secondary city in the southeast. Noether is a tertiary town not far from it."

The rest of the group began chatting about the movie again while Marcus continued his discussion with Priya. "How far away is Carver?" he asked.

"Not far. Maybe a twenty-minute drive tops, but it is in farm country, and Nikola's family's farm isn't near a train station."

"Farm country?" Marcus asked. "Ugh. Had I known that..."

"Do you have allergies?" Priya asked.

Marcus shook his head. "How do they treat..." he paused. "People like us there. People with some color in their skin."

Priya's head tilted, and her eyebrows pinched together, making her almost look like she had a unibrow. "What do you mean?"

"My experiences in...well. Never mind. I guess if you, Nasir, and Malala are fine with this place, then I shouldn't worry."

"Nikola's family is really nice. Don't worry, they'll treat you well. And I think you'd really enjoy talking with Nikola. I remember seeing on your bio-sheet at the office that you are a gridiron athlete. Nikola plays gridiron too."

Marcus nodded as he returned his gaze to the front window. The scenery outside had changed from cityscape to woodland while his attention had been diverted. His attention was diverted briefly a second time as he pulled his phone out of his pocket to see why it had vibrated. It was a text from Havana. "Kelsey is about to come over so we can go to dinner. You doing OK? I can still call off K if you want to talk."

He quickly typed a response. "Go out with K. I'm fine without you."

He stuck his phone back in his pocket and looked back out the window. It suddenly changed again from the dimly lit wooded area to farmland fully bathed in evening light. They passed one pair of farmhouses and barns on opposite sides of the road, then the van accelerated to what must have been 100 miles per hour as it drove past what seemed like miles of a mixture of agricultural, solar panel, and wind turbine farms before slowing back down as they encountered another set of four farmhouses and barns at the four corners of an intersection.

The van pulled into a driveway in front of one of them. The red barn at this one was especially large and elongated. Marcus peered at a two-word sign on the front façade. The first word he could easily read as "Big." The second word took him a few seconds to realize that the first and last letters were capital T's that had their horizontal arms extended and connected, creating a canopy over the top of an "en," creating the word "TenT."

The group exited the van and entered the bar area of the restaurant. Marcus stopped behind Nikola, who was leaning over the bar to hug the female bartender. He looked around at the decorative rough-hewn timber framing and the small tables made from granite slabs sitting on oak barrels, then at a side-lit enameled mirror centered behind the bar. The "Big TenT" logo was featured prominently on the mirror, along with a row across the top of multicolored triangle shapes dangling like icicles.

Marcus's eyes nearly doubled in size as a red and gray triangle inscribed with the words "Ohio State" caught his eye. He looked over the other pennants. Each had the name of a school he recognized from either EUS or WUS. Purdue and Michigan State from EUS. Minnesota and Iowa from WUS. He looked to the spot where he had last seen Priya, only to discover that the group had continued on to the restaurant area already. He hurried to reconnect with them.

Marcus followed the group as they walked from the one-story bar area into a cavernous two-story-tall restaurant area. He tilted his head back to look up and admire the colorful fabric canopy draped over the room. Colored triangular wedges radiated around a center chandelier. The high end of each wedge hung from above the chandelier, and the low points connected to the barn walls above the windows, creating an elongated octagon of catenary ceiling panels.

The group was seated at a long table along one edge of the room. Marcus sat at one end next to Priya. A minute later, Nikola sat down across from him.

"We were seated immediately," Marcus said to Nikola. "I'm guessing you have a little pull with the owners?"

Nikola laughed and pinched two fingers together so they were nearly touching. "A little bit! But I texted my dad at the same time I ordered the van to make sure we had seating available too. I wouldn't have brought us here if it had been too full."

"So Priya tells me we both play gridiron."

"A fellow ironman?" Nikola exclaimed giddily. "No way! Where do you play."

"Well, I guess I still kind of play for Miami University. It's kind of a vague situation, though. Until I left home, I played at New Rochelle High School in NEUS. I had a verbal offer to go to Ohio State in a year, but then I ran away from NEUS. My friend and I ended up at Miami and are on the practice squad, but everything is kind of in limbo right now. How about you? Where do you play?"

"I play for the Whips. Western Puerto Paz. In the bar they have a sports program on the TV where they are showing highlights of the Whips from last season. After we order, we should go to get beer and wine for the table and we can check it out together. Maybe they'll even show a highlight of me!"

"Sure. Speaking of the bar, I noticed an Ohio State pennant on the mirror. What's up with that?"

"You know, I should explain that to the whole group." Nikola picked up a spoon and clanked it gently on a glass a few times before addressing the whole table. "Guys and gals, so awesome to have you all here! Marcus was just starting to ask me about our restaurant, and I figured I would tell the whole group about this place since I know this is the first time here for many of you. The farm land we are on now was founded by my Grandpa Max. He was a farmer in Indiana until Puerto Paz was declared habitable after the Annihilation. He grew up in pre-partitioned USA, but after Indiana became part of NEUS, he was persecuted and ostracized for being gay.

"My other grandpa, Grandpa Heike, was murdered in a hate crime, which drove Grandpa Max to move here with my mom and uncles the very first year of Puerto Paz's existence. Together, they ran this farm and have been helping feed the people of New Athens for twenty years. A few years ago, my grandpa retired, and my mom took over the farm, and my dad, a chef, started this farm-to-table restaurant and market.

"My Grandpa Max grew up a huge sports fan, specifically of Midwestern college sports. The Big Ten Conference was the sports conference that mattered most to him, so in honor of him they used the words "Big Ten" in the naming of this restaurant. They added a "T" to the end to make it "Big TenT," in reference to the inclusive culture that has allowed my grandpa to thrive here, which stands in polar-opposite contrast to what he had to leave behind in NEUS. It also refers to the eclectic menu that features dishes from around the globe." Nikola then looked up and pointed. "The ten tapestry panels you see overhead also form a tent of sorts, and each represents the color of one of the original Big Ten schools. They are arranged in rainbow order to also represent the gay pride flag. So, it is with great *pride* that I welcome you all to my Grandpa Max's Big TenT!"

The group started clapping and tossing out whoops of "To Grandpa Max!"

Nikola looked down at the glasses on the table and exclaimed, "I should have waited to tell my story until after we had beverages to toast with! I'll go get some now!" He looked over to Marcus and nodded his head toward the bar. "Want to come with?" he asked.

Marcus stood up and walked with Nikola to the bar. "Is she your girlfriend?" Marcus asked, pointing at the bartender after Nikola told her which wine and beer he wanted for the table.

"Sister!" Nikola said with a laugh. "She's in grad school by day and helping run the bar by night."

"Do a lot of people live out in the rural areas in Puerto Paz? I didn't see many houses on the way out here."

"Nah. Mostly just a few farming families here and there. The rural areas are almost entirely a mix of farmland, energy farms, and nature preserves or parklands. Most people live in the city. It's more environmentally friendly, plus more cost effective for providing services."

"Must have been a lonely childhood out here," Marcus said.

"Not really. I went to school on the edge of the city and had a lot of friends there. And here at home, I was tight with my siblings. My sister here throws a mean Hail Mary. She helped me become the tight end I am today." He looked up at the TV in the corner of the room. "There I am!" he shouted. "Number eighty-seven!"

The two young men stood there watching the football highlights on TV for a few minutes and discussing the rules differences between EUS and Caribbean football, and then Grandpa Max's disappointment at how the partitioning of the USA had split apart the Big Ten conference. Marcus said he could relate, mentioning the splitting of EUS conferences along north-south lines. As they were watching, Marcus felt a vibration in his pocket again. He furled his eyebrows in annoyance, assuming it was Havana again reconfirming that he was okay, but this time it was Dylan.

"DUDE!!! Get to a TV! Puerto Paz football is on. It's hilarious! PUSSYBALL!

"I'm looking at it right now. It's not so bad," Marcus texted back.

"I thought they didn't allow TVs in dorm rooms. Where are you watching it?"

"At a bar."

"WTF? Thought you weren't interested in going to bars tonight."

"The bar is in a restaurant. Ran into Priya from Immigration. Got sucked in to dinner out on a farm with her and some students from the dorm after a movie in the lounge. You should come out here. We haven't even ordered dinner yet. Plenty of time for you to get here for dinner. Big group. I'm actually standing next to one of the football players you're seeing on TV. Come out and I'll introduce you to him. He's a tight end. We're getting drinks for the table now."

"So you're out at some farm, far from the dorm, drinking in a bar with a bunch of people? After telling me you didn't want to join me far from the dorms for drinking at a bar because you felt like being a loner? DICK!"

"Chill! I got sucked in and have been feeling more recharged and social as the day goes on. Don't be so butt-hurt. COME JOIN US!!! It would do you some good to go someplace other than Playa. You're turning into an alcoholic hermit out there."

Marcus's phone went silent. He stuck it back in his pocket to help Nikola carry pitchers of beer and bottles of wine back to the table. Their server came to take their orders and everyone except the three vegetarians and Marcus ordered the Wednesday night special stew that Nikola had brought them there for. Marcus chickened out, not feeling like experimenting with something new, and ordered a burrito.

As appetizers arrived and the group started passing them around the table, Marcus handed Priya a dish, and while he had her attention stammered a question. "So, Priya.... Can I...can I ask you a personal question?" Priya nodded and Marcus continued. "I don't mean to be insensitive or anything. You're like, of Indian heritage, right?"

"My parents are from India, yes. I'm second-generation Puerto Pazian."

"Are you non-Christian? What religion are you?"

"I'm loosely Hindu. Like, Hindu Lite or something. Hindu-nostic? I don't follow my parents' religion strictly. I meditate daily, but that isn't really a religious practice to me. I guess once in a while when I'm feeling frustrated with something in life, I'll perform a puja, a customary prayer where I bathe, make offerings to one of the representations of god, and say a Vedic prayer. Intellectually I know it is unlikely to have any impact on my life other than as a placebo, but it can feel like I'm doing something when there is nothing to be done, and it makes me a little happier when I have done it."

"Again, I don't mean to be rude, but that sounds so...I don't know."

"Different than what you are used to?" Priya said, smiling.

"I think I was going to say weird," Marcus admitted.

"You only know what you know, and new knowledge always seems weird at first."

"Yeah. I guess it reminds me of how I felt about this tribe I met in Wyoming. They put their faith in where the stars aligned and in ritual chants. It seemed so weird to me then too."

"I'm guessing you are Christian?" Priya asked. Marcus nodded. "Imagine how a non-Christian feels about your beliefs and rituals. Virgin birth? Drinking the blood of your savior? Admittance to Heaven being dependent on whether you believe that something that happened over two thousand years ago was divine magic, despite unreliable historical documentation of those events?"

Marcus nodded. He listened to the chatter of the other conversations for a minute, then pressed Priya again. "I don't think I've seen any churches while here. They don't ban organized religion here like they do in San Francisco, do they? Do you have to do your prayers in secret?"

"Our government might be secular, but organized religion is not banned. We have a policy of tolerance of all religious beliefs so long as they don't harm society, but we also believe in keeping our religion and our politics separate and not trying to force our own religion onto everyone else. Proselytizing is self-righteousness. There are plenty of religious people here, including Christians, but it is a smaller percentage of people who participate here than what you likely experienced in NEUS. The more people are struggling, the more they turn to religion to try to alleviate their pain. In healthier societies, people tend to have a more personal spirituality that acknowledges that there are a lot of unknowns in this universe, and that they don't need to solve those unknowns with supernatural stories. Church attendance here tends to have a fairly high percentage of new immigrants. You probably have walked past a few but just haven't noticed them because they aren't as ostentatious as in other countries. They tend to blend in with the surrounding architecture."

Marcus munched on a vegetable empanada, admiring the pinwheel of colors overhead. His attention briefly turned to the three red panels, realizing that one of those represented Ohio State. He turned back to Priya and politely waited until she was finished chewing her bite of empanada before prodding her again. "So, are there many other Hindus here in Puerto Paz?"

"Some, but it's a fairly small percentage."

"Does that make dating hard for you, being in a religious minority?"

"Not at all. I don't really care about the religion of the guys I date, so long as they aren't a part of some creepy cult that wants to harm society. Why should their weird, unverifiable beliefs be any more of a detriment to me dating them than mine are to them dating me?"

"And interfaith dating doesn't make you feel…I don't know, like you aren't staying true to your heritage? Your culture? To yourself?"

"Not one bit. Culture isn't something you can own or inherit. My culture is whatever I choose it to be. I don't owe anything to anyone. My life is mine to live as I please, so long as I'm not harming others in the process."

"Hmm," Marcus said as the waiters began serving the main course. "So, it sounds like you consider yourself a staunch individualist. Kind of like the people in SEUS? Not a team player like people in NEUS?"

"Oh, god no!" Priya said. "Not at all. I think it is somewhere between the two extremes. I'm an individualist in the sense that I don't let anyone define who I am except me, but I'm a team player in that I want everyone around me to succeed with me, and I want to jointly improve society. I want symbiotic relationships, not the destructive, parasitic relationships of SEUS."

Marcus nodded and jealously eyed the stew Priya was scooping out of a shared serving bowl into her own bowl.

"Would you like to try some?" Priya asked.

"I didn't order that."

"So what? I'm offering you some."

Marcus shrugged and said, "Sure." Priya passed him her bowl, and he took a spoonful. "Delicious!" he exclaimed.

Maria, who had been sitting on the other side of Marcus, asked if she could try some stew too, and Priya passed her a bowl via Marcus. Maria then eyed Marcus's meal before asking if he was interested in trading bites of his burrito for bites of her gnocchi dish. Marcus shrugged and agreed, figuring he might as well go all in on the Big TenT philosophy and sample the diverse flavors.

He re-engaged in the conversations going on around the table. The topics wandered from recounting the funniest moments in the movie they had watched together, to whether a scene in the movie violated the laws of physics, to how they might have engineered that scene, to the ethics of robotic circuitry being embedded into humans, a theme that had featured prominently in the movie. They moved on to some of the projects the students had worked on in school the past year. Marcus learned that the group had a diverse range of majors including engineering, philosophy, childhood education, political science, and, of course, Nikola was studying agriculture in preparation for improving and taking over the farm.

The evening ended with another toast and hugs all around, before people split up into different autonomous cars to go to their various final destinations for the night. Back in his peaceful dorm room, a full six hours after he had ventured out with his new friends, he lay in bed digesting his meal and the evening's experience. Drifting off to sleep, he found himself thinking of Mamaroneck friends he had made at summer football camp back in New York a couple of years earlier.

Chapter 10: Sacred Heart

A seemingly rare rainstorm washed out much of Marcus's ideas of what to do Thursday while Havana was busy shadowing doctors. Marcus downloaded the Puerto Paz app to his phone to check the weather and was relieved that it was only part of a tropical depression and not the precursor to a hurricane.

He explored the app a bit more and was surprised to find that the *Renaissancity* game was still alive and well, and was listed in the app's menu. A few clicks later, he discovered it was used as a geospatial data model to keep track of city information, and as a way to game out "what-if" scenarios, such as new buildings or businesses, for both the government and public alike. He began exploring the options for making his own virtual reality avatar, including how high or low he wanted to set artificial intelligence predictive decision-making for his character when he wasn't actively using the game, and how often to get summaries of those AI decisions, but the initial setup began to get a bit elaborate, and he lost interest. He left his room but couldn't find any of his new friends in the dorm, so he spent part of the morning alone in the lounge watching modern movies on-demand. Eventually he got bored and headed to the basement, where he had heard there was a doorway to the underground tunnel system.

He found the doorway easily and explored the busy tunnels for a while. He quickly found himself outside the windows of a store built into the wall of the tunnel called "UNA Ift Shop: Thrifts and Gifts." He peered through the window at the variety of new and antique trinkets. A display of shiny metal keychains in the window caught his interest. At the center was a beautiful replica of the Puerto Paz symbol. He continued around the display until a pair of keychains along the edge startled him. They were very old-looking medallions, one featuring the New York Yankee's logo, the other the Boston Red Sox, dangling side by side.

Clearly the shop owner knows not the blasphemy of their display, Marcus thought.

He continued on, thinking he would amuse himself and pass the time by playing a game of getting himself lost and trying to find his way back, but there were maps on the walls at each intersection and signs pointing out major landmarks and directions everywhere. It was practically impossible to get lost. Much of the city seemed to have the same idea to go underground during the inhospitable weather.

The tunnel traffic was fairly orderly, with different lanes of travel identified by different colored tiles. Opposing center lanes were for the pedestrians, who all seemed to be walking at nearly the same steady pace. Lanes to the outside of those seemed to be for a variety of sizes of portable wheeled boxes, the same boxes he had seen at the subway tracks his first day in New Athens. Some were either manual-push or non-autonomous motorized boxes, but most were fully autonomous versions that either wandered alone or shadowed their human leader like droids from *Star Wars*. The outer lanes against the tunnel walls seemed to be some sort of slow-speed on-off ramp for people and boxes trying to get into or out of the tunnels. When Marcus matched the speed of the surrounding people, everything went smoothly, but when he got impatient and wanted to walk faster, he found his expedition turning into a game of human *Frogger* as he tried to navigate the crowded aisles without bumping into anything or anyone.

Typically it was fairly easy to jump into the moving box lane, speed up to pass people, then dart back into the center pedestrian lane, but at intersections he found his experience as a running back being put to use. Eventually he decided there was no point in rushing, so he slowed down a little to match the pace of the people around him.

After a few random turns at intersections, Marcus spotted one of the autonomous boxes change to the outer lane, slow down, then exit the tunnel through a sliding door that had opened for it. He followed it through the doors into an underground parking garage. It was crammed full of cars all jammed together and stacked on racks, with only a single narrow path through them leading up a ramp. Some of the cars on the racks were fully assembled, others were just flat chassis with wheels, and others were just car bodies with no chassis. He watched a robotic arm pull a car body off the rack and press it down into a chassis that was already on the ground until it clicked. The assembled car drove itself toward Marcus, then turned toward the ramp, revealing a missing rear end with just fins sticking out on both sides of the car. The automated box Marcus had followed then mated with another box and maneuvered into position behind the car. A forklift system extended from the back end of the car, scooped up the interconnected mobile boxes, and pulled them tight to the car with an audible click as the mobile boxes locked into place and turned into the car's trunk.

"Excuse me," a voice from behind Marcus said.

Marcus turned around, then stepped aside to allow a man to walk past him. He watched as the man climbed into the car, and the car drove off up the ramp.

Marcus was about to turn around and head back to the tunnels when he heard another voice.

"You look lost. Need any help?"

Marcus looked back over to where the car body and chassis had been assembled and spotted a man in overalls standing next to a bodiless car chassis that had cables connecting it to a computer.

"I'm sorry?" Marcus asked.

"You look lost."

"I've been getting that a lot lately," Marcus said.

"Need any help?"

"I don't think so. I'm kind of intentionally trying to get lost. I followed one of those portable trunks in here and was checking things out. I've never seen a garage like this before."

"Are you from out of town?" the man asked.

"Yeah."

"Welcome to New Athens!"

"Thanks. So, what are you doing over there? Are you a mechanic?"

"I am. You want to come over and see?"

Marcus walked over to look at the computer monitor. The man wiped off his hands and extended one. Marcus shook his hand. "I'm

Paul. Paul Hawking. But all my friends call me Hawk."

Marcus introduced himself and asked again what he was doing.

"Just a basic inspection and maintenance for this chassis."

"I'm surprised that a place so high tech wouldn't have wireless connections," Marcus said, pointing to the wires attaching the computer to the car.

"It is for security. The core computing functions of the car are segregated from the less-essential ones to prevent hacking. Only the less-essential functions have wireless."

"Makes sense. So do these things have a good safety record? I rode in a City Van for the first time last night. It was a little nerve-racking."

Hawk nodded. "Better than humans. Crashes are rare, and when they do happen, usually they've managed to slow down enough to make them not too serious. You are welcome to stick around for a while and watch if you want."

Marcus declined, saying he had more exploring to do, and headed back into the tunnels.

He renewed his attempts to get lost. He was trying to ignore all the maps and signs, but a few intersections away from the garage, a sign with a cross symbol caught his eye: It marked the entrance to the Sacred Heart Catholic Church. He got back into the outer lane, stopped walking, and paused to look at the sign, triggering the sliding door to open. Marcus was certain that if he stood there looking at the sign much longer it would instigate another stranger approaching him to tell him he looked lost. *I have been feeling lost,* he admitted. *For the last couple of days. No, since running away from NEUS. No, since before that. Since I can remember. I feel like I've been stumbling through life, only able to focus on putting one foot in front of the other and continuing moving forward without tripping, but never really knowing what direction "forward" is supposed to be, or what my final destination is. I felt more confident in my path until a couple of days ago though.*

He hadn't set out this morning with a specific destination, but looking at the sign, he felt like maybe he had found what he had been unconsciously looking for. Something had been silently gnawing at the back of his mind for the last couple of days. As he looked at the sign, it percolated into his consciousness. *Havana isn't*

Christian. He walked through the doors far enough for them to close behind him, isolating him from the rest of the city. *Does Havana's religion matter? Why is this bothering me? I couldn't stand having religion crammed down my throat back home.* Catholicism wasn't his brand of religion, but his path had led him here. *Maybe it's time to heed Mom's parting advice and to pray on things to find peace.* He ascended the stairs to the church, hoping to find another sign of sorts inside.

At the top of the stairs, he entered a small lobby. He pushed open another set of doors that led to a dimly lit nave. He inhaled the church's scent deeply. No matter where he went, all churches seemed to have a similar odor: some sort of musty wood mixed with old incense. Childhood memories began to flood in. The time Reverend Fallar had whipped him and Dylan with a cane in junior high after they were caught sneaking into the room where they stored the wine for the Lord's Supper. Reverend Wegener screaming at him that he was a sinner who would go to Hell. The mandatory daily prayers to start off the school day and again before they were allowed to eat lunch, and the time Dylan had defiantly gone on a hunger strike while refusing to say his lunchtime prayers during his "angry at God" phase after his mother had died. Marcus could recite those prayers backward and forward while juggling flaming batons if he wanted to.

More recent memories peeled away to reveal older ones, from before he had met Dylan, of his own mother teaching him those very prayers, and to his dad, who was always on his best behavior and was relatively nice to Marcus while they were in public at church. He thought about his family's home in New Rochelle and mentally inventoried every cross they had on display. Did he miss his church and his religion? Or did he miss the connections to people that religion helped bring him closer to? Why did his religion suddenly seem to matter so much?

If I were brought up in a Hindu culture, would I be a Christian right now? Marcus wondered. *Or if I was brought up in a more agnostic culture, would I still be a Christian right now? Am I only Christian now because I was raised in a Christian culture? And if I weren't Christian now, would I view Christianity as bizarrely as Havana does? The same way I viewed the hippies in Wyoming's beliefs as bizarre? Or Priya's Hindu rituals as bizarre? Do I only view those as bizarre because they're not my beliefs, the ones I'm accustomed to? Because they're not from my tribe?*

He looked around the empty church. It was a surprisingly small room, with fairly simple architecture and décor. As he walked toward the center aisle, he briefly looked up at the lit crucifix suspended over the sanctuary under the tent-like cathedral ceiling. He turned toward the front entrance of the church. The dark skies outside intensified the dimness of the interior, but the church's selective lighting accentuated its most sacred details. A backlit, circular stained-glass window over the front doors glowed brightly, making it the most conspicuous object in the room. Marcus studied it. Shards of orange and yellow glass radiated outward from a golden center, simulating a fire. The orange and yellow diffused into blues and purples around the circumference of the window. In the middle of it all, surrounded by gold-colored glass, was a blood-red heart wrapped in thorns and with a cross planted in the top that was engulfed in a smaller flame emanating from the top of the heart.

He closed his eyes momentarily and prayed, asking God for the wisdom to settle his mind. He opened his eyes again and looked at the stained glass, trying to soak in its overall beauty this time rather than inspecting every detail. A heart on a gold background. Echoes of Nigel's voice began to reverberate in his head. "I have met far too many atheists and agnostics with hearts of gold..."

"Havana has a heart of gold!" Marcus whispered.

He looked up at the ceiling and thought back to Priya the night before saying, "Why should their weird, unverifiable beliefs be any more of a detriment to me dating them as mine are to them dating me?"

He nodded to himself and said out loud, "Tribes be damned, I love her. My culture is whatever I choose it to be."

He stood there smiling, looking back at the stained glass until the church's bells began to chime twelve. His shoulders sagged as he released the tension in his neck and upper back, and he sighed before walking casually toward the front doors. He fished a small bill out of his pocket and dropped it in a donation bin at the entrance before opening the front doors and exiting to an arcaded sidewalk along one of the main avenues.

He stood in the arcade outside the church for a few minutes, just enjoying the fresh, earthy scent of the rain stirring up the grass and leaves of the linear park in front of him. He hadn't even thought to hunt for an umbrella when he left the dorm, but it was mostly dry under the cover of the arcade vaults, with only an occasional gust of wind blowing a mist of rain nearly horizontally into the walkway.

He began to stroll, and soon heard faint music. He followed the sound and ended up in a pub where a quartet was playing bluegrass music. It was not a style of music he was terribly familiar with, nor was it one that he would normally have selected to listen to, but it intrigued him. As much as he despised country music, and as similar in nature as this was to country music, somehow he found this music pleasant. He sat down, ordered lunch and a beer, and listened to the overlapping melodies of the banjo, guitar, and mandolin that dovetailed together seamlessly over the steady rhythm of the stand-up bass.

As his meal was arriving, he felt his phone vibrate. It was Dylan texting, "K's taking a nap. Bored. Come over for drinks? You owe me for ditching me last night." Marcus shook his head and put the phone face down on the table before taking his first bites of his sandwich.

As he ate, he studied the bass player, sensing something familiar about him. He nearly choked on his beer when he realized it was that the bass player resembled a younger version of Reverend Wegener. He hadn't noticed it until the guy stopped smiling briefly between songs as the band discussed what they'd play next.

As they resumed, Marcus looked over the band and then surveyed the small crowd that had grown around them to listen to this happy, beautiful music. *The bass player might look like the reverend, but these musicians are the ones doing the Lord's work, not Wegener*, he thought.

Marcus shifted in his seat and suddenly thought of Dylan kneeling at the school cafeteria table freshman year because his butt was too sore to sit after Wegener had caned him. He flipped his phone back over and re-read the message from Dylan. *Maybe I do owe him one. That caning was because of me. How do I reach out to someone so rebellious though?* He remembered what Nigel had said about having gone through a rebellious period in his life, and how a steadfast mentor had altered his path for the better.

He picked up his phone and responded. "You should come into the city. There is beer here too, and great live music."

After finishing his meal and seeing no response from Dylan, he headed out, finding his way back to the tunnel system near Sacred Heart. He retraced his steps from near the church back to the garage where he had met Hawk and poked his head in to see whether the mechanic was still there. He was, working away on a chassis. He looked up and spotted Marcus.

"You again! Succeeded in getting yourself lost finally?"

"No, quite the opposite. I was on my way back home but thought I'd stop in to ask you about something."

"Ask away," Hawk said, setting down his wrench and giving Marcus his full attention.

"It's kind of a personal question. I hope you aren't offended. I was curious whether mechanics make a decent living here. I know there is the symbiotic capitalism thing here.... Does that mean you make a reasonable income?"

"I'm not offended in the least by that. I don't know how you do it where you are from, but here our salaries are public information. You can't establish fair salaries without knowing what others are making, and yes, I make a good living doing this, and more importantly, I love doing it. Is becoming a mechanic something you are considering?"

"Not really. But I have a friend who is. He's more into gas-powered, human-driven cars, so I'm not sure how he would do with these electric autonomous ones. He's a tinkerer in general, though. He fixes all sorts of stuff like old DVD players and VCRs. I imagine these are a lot more complex though."

"Yes and no. There is a complex array of computers, sensors, electric drive systems, battery systems, and such built into the chassis, but there are only two types of chassis manufactured, so once you learn those two chassis, you are essentially done. There are a lot of different body styles that fasten to the chassis, but the only complexity with those are the fastening system, the HVAC system, and the display monitors, and they are all fairly standardized too."

"Is the training to learn all of that hard?"

"Mechanics get a college degree just like everyone else, but our curriculum skews toward the mechanical, electrical, and computing side, especially in the final years. We usually start as apprentices too. I could talk to your friend about it more if you want."

"That'd be great! I'll suggest it to him," Marcus said. He thanked Hawk for his time and headed back into the tunnels.

Nearly back at the dorm, he encountered the Ift Shop again. This time he decided to go in and have a look around at the various salvaged treasures that people had recycled. He gravitated back to the window display in the end and picked up the keychain that featured the Puerto Paz compass symbol on it. He got his own keychain out of his pocket and looked at the Ohio State Football medallion. He laughed. The first line of text had originally read "Ohio State" and the second line had read "Football," but he had nervously rubbed the medallion so many times that he had worn off the text down the center of the logo, and it now read "Ohio ate Foo ll." *I wasted so much emotional energy the last couple of years worrying about getting to Ohio State.... Ohio ate fool indeed*, he thought. He purchased the new medallion and attached it to his old keychain next to the Ohio ate Fooll medallion and headed back to the dorm.

He peeked in the lounge. "Hey, Nikola! How's it going? Is that a rerun of the Pippa Awards you are watching?"

Chapter 11: Pre-Immigration Testing

Friday morning arrived, and after breakfast and a shower, Marcus had plenty of time to get to the Department of Immigration for the testing, so he decided to try something new. He used the Puerto Paz app to reserve a city bike from the rack outside the dorm, and he rode the bike up the protected bike lane of South Avenue into Central Park, then rode around Central Park a bit before heading out West Avenue to Nigel's office. He marveled at how liberating it felt to be able to ride a bike without fear of being hit by a car. Perhaps a bit too liberating, as he lost track of time touring Central Park and ended up a few minutes late for his appointment.

He arrived at the building, parked his bike, and was ushered into Nigel's office where he was relieved to find that Dylan and Kelsey had both already arrived. Nigel walked into the room and did his usual smile and handshake with each of them, but then quickly went into business mode. No stories from his past or idle chitchat today. He explained to them the purpose of the pre-immigration testing, how long it usually took, what the different parts of the exam were and how they worked, and what they could use the exam results for later.

After asking the three teens whether they had any questions and then confiscating their phones, he led them to the top floor of the building to the testing room and assigned them each a small, noise-proofed room in which to take the exam.

The exam began with the multiple-choice portion. There were a lot of questions about personal preferences, opinions, beliefs, and situational what-would-you-do-if type questions. There were often questions where multiple answers could be selected, and almost every set of multiple-choice answers for yes-or-no questions included options for "I don't know" or "I'm not sure" or "Not enough information to determine an answer" or "Both yes and no to some degree."

One question that stuck out in his mind because it made him think about both Havana and Lily from the Wyoming tribe was about the medical field.

> *How do you view the current state of the medical field?*
> > *A) It has come a long way and is now highly advanced.*
> > *B) It has a long way to go and is still primitive.*
> > *C) Both A and B simultaneously to some degree.*
> > *D) I'm not sure/I don't know.*

Another question asked:

> *A government employee discovers evidence that the government is doing something illegal and immoral. The employee does something illegal to disclose that evidence and expose the wrongdoing. The government finds the employee guilty of treason. Was what the employee did:*
> > *A) Wrong.*
> > *B) Not wrong.*
> > *C) Both wrong and not wrong simultaneously.*
> > *D) I'm not sure/I don't know.*

The next portion of the test required short essay answers to philosophical questions, including one that asked for a description of the difference between a stranger committing murder versus a family member committing murder. The third part of the test asked numerous questions about his own personality, as well as Dylan and Kelsey's personalities, and had responses that required him to rate things on a scale of one to ten, along with an "I don't know" option, to indicate how much that description applied to the given person.

The final portion of the test was a video-recorded personal interview. Marcus's interview was administered by Priya, and it was relatively casual. They mostly talked about his experiences, likes, and dislikes as he traveled through EUS, WUS, and Puerto Paz.

Overall the testing took under an hour, and at the end they were given a free lunch in the building's small cafeteria, where their phones were returned to them.

While eating lunch with Dylan and Kelsey, Marcus turned his phone back on and saw that he had a recent text from Havana asking whether he was still at Immigration. He texted back confirmation that he was eating lunch in their cafeteria. A few minutes later, he picked up his phone to see whether he had missed a response from her, when suddenly she sat down next to him.

"Oh my god!" he exclaimed. "You are here!" He leaned over and kissed her on the lips before she exchanged hellos with Dylan and Kelsey.

"Well, you certainly seem to be in a better mood than a couple of days ago," Havana said. "Yeah, they let us out early to get a jump on the weekend. I wanted to surprise you. I have another surprise for you too. I got us theater tickets for tonight. You seemed so glum a couple of nights ago that I figured I'd get some tickets to cheer you up."

"Awesome! Is it in your favorite theater? What show?" Marcus asked.

"The tickets are for *Fiddler on the Roof.* It isn't in the big Debroux Theater, which is the most beautiful theater in town, but it is one of my favorites."

"So, you just got tickets for you and Marcus?" Dylan asked. "Didn't bring enough for the rest of the class?"

Havana turned to Dylan and Kelsey. "Sorry, guys. Kelsey and I just went to the theater a couple of nights ago, and Dylan, I assumed you would think theater was too gay and wouldn't be interested. I'm sure there are still tickets available if you want to go, though."

"Nah, theater *is* gay. Plus, me and Kelsey are going to check out a couple more bars on the other end of the beach tonight. You guys are welcome to join us for drinks after your little show, though." Dylan held his left wrist limply in the air as he said "show."

"More drinking? Can't say I'm in the mood for that," Marcus said.

"How about we all get together this weekend. Maybe volleyball on the beach tomorrow afternoon and a few drinks after?" Havana suggested.

Dylan held up his right hand, his cast now covered in a light-gray layer of dust and dirt. "Yeah, thanks. Great."

"It doesn't have to be volleyball," Havana said. "We could modify it and either play hands-free football-volleyball, or play volleyball with a beach ball. Or go snorkeling or something."

"I can't get my cast wet, so water sports exclude me too," Dylan said.

"We could stop at the hospital and get one of the doctors I'm working with to cut that one off and put a waterproof one on if you want. Whatever. The point would be the four of us all together, doing something we all find enjoyable."

"Sounds nice," Kelsey said.

Dylan shrugged. "Sure."

That evening, Marcus and Havana headed to the theater district, and after a glass of wine and some appetizers at a Spanish tapas bar, strolled to their theater to see *Fiddler on the Roof*. After they took their seats in the theater, Marcus had a few moments before the lights dimmed to marvel at the ornate proscenium arch and theater ceiling. He could see why Havana chose this venue.

There was electricity in the crowd as the lights dimmed and the musical began. Seeing the actors in front of him, exposing their souls and risking mistakes during a live show, amplified that electricity far beyond any TV show or bootleg movie.

As the show progressed, he began to suss out the themes and plot, and he began to doubt his previous convictions about Havana having chosen this particular musical based on the aesthetics of the theater it was in. The musical had themes of tradition versus modernization, of daughters forging their own paths contrary to their father's desires for them, with one of them even leaving her home town and traveling far away to be with her love. During the song "Far from the Home I Love," he looked over at Havana, checking to see whether he could see any sign of self-satisfaction in having chosen a musical with themes mirroring Marcus's own life. She seemed fully engrossed in what was transpiring on stage. *You know, I don't think I really care whether Havana chose this musical based the applicability of its themes to my life*, he thought. *It is a spectacular show, in a beautiful theater, and she is an amazing young woman choosing to sit next to me.* He slipped his hand over the armrest and clasped her hand. She looked over briefly and smiled as she clasped his hand in return.

After the theater, they headed down the street to an Asian-inspired restaurant for a proper dinner, chatting about what they loved and disliked about the show. As they sat reviewing the menu, Havana lowered hers, tilted her head, and asked, "Competitive food ordering?"

Marcus laughed. "We could, but I think I'd have to declare you the winner no matter what, given that you inspired what I'm about to order, and I would owe you at least half of my points even if my dish won. Maybe tonight instead we do collaborative food ordering?"

"What are you ordering?" Havana asked.

"Same thing you ordered at Alta. Vegetable pad Thai. I've been craving a full dish of it ever since!"

"Oooh, yummy! So we'll go halvsies and split our orders? Are you okay with me ordering something I've never had before? It might be a bit exotic to our taste buds."

"So long as it doesn't have insects in it, sure. I'll give it a shot if you agree that if I hate it, but you love it, then I'll eat more of the pad Thai."

"Deal!"

As they waited for their meals to be cooked and delivered, Marcus cleared his throat and asked, "Havana?"

She looked at him. "Yeah?"

"I have a confession to make. The reason you sensed something was off with me the last few days is that I was trying to work through an issue I was having. I feel like I've successfully worked through it, but that I owe you an explanation."

Havana nodded.

"My whole life I've been a Christian, and I've been surrounded by nothing but Christians. I've been told that my religion is the one true religion, and that everyone else is wrong and a sinner. I haven't always enjoyed having Christianity forced on me against my will. In fact, the more distance I get from that life, the more I feel a weight is being lifted, but it has always been a part of my identity, for better or for worse. I was struggling for a while there with the idea of having a romantic partner who..."

"Who wasn't part of your tribe?" Havana asked.

"I was going to say, 'Who didn't share that identity with me,' but you might be right. Nigel described tribalism as rabid Yankees fans versus rabid Red Sox fans. I think I was raised to believe that anyone who wasn't a Yankees fan isn't a good person, but I'm starting to see that Red Sox fans can be good people, and Yankees fans can be bad people, and which team they support doesn't really matter."

"After our walk in the park, I was a bit worried that your Christianity might be more extremist than our relationship could handle," Havana admitted.

"From your perspective, is it like dating a creepy cult member or something?"

"I wasn't quite sure what to think of it. It was the first time we had ever really discussed religion, and obviously it didn't go very well. I know that you are a smart, sensitive, good guy with a good sense of humor, though, and that's what matters to me. The last few days, I have been hoping for the best but kind of preparing for the worst."

"Well, I still find it a bit weird that you don't have the same faith as me, but you are a wonderful, amazing, beautiful woman, and over the last few days I've come to realize that's what matters to me. You walk the walk of a good Christian even if you don't talk the talk."

Havana reached over the table to hold hands with Marcus. "Thank you. Thank you for gently confronting me, and for sharing your thoughts and feelings. This is such a relief. I had some doubt about you too...about your ability to confront your closest friends about things that are bothering you, about whether your NEUS upbringing had repressed your ability to get in touch with your feelings. You confronting me about this religion issue that was troubling you means a lot to me."

"I feel safer telling you these sorts of things than I have with anyone else in my life. Being with you challenges me...my weaknesses get exposed, but I feel like you are there to help me with those weaknesses, not to exploit them or ridicule me for them. You are the perfect teammate."

Havana leaned over the table, and Marcus met her halfway. They kissed and held hands until their waitress broke up their public display of affection to set their dinners on the table.

Chapter 12: Regresa a la Playa

On Saturday afternoon, after a rather steamy night and extended morning in Marcus's dorm room, Marcus and Havana kept their promise and headed out to Playa Nueva to hang out with Dylan and Kelsey. After greetings in the shade under the canopy of an open-air picnic structure, Kelsey became unusually chatty, asking Havana what musical she saw with Marcus the previous night. She turned to Marcus. "So, did you like it?"

"I loved it," he said. "It was as if it were made just for me. And the theater was beautiful too. How was the one you saw on ladies' night?"

Kelsey's forehead and eyebrows scrunched into a look of pain or worry, but her voice sounded happy and excited. It reminded Marcus of her behavior in New Miami when talking about the big frat party. "Oh my god. Like, oh my god. It was so awesome!" She made a smile that looked forced, but Marcus was certain she was actually happy. "It was called *Take Us to Your Leader*. It was so awesome! It was, like, totally done in a cheesy 1950s sci-fi movie style, where like, the entire set, the costumes, and the makeup were done to make it look like a black-and-white TV show, but it was, like, a totally modern production, and um, like, it was about a small group of aliens who, like, made a wrong turn on their way to a different planet, and um, they landed here on Earth by mistake and..." Kelsey took a deep inhalation that had Marcus mildly worried that she was going to start hyperventilating until she continued. "And, like, they didn't realize they were on Earth instead of the other planet, and, like, they started trying to negotiate the peace talks that they had intended to have on the other planet, and like, I don't know."

"And hilarity ensued," Havana said.

Kelsey giggled. "Yeah, and hilarity ensued! It was awesome."

Marcus turned to Havana to make a comment about having sucked it up to go to a modern production, but he heard Dylan's sarcastic voice before he could say anything.

"I think I'm experiencing a 'gaylien' invasion right now with the three of you all yapping about musicals."

"Huh, another 'gay' comment," Kelsey said to Dylan, her tone changing from happiness to match his sarcasm. "You make a lot of those comments. Maybe *you're* gay?"

"Says the chick I've been banging for the last few weeks," Dylan snapped.

"Maybe you're closeted. Or bi. Who knows. It's just, like, you won't stop talking about how everything is gay."

Havana interrupted. "Okay, Dylan didn't get to experience the theater the way the three of us did, so why don't we drop the theater talk for now and do something that all four of us can enjoy. Shall we head to the storage shed to see what's available?"

Havana led them to the shed at the back of the bathhouse and lifeguard station. There they found a vast array of beach toys for adults and children. Beach balls, volleyballs, footballs, and soccer balls, snorkeling equipment, flotation rafts and toys, kayaks, and even shovels and pails. Havana pulled out a beach ball and topped it off with a little more air. "Beach ball volleyball?" she asked.

Marcus and Kelsey nodded. They headed over to the sand courts and began playing two on two.

After a few rounds of volleys, Dylan point off to a group of people approaching in the distance and shouted, "Liam! You wanker!"

The group got closer and finally reached the courts. After a bald-headed man began speaking, Marcus finally recognized him as one of the Australians who had joined Dylan in the bar the other day.

"Dylan! Finally got your alcoholic bum off the barstool, eh?" Liam said.

"Yeah. Ladies talked me into playing some volleyball," Dylan said.

"That's not a volleyball. This is a volleyball." Liam thrust forward a regulation volleyball.

Dylan held up his right hand and pointed at the cast.

"Aww, excuses, excuses," Liam said.

The Aussies headed to a nearby court to start their game. Dylan looked dejected and began moping. "I don't want to play pussy volleyball anymore," he said.

"Oh, come on, D!" Marcus said. "It's just a game. All games have arbitrary rules. Playing volleyball with a beach ball makes just as much sense as playing it with a regular volleyball. Who cares what anyone else thinks?"

Dylan continued to refuse to play with the beach ball, though, so Havana proposed they play left-handed volleyball, where everyone was required to play with their left hand, only using a regulation volleyball. Dylan agreed to that, but the game devolved into an unfulfilling series of hits out of bounds and occasional aces.

Dylan finally just said, "Go ahead and use both hands. I'll stay next to the net and try to block and spike one-handed."

The game continued, Marcus and Havana against Dylan and Kelsey, but with Havana's skills, Dylan's handicap, and Kelsey's lack of skill, it got lopsided quickly. Marcus had to stifle giggles as he watched Kelsey try to bump the ball. She would stand three feet away from where the ball was going to land, and with a terrified expression on her face, stick her arms out like she was holding a dirty diaper as far from her nose as possible and turn her head away as the ball got closer, usually completely missing the ball entirely. Havana finally proposed girls against boys and interrupted the game to give Kelsey some help.

"Kelsey, you are acting like the ball is going to hurt you. Here. I'm going to hold the ball out steady, and I want you to put your hands together like you are going to bump, and then just swing up at the ball, knocking it out of my hands."

Kelsey tried it and succeeded in hitting the ball a few feet in the air. They repeated that drill a few times before Havana said, "You see how harmless the ball is? Now I'm going to stand back a few feet and gently lob the ball right in front of you, and I want you to do exactly the same thing you were just doing."

Kelsey whiffed on the first one.

"Keep looking at the ball," said Havana. "See it into your hands. If you keep your eyes on it, then you can control what part of your body strikes it, rather than letting it randomly strike you."

Kelsey tried again and connected with the ball, sending it mostly sideways. A few more tries, and suddenly she was bumping considerably better than before, albeit inconsistently.

"I'm getting it!" Kelsey exclaimed.

"I knew you could do it," Havana said.

The game resumed, but it didn't last long, as Dylan was losing interest. As they wound down, Marcus overheard Kelsey say to Havana, "You know, I think I might take your advice and look for a psychologist when I get back to New Miami. I'd really like to work on my fear of heights and anxiety in general."

Marcus felt the briefest sense of amazement before Dylan laughed. "A shrink! You're going to see a shrink? I thought you were a psycho, and this cinches it."

Marcus saw Kelsey's face turn red with anger before she erupted with a shout. "Shut up, you tool! You need a shrink more than I do." She stormed off toward the water's edge.

Dylan shrugged and headed toward the topless sunbathing area that was beginning to fill in with people.

Havana and Marcus looked at each other. "Why don't you go ask Kelsey if she wants to go snorkeling with you?" Havana asked. "She mentioned interest in that on ladies' night, and I know you love swimming in the ocean."

"She's actually willing to get her hair wet?" Marcus mumbled to himself.

"I'll go hang with Dylan for a bit. I think he needs a timeout," Havana said, looking in his direction with a concerned look.

Marcus caught up with Kelsey and invited her to go snorkeling with him, noting the blue-striped fish he had seen during his swim earlier in the week. She agreed to it, and they hunted in the storage shed for gear before heading out into the ocean. He took a peek back at the beach while standing in shallow water to see how Havana and Dylan were doing. He could see Havana rubbing sunblock on her body.

"Is she topless?" Marcus asked.

Kelsey turned to look. "I think so. Most of the ladies here are. I've been seeing boobies all week. I'm starting to get used to it. We have some nude beaches back in New Miami too, but I'd never been to one before, so it was kind of a surprise for me too."

"Yikes. Not sure how I feel about my girlfriend's exposed boobs that close to Dylan."

"Do you distrust her?" Kelsey asked.

"Her? No. Him? Maybe."

"Don't worry. Dylan is mostly hot air and bluster. Besides, I think Havana could take him in a fight."

Marcus laughed. They put on their masks and snorkels and plunged underwater, quickly finding and following a school of small fish out to an underwater man-made playground. They came up for air.

"Did you see it?" Marcus cried. "The blue-striped fish? It's just like the one I saw the other day!"

"It's beautiful!" Kelsey yelled back.

Marcus swam closer to her. "God, I could do this all day! Now I'm starting to wonder about getting scuba lessons so that I can explore without having to come up for air."

"I know! It's so peaceful and relaxing," Kelsey said.

"This whole city is pretty amazing."

"Yeah, I could, like, totally see moving here after college or something. Everyone is so nice," Kelsey said.

"I could see moving here too," Marcus said.

They swam with the fish for a good half hour before returning to shore. Marcus looked toward where Dylan and Havana had been and only spotted Dylan alone. A waving arm from the covered picnic area led his attention to Havana. Marcus and Kelsey returned their gear and rejoined her.

"Did he behave himself?" Marcus asked.

"Yeah. I caught him ogling my breasts a little, but he wasn't feeling chatty. After fifteen minutes, I wanted to get out of the sun, so I came over here. He's insane sitting in the sun like that. He refused my offer of sunblock."

"I'm going to go over and chat with him," Marcus said. He walked out into the hot sun and planted himself on the beach next to Dylan. "So, what'd you think of Havana's tits?"

"A bit small for my taste, but all tits are good tits. What was it you said in Wyoming about Lily? I feel like now I've seen as much of her as you have and now she's my girlfriend too?"

"Yeah, the difference being that you kept insisting that Lily wasn't your girlfriend. I definitely call Havana my girlfriend."

"Don't worry, dude. I have no desire to be henpecked the way you do."

Marcus shook his head and looked around for inspiration for a new topic of conversation. "You know, I finally rode in one of those autonomous vehicles the other day. A van. Out in the country, it got up to probably a hundred miles per hour. It was pretty impressive."

"Their cars aren't much sexier than WUS's."

"I think they look way better," Marcus said.

"But they don't have any muscle. They aren't masculine," Dylan complained.

"Maybe you could be the guy who brings masculine sexy back to the electric car industry. I was in one of their garages the other day and saw how the bodies are all removable from the chassis. You could design sexier bodies for them. I met a mechanic down there too. He seemed like a nice guy. I could introduce you to him."

"I don't want to talk shop while on vacation."

"Man, you don't seem to be interested in doing or talking about anything." He cringed, uncertain whether he should have said that, and he looked over at Dylan to see if any damage had been done. "Is there anything you *do* want to do here besides drinking?"

Dylan shrugged. "I dunno." He thought for a minute. "There was a football in the shed. We could practice the trick play."

"With a broken hand?"

"I'll catch it one-handed. It'll be good practice. In a game situation, I might need to catch it one-handed anyway because you'll probably be so amped up that you'll overthrow the ball."

They got up, sauntered over to the shed, and got the football out. They lined up at an imaginary line of scrimmage. Dylan played center and hiked the ball. Marcus set the ball down in the sand like he was readying it for a field goal kick. Dylan circled around to play kicker, ran at the ball, and intentionally whiffed the kick before running around an imaginary lineman and down the beach. Marcus picked up the ball and curled around toward the opposite side of the imaginary linemen. He untucked the ball and launched it toward Dylan. Dylan reached out for it with one hand and lost his balance. He went crashing to the beach, attempting to brace his fall with his hands. The ball sailed past him.

"Fuck!"

"You okay?" Marcus shouted as he began running toward Dylan. Dylan had rolled over on his back and was clutching his cast. "You okay?" Marcus repeated.

"Yeah. I think so. It just hurts like a mother."

"You want me to get Havana to look at it? Should we go to the hospital?"

"No. I'm fine. I don't think I rebroke it or anything. I just tweaked it. The cast mostly protected it. The pain is nothing a beer can't numb. Let's go get a drink."

"You know your hand would heal faster if you didn't binge drink all the time. It slows healing."

"I'm not going to let my hand ruin my vacation," Dylan said as he stormed ahead toward the bar.

Marcus passed Havana and Kelsey at the picnic area. "I guess we're getting a drink," he said to Havana, rolling his eyes. "Come with?"

"Be there in a minute," Havana replied.

Marcus followed Dylan into the bar and ordered three more beers to go with the one Dylan had just ordered. "There are a lot of fun things to do in the city that won't affect your hand. Don't you get bored out here just drinking all day? You've never struck me as the kind of person who would just repeat the same thing day in and day out, never trying anything new."

Dylan looked over at Marcus with a scowl. "Hey, MC, remember how I broke this hand? How I stepped in and knocked Apollo out and saved your ass?"

"What's that got to do with anything?"

"I don't know. Maybe you could lay off me with the nagging about seeing the city, given that I saved you a trip to the hospital?"

Marcus scowled back at Dylan. "Hey, Dylan, remember how Apollo's crew started cheering instead of ganging up and attacking us? Remember how shocking that was? I wonder if, given my military self-defense training, I could have taken him without—"

Marcus was startled by an arm slipping around his waist. "Sorry to interrupt," Havana said. "Could you grab our beers and come out to the patio with me? Please? Now?"

Marcus shook his head then grabbed the freshly delivered beers and followed Havana out. "What's up?" he asked as he ducked under an umbrella and sat down at a table with Havana.

"It seemed like it was your turn for a timeout," Havana said. "Have a beer with me, enjoy the scenery, and chillax." She leaned into his shoulder and put her arm around him.

"I'm trying to reach out to him, but he's being impossible," Marcus said.

"Getting angry and arguing isn't going to help with that," Havana replied.

Marcus sighed and reciprocated the cuddle.

Chapter 13: Test Results

Monday afternoon, Marcus rejoined Dylan and Kelsey at the Department of Immigration to discuss test results with Nigel. The three of them waited in Nigel's office as usual, but instead of Nigel joining them, they were called one by one to another room. First Dylan, then Kelsey, but Dylan didn't return when Kelsey was called. Finally, Marcus was called. Priya escorted him down a corridor to a small meeting room, where Nigel was sitting alone. Priya gestured for Marcus to take a seat. Nigel skipped the usual smile and handshake and got right to business.

"Marcus, good afternoon. Given that the three of you are traveling in a group, and testing as a group, we are asking each of you individually whether we have your permission to discuss your results with the others. Doing so could potentially bring up sensitive personal information, and we wanted to know if that is acceptable to you, or if there is anything you want to remain confidential. Is discussing these things with the others acceptable to you?"

"Sure," Marcus said. "I have nothing to hide."

"Have you discussed with them that you are considering moving here, either for college or permanently?"

"No. I haven't gotten to that yet. I was going to wait until after we got the testing results. I guess I would appreciate that not being brought up with them."

Nigel looked down and jotted some notes on the sheet of paper in front of him. "Okay. Follow me, please." Nigel stood up and opened a door into the adjoining room, a larger conference room, where Dylan, Kelsey, Priya, and a couple of other members of the department were waiting at the table. Marcus took a seat next to Dylan.

Nigel began the conversation. "So, you have all taken the pre-immigration testing, and we are here to discuss your results and what those results mean for your future opportunities to visit Puerto Paz. As I suspect you already know, visitors are welcome here for short-duration vacations or business trips, but if you want to visit frequently within a relatively short window of time, or if you want to stay longer than the typical two-month limit, then you need a visa.

"Pre-immigration testing is a step towards that visa. It can also be used as a step towards citizenship, if that were something you were interested in pursuing. The majority of our applicants for visas are individuals traveling alone. When it comes to groups of friends or family, though, we tend to treat the application a little differently, as we do not like to split up groups. Sometimes if there are people in the group found strongly incompatible with our culture, we will allow them in with the rest of the group anyway, with conditions, and other times it tips the balance in the opposite direction, and we end up rejecting the group as a whole."

Marcus felt a lump in his throat. He wondered how seriously Dylan had taken the testing and whether he had jeopardized his own chances at a visa or more. He peeked over at Dylan, hoping for a clue, but couldn't get a read on his body language.

Nigel continued. "You have all indicated that you are considering visas for more frequent visits to Puerto Paz. The criteria for getting visitor visas is considerably less stringent than for longer-term visas or for citizenship. We have decided that for a one-year frequent-visitor visa, we will qualify all three of you."

Marcus breathed a little easier. "For Dylan and Kelsey, however, the visas are flagged as conditional because of your history of public drunkenness complaints and other alcohol and behavior concerns. If you continue to gather complaints like those, then your visas would be rescinded. A big part of why your application for a frequent-visitor visa would be accepted is because you are applying in a group with Marcus. Marcus had a very high degree of compatibility with our culture, Kelsey a medium level of compatibility, and Dylan a low level of compatibility."

Nigel looked down at a sheet of paper before continuing. "Another item in the plus column for both Dylan and Marcus is that you have traveled through multiple types of societies and experienced different cultures, which is experience that Puerto Paz values highly. Nothing is more detrimental to the world than when pockets of isolation develop and people don't mix. Xenophobic nationalism will destroy the world."

Nigel closed his eyes momentarily. "But, as usual, I digress. Getting back to the matter at hand, in terms of longer-duration stays or citizenship, there is still a path available for everyone, but it would require some serious effort on your part. Quite honestly, if Marcus were applying alone for a longer-term visa or citizenship, his application would be accepted. Kelsey alone would be borderline but likely accepted. Dylan alone would be rejected. Dylan tests high in rebelliousness and low in intellectual curiosity, compassion, and fairness, and we've seen no evidence of a willingness for introspection or a desire to improve himself. We do recognize that a lot of Dylan's issues are a direct result of parental abuse and neglect, so we are willing to make a compromise in order for all three of you to obtain longer-term visas or citizenship. The compromise would involve each of you going through mandatory psychological therapy."

Marcus spoke up, covering up an exasperated huff from Dylan, and like a courtroom objection by a lawyer, said, "I would have to go through therapy? Even though I tested highly compatible?"

"Yes," Nigel replied. "If you were applying alone, it would be borderline whether we asked you to go through therapy, but as a group wanting to move here together, we would want all three of you to go through the therapy experience together. There are good reasons for you to go through it too, regardless of whether the other two applied with you. You would be emancipating from your parents, which can be traumatic. You ran away from home, which can be distressing. Whatever tribulations you experienced that caused you to want to run away has undoubtedly left you with some psychological issues to work through. You have a father who you feel treats you more like his cadet than his son, which is not healthy parenting. There is also the issue of avoidance of difficult conversations and deception or a lack of openness and honesty that we would want to explore with you, since we value openness and honesty so highly. Additionally, we detected in your personality testing a potential bias against rural folks that we would want to work with you on, even though our rural population is very small."

"What difference does it make?" Dylan asked. "We're not moving here. We'd just be vacationing here once in a while so that the two of them can hang with Havana while I chill on the beach. We're not interested in anything more than the frequent-visitor visas."

Nigel looked at Marcus briefly before looking at Dylan. "We just want to be sure we have all bases covered. Pre-immigration testing can be used for many purposes, and we wanted you to be aware of what the test results can and cannot do for you."

"Well, I'm not going to sit here and listen to you criticize us for no good reason. I've told you before we're not looking for long-term visas or citizenship. You said we qualify for the short-term visa, so why do you feel the need to keep talking and insulting us? You know what? I'm outta here. I'm sick of this shit." Dylan got up and walked out the door, leaving Marcus flabbergasted.

Kelsey sat there looking confused and uncertain whether to follow the majority still sitting there or to get up and follow her kind-of-sort-of boyfriend out the door.

Finally, Marcus turned to Nigel. "I think I should go after him and talk to him one-on-one."

Nigel nodded, and Marcus got up to chase after Dylan. He speed-walked to the front door but couldn't see any sign of Dylan. He got out his phone and texted him as he walked toward the nearby subway station. "Where are you?" A couple of minutes later he got a reply saying Dylan was walking to Central Station to try to cool his head before taking the train back to Playa Nueva. "Wait up," Marcus texted back. Marcus started half trotting, half speed-walking toward Central Park, trying to catch up with Dylan before he got on a train.

Dylan texted back. "Standing at the edge of Central Park. I just want to go get hammered. Beers at the beach?"

A couple of minutes later, Marcus was at the edge of Central Park, looking around for Dylan. He spotted him under a tree and walked over to him.

"Dude, why'd you walk out like that? It was kind of rude," he asked Dylan as he approached.

"Nigel is an asshole. You heard him. He just kept hurling insult after insult at me. I wasn't going to sit there and take it from that fucker."

"He had some critical comments about me too, and you didn't see me getting bent out of shape about it, did you? He's not an asshole. He's a good guy, and what he was saying probably had a lot of truth to it. We *have* been through a lot of trauma in our lives. Running away from home was stressful. Maybe it would be best if I went through therapy. Maybe it would be best for you too."

"You're taking his side on this? What the fuck?"

"I'm not taking any side. I'm just saying the guy is wise, and he makes some valid points. You don't have to get all defensive about it. He wants to help us."

"What is he, your gay lover or something? Are these commies brainwashing you? You've been spending more time with him than you have been with me. You're supposed to be my best friend, man. You gotta have my back when someone starts insulting me like that. I had your back at the Alpha Sigs party. Don't give me this bullshit about maybe we should all hold hands and go through therapy together."

"If going through some harmless therapy gets me what I want, then I'll go through the therapy. It's not that big of a deal."

"What do you want, anyway? I thought therapy was only needed if you wanted more than just the frequent-visitor visa."

Marcus felt the same sensation now that he felt at the supper table with his dad the night he ran away from home. That welling up of pent-up emotion about to explode. The feeling that he was going to lose the control that he so highly valued. "I think I want to live here," he blurted out.

"What the fuck?" Dylan cried. "In Commie Central? Are you fucking kidding me? We're *not* moving here. Our lives are in New Miami, man. We're on the Miami football team. We got into college early there. We get to party our brains out without some fucking commie minders keeping track of complaints against us for public drunkenness. What the fuck more could you want?"

"How about a culture that doesn't make me want to vomit? A society where people give a shit about the people around them, even complete strangers. A place where I can fucking swim in the ocean because they don't dump all their toxic waste into it. A place where I don't *need* you to punch anyone for me because the guys aren't a bunch of macho, roid-raging assholes."

"You're nuts! New Miami is fucking awesome! We're going to be kings there! I'm already a god at Alpha Sigs. We can drink whenever we want there too, and the parties are way better. You can't get that here. You can't get real football, either. Football here is ridiculous. It's pussyball. You can't give up on your dream of football, for Christ's sake! Football is your life!"

Spit was flying from Dylan's mouth as he talked. His voice was getting louder and louder with each sentence.

"Dylan, I hate New Miami. It's the worst place we've been. I hate it more than New Rochelle. I'm willing to give up EUS football for this. I'll find other things to do. Track and field, their version of football, open-water swimming, whatever."

"Well, what about Wyoming. You liked the tribe, didn't you? We could go there."

"They were nice people, but they were fucking nuts, and I want to become an engineer. No way am I going to live like that. D, man, everywhere we've been, I've hated it. Everywhere we've been, I've felt like a fish out of water. I hated home. I would be miserable in Wyoming with no future in engineering, wiping my ass with leaves and watching friends die of preventable diseases while my life spins around in the same hamster wheel of rituals every day. I would be miserable in San Fran with their ridiculous, overprotective rules. I'd be most miserable in New Miami, though. The people there are horrible. This place makes me happy. Havana makes me happy."

"Havana. Fucking Havana. It's always Havana with you. You've only been dating her for less than two months. You're going to choose her, a chick you've been boning for a couple of months, over me, your best friend for the last decade? That's insane, you fucking disloyal asshole! She's fucking brainwashing you, dude."

"Don't try to pin this on Havana or Nigel. They are the only reasons I made any effort to spend time with you while we were here. You were being such a dick that I didn't want to be around you, but they kept encouraging me to reach out to you."

Dylan had seemed to calm down for a second after his Havana tirade, but he suddenly stood tall and leaned back, and his eyes got wide. "How long have you known you wanted to live here?" he asked. "Was your answer at the Port Camille kiosk even a mistake?"

"It has been a possibility for a few weeks, but coming here for vacation was a sort of trial run to see if I liked it here enough to want to live here. I've only realized in the last couple of days that it's what I want for certain, and it's not just for Havana. I would want to live here even if Havana and I broke up. You've always believed the EUS propaganda that this place is some awful communist wasteland. You are so damned stubborn that I didn't think I could say anything to you without getting this kind of reaction, and I was hoping that if you just saw the place with your own eyes, you would see how incredible it is."

"Traitor!" Dylan shouted as he lunged at Marcus, attempting to throw a wild right hook, cast and all. Marcus's quick reflexes allowed him to jump out of the way. He leapt forward at Dylan, tackling him to the ground and pinning him down on his back.

"I don't want to fight you, Dylan," he said calmly. "And I don't have to choose her over you. You could live here too. You choosing New Miami over me and Puerto Paz would be just as disloyal as me choosing Havana and Puerto Paz over New Miami."

"Fuck you, you fucking pussy!" Dylan screamed. He tried to spit at Marcus, seeming to forget about gravity, and the spit landing on his own shoulder.

"I'll let you up, but you gotta calm down and talk with me without throwing punches. Can we do that?"

Dylan squirmed a bit but relented. Marcus let him up.

"I can't live in a place where they don't even let you drive your own fucking car," Dylan said. "And speaking of cars, if you stay here, you'll be broke. Ever think of that? The money we have is all from the sale of my car. You want to stay here, you get none of it."

"I don't care. I'll figure something out. They don't let people starve to death here."

"I should have known better than to become friends with a fucking disloyal nigger. You're a fucking piece of shit. After everything we've been through together, you're just going to ditch me for some commie vagina? Traitor! I should have sold you instead of the Dean!"

Marcus had been trying to maintain his cool and take the high road, but Dylan calling him a nigger and making a slave reference was the last straw. "Maybe our friendship was just a friendship of convenience," he said in his cold-blooded mercenary style, as Dylan had put it earlier in their journey. "We have nothing in common except football. Maybe I should have known better than to befriend someone who was such damaged goods and so fucked up in the head. Someday you're going to have to grow the fuck up and make adult decisions."

Marcus saw Dylan clench his left fist, and he took a small step back. A couple of police officers on bicycles skidded to a stop next to them, laid their bikes down, and told Marcus and Dylan to step away from one another. The female officer asked them what was going on.

"Nothing," Dylan said. "Just the end of a decade-long friendship. It's over now though."

The male officer escorted Dylan away while asking him some questions, and the female officer walked Marcus in the opposite direction. Marcus explained to her what had happened. She checked his ID and jotted down some notes before telling him he could go, but to go in the opposite direction of Dylan and that there would be a follow-up call the next day from a counselor.

Marcus dusted the grass and dirt off of his knees and headed back to the Department of Immigration. The meeting had adjourned, and Kelsey was gone. Priya led Marcus to Nigel's office where he filled Nigel in on what had transpired. Nigel uncharacteristically didn't have much to say. He mostly just nodded and sighed before scheduling an appointment with Marcus to follow up on his desire to apply for a long-term visa and possibly be put on a track to citizenship.

He left the Immigration building and suddenly felt an overwhelming sense of loneliness. Blurry eyed from fighting back tears he was barely able to read the words on his phone as he texted Havana, "I need you. Please meet me at my dorm room. Things exploded with Dylan."

Havana responded nearly immediately that she had just finished at the doctor's office and she'd be there as soon as she could.

Back at his room he reunited with Havana and they cuddled in bed, with Marcus occasionally burying his head into her torso while silently crying. He tried to flex every muscle in his upper body to prevent his intermittent gasps for air from shaking the bed.

"It is okay, Marcus," Havana said gently. "You are safe with me.

It is okay to let it out. You don't need to hide from me."

Marcus's body trembled. "He called me the N-word and said he should have sold me instead of the car," he blurted out before bursting into uncontrollable sobs.

Havana pulled him tighter. The tears poured out of him. Several minutes passed before he could even speak again.

"I should have known. I should have known since at least back at the gas station near Denver. He called that guy a Spic. I should have known it would come to this." He yanked on the sleeve of his T-shirt and dried his cheeks off with it. "Sorry about your shirt."

"No problem. It is just saltwater. Not much different than getting a little ocean water on it."

Marcus grabbed a tissue and blew his nose. "Back in Denver he said he wasn't racist. He said he only said racist things to piss people off. But saying that shit to me? How could he? How dare he? How could he say that to his best friend?"

"That's exactly why he did it to you. He wanted to hurt you."

"Well he succeeded," Marcus shrieked as he burst into tears again. He felt his soul split open and more than a decade's worth of repressed emotions were now spilling out.

"Give it some time," Havana said, pulling him close again.

After a few more minutes, Marcus began to settle down. Havana still wrapped around him, he closed his eyes, the warmth of her body radiating into his, enveloping him like a blanket, and the steady rhythm of her breath lulling him to sleep.

At 2:45 a.m. a message alert on Havana's e-glasses woke them up. Marcus stirred, then went back to sleep. Another alert woke him up again.

"Don't you have that thing set to be silent during sleeping hours?" he grumbled.

"Yes, but the messages were from a known contact and were set as 'important,' so they overrode it."

"Important? How important?" Marcus asked.

With one arm still wrapped around Marcus, she grabbed her e-glasses off the nightstand, set them on her belly for a moment, and wiped the rheum from her eyes before putting them on to check the message. She sat up suddenly.

"We need to go to the hospital. It was from a nurse I met while shadowing." She handed him her glasses to read the messages and started rousing herself.

The first message said: "Working detention. Tall white kid from EUS named Dylan here under restraint…is he your BF's friend?"

The second message said: "Just found out white blonde girl from EUS named Kelsey here too. Alcohol overdose and broken nose. In bad shape. Think she's the girl you mentioned other day?"

Marcus handed the glasses back to Havana, and she exchanged a few messages with the nurse. "Are they okay?" Marcus asked.

"Don't know for sure. Sounds like Dylan might be physically okay but in trouble with the law. Kelsey sounds like she's in rough shape."

By 3:30 a.m., they were walking in the hospital door. Havana did the talking at the check-in desk to find out where Dylan and Kelsey were and whether they were taking visitors. They agreed they'd split up and meet back at the cafeteria later, and Havana gave Marcus directions to the detention unit at the back of the hospital before heading to the ward Kelsey was in.

Marcus approached the security desk at the detention unit and asked the guard through a glass security window whether he could see his friend Dylan, noting that they were in the same travel party from EUS. The guard checked his ID and directed him to sit in a waiting area while he checked with a superior.

Marcus sat down and waited a few minutes before the guard called his name. He was let into an air-lock corridor, where he walked through body scanner similar to the ones at Port Camille before being let into the detention ward and directed to Dylan's room. He walked in and saw Dylan propped up at a slight incline with his wrists handcuffed to the railings of a gurney. His eyes were closed, and he had an I.V. tube and various monitor wires fastened to his body. The guard told Marcus to wait at the curtain drawn around his area and then announced to Dylan that he had a visitor. Dylan opened his eyes. They were bloodshot.

"Liam?" he asked, looking like he was having difficulty focusing on Marcus.

"It's me, Marcus."

Dylan closed his eyes and turned his head away, smushing the side of his face into the pillow. "Fuck off. I don't want to see you.

Fuck off forever."

"What happened, man?" Marcus asked.

Dylan snapped his head back toward Marcus and screamed, "FUCK. OFF!"

The guard stepped in and insisted that Marcus exit the room. Visiting time was over. He walked away as the heart monitor alarms hooked up to Dylan began to scream with incessant beeping. Marcus crossed paths with a nurse who was headed toward Dylan as he left the room. He sat down in the waiting area again to collect his thoughts.

Not knowing what to do next, he defaulted to going to the cafeteria to wait for Havana. When he got there, he immediately recognized a small group of people huddled around a table sipping coffees as part of the group of Australians Dylan had been hanging out with at the beach. He asked if he could join them, and they pulled up a chair for him and offered to get a cup of coffee for him. He declined the coffee and asked for information instead.

"Liam, right?" Marcus asked a burly, bald white guy. "What happened?"

"Your mate got out of control," Liam said. "He got as drunk as the bartender would let him at one bar, hopped to another bar and did the same, and kept doing that until finally he was too drunk to convince a new bartender to give him a drink. Then he yelled at the last bartender and threatened to punch him, swiped a couple of bottles off the bar and ran out the door. His girl, what's her name?"

"Kelsey," said one of his female companions.

"Yeah, Kelsey," the bald Australian continued. "Kelsey was completely shit-faced. She had her wobbly boots on and stumbled out the door after him. A couple of our ladies here followed her out to try to talk her into staying with us because your mate was starting to get violent, and they found her face down on the sidewalk with blood gushing from her nose. Your mate just left her behind. That fucking derro cunt just abandoned her and left her for dead! We called the ambulance and then came here to check on her. We've been texting with some of our mates who were at another bar who said that your mate was arrested after the police caught him pissing on the side of a building. Your mate is a total wanker!"

"I don't know if he's my mate anymore," Marcus said. "We had a big fight yesterday. So…did Dylan punch Kelsey?"

"Nah, mate, I don't think so. I don't think Kelsey ever caught up to him. I think she just passed out on her face. Still, you can't leave your woman behind like that, especially in the condition she was in. A total fuckknuckle move."

Marcus was about to ask whether they had any news on Kelsey's condition when he spotted Havana walking toward him. "How is she?" he asked.

"She'll live, but she's prepped to get her nose reset and won't be able to talk for a while. She looks awful."

Marcus filled Havana in on what the Aussies had told him. The Aussies stayed a bit longer to be courteous and make small talk with Havana, but acknowledging that Dylan and Kelsey now had familiar people there to watch after them, they excused themselves to go back to their hotel to get some sleep. Marcus and Havana's skipped supper finally caught up to them, so they grabbed a meal and chatted while eating.

"I don't know what to do about Dylan," Marcus confessed. "He's out of control. I think I'm going to have to cut him loose, but part of me would feel guilty."

"Wait until later this morning," Havana proposed. "He still has a lot of alcohol in his system right now. Let him sleep it off and get the benefit of the intravenous, then try again."

"Yeah. I guess. But if he is still hostile, then I think I need to prepare myself for the possibility that our friendship is over. There is only so much I can do. Loyalty has its limits. He has to choose the friendship. I can't force it."

Havana nodded.

After their meal, they went to a waiting lounge with a TV and cuddled on a loveseat, watching TV for several hours until Havana got a message from her nurse friend saying that Kelsey was awake and had her tube out. Havana went to go see her, and Marcus headed back to the detention unit to try one more time with Dylan.

He walked past some exterior windows and felt discombobulated by the sight of daylight. The hospital had transitioned to daytime life, and a fresh shift of doctors and nurses had injected new energy into the air. He went through the security procedure again and was let in to see Dylan. The fire in Dylan's eyes was gone. It was replaced with a look of defeat and exhaustion. He saw Marcus approaching and turned his head away again.

"What the fuck are you doing here?" he asked. "I told you to fuck off. You're dead to me."

Marcus sighed. So it was over. "Listen. If you ever change your mind about this place…if you realize that Puerto Paz is a really great place or if you want to reconnect with me…whatever. If you change your mind, you know how to reach me, and I would welcome you back into my life. I'll miss you. Take care of yourself."

Marcus turned around and walked out the detention unit door, a mix of conflicting emotions swirling in him. Guilty but liberated. Defeated but optimistic. Like he had just experienced both death and birth.

Chapter 14: Port of Peace

Marcus walked down the rock staircase hugging the cliffs along the northern shore and sat at a table at the de Grasse Café, placing a cardboard box on the table. A waiter came out of the cliffside tunnel and took his breakfast order. He sat there savoring the salty air and listening to the murmur of conversations around him over the sound of steady waves crashing below. He looked over to near the yellow bathhouse at the popular cliff-jumping area but was disappointed to see no one there.

His breakfast arrived. He munched his avocado toast and sipped his mimosa and continued to admire the view. After he finished his toast, he took the lid off the box, pulled out a sheet of paper, and set his keychain on it to keep it from blowing away. He pulled out a pen, an envelope, and one of dozens of identical cards, all with a copy of a painting of the very coastline he was sitting at now printed on the cover. He inverted the box lid and set the box into it, then brushed the crumbs off his plate and set it on top of the remainder of the cards to serve as a paperweight.

He looked at the painting on the card, then at the real-life scene splayed out before him, comparing art to reality. This was his favorite place in all of Puerto Paz. Beyond its physical beauty, it had sentimental value. It was here where, nearly five years earlier, he had first swum in the ocean. It was these rocks where, four years earlier, he had leapt off the cliff into the water in what he considered a ceremonial baptism of sorts to celebrate becoming an official citizen of Puerto Paz. As he liked to tell it, it was where he "took the plunge after taking the plunge." It was also here where, just a few months earlier, Havana had said "yes."

He looked at his wedding invite list. He had agreed with Havana that since she had more people to invite than he did, he would write the personal notes on invitations to their mutual friends in addition to his own family and friends. At the top of the list was his parents. He printed "Mr. & Mrs. Abraham Coleman" on the envelope, began writing their address, then stopped, ripped the envelope in two, and stuffed it back in the box. He pulled out a second envelope and addressed it "Mrs. Wynona Coleman," then wrote their address. He opened the card and wrote "Mr. & Mrs. Abraham Coleman" in the blank space for the invitee, then read the preprinted portion.

Havana Lamarr & Marcus Coleman
Request the pleasure of the company of
<u>*Mr. & Mrs. Abraham Coleman*</u>
to share in their joy as they exchange marriage vows on
Sunday, the First of September, Two Thousand and Fifty-Eight
at Two O'clock in the Afternoon at
The Big TenT Farm, Carver, Puerto Paz

He twirled the pen in his hand, trying to come up with the words for a personal message to write on the empty page of the card. He had called his mom a few times over the last five years. His calls were, as his sister had always done, covert communications made during the middle of a workday, when his dad wouldn't be home.

They always had light, fluffy conversations about pleasant topics that avoided the elephants in the room. He had told her he was attending college tuition-free, pursuing an engineering degree. She didn't yet know that he had just graduated with a Bachelor of Science a week earlier, and that he was preparing to enter the first year of his Master's in Mechanical Engineering program at UNA. He had told her that he was playing professional gridiron and making money to supplement his stipend, including a bonus he had received for being league MVP that season. He had told her he had narrowly missed a spot on the 2056 Olympic track team only four months after recovering from a hamstring strain and was looking like a sure bet for the 2060 team.

Every bit of good news he had from Puerto Paz seemed to make her sound melancholy, or worse, provoke some sort of passive-aggressive concern about whether it was really good news. She seemed to enjoy hearing his voice, just as he enjoyed hearing hers, but any topic of conversation beyond the mundane and trivial seemed problematic. He consulted with Sharon about it, and she said it had taken at least five years after she had run away from home before their mother even remotely began to accept the situation.

Marcus had hoped that maybe with the second runaway, the process would happen a little faster, but here they were, five years later, still unable to have a true heart-to-heart. They had never broached the subject of Marcus having run away from home, nor his frustrations with NEUS culture, nor his anger at the way his dad had treated him and raised him, nor his mother's complicity in it. He had avoided telling her about Havana out of fear that it would trigger questions he didn't want to answer. He could just imagine how it would go.

"Where does she live, Marcus?"

"Oh, Mom, we're just living in sin, together in our off-campus intergenerational apartment complex."

"How could a good, Christian girl agree to live with her boyfriend unmarried, Marcus?"

"Well, Mom, thing is, she's not Christian."

He knew that his mom might see his marriage to a Puerto Pazian as the nail in the coffin, entombing her hopes of him ever moving back to NEUS.

His most recent call home had been almost a year prior, before he had proposed to Havana. It was the middle of a workday, yet his dad had answered the phone, so Marcus quickly hung up without saying a word. He couldn't remember his dad ever taking a sick day in his life and was completely unprepared to hear his voice.

Part of Marcus wanted to call his mom now and tell her about the wedding verbally, rather than in writing. "Opportunity to practice gentle confrontation," Havana had said when he had expressed his trepidation to her. "Much easier with Puerto Pazians than with Eastern Americans," Marcus had replied.

Still with nothing in mind, he grasped the pen and prepared to write, the tip hovering over the paper in case inspiration suddenly struck him. His hand began to tremble. He jerked it away from the table as it twitched, almost staining the paper with a stray mark. He set the pen down, sighed, closed the card, and tucked it with its envelope along the edge of the box, perpendicular to the rest of the cards. He slid his keychain to the side to see the next name on his list, figuring he could write a few easier, warm-up cards before returning to his parents' card.

Touching his keychain, he was briefly reminded of the box tucked away in his closet, where the Ohio State Football medallion had long since been relegated. He looked at his current medallion, the one with the Puerto Paz symbol on it that he had bought his first week in New Athens. He felt his throat swelling and briefly closed his eyes and looked away. *Maybe I shouldn't have ordered the mimosa,* he thought, then he snorted. *Who am I kidding? It isn't the mimosa.*

He refocused on the task at hand. Sharon and Elena were next on the list. This invitation was just a formality, since he had already asked Sharon to be maid of honor during one of their regular phone calls. After Sharon came his brother Saul. He didn't have Saul's address and figured that if their father had disowned Marcus, then surely Saul would have disowned him too. He wrote in Saul's name on a card, skipped the personal note, and stuck it with the card for his parents to send in the same envelope.

Next up was Kelsey. As he wrote her name, he shook his head in shameful disbelief at how his opinion of her had changed since he first met her. He had never misjudged someone as badly as he had misjudged her. He paused a moment, then changed his mind about that. He had never misjudged someone's *potential* as badly as he had misjudged Kelsey's potential. He had judged her correctly for who she was when he first met her, but she had changed a lot since then, and he hadn't seen the change coming.

She had been visiting New Athens a few times per year, and every visit she seemed a bit more mature and self-confident. During her most recent visit, she had even suggested dining at Alta and stood at the observation lounge windows for a full minute before retreating to the interior. She was less desperate for attention and popularity. Less obsessed with boys and fashion. Her forehead didn't have that wrinkle of worry as much. She also had grown a bit cynical about New Miami and had been hinting the last few visits that she was considering moving to Puerto Paz. He knew that Havana had recently helped her revise her résumé to make it more appealing for local companies, a sure sign that she was getting serious about the move.

Every time Kelsey visited, it seemed like he spent more and more time with her and Havana than the previous visit, and she subtly slipped from being Havana's friend to being a mutual friend. Not bridesmaid-level friend, but a good friend. He put pen to paper. "It has been quite the adventure the last few years.... We hope you will join us as we embark on our next adventure. Marcus and Havana."

The next name on the list was written "Dylan ???" Marcus hadn't spoken to him since the day he left him at the New Athens hospital after his arrest. Kelsey hadn't seen him since then either, nor did she have any interest in ever seeing him again. Marcus had checked Miami University football game stats a few times, but he'd never seen mention of Dylan. Internet searches turned up empty. He had tried to track down Dylan to ask him to be his best man but was unable to find him anywhere. When it came time to select the wedding party, he finally had to give up on having Dylan as best man. That was when Marcus and Havana agreed that Sharon would be the maid of honor, and one of Havana's male cousins, who she was particularly close to, would be the best man. Marcus had kept Dylan's name on the invite list in case of a miracle, hoping that maybe in time Dylan would have begun making the sort of transformation that Kelsey had, but now he felt compelled to cross Dylan's name off the list.

Next came the invite to Nikola and his family. Another invite that was just a formality, since the wedding and reception were being hosted at their farm and restaurant. Nikola, Marcus's gridiron teammate and his best friend outside of Havana, had put together quite the sales pitch after he found out that Marcus was considering his farm and restaurant as a possible venue for the wedding, including insisting that hosting the event would be his family's wedding gift to Marcus and Havana.

The Big TenT venue had also appealed to Marcus as a way to compromise with Havana between the marriage in a church that he had envisioned and the civil union ceremony at City Hall that seemed to be the local custom.

The invite for Isaac, his seatmate on the plane ride from San Francisco to New Miami, came next. During the summers, he typically worked as an engineering intern with Isaac. He had originally contacted him to ask whether he would be a reference for Marcus's application for a long-term visa, and later for his citizenship application, and they had struck up a friendship that had continued to this day.

The invite for another older male, Nigel, came after Isaac's. Marcus had briefly lived with Nigel until the government decided that Marcus was a suitable candidate for living in the UNA dorms while attending his senior year of high school, but even since then, he had continued to have occasional dinners with him. The dinners were less frequent now, but Marcus and Havana still saw Nigel sporadically at triathlon training workouts that they used for cross-training. Marcus laughed as he recalled Nigel informing him about sprinter's triathlons, involving short sprints with plenty of rest between each segment, after Marcus had complained to him about Havana always whooping his butt at endurance events. In one last vestige of his NEUS sense of "manliness," he had insisted that Havana do a sprinter's triathlon with him so that he could crush her in an athletic event for a change.

Priya was next on the list. He considered her a close friend too. Had he met her at the Miami University admin building instead of Havana, he could easily see himself writing out wedding invitations that said "Priya and Marcus" on them right now. He had secretly rooted for her and Nikola to hook up but was disappointed that the chemistry just wasn't there. They seemed to see each other more as brother-and-sister-type friends.

After a few more invites to extended family and college friends, he returned to the card for his parents. He closed his eyes and mentally scanned his body, identifying which muscles were tightening in response to the task at hand. He focused on his breath and progressively released muscles in his neck and shoulders. He thought of the last time he had seen his mother in person, the night he had run away from home. He recalled her last words to him that night. He opened his eyes, pressed the tip of the pen to the paper, and wrote:

"Mom, I've found peace."

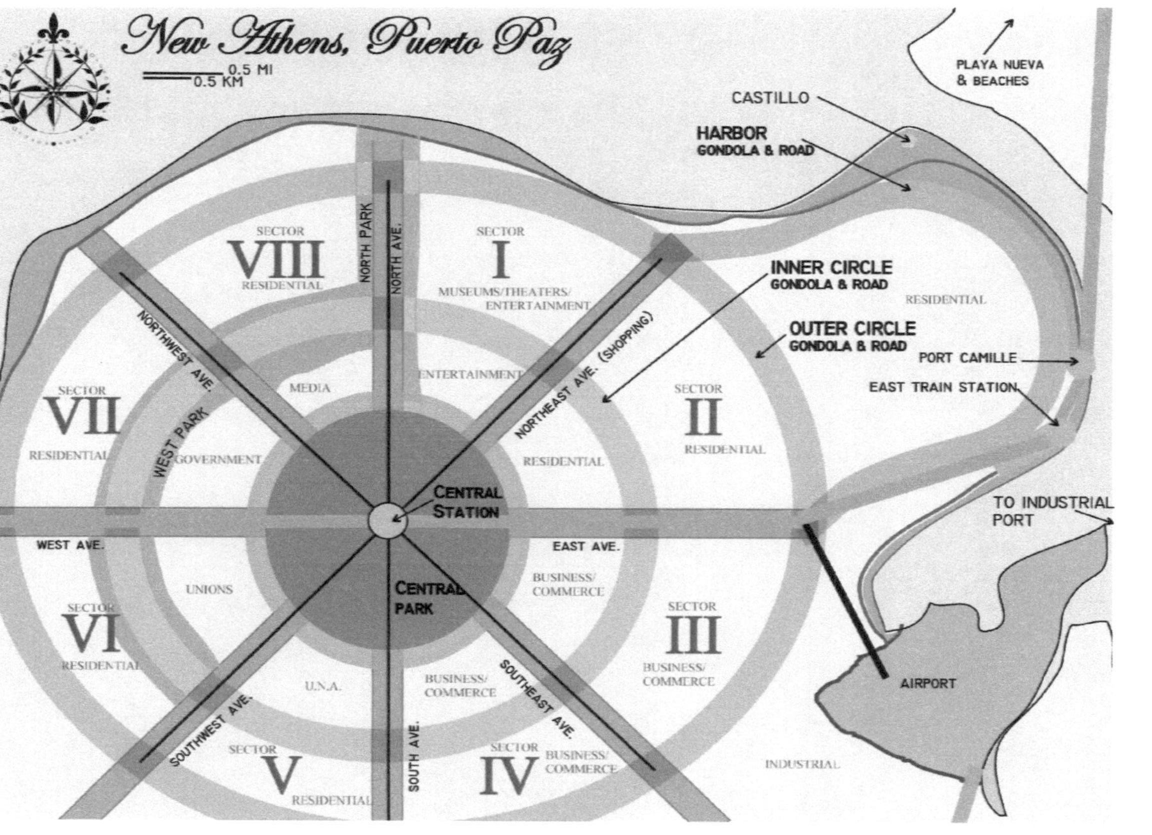

New Athens, Puerto Paz
0.5 MI
0.5 KM
PLAYA NUEVA & BEACHES
CASTILLO
HARBOR GONDOLA & ROAD
INNER CIRCLE GONDOLA & ROAD
OUTER CIRCLE GONDOLA & ROAD
RESIDENTIAL
PORT CAMILLE
EAST TRAIN STATION
TO INDUSTRIAL PORT
AIRPORT
INDUSTRIAL
SECTOR VIII RESIDENTIAL
SECTOR I MUSEUMS/THEATERS/ENTERTAINMENT
SECTOR VII RESIDENTIAL
SECTOR II RESIDENTIAL
SECTOR VI RESIDENTIAL
SECTOR III BUSINESS/COMMERCE
SECTOR V RESIDENTIAL
SECTOR IV BUSINESS/COMMERCE
NORTH PARK
NORTH AVE.
ENTERTAINMENT
NORTHEAST AVE. (SHOPPING)
MEDIA
WEST PARK
GOVERNMENT
RESIDENTIAL
CENTRAL STATION
CENTRAL PARK
WEST AVE.
EAST AVE.
UNIONS
BUSINESS/COMMERCE
U.N.A.
BUSINESS/COMMERCE
SOUTH AVE.
SOUTHEAST AVE.
SOUTHWEST AVE.
NORTHWEST AVE.

<u>Appendix 2</u>
Puerto Paz Primer
American English Version: Primer text reproduced with permission of the Puerto Paz Department of Immigration. Refer to the website <u>www.PuertoPaz.com</u> for revisions, addenda, and additional commentary.

<u>CORE PHILOSOPHIES</u>

A functional society depends on a social contract among its citizens. These Core Philosophies outline that social contract for Puerto Paz:

1) <u>Society matters</u>: Life is an interdependent, interconnected web. Recognize the needs of the many. This needs to be balanced with respect for individual liberties.
   a. What one person does impacts everyone around them.
   b. Have respect for everyone. Avoid "us versus them" mentalities. Cooperation and coordination are important for a healthy, functional society.
   c. The world is getting increasingly specialized, and we depend on others to compensate for areas outside our specialties. This needs to be balanced with an awareness of the big picture.
   d. Engineer environments that make healthy decisions easier and unhealthy decisions harder. Recognize that humans are more susceptible to environment than they care to admit to themselves.
      i. *Commentary & Examples: Studies show that people's food choices, both quantity and quality, at a buffet are affected by plate size and the order in which the food is presented.*
   e. The Commons are to be shared and protected by everyone.
   f. Climb Maslow's Hierarchy to best of ability. Recognize that the lowest levels of Maslow's Hierarchy are the highest priority for society as a whole, and the highest levels of Maslow's Hierarchy are lower priority.
   g. Restrictions on freedom should progress up a 3-tiered system of boundaries based on the damage those freedoms cause to society: If the freedoms do not cause damage to society, then they should not be restricted. Tier 1, for the least severe problems, is "incentives and disincentives", where the state tries to guide people to desirable, healthy behaviors by means of making the good choices easier and the bad choices more difficult. Tier 2 is regulation. Tier 3 is prohibition.
      i. *Commentary & Examples: Tier 1: Rebates, like free subway transportation, and taxes, such as taxes on simple-carbohydrates to promote health.*
2) <u>Balance. Non-extremism</u>.
   a. The world is not black &white. Recognize that you don't know the answers with certainty. Acknowledge the subjective nature of humans.
   b. Balance loyalty to ideas with loyalty to people. Excessive loyalty to either can be damaging.
      i. *Commentary & Examples:*
         1. *Examples:*
            a. *Loyalty to Hitler and the Nazi's during World War 2 led to German soldiers participating in the genocide of Jews. Loyalty to President Skrellin in EUS led to the nuclear annihilation of Cuba in 2029. When patriotism becomes national narcissism that turns every other country into an enemy. Or misguided loyalty to mobsters, gangs, or jihads that damage society.*
   c. Balance pragmatism with idealism: Keep the pendulum of opinion

from swinging violently between extremes based on recent events. Excessive idealism leads to unattainable goals. Excessive pragmatism leads to the status quo never improving.

    d. Balance simplicity with descriptiveness: Keep it simple. Don't make regulations or instructions excessively complex when something simple would suffice.

    e. Political debates should begin with extremism exercises. Determine the most extreme positions in the four political categories (order-conservative, order-liberal, freedom-conservative, and freedom-liberal), then progressively work out less extreme positions leading to a center, moderate position. From there debate whether the center position should be nudged further towards one of the extremes.

3) <u>The State</u>: A State is needed to protect The Commons and protect against discrimination. The State must balance order with freedom, societal needs versus individual liberty.

4) <u>Respect</u>: Treat others with respect. Recognize everyone's' importance. Recognize that you are no more, nor no less important than any other person and avoid an egotistical, VIP mentality. Treat janitors as well as you treat bankers. Everyone plays an important role. Society needs janitors, and we can't have a society of nothing but CEO's and no janitors.

5) <u>Transparency</u>. Free flow of information so that decisions can be made based on facts. Sharing of information. Higher value on knowledge than on the money made from selling that information.

6) <u>Income's relationship to Priorities and Value</u>: Individual Citizens have a responsibility recognize priorities in relation to Maslow's Hierarchy. Base levels of income should be associated with value, and those advancing society's highest needs and priorities should be compensated more highly. Income can be adjusted from the base levels by specific types of bonuses based on qualities such as difficulty of job, level of training required, skill or ability, and how hard working a person is. The highest incomes possible shall not be extraordinarily higher than the lowest possible incomes. The State will use income taxes to regulate the above. The health of Individual Citizens, and society as a whole, trumps the desire for higher profits or income.

    a. *Commentary & Examples:*

        i. *Examples of high priority careers that should have higher base incomes based on society's needs: Farmers (food), Public Works (water and sanitary), police and fire (safety), doctors and nurses (heath), construction workers and engineers (shelter),*

        ii. *Examples of lower priority careers that should have lower base incomes based on society's needs: artists, athletes, entertainers.*

7) <u>Pursuit of knowledge and Truth</u>:

    a. Citizens with intellectual curiosity are desired. Question traditions to keep what makes sense and purge what doesn't make sense.

8) <u>Overcoming Irrational Fear</u>: It is important for people to overcome the aspects of their fears that lead to behaviors that are detrimental to society.

    a. Fear leads to much of peoples' misbehavior. Fear of not being liked. Fear of not making enough money, survival.

    b. Fear can also be motivational and serve good purposes, so as with all things, balance is necessary.

9) <u>Communication</u>: Openness, honesty, and the free mixing of ideas is critical to a healthy society. Interact with people who are different than yourself.

***

<u>**POLITICAL ORGANIZATION**</u>

Political Groups are the major categories of the participants in the political system who have unique political interests. They are intended to provide checks and balances on one another such that no one group forms a monopoly or no two groups form a duopoly. These are static groups, unchanging in nature throughout time, although they may change in membership and size. There are 7 Political Groups, 4 of which are Primary Political Groups (Individual Citizens, The State, Corporations, and Public Media), and 3 of which are Secondary Political Groups (Citizens Advisory Group, Citizen Union, Corporate Advisory Group).

Political Parties are the alliances of citizens, which can be from various Political Groups, formed to promote and advance their own political agendas and ideas. These are dynamic groups that can change throughout time. *Examples: Democrats and Republicans.*

<u>**Structure of the Political Groups**</u>:
1) <u>**Individual Citizens**</u> (Primary Group)
    a. Membership: Open and mandatory: Everyone, including those in other Political Groups, is included in this group.
    b. Responsibilities:
        i. Uphold and value the Core Philosophies.
        ii. Communicate with other groups
    c. Controls over self:
        i. Private groups and relationships that apply peer pressure
        ii. Dispute boards, arbitrations, and lawsuits
    d. Controls/Checks against other Political Groups:
        i. Vs. The State:
            1. Elections
            2. Referendums
            3. Published Reviews of State
            4. Citizens Advisory Group
        ii. Vs. Corporations:
            1. Citizen Union
            2. Individual Published Reviews
            3. Consumer spending choices
        iii. Vs. Public Media
            1. Libel/Slander lawsuits.
2) <u>**Citizens Advisory Group**</u> (Secondary Group, under the domain of Individual Citizens)
    a. Membership: Closed: Membership is open to any Individual Citizen, except those who are members of The State, Corporations, Public Media, or the Corporate Advisory Group Political Groups.
        i. Funded by a government mandate through State taxes. Funding amount is voted on yearly by public referendum. The State may, at their discretion, choose to increase funding, but may not decrease funding. Additional money may also be obtained through public fundraising efforts.
    b. Responsibilities:
        i. Uphold and value the Core Philosophies.
        ii. Provide more formal Communication (beyond everyday informal communication) between Individual Citizens and The State. The Citizens Advisory Group communicates Individual Citizen needs and concerns to The State.
        iii. Seek a state of balance among the 3 groups: State, Corporations, & Individual Citizens.
    c. Controls over self:
        i. Elections by Individual Citizens who are not members of other closed Political Groups.

        ii.   Term limits.
    d. Controls/Checks against other Political Groups:
        i.   Published Reviews and Editorials
        ii.   Boycotts and Protests.
        iii.   Can initiate impeachment referendums for members of the
                State.
        iv.   Vs. Public Media: Libel/Slander lawsuits.
    e. *Commentary & Examples: The State, Corporations, and Public Media all
        possess strength in numbers and organization. As organized groups they possess
        an unfair advantage versus ordinary, unorganized Citizens. This sub-group is
        intended to bond Citizens together in an organized, united front to fight against
        abuse and corruption in the State.*

3) **Citizen Union Group** (Secondary Group, under the domain of
    Individual Citizens)
    a. Membership: Closed: Membership is open to any Individual
        Citizen, except those who are members of The State, Corporations,
        Public Media, or the Corporate Advisory Group Political Groups.
        i.   Funded by a government mandate through State taxes.
                Funding amount is voted on yearly by public referendum.
                The State may, at their discretion, choose to increase
                funding, but may not decrease funding. Additional money
                may also be obtained through public fundraising efforts.
    b. Responsibilities:
        i.   Uphold and value the Core Philosophies.
        ii.   Provide more formal Communication (beyond everyday
                informal communication) between Individual Citizens and
                Corporations. The Citizen Union communicates Individual
                Citizen needs and concerns to The Corporations, including
                both needs and concerns as consumers of their products via
                the **Consumer Union** sub-group, and as employees of their
                businesses via the **Worker Union** sub-group.
        iii.   Seek a state of balance among the 3 groups: State,
                Corporations, & Individual Citizens.
    c. Controls over self:
        i.   Leadership Board elections by Individual Citizens who are
                not members of other closed Political Groups.
        ii.   Term limits.
    d. Controls/Checks against other Political Groups:
        i.   Published Reviews and Editorials
        ii.   Boycotts, Worker Strikes, and Protests.
        iii.   Lawsuits.
        iv.   Vs. Public Media: Libel/Slander lawsuits.
    e. *Commentary & Examples: The State, Corporations, and Public Media all
        possess strength in numbers and organization. As organized groups they possess
        an unfair advantage versus ordinary, unorganized Citizens. This sub-group is
        intended to bond Citizens together in an organized, united front to fight against
        abuse and corruption in Corporations.*

4) **The State** (Primary Group)
    a. Membership: Closed: members of this group must not also be
        members of another closed group. Membership is based on election
        by Individual Citizens.
    b. Responsibilities:
        i.   Uphold and value the Core Philosophies.
        ii.   Protect the Commons, especially the environment. Provide
                public transportation systems, communication systems,
                public works and utilities, and education systems.
        iii.   Impartial arbitration of disagreements in the other Political
                Groups or among Citizens. Define (collaboratively) &
                enforce boundaries of acceptable/preferred behavior.

Prohibit discrimination. Seek resolutions that result in the healthiest and best functioning society possible.
   iv. Prioritize the bottom layers of Maslow's Hierarchy including security of body, security of property (Police, Fire, military); Public Works (sewer, water); Transportation (highway, transit); Communication (internet, phone) or at least regulation of it.
   v. Communicate with other groups, including foreign states. Transparency. Publish yearly reports of income and expenditures.
   vi. Recognize its own limits. Seek a state of balance among the 3 groups: State, Corporations, & Individual Citizens.
   vii. Government itself is secular humanist agnostic while individuals may privately choose own beliefs.
   viii. Explain WHY rules are what they are (law commentary)
   ix. Regulate income via an income tax per the Core Philosophies of Puerto Paz.
   x. Provide law and order.
c. Controls over self:
   i. Internal checks and balances of sub-groups of Executive, Judicial, Congressional branches.
   ii. An independent judicial system
   iii. International laws and foreign pressures.
   iv. Term limits.
d. Controls/Checks against other Political Groups:
   i. Vs. Individual Citizens:
      1. Laws and enforcement
      2. Taxes
   ii. Vs. Corporations:
      1. Regulations/laws and enforcement
      2. Taxes
   iii. Vs. Public Media
      1. Libel/Slander lawsuits.

5) <u>Corporations</u> (Primary Group)
a. Membership: Closed. For businesses only and consists of a business's CEO's and leadership boards.
b. Responsibilities:
   i. Uphold and value the Core Philosophies.
   ii. Balance prosperity/greed with what is best for society (includes durability/quality to avoid planned obsolescence environmental problems)
   iii. Provide jobs
   iv. Make sure competition is healthy and non-destructive. Seek out collaboration vs competition wherever possible.
   v. Communicate with other groups.
   vi. Do not damage the Commons or the environment.
   vii. Improve society through new technology and innovation.
   viii. Private media corporations are required by law to provide minimum access levels (as determined by The State) to the publicly funded Media Group and to the Citizen Union Group. (for example, all private TV stations required to provide minimum 1 hour per day of public media programming, and 30 minutes of Citizen Union programming.)
c. Controls over self:
   i. Competition with other corporations
d. Controls/Checks against other Political Groups:
   i. Vs. Individual Citizens:
      1. Jobs and wages

2. Product supply and prices
    ii. Vs. The State:
        1. Private media coverage (except for mandatory minimum exposure provided to Public Media, Citizen Union, and Citizens Advisory Groups)
        2. Published Reviews of State
        3. Lobbying the State via the Corporate Advisory Group. Individual Corporations are not permitted to lobby the State, all lobbying must be performed via the Corporate Advisory Group.
    iii. Vs. Public Media
        1. Libel/Slander lawsuits.
6) **<u>Corporate Advisory Group</u>** (Secondary Group, under the domain of Corporations)
   a. Membership: Closed: members of this group are elected by members of the Corporations Group and must not also be members of another closed group.
       i. Funded by Corporation membership dues.
   b. Responsibilities:
       i. Uphold and value the Core Philosophies.
       ii. More formal Communication (beyond everyday informal communication) between Corporations and The State.
       iii. Seek a state of balance among the 3 groups: State, Corporations, & Individuals.
   c. Controls over self:
       i. Mandatory that all meetings open to public with meeting minutes published.
       ii. Internal elections system.
       iii. Term limits.
   d. Controls/Checks against other Political Groups:
       i. Vs. State, Corporations, and Individuals: none
       ii. Vs. Public Media
           1. Libel/Slander lawsuits.
   e. *Commentary & Examples: Historically there have been problems caused by the most powerful Corporations exhibiting excessive influence on the State and elections at the expense of both smaller businesses and ordinary Citizens, due to their wealth, power, and organization. This subgroup is intended to force Corporations to work together to find mutually beneficial lobbying efforts, and to provide an official and transparent method for Corporations to lobby the State in blocks by industry.*
7) **<u>Public Media</u>** (Primary Group)
   a. Membership: Closed. Open only to trained journalists. Operated similar to a Corporation, except funded by a government mandate through State taxes. Funding amount is voted on yearly by public referendum. The State may, at their discretion, choose to increase funding, but may not decrease funding, to Public Media. Additional money may also be obtained through public fundraising efforts.
   b. Responsibilities:
       i. Uphold and value the Core Philosophies.
       ii. Maintain independence and objectivity.
       iii. Investigate and expose corruption and misbehavior.
       iv. Report the news.
   c. Controls over self: Internal elections system.
   d. Controls/Checks against other Political Groups: Media coverage and editorials.

<h1 style="text-align:center"><u>ELECTIONS</u></h1>

An independent election commission shall oversee all elections. The United Nations and the Public Media shall be invited to observe and report on all elections.

<u>Key election features:</u>

1) <u>Instant Runoff Voting</u>: Voting is to use the instant runoff voting system where each voter ranks the candidates in order of preference. Candidates are not permitted to swap votes.

   a. *Commentary & Examples: In the former United States of America, the destructive 2 party system that led to its downfall was inevitable because of its winner-take-all voting system. Duverger's law predicts this result, but in the former USA the 2 parties became so strong that the election system could not be reformed from within the government.*

2) <u>Voting district boundaries</u>: All voting districts shall have boundaries determined by mathematical formulas and geographical boundaries to avoid Gerrymandering. The election commission shall hire trained mathematicians and geographers for development of boundaries. Residents of a district may appeal based on cultural differences within a district.

3) <u>Candidate equal access to publicity</u>: Private media corporations shall provide an equal amount of time (video) or space (text) to each candidate who has met the election commission's qualifications as a "viable candidate". Public spaces shall be designated by The State in each district that permit an equal amount of space per candidate for election posters.

4) <u>Candidate funding</u>: All campaign funding shall be from a public campaign election fund that is funded by State taxes and distributed equally among all candidates. No private funds are permitted for campaign activities.

   a. *Commentary & Examples: In the former United States of America, politicians were spending more than half of their time fundraising for elections rather than governing the country or trying to reach bipartisan deals. The lack of public funding of elections, or even campaign finance regulation, led to elections being a non-stop fundraising effort, distracting the government from accomplishing anything. As campaigns were further deregulated it led to a pay-per-vote lobbying system where privately funded wealthy corporations had an unfair influence on government, effectively buying legislation that favored them at the expense of citizens who couldn't afford to buy the same legislation.*

5) <u>Voting Day</u>: All major elections shall be on a day declared a holiday to give all workers an opportunity to vote. Major elections shall be held at adequately prevalent and adequately equipped voting stations throughout the voting region. Minor elections may use technology to vote electronically from the voter's home.

   a. *Commentary & Examples: In the former United States of America, being 'too busy' or encountering 'transportation problems' were the reasons why 28% of people making less than $20,000 did not vote in 2012.*

6) <u>Vote Tabulation</u>: All electronic or computerized voting systems shall produce 2 paper Vote Receipts per voter. Vote receipts identify the voting location and time and have a unique vote number, but do not identify the voter. Vote Receipts are printouts showing the voter's selections. One copy shall be retained by the election commission in case of a recount or concerns of electronic voting machine tampering or other failure. One copy shall be provided to the voter to confirm that the machine registered their votes correctly.

<u>**TAXES**</u>

- Taxes are used to smooth out the flaws inherent in a free market economic system and to make a functioning society.
  - o The redistribution of wealth via taxes acknowledges that those in power often try to keep more than their fair share because they can, not because they deserve to. A free market is allowed to function within healthy and safe boundaries with minimal economic intervention, but Taxes are used to redirect the flaws in human nature to provide a more fair, just, and healthier society.
    - *Commentary and Examples: Studies have shown that when any two people play a game of Monopoly where one person is arbitrarily given a tremendous amount of free money at the start of the game, but the other person isn't, the benefactor of the free money wins the game and claims it was because they played the game smarter, and behaves as if they deserved the free money at the start.*
  - o It acknowledges that every single corporation builds itself on a foundation of public Commons administered by the State, and that those Corporations owe their fair share to maintain the Commons.
  - o It acknowledges that every human being has a right to survive and meet the lowest levels of Maslow's Hierarchy, and uses a Negative income Tax used to supplement lowest income citizens. It acknowledges that there is a limit to how much more those in power should be compensated relative to those without power, and that a society with nothing but CEO's cannot function.
  - o Taxes are primarily done through payroll taxes where the tax is levied before it even reaches the employee. Once per year an employee can file for credits to claw back some of that money, but the money owed is taken from the paycheck to reduce the sense of loss.

<u>**LAW & ORDER**</u>

Laws are separated into three prioritized categories: General Laws, General Laws Commentary, and Specific Laws.

1) The General Laws are vague and general principals. These are what citizens are expected to know. They are kept brief, and few in quantity. They are the highest laws of the land though, and are the ultimate authority. They typically correlate with Puerto Paz's Core Philosophies.
   a. Examples include:
      i. Do not harm the earth.
      ii. Do not harm others
2) The General Laws Commentary is further description of the General Laws. They describe why each General Law was chosen and what each law is meant to be, and gives a history of the Law. The Commentary is also covered extensively in Civics classes, but not necessarily meant to be memorized for life.
3) The Specific Laws are specific examples and case histories that fall under each General Law. It is meant to be more black & white clarification of the vague General Laws. For example, under the General Law of "Do not harm others" would be Specific Laws such as murder, and exceptions such as self-defense. General Laws trump Specific Laws so that people can't use Specific Laws as loopholes for complex situations.

Any time the State votes on a law, the citizens get to take a voluntary, informal, non-binding poll (via at-home technology) before the State's vote on that legislation to see if the State is mirroring popular opinion. There is a locked version of the Citizen Poll that reflects opinions at the time the State Votes, but then there is after-vote polling that continues the polling process after the State has voted in case one side of the argument was underrepresented because of lack of poll-taker turnout. This gives the State an opportunity to revisit issues they've voted on to make sure they are representing the citizens' interests, but still maintain the control with the State which is supposed to have a professional alta-vista that can overcome unhealthy popular opinions. *For example, if the majority of citizens who participate in a poll asking whether chocolate should be the only food served at restaurants say yes, then the State can see that this is what the citizens want, but can still override it and say that chocolate should not be the only food served because it is unhealthy to do so.* Technology plays a strong role in allowing this to happen because citizens polling is done through mobile technology with secure login to make it as easy as possible for citizen participation.

The general policy is for the State to provide a balance between freedom and order that allows Citizens to feel safe and healthy yet free. Citizens who violate the laws and Core Principals of Puerto Paz and are disruptive to society will be subjected to various levels of order based on their crimes:

1) Violent offenders who are deemed a risk to society are imprisoned. The State will make all attempts reasonably possible to rehabilitate and to provide psychological therapy to all violent offenders while they are imprisoned.

2) Non-violent offenders who habitually reject the Core Principals or Laws may be ostracized. The State will make all attempts reasonably possible to rehabilitate with civics lessons explaining why the Core Principals and Laws are a necessary part of a functional society, and to provide psychological therapy as needed to all offenders. Citizens who reject rehabilitation, or who continue to reject the Core Principals and Laws and are considered disruptive to society may be ostracized at the State's discretion, as determined by the judicial branch. Ostracization shall begin with all reasonable attempts made to relocate the Citizen to another country that more closely matches with that Citizen's beliefs and philosophies. If no country will accept the Citizen, then the citizen shall be relocated to the Isla de Juventud, an island off the coast of Puerto Paz that is reserved for ostracized citizens.

NOISE ORDINANCES

The various zones, neighborhoods, and districts in each city are zoned for varying permissible noise levels. In accordance with the Core Philosophies of treating everyone with respect and acknowledging that what one person does has an impact on everyone around them, the default status is that Citizens are not permitted to subject the people around them to loud, disturbing noises unless they have the specific permission of *everyone* affected by the noise. Various zones in each city will be established that allow more noise to accommodate Citizens who either like living in noisier environments, or for Citizens to go to in order to participate in noisier events. In areas that are not zoned for higher noise levels, condominiums, apartment buildings, and housing developments are required to have a neighborhood community building or a noise-proofed community room for events or parties that are noisier than a small cocktail party with music at low levels. Citizens are encouraged to host their parties at community buildings and community rooms in areas zoned for higher levels of noise rather than in their homes. Multi-family residential buildings are also required to incorporate minimum standards of noise-proofing construction methods.

DRUGS

Recreational drugs are legal, but training on their effects is a part of civics classes. The State controls distribution of dangerous drugs. Hard drugs are required to be taken in specially controlled buildings staffed with emergency personnel. The goal is to discourage use, but to provide a safe environment for those who still choose to use, and to provide counseling and rehab to try to avoid use or deal with addiction, and prevent a black markets controlled by gangs that happens whenever there is outright prohibition. Alcohol, tobacco, and marijuana are considered soft drugs that are taxed by the State, and are minimally regulated other than having minimum ages for use for all except beer and wine.

NATIONAL HOLIDAYS

1) January 1: New Year's Day.
2) February 1: Puerto Paz Day. A holiday to celebrate the cleansing of the radioactive material from the soils and the birth of the country.
3) First Mondays of March and September: Poll Days. 2 polling days where citizens take time off to answer Public Media polling questions asking things like is the government exceeding its authority or not, and how they feel about current issues. Polling days seek out signs of abuse or corruption by any of the Political Groups and allows the State to monitor whether their work reflects the views of the population.
4) April 22: Earth Day. A day to consider environmental issues.
5) First Monday of May: Election Day holiday. *In May to avoid hurricane season.*
6) First Monday of June: Diversity Day: A holiday for socializing with people different than oneself to avoid living in bubbles and to promote the exchange of ideas.
7) July 31 and August 1: Past and Future Days. A day to reflect on the past followed by a day to think about the future.
8) First Monday of September: 2nd of 2 Poll Days, see March.
9) First Monday of October: Global Perspective Day. A holiday to reflect on how Puerto Paz as a whole, businesses as groups, and citizens as individuals can help make world a better place.
10) First Monday of November: Thanksgiving Day. A day to be grateful for what you have.
11) December 25: Family Day. Intentionally coincides with Christmas Day to allow Christians the day off but without making a religious holiday an official government holiday.

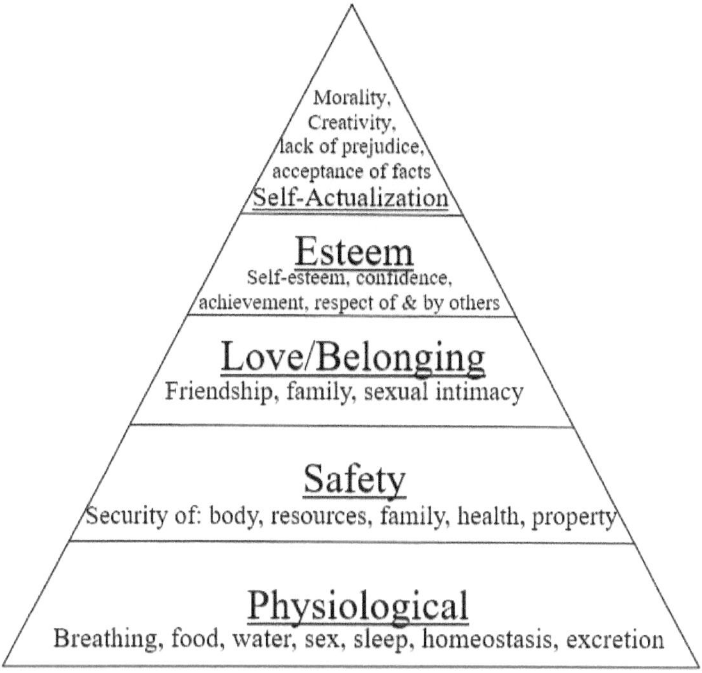

Maslow's Hierarchy of Needs

<u>Appendix 3</u>
Letter

sɛpˈtɛmbər 1, 2059

dɪr həˈvænə,

ˈhæpi ˌænəˈvɜrsəri! ju ər ðə lʌv əv maɪ laɪf, ənd aɪ əm soʊ ˈlʌki
tə həv mɛt ju. ju meɪk mi ˈhæpiər ðən aɪ həv ˈɛvər bɪn bɪˈfɔr. ɪt
əz ˈfɔrtʃənət, ˌhaʊˈɛvər, ðæt wi sərˈvaɪvd ˈaʊər fɜrst deɪt ɪn nu
maɪˈæmi. aɪ həv bɪˈkʌm ˈfʊli vɜrst ɪn ðə rulz əv kəmˈpɛtətɪv fud
ˈɔrdərɪŋ ənd əm naʊ əˈwɛr ðət an ˈaʊər fɜrst deɪt ju wər ˈtʃitɪŋ. wi
boʊθ noʊ ðət meɪn ˈdɪʃəz kaʊnt fər mɔr pɔɪnts ðən saɪd ˈdɪʃəz
ənd ðət aɪ wʌn ðət naɪt. soʊ, ju ər nat ˈpɜrˌfɪkt. ðər ɪz noʊ sʌtʃ
θɪŋ əz pərˈfɛkʃən, bət ju ər əz kloʊs tə ˈpɜrˌfɪkt əz ˈɛni ˈwʊmən
kən gɛt ənd aɪ lʌv ju.

ˈmarkəs